STARRYCARD CREEK BACHELORS

CW01506558

THE
Birthday Card
BOYFRIEND

KRISTA SANDOR

USA TODAY BESTSELLING AUTHOR

CANDY CASTLE BOOKS

CHAPTER

One

IZZY

"IZZY, YOU'RE FUCKED."

"You can't be serious?" Isabelle "Izzy" Adaire replied, her voice rising an anxious octave as she held her translator's gaze. As an environmentalist, Izzy's career was built on gauging the delicate balance of ecosystems and penning reports that could sway the fate of entire regions. Martina Suarez had been her translator in the trenches of South America for three solid years. Yet, in all that time, Martina had never dropped an F-bomb.

Martina's rich mocha skin bloomed a deep scarlet. "I am dead serious."

Despite a chill in the mountain air, a bead of perspiration trickled between Izzy's breasts. "How fucked do you think I am?"

Martina's eyes widened. *"Mucho fucked,"* she whispered through a rolling Spanish accent.

Izzy plastered on a nervous grin.

Mucho fucked? That couldn't be good. In fact, it sounded quite perilous. Still, it wouldn't change her assessment of the environmental conditions she'd been assigned to evaluate. And she sure as hell wouldn't be backing down. She'd made that mistake once before and vowed never to allow her judgment to be swayed again.

Izzy schooled her features and shooed away a mosquito buzzing at her ear. She surveyed the stern-faced elderly indigenous women gathered around a wobbly table. Atop a Peruvian mountain at an elevation just shy of eleven thousand feet, the clouds hung low as the group stood in a clearing not far from a trickling river.

She adjusted the straps of her worn backpack and brushed a lock of golden hair from her cheek.

There had to be a misunderstanding.

"Martina, did you relay exactly what I'd said to the women?"

The translator nodded. Her jet-black bob swished past her chin. "I did. I told them they cannot build in the area adjacent to the water."

Izzy studied the village elders. They wore wool shawls and ponchos in an array of lively hues—deep reds, stormy blues, lush greens, and vibrant violets. The colors popped, setting them apart from the tufts of wild grasses and low shrubs clinging to the rocky terrain. This collection of ten stone-faced women in wide-brimmed hats eyed her like they wouldn't mind if she tripped and fell a few thousand feet. Standing together, they resembled an angry rainbow. From the second she'd set foot in their small village of Encanto de las Alturas, which translated to Enchantment of the Heights, they'd regarded her with a mix of curiosity and uncertainty, which made sense. At five foot seven, she towered over every villager. Add in her blond hair, and she stood out like a sore thumb in this indigenous mountain community.

But her appearance didn't matter. She'd been sent to do a job. This, however, was usually the moment when she'd be asked to leave—and told never to return.

Izzy met Martina's gaze. "You let them know they can't build on the land because it's home to an endangered bird species, correct?"

"Yes, but there's more," the woman answered warily.

Izzy toyed with the sleeve of her white linen blouse. "What more could there be?"

Martina spoke softly to a woman draped in a violet poncho with deep lines etched on her face. "Elder Pachamama says they're upset because you shared this information with the local government."

Here it comes.

"Of course, I informed the authorities." Izzy eyed the town elder, then flicked her gaze to a trio of men from a local construction company the elders had brought in to build a structure beside the stream's flowing waters. A knot twisted in her belly as she watched the men gesture to a series of architectural plans scattered on the table. But they couldn't fool her. Izzy lifted her chin. "Tell them their fate was sealed when I identified the endangered bird. These men won't be building today—or any day."

Martina sighed and rattled off the translation. She'd barely finished speaking before the men erupted into boisterous conversation. Izzy didn't have to speak the indigenous language to know they were well and truly pissed off. The men muttered, tossing pointed glances her way as they gathered their plans. They stomped off and headed for a beat-up Jeep. Barely a minute had passed before they took off down a pitted dirt road.

Izzy bit back a grin. The rumble of the engine and the grind of the tires meeting the dirt path were music to her ears. Excellent! She didn't have to worry about these guys giving her any trouble. Perhaps relaying the bad news would be easier than she'd thought.

Elder Pachamama waved in Martina and spoke softly.

Izzy studied the tiny elder. She had to be in her seventies or eighties. Years spent working and living in this unforgiving yet beautiful terrain had etched a story of hard work on her weathered face and wrinkled hands. And there was something else. Izzy had noticed it the day she'd arrived. Wisdom laced with mischief had glinted in the elder's eyes when she handed her a basket of *mortiños*, blueberries from the mountainous region. It was clear that Ms. Violet Poncho, Elder Pachamama, was in charge. But she was just a little old lady. Yes, she was disappointed. But how much trouble could she make?

The translator nodded as the elder spoke in a low, rolling rasp, her words sounding more like an incantation than a conversation.

"What is it?" Izzy asked after the old woman finished speaking.

"The Elder Pachamama says she wished you would have come to her first," Martina explained and shared a look with the elder. "She didn't ask Earthwise Consulting to brief the government. She wouldn't have agreed to work with your company if she'd known you'd be doing that. She thought you would help them. She thought you'd be sympathetic to their cause. She's frustrated because they're trying to be proactive and do the right thing. Instead, she says you've thwarted their growth and will impede their ability to provide for the village."

Izzy had heard this before. Everybody wanted to care about the environment until doing the right thing meant they couldn't have it their way.

"Tell her there's nothing I can do. There are rules and mandates. That's my professional assessment. She and her people will have to figure out another plot of land to destroy."

Martina frowned, her eyebrows knitting together.

"I mean *develop*," Izzy corrected and chastised herself. She had to keep it professional.

Now, should this piece of land be entirely off-limits to development?

The short answer was no.

But—and this was a huge but—it would take serious attention to detail and the use of specialized materials and processes to protect it. She couldn't trust some random local builder. And once one small building was constructed, what would stop some greedy developer from swooping in and exploiting the fragile ecosystem? This land was breathtaking. Between the babbling stream and the stunning panoramic views, there was probably some asshat out there who would love to steal this land out from under the villagers and smack a luxury resort on it—ruining everything for the environment and the indigenous people who called this place home.

Once a greedy developer wanted something, nothing would stop them.

She knew that better than anyone else.

She had to stand her ground. The elder might be frustrated, but she'd be utterly heartbroken if she lost everything.

The elder came around the table. Only a few feet separated them. Izzy had never been this close to the woman. Over the last couple of weeks, she'd noticed the hunched senior in the violet poncho checking up on her. Izzy would give the woman a polite nod, but she made it clear that she worked alone as she documented and observed the environment. And she always kept her distance. It was the hard and fast rule she lived by—professionally and in her romantic life. Scratch that. She didn't have to apply it to her romantic life because she didn't have one—nor did she want one. She envisioned a pair of gray eyes accompanied by a slippery smile she'd misinterpreted as charming. A disconcerting prickle spider-crawled down her spine. Romance would never be in the cards for her. No way! She had her work. And she would not allow herself to be swayed or manipulated. She wasn't that stupid young woman anymore.

The elder spoke softly. The lines etched into her dark, papery skin deepened as she conversed with Martina. The old woman touched her poncho, then gestured toward a fenced-in area where alpacas chomped on spotty patches of natural grasses.

The translator nodded to the woman. "She's telling me they want to develop this land to ensure their livelihood. While they make some income from selling the mortiños, they need to expand their alpaca wool business. Elder Pachamama says they would never want to harm their lands or the creatures who live here."

Izzy pursed her lips.

She'd heard that before.

She felt for her locket and clutched the bit of gold in her hand. Drawing strength from the object, she looked the old woman square in the eyes and shook her head. "No, you cannot build on this land."

The elder eyes narrowed into fiery slits.

Good! The woman appeared to get the message loud and clear.

The old woman spoke to the translator.

Izzy knew this song and dance, too. The lady was probably rattling off a million reasons why this project was essential.

"There's nothing more that can be done," she said and released her locket. "You don't need to explain why you want to develop this land."

"That's not what she's saying," Martina offered.

What the heck else could the elder be going on about?

Izzy met the old woman's gaze. "What is she saying?"

"She says she can sense you've hardened your heart," Martina relayed softly.

Izzy took a step back, the breath catching in her throat. "What?"

The elder spoke, keeping her voice low.

Martina nodded. "She says she can see you're hiding behind . . ."

"Behind what?" Izzy asked, transfixed on the slight woman.

"Anger and guilt. She says your icy blue eyes match your heart."

What a thing to say! And was it a correct assessment?

Izzy stood there, speechless.

"She says you weren't always like this," Martina continued. "She says the ice blue in your eyes doesn't have to mean anger. It can mean justice and perseverance. It can mean fighting for love. She wants you to know, and I'm translating this word for word."

"What does she want me to know?" Izzy pressed, her voice barely a whisper as anticipation hung thickly in the thin air.

"The lone bearer of burdens shall find their own demise. She wanted me to tell you that part word for word," Martina added, concern marring her features.

Izzy exhaled a shaky breath.

The lone bearer of burdens shall find their own demise.

The foreboding statement hit like an arrow to her battered heart.

Was this lady an alpaca wool maker or a witch . . . or both? Could she see through her? Could she look into her soul and assess the weight she carried—the invisible load that never lightened?

No, that was ridiculous.

And there were no such things as alpaca wool-making witches. Elder Pachamama was simply another client—an upset client with one hell of a way with creepy, prophesy-esque declarations.

Yeah, that had to be it.

Or was the elder spot-on in her interpretation?

"I'm not any of those things," Izzy stammered, feeling every pair of eyes fall on her. "Please tell her that, Martina. Tell her, when it comes to my life, I'm a very . . ."

A very what? A very *happy* person? A very *fulfilled* person? Sure, that could be true. She had one good friend, and that counted for something. And her work protecting fragile ecosystems and endangered animals meant everything to her.

Before she could come up with a response, the old woman spoke to Martina.

"What is it now?" Izzy asked, her heart racing.

"She says you're trying to right a wrong from your past, and punishing them isn't the way to make peace with yourself."

Who the hell was this little old poncho-wearing woman?

The elder continued speaking to Martina, and the translator's cheeks again bloomed crimson.

"What is it?" Izzy pressed.

Martina chewed her bottom lip. "I'm trying to figure out a delicate way to translate her words."

Izzy didn't look away from Elder Pachamama. "You don't have to sugarcoat it for me."

The elder adjusted her wide-brimmed hat and squinted her eyes. "You need sex," the woman blurted in choppy English. "You like the boys or the girls?"

"What?" Izzy stammered.

"I say, boys or girls or both?" the elder demanded.

She spoke English.

"Boys," she offered meekly.

Was Elder Pachamama the Peruvian version of Dr. Ruth?

"You need lots of sex," the elder exclaimed, her words echoing off the mountaintop. "Get some dick and make new report. We need build. We protect birds and make wool. Big dick make you smile. Get some boom-boom action, and all will be good. That *my assessment.*"

Wowza!

From dishing out foreboding forewarnings to promoting flaming-hot fornication, Elder Pachamama was hella proficient in English. *And holy shit!* Those were the last words she'd expected to fall from the woman's lips.

Izzy cleared her throat. She had to reply. "I've gotten plenty of dick. All the dick. Every dick. Here, a dick. There, a dick. Everywhere, a dick, dick," she stammered. *What was wrong with her?* Actually, there was plenty wrong with her. Not to mention, her *dick-dick* word salad was a complete lie. There had been no dicks. No dicks here. No dicks there. Isabelle A. Adaire had no man vying to give her some *D* and rip off her underwear.

Was she losing her mind? Was twisting children's rhymes into dirty verses a sign of a complete mental breakdown?

No, she was perfectly sane and perfectly happy without a boom-boom dick bonanza. She didn't have time for it.

Okay, that wasn't exactly true either.

She certainly wouldn't mind the company of a man to engage in a bit of carnal release. But she was not about to take dating advice from a woman who knew nothing about her. Well, besides the parts about no dick, crushing guilt, and simmering anger she couldn't figure out how to quell.

Maybe Elder Pachamama was a mind-reading witch.

Mischief sparkled in the woman's deep brown eyes. She turned to her flock of brightly colored companions and barked what appeared to be orders in their indigenous language. And yep, they had to be orders. Martina gasped as the women fanned out. A few of the old lady rainbow brigade moved toward the alpaca enclosure while others darted toward her like a military regiment prepared to pounce.

Izzy peered over her shoulder at the road. A little more than a kilometer down the rutted path, a helicopter waited to take her to Lima. From there, she'd contact Earthwise, get her next assignment, and be off to another part of the world. She just had to make it out of this village in one piece. She surveyed the group. Sure, there was something ominous about having ten pairs of eyes trained on her like a pack of wolves hunting a lone rabbit. But these wolves were senior citizens who weren't tall enough to ride a roller coaster at Disney Land. Really, what could ten alpaca wool witches do to her?

Martina's gaze was piercing, urgency etched into her every feature. The air crackled as terse commands flew between the angry senior citizens. Martina snatched the satellite phone from her pack. "Izzy, I've got to report this—now! You must leave immediately."

Perhaps these wool witches were more powerful than they appeared.

Izzy's pulse kicked up. "Please, Martina, do not call this in. The helicopter is already waiting for me."

Calling in a rapid extraction was supposed to be the last resort. Hardly anyone in the company had to revert to this extreme measure—well, besides her. This would be her third rapid-extraction request in less than six months. She was already skating on thin ice at work. Her boss would absolutely lose her shit if it happened again.

"Earthwise needs to know, Izzy," Martina said, holding the receiver to her ear.

"Martina, Pamela will have my head on a platter if she learns things have gone south with another one of my assignments."

Martina threw a nervous glance at the fuming rainbow brigade. "I'm sorry, Izzy. The elder said something I didn't translate because I didn't want to scare you. And I wasn't sure what it meant. But now that I see a few villagers by the alpaca gate, I know what they're about to do. I have to call it in if you're in danger. It's company protocol."

There's a statement a person never wanted to hear from their translator.

Izzy stepped back. "Tell me. At least I can be ready for it."

"They have a tradition in this village. When a person's spirit is hindered by guilt, anger, or extreme sexual frustration, they believe the alpacas are the key to clearing the negative energy blockage."

"What does that even mean?" Izzy stammered. Warily, she eyed the enclosure with at least two dozen big-ass alpacas. *Were they glaring at her? Did alpacas glare?*

"I'm not sure," Martina answered and mustered a weak grin. "But they mentioned it was a good thing you're wearing hiking boots."

What were those mind-reading wool witches planning?

Izzy had to prove she didn't need alpacas to unblock her—whatever the heck that meant. What could she do? What could she say? What could she show them?

She adjusted her pack and felt the answer against her left shoulder blade.

She might not have been getting any dick, but she had a Bob. Izzy removed her pack, unzipped it, and rustled through the contents. In her wild haste to retrieve her battery-operated boyfriend, a treasured birthday card slipped through her fingers. It fluttered to the ground and landed on a tuft of dense grass.

"No!" she exclaimed, panic tearing through her chest. She

could not lose that card. She crouched to pick up the item, but tiny Elder Pachamama was closer to the ground and got to it before she could.

With a gentle touch, the old woman plucked the card from the earth. She brushed her thumb across the fibrous paper. With tiny flecks of indigo dotting the cream-colored card, its unique appearance drew people in. Elder Pachamama appeared to be under its spell. But it wasn't just the paper that made this card unique. The woman studied the image painted on the front. "Butterfly," she said, again employing English as she pointed to the delicate creature adorning the cover. "You like butterfly, Isabelle A. Adaire?"

How did this wool witch know her middle initial?

Izzy pushed aside the thought and nodded, momentarily calmed by the card. "I do. And what you're holding is a birthday card from my family. It . . ."

It reminded her of a time when she believed in people—believed in herself, believed in love.

She wasn't about to say that, though.

Wrapped up in this crazy moment, she stared at the hand-painted butterfly. Deep violet wings dotted with iridescent icy silver markings mimicking a starry night sky made this winged creature look like something out of a fairy tale. In the picture, the hauntingly beautiful butterfly perched on a log near a pool of sky-blue water. A slight haze rose above the placid surface. Over the years, she'd spent hours staring at this card, marveling at the intricacies. The insect looked so lifelike—like it was waiting for the right moment to flutter its wings and emerge from the textured paper.

The elder handed Izzy the card, snapping her out of her butterfly stupor.

"That's not what I meant to show you," Izzy mumbled as she carefully tucked the card into the pocket of her pack. She felt around and gripped the one thing she hoped would call off the alpaca intervention. "I might not be having much sex, but I've got this. It's called a Wham Bam." She activated the vibrator and waved it around like a dildo sorceress. She stilled. "I don't know why I did that. I'm not sure if you get a lot of these in your neck of the woods. This is a device for making orgasms. No dick needed for the modern girl."

No dick needed for the modern girl?

Stop talking. Stop talking.

Elder Pachamama eyed the buzzing tube, then glanced at her companions. The woman hooted and hollered, exploding into boisterous laughter.

At least somebody was having a good time.

Elder Pachamama regained her composure and spoke to Martina.

"What is she saying? Am I in the clear?" Izzy asked.

"She says you've proven something to her."

Izzy pressed the still-vibrating battery-operated boyfriend to her heart. "Oh, good."

"No, it's not good news. She says—"

"You need real dick," Elder Pachamama exclaimed. She whipped the dildo out of Izzy's hand and tossed it to another woman, who spiked it like a quarterback into a steaming pile of alpaca poop.

Izzy watched the Wham Bam sink into the animal excrement. "That was Bob, my battery-operated boyfriend," she whimpered.

"That not boyfriend," the elder admonished. She spoke to a woman draped in a green wool shawl. The woman in green hurried inside one of the stone dwellings. Seconds later, she emerged with a bowl.

Izzy eyed the crockery, then met Martina's gaze. "Why is she holding a bowl of blueberries?"

"*Mortiños,*" the elder corrected.

"Why do you have those mortiños?" Izzy stammered.

The elder plucked a berry from the top of the heap and held it to Izzy's lips.

"She wants you to eat it," Martina explained.

Eat it?

"This feels very dark fairy tale-ish. Like I'm about to ingest a poison berry and fall into a deep sleep," Izzy murmured, working to keep her lips from opening as she spoke.

"You already asleep, Isabelle *A*. Adaire. You sleep through life. Only wake to bad parts. You think you are alone. You wrong. Eat berry. Get energy. Clear blockage," Elder Pachamama ordered.

Izzy grimaced. Unsure of what to do, she parted her lips. The old woman slipped the fruit into her mouth. Like she was about to bite into a stick of dynamite, Izzy chewed cautiously, then swallowed. She waited for a beat, then another. She was still alive—at least for the moment. "Okay. I ate the berry. *Mmm . . .*" She rubbed her belly theatrically. "I'm feeling that fruity energy," she blathered, unsure when this situation had gone from tense to absolutely bonkers.

But this berry ritual weirdness wasn't over.

Elder Pachamama dipped her hand into the bowl. She called out in a raspy voice, employing her native tongue. *Was this the part where she cast a wool witch spell?* Izzy could hear Martina calling Earthwise, but she couldn't take her eyes off the tiny, wrinkled woman. The elder made a fist and squeezed the handful of mortiños. The juices trickled between her fingers as a sweet, aromatic scent floated in the air. The alpacas emitted a foreboding, high-pitched hum and stomped their hooves. The frenzied alpaca vibe rippled across the village.

"What's happening, Martina?" Izzy eked out.

"From what I can gather, they give these berries to the alpacas as a treat. The animals rarely get them. When they smell them, they go kind of *loco*."

"*Loco* like crazy?" Izzy got out.

"*Mucho loco*," the translator replied.

Mucho fucked.

Mucho loco.

Enough with the mucho.

Elder Pachamama removed her dark, wrinkled hand from the

bowl. It dripped with deep purple juices and lush pieces of indigo berry flesh.

"Do you want me to eat that like a hand-smooshed smoothie?" Izzy asked. Maybe that was the deal. To clear her blockage, she was supposed to eat like an alpaca. It was certainly odd and not entirely sanitary, but not awful.

In the blink of an eye, and with a movement straight out of one of those horror movies where the witchy woman plunges her fist into the victim's chest and rips out the poor fool's beating heart, the elder pressed her berry-juiced hand to Izzy's heart. Izzy shrieked and closed her eyes. Turning away, she sipped sharp breaths, waiting for her still-beating heart to be yanked from her body. But that's not what happened. Cautiously, she opened her eyes and observed the elder smear the sticky berry mixture onto her white linen shirt.

Mischief glittered in the woman's dark eyes. "No eat. No smoothie. And take this for luck," she continued. The elder pressed a Peruvian coin into Izzy's hand—a one-sol coin minted with an alpaca.

"Thanks?" Izzy replied, eyeing the sticky mess on her shirt. She slipped the coin into her pack as the chances of getting out of this village in one piece seemed to be slipping away.

The whine and clink of a metal latch opening pierced the dry air.

She eyed the animals. "Are they coming for me? I'd love it if they weren't. I'd like to make it to my twenty-sixth birthday."

The elder cocked her head to the side. "When your birthday?"

Izzy shifted her stance. "It's a few weeks away."

Elder Pachamama tapped her chin. "Not sure you make it that long. It depends on one thing."

Izzy swallowed hard. "What's that?"

The little wool witch schooled her features and waved her in. "Depend on how fast you run."

Damn it! She was afraid the elder would say something like that.

The old woman winked at her, then bowed.

Izzy chewed her lip. Should she bow? Or was that an elder thing?

What could she do?

She could curtsy.

It was better than nothing. Perhaps a show of respect would persuade the elder to call off the alpaca anger cleansing. She lowered into a semi-squat.

The elder frowned. "Legs broken, Isabelle A. Adaire?"

"No, I'm . . ."

She was curtsying like a psychopath.

"This isn't *Pride and Prejudice*, Izzy. You've got to run!" Martina exclaimed.

Run! Izzy couldn't dwell on wool witches, or the creepy berry smoothie splattered across her chest, or her vibrator encased in alpaca shit, or her creepy curtsy.

The animals surged out the gate in a rushing wave of brown, cream, and oatmeal. Their hooves echoed, carrying across the mountaintop.

"The pilot's ready for you." Martina edged backward, moving out of the way. "Izzy, you need to run! You smell like a walking, talking slice of Alpaca Mortiños Surprise."

Izzy gasped.

She was literally on the menu.

Still questioning if she could believe her eyes, she stumbled a few feet. The docile creatures had meandered around the enclosure during her time in the village. They'd barely done more than trot from trough to trough. But there was nothing passive about these beasts now. Blood whooshed through her ears, and adrenaline coursed through her veins as the alpaca pandemonium caused the mountain to shake.

"Goodbye, *butterfly*. Spread your wings. You get dick. Unblock energy. Send new report," Elder Pachamama called.

Despite her limited English, the woman had a way with words.

On the other hand, Izzy had no words.

"Girl, how much more mucho fucked do you want to get? Run!" Martina roared.

Izzy snapped out of her alpaca haze. Smelling like a slice of blueberry delight, she spun on her heel and sprinted toward the road. Her feet hit the rugged, rocky earth, kicking up plumes of dirt. *Crunch, crunch, crunch.* Her locket slapped against her chest. Her pack bounced from side to side. She gripped the straps. Lungs burning, she pushed her body to the limit.

One foot in front of the other.

Just keep moving.

But the beat of the alpaca blockage posse drew closer.

Heaven help her! Those animals could move when motivated, and she was not about to have *trampled by a horde of blueberry-obsessed alpacas* written as her cause of death.

She came around the bend, and the *whoop-whoop* of rotor blades drowned out the pounding of her feet and rasp of her breath. She peered into the helicopter. *Thank God!* She knew the pilot. Delores Sanchez had flown her into the remote region. Izzy waved her arms, booked it toward the aircraft, and dove into the barebones chopper. Her elbow smacked into a fire extinguisher secured against the wall. "*Ouch! Dammit!* That'll leave a mark," she hissed as sharp pain engulfed her appendage. Still, a little bruise was better than death by a thousand alpaca bites or licks or whatever alpacas did to take out a blueberry-smeared target. She ignored her throbbing elbow and brushed the hair out of her eyes. Slipping on a headset, she studied the gaggle of alpacas—the motionless gaggle of alpacas.

Why had they stopped their frenzied stampede? Did the helicopter scare them?

"You must have made one hell of an impression on Elder Pachamama. She doesn't send the alpacas after everyone," Delores said through a chuckle.

Izzy shrugged off her pack, set it on the floor, and strapped into the seat next to the woman. "I don't know why you're laughing. I barely made it out alive."

"You were never in any real danger. The alpacas know to stop at the entrance to the helo pad," the pilot said, maneuvering the chopper into the air as the animals remained a safe distance away on the road.

Chest heaving, Izzy worked to catch her breath. "Nobody mentioned that."

"The elders were messing with you. You must have really pissed off Pachamama."

"I did. And they owe me a new Wham Bam. But it's over. I filed my report. I'm in the clear." Izzy peered out the window as they flew past the village. A shiver passed over her, and she felt for her locket, taking comfort in the cool metal.

Delores glanced at her. "You're not in the clear quite yet. Pamela wants to be patched through to your headset."

Izzy groaned and dropped her hands to her lap. "Not Pamela. I'm not sure what's worse. Enduring her wrath or being eaten alive by two dozen two-hundred-pound blueberry-obsessed herbivores." She rubbed her bleary eyes. "I'd trade my soul for a giant slice of cake and a mind-blowing orgasm right about now." She picked a pulpy remnant from her shirt and popped it into her mouth as a booming voice cut through the headset.

"I heard that."

Pamela!

Izzy cringed. "Even the cake and orgasm part?"

"Yes, and that's the least of your problems."

Izzy braced for impact.

"Another extraction, Isabelle? Are you trying to set a record, or do you enjoy seeing how high you can spike my blood pressure?" Pamela thundered.

Izzy deflated into the threadbare seat. "This extraction was due to . . . more of a joke—a prank."

"A prank?" Pamela shot back.

Izzy inhaled a tight breath.

"Upsetting the elders of an indigenous tribe isn't a joke." Pamela huffed, and the sound crackled through the speakers. "If it wasn't for your parents and grandparents, God rest their souls, I'd fire you for this shit. What were you thinking? This was a no-brainer assignment. Earthwise has worked with Elder Pachamama and her people for decades. They welcome university students to their village. They're committed to their culture and care for their land. Your job was to help them make an ecologically responsible plan for expanding their business."

The anger and guilt Izzy pretended didn't vex her built like a gathering storm in her chest. She pulled herself up and perched on the seat like an iron rod had been inserted into her spine. "I observed two Yellow-eyed Juncos and a nesting area where the villagers wanted to build a structure. Deforestation has decimated much of the mountainous region. I had to tell them they couldn't build that close to the stream. I stand by my work."

"It's not just *your* work, Isabelle. We're an environmental consulting group. Governments and businesses ask for our opinion—our unbiased, objective opinion. We're part of the team. You're not some lone environmental vigilante taking on the world."

Lone.

Izzy shuddered. "The lone bearer of burdens shall find their own demise," she murmured as the elder's words looped through her mind.

"What was that, Izzy? I couldn't make out what you said," Pamela replied.

"Nothing. I gave them my opinion. My professional opinion."

"And you lied to them," her boss hissed.

"I didn't lie . . . exactly." Dammit, she sounded like a schoolgirl trying to dodge detention.

"You know as well as I do that they're allowed to build as long as they adhere to the restrictions and follow building protocols."

Izzy squeezed her hands into tight fists. Her nails dug into her palms. "I couldn't trust that they'd do that. The builders they'd chosen were sketchy. They could have been out for themselves. Most people don't care who they hurt or what they destroy. It's our job to protect the parts of our world that can't speak for themselves."

"No, honey, you're wrong," Pamela said, her tone softening. "Most people want to do the right thing. They also want to provide for their families. Our clients come to us for guidance. I gave you this assignment because . . ."

"Why?" Izzy asked, a knot forming in her belly.

"Because it was an easy case, and I couldn't trust you with anything else. You've been a loose cannon. You run on pure passion. It's driven you your entire life. You're very much like your mother and grandmother. Passion can be an admirable quality—especially for an environmentalist. But if you don't control it and learn to remain level-headed, there's no place for you at Earthwise."

Izzy relaxed her fists and exhaled a shaky breath. Still, her pulse raced, but she had to tread carefully. "I'll be more objective, Pam. What's my next assignment?"

"You should take a break, kid. You haven't used a day of your paid time off."

Anxiety surged through Izzy's veins, quickening her already hammering pulse. "No breaks. I need an assignment. I have to work. If I'm not working, I can't . . ." She pictured a cemetery and four headstones. The emptiness hit like the air had been sucked from her lungs.

"Izzy, you have to stop beating yourself up. What happened with your family's business wasn't your fault."

Pamela was right about almost everything else, but she was dead wrong about this. Isabelle Adaire had decimated her family's name and legacy with one stroke of a pen.

"But it is my fault. The damage that's been done to so many. Your daughter . . . those towns . . . those people. And I can't say anything. I can't do a damned thing. I've lost . . . He took everything." Izzy said, the words tumbling from her lips as guilt clutched her heart.

"Enough, Izzy. What's done is done," Pamela barked, but a forlorn thread was woven into her harsh words.

"I know." Izzy closed her eyes as if the action could shield her from her mistakes. "What's my next assignment, Pam?" she asked, willing her voice to remain steady.

A long stretch of silence crackled.

"Pamela?"

The woman sighed. "Colorado. You'll fly into Rocky Mountain City and drive to the town from there."

Izzy clenched her hands again, tightening like a vault. "I don't take jobs in Colorado, especially not in Rocky Mountain City. You know why."

"You can't live like that," the woman shot back. "And this isn't up for debate. If you want to work, this is the assignment. It brings me no pleasure to say this, but it's your last chance to turn things around, Isabelle. I'm doing this as a courtesy."

"But . . ." Izzy blathered, "I know there are requests for evaluations in Costa Rica and Brazil. I could be on a flight to—"

"They don't want you," Pamela snarled. "They've asked for anyone *but you*."

Heat burned Izzy's cheeks. Humiliation and anger—that damned anger—ignited a prickly inferno, scorching what was left of her heart.

"You're going to Colorado. It's that, or you're fired." Pamela paused, keyboard clacking. "Hold on a second. There's a note on this assignment."

"What is it?" Izzy asked.

The clicks ceased.

"You were requested."

Izzy balked. "In Colorado? By whom?"

"It doesn't say. It could have been entered into the system incorrectly. But it doesn't matter. There's nowhere else for you to go. You still want to be employed, don't you?"

A coppery taste invaded Izzy's mouth. "I do."

"I'll email the details to you as soon as I can. It may take a couple of days. I'm waiting on one last piece of information. Here's what I can tell you now. It's a cut-and-dry case—a technicality required by a small mountain town's charter. You're there to work with the town manager and provide guidance. *Simple guidance and play nice with the town manager,*" she emphasized, speaking slowly.

Oh, hell no! Isabelle A. Adaire was no rubber stamp. This town manager was about to learn the definition of misery.

"Isabelle?" Pamela snapped.

"I got it, Pam," Izzy muttered, allowing that damned streak of anger to take control.

"Do you? Because you need to know your job and reputation are hanging by a thread," Pamela fired back. A sharp click echoed in her headset. Pamela had cut the connection.

Izzy's jaw set with determination. A storm brewed in her ice-blue eyes. This mystery town manager had no idea what was coming. She'd blow into that Colorado mountain town, riding high on a righteous wave of environmental justice. "Brace yourself, town manager," she whispered like Elder Pachamama reciting a spell. "This badass Earth-loving bitch is headed your way. You're about to get mucho fucked."

CHAPTER

Two

KIERAN

KIERAN STARRYCARD SAT at a table in an isolated corner of the swanky bar inside The Pike, a boutique hotel in the heart of Colorado's Rocky Mountain City. He took a sip of his whiskey, caught the eye of a tall brunette sitting at the bar, then returned his gaze to his cell phone's screen as his young niece sang her little heart out.

"Happy birthday, Uncle Kieran!" McKenzie Starrycard-Dunleavy belted as she approached the final bars of the tune. She paused dramatically, palms up, like an imaginary spotlight held her in its glow, giving him a second to lower the sound on his earbuds. "Happy birthday," the little girl crooned at the top of her lungs while completing a cartwheel. "To," she exclaimed, surely frightening—or possibly communicating—with any dog in the vicinity. "My uncle Kier!" She finished with a twirl. Spinning past a bowl of fruit, she plucked a berry from the top and popped it into her mouth. Sparing no drama, she leaned forward and bowed like she'd finished her first night starring on Broadway.

Cheers, clapping, and laughter followed the seven-year-old's rendition of the birthday staple. A staple Kieran had learned was best experienced via video call many miles from his hometown of Starrycard Creek, Colorado.

"Did you get that, Goldie?" the child asked, turning to the Starrycard matriarch.

The woman grinned, the skin crinkling at the corners of her eyes. "I did, little star. It's your first video."

"Goldie is letting me use her old phone to take pictures and videos for the summer," his niece chimed, holding up the cell. "I'm gonna make a million movies. I'm gonna record myself doing cartwheels and climbing trees and playing by the creek."

"That's exciting, Kenz," he replied, manipulating his features to project enthusiasm.

The image on the screen changed as his sister panned her phone across the back porch of Starrycard House, his childhood home and where his mother and father still lived. He observed the screen, taking in his parents, cozied up on one of the outdoor hanging swings. His grandparents, Rex and Goldie, were settled on one of the outdoor loveseats. Next up, his brother, Owen, and his brother-in-law, Jack, sat at a long rectangular table. The men held up beers, toasting the occasion.

"Make it so Uncle Kieran can see me," McKenzie called and pounced into the frame. She peered into the camera, moving close enough for him to see the three freckles on her sun-kissed left cheek. "What did you think of my singing, Uncle Kier? I've been practicing all day long. I've been singing and singing and singing because it's summer break, and I don't have to go to school until summer enrichment starts, but that's only two hours a day," the child rattled off, not taking a breath.

The girl could give a fast-talking auctioneer a run for the money.

"And I've been popping ibuprofen along with a couple of bottles of wine all day long. Medicating, medicating, and medicating," his little sister and McKenzie's mother, Eliza, added with a twist of a grin.

He recognized his sister's expression. He'd deduced this crafty smile, laced with exasperation, expressed that while the trappings of motherhood could be tiresome, they were also highly rewarding. He'd borrowed this expression and had utilized it quite successfully when reacting to people speaking about labors of love.

But as much as he would have liked to pick apart the facial movements and quirks that completed this expression, he'd learned he couldn't dwell on this exercise. The conversation would move on, and he'd need to be prepared to react. Experience had taught him he had roughly seven seconds. It was, however, easier to anticipate what was coming when it came to his family. As the oldest of six, he'd spent much of his childhood caring for and observing his siblings. The truth is, he probably knew more about them than they knew about themselves.

He curtailed those assertions and returned his attention to his niece. "Would you like my honest assessment of your performance, McKenzie?"

The child clapped—because that was what Starrycards did. Every Starrycard, save for him.

"Yes!" his niece exclaimed effusively. "And say it in your robot voice."

His robot voice was his actual voice, but he didn't mind her calling it that. He didn't even mind having his demeanor described as robotic. Robots were efficient, reliable, and precise. All qualities he possessed and admired.

He cleared his throat. "This year, you added a cartwheel to your presentation, which increased the level of movement and vigor. Overall, the effort put forth, combining singing, gymnastics, and the consumption of fruit, proved to be an enticing and electrifying ensemble."

Wide-eyed, McKenzie gifted him with a toothy grin as she took up the entire frame. "Does that mean you liked it?"

He mimicked her expression but modified it, reducing it by fifty percent. "I'd venture to say it might be the world's best performance of the 'Happy Birthday Song' ever completed by a seven-year-old in Starrycard Creek, Colorado."

This statement was factually true. Now, had any other seven-year-old ever serenaded him on his birthday, nearly blowing out his earbuds in the process? No, but that was a moot point. McKenzie enjoyed the activity, and he appreciated her effort.

"I'm getting real good at cartwheels and eating. Great-Grandma Goldie said I might eat every wild blueberry in Starrycard Creek. But I was wondering something, Uncle Kier," the child continued, her expression dimming.

"What's that?" he asked, studying the girl's face. *Had he not responded appropriately? Had he unintentionally led her to believe there was a deficiency in her performance?*

"You're always away from Starrycard Creek on your birthday," McKenzie mused.

This was an accurate assessment. But from the crease of her brow, he deduced that he needed to reassure her that his absence had nothing to do with her.

"I'm on official business for the town," he answered, which was true but not the entire story. Still, it was enough information for a child—and the rest of his family, for that matter. He dedicated his life to his hometown, and he did this with his whole heart. But what he did on his birthday was for him. It required privacy and anonymity that wasn't afforded to him in the small mountain town where everyone knew each other. Again, he glanced up and found the brunette at the bar, tossing a glance his way. A very promising behavior, clearly indicative of carnal interest.

"Your uncle Kieran is away on business as the newly elected town manager," his mother, Maeve O'Leary-Starrycard, added.

He returned his gaze to his cell. His mother's words had ushered in another round of applause from his family. He hailed from a lineage where applause, laughter, and celebration were as natural as breathing. Not to mention, as far as families go, his was quite effusive, possibly overly effusive. Sometimes, gratingly effusive, while other times, endearingly effusive.

This time, it was endearing and predictable. He knew what was coming, and that brought peace of mind.

Eliza propped up the camera, allowing everyone gathered on

the porch to be included in the frame. The creek, Starrycard Creek, named after his ancestor William Starrycard, who founded the town in 1880, rushed past the outdoor seating area. Fed from Starrycard Mountain's hot springs, the gurgling waters offered a comforting melody and a steady, reassuring presence in his life.

He waited for Owen to ask a snarky question—because that's what the man did.

"How many titles do you have now, bro?" Owen pressed.

There it was.

And it was an easy question to answer.

"Five. Councilman, school board member, Chamber of Commerce president, co-owner of Starrycard Creek Legal Services, and now Starrycard Creek's town manager."

He waited for a beat, knowing his niece would think of something to add to the list and disagree with him.

"No, you have six titles," McKenzie countered.

There she was.

"What's my sixth title?" he asked, relaxing into the cadence of conversing with his family.

"You're also my old-man uncle."

"Old-man uncle? I'm thirty-three." Kieran balked but added a slight upturn to the corners of his mouth so the child could ascertain that his words were in jest.

"You're my *oldest* uncle," she corrected. And she was correct.

Kieran didn't speak. As the child's old-man uncle, again, he knew what was coming—a list most likely followed by a family update.

"It goes you," McKenzie continued, counting on her fingers, "Uncle Owen, Uncle Finn, Uncle Christian, then my mommy, and then Aunt Caroline. But I'm gonna have another aunt when Uncle Finn marries Hailey. Uncle Finn and Almost-Aunt Hailey are in Arizona camping. Did you know that?"

He'd predicted correctly, and yes, he knew the location of his brother and his brother's fiancée. He made it his business to know everything when it came to the town and his family.

"I did know about the camping trip. Finn and Hailey called early this morning to wish me a happy birthday. They'll be camping in a remote setting and won't have cell phone service for a few days."

"Uncle Christian and the Rattlers are playing baseball in Chicago, and Aunt Caroline told me two days ago that she might be home for Christmas. Did they call to wish you a happy birthday?"

"They did earlier today," he reassured the child.

McKenzie nodded, then gasped.

"What is it?" he asked, noting the child's wide eyes and parted lips as he patted a slim notebook in his pocket. That was the face McKenzie made when she'd had an epiphany. He'd labeled it *MSD 15* in his notebook. It stood for McKenzie Starrycard-Dunleavy. The fifteen simply represented where it fell on the list. While his family owned Starrycard Creek Paper Company, an artisan papermaking business, the notebook he kept with him wasn't from their shop. It was a nondescript notepad, something he purchased years ago without his family's knowledge.

He mirrored her expression, again dialing it back fifty percent. This allowed him to express enough emotion to show her he was invested in whatever discovery the child had uncovered. However, these discoveries were often peculiar musings, but they didn't stop him from enjoying the interactions. In fact, despite his niece's often outlandish contemplations and the girl's tendency to request an excessive amount of ice cream, which he always allowed her to consume, McKenzie, with her swishing pigtails and toothy grin, was one of his favorite people. It was also quite helpful that many of McKenzie's expressions mirrored her mother's. The overlap between his sister and his niece helped reduce notebook entries.

"I remembered what Grandma Maeve told me. You have the same birthday as William Starrycard," McKenzie announced.

Again, she was correct.

"I do."

"And he got to Starrycard Creek before it even had a name. And he got here on his birthday."

Kieran nodded. "You know your town's history."

"And that's the day he saw Fiona Donnelly, and they fell in love. Are you going to fall in love today, Uncle Kier? They say love is in the cards in Starrycard Creek. Right, Goldie?"

"Indeed, they do, little star," his grandmother replied, catching his mother's eye.

Anytime his mother and Goldie exchanged knowing looks, it often meant they'd devised a plan to meddle in a Starrycard's life. Over the years, his mother and grandmother had abundantly clarified two facts. His mom wanted more grandchildren, and his grandmother loved love. That's why his absence was particularly advantageous. But he would not fall in love today or any day.

He willed himself to smile. Nothing over the top. Simply a movement to mask a hollowness brought on by his niece's question. An odd reaction for him. But he couldn't convey that the child's words had struck a nerve. "I can't fall in love. I'm not in Starrycard Creek. I'm two hours away in Rocky Mountain City. Given those conditions, love is *not* in the cards for me."

And it never would be.

His job was to make sure the town remained solvent and vibrant. As the town's manager, it fell to him to secure the future of his family's business, the other businesses in town, his niece, and every child growing up in his hometown.

Except, despite emanating a cool, reassuring confidence—an expression that had served him well and led him to hold several prominent posts in Starrycard Creek—he'd fucked up.

And he didn't like fucking up.

He'd worked his ass off not to fuck up.

He craved order and consistency. That's what he provided for the town. A steady hand. Unbiased, accurate assessments and opinions. Close attention to detail.

But he'd neglected one significant element in the town's charter. He'd missed a submission date, and that uncharacteristic oversight had triggered the shitstorm he was trying damned hard to quash.

It was another reason he was spending his birthday in Rocky Mountain City.

"Can we go on a Kenzie and Uncle Kier treasure hunt when you get back? Will you draw a map for me?" the child asked as she bounced over to Rex and Goldie and settled herself between the pair. "Uncle Kieran makes the best maps, and I'm his favorite treasure hunter. He knows all the good spots."

Goldie patted McKenzie's cheek. "I believe he's known about them since he was around your age. He liked to make maps for his brothers and sisters to find little trinkets. Didn't you also have a portable easel with you?" she asked, staring into the cell's camera.

Goldie knew damned well he used to hike with the portable easel. She'd given it to him.

He ignored the part about the easel and focused on his niece. "Yes, McKenzie, I can create a map, and we can hike."

"I like to call it treasure hiking," she replied.

He borrowed Eliza's labor-of-love expression. "It doesn't matter what you call it as long as we understand the meaning and intention behind the act."

She cocked her head to the side. "What?"

"It means we'll go on a treasure hike," he clarified. He had to remember to employ directness with her.

"Woo-hoo!" McKenzie exclaimed. The kid shot to her feet, knocked out another cartwheel, popped a handful of berries into her mouth, and clapped.

Damn, she was endearingly effusive.

He recognized his grandmother's tone and the twitch of a grin. She often spoke with a lilt and a cadence that resembled a spider spinning its web. Goldie crafted word webs to pose a question or make an assertion she also meant to serve as a revelation. However, her line of thinking often bordered on the magical and mystical—especially when it came to Starrycard Creek folklore.

And while her farfetched musings on matters of the heart could pertain to others, they would never apply to him.

"I'm sure your uncle Kieran has Starrycard Creek paper with him. We know that having that bit of magic with you can steer you toward your destiny." She turned to her husband and kissed his cheek. "I was many, many miles away from Starrycard Creek when my destiny was revealed."

McKenzie clapped. "Do you have Starrycard Creek paper with you, Uncle Kieran?"

Kieran looked up, but he didn't check on the brunette. Instead, he glanced across the hotel lobby and into the gift shop. He'd picked this spot in the bar precisely because it allowed him to be on the lookout for a birthday companion and observe what was happening inside the bustling shop. But this was no ordinary hotel gift shop. The Pike Hotel had one amenity other hotels didn't. It maintained sprawling botanic gardens on its grounds. And this gift shop offered an array of botanical-themed merchandise made by local artisans and craftsmen. He peered at a box next to the cash register. A female gift shop employee carefully opened the flap and removed a stack of folded cards and envelopes. She showed the items to another employee, who placed them on a rack. Within seconds, a couple migrated toward the new cards.

Kieran returned his attention to his cell's screen. "Alas, I am not in possession of Starrycard Creek paper." He checked his watch. "And I need to bring this call to a close. I have an appointment."

"Is it the appointment with your friend from law school? The one you asked to review the town's charter?" his mother asked.

He took in the crease between her brows. She required reassurance.

"Maybe I should stay on the call," she mused. "I am the mayor of Starrycard Creek. If there's a problem—"

"There's no problem, Mom," he said, taking control of the conversation. "I'm simply here to consult with a colleague. I've got everything under control." He maintained his cool exterior, which was not a small feat since he was lying. His heart pounded in his chest. The fear of losing control nearly chipped away his calm demeanor.

The crease on his mother's face disappeared. "You always do, dear. Happy birthday to my firstborn. My darling, Kieran."

"Happy birthday, Kieran!" the rest of his family called, smiling, and, of course, clapping.

He removed his earbuds, pocketed his cell, and glanced toward the gift shop. He wasn't sure what pulled his attention that way again until a swish of blond hair caught his eye. He observed a woman in sandals, a slim-fitting black knit skirt that hit above her knees, and a white button-down blouse. Her attire wasn't explicitly seductive, yet it accentuated her slender silhouette. He couldn't see her face. She was turned away from him, but that had its advantages. He could make out the curve of her ass beneath the dark fabric. And it was a fucking gorgeous ass. Desire sparked. It wasn't just her toned legs and inviting curves that captivated him. She moved like a lynx, effortlessly winding through the shop, drawing her fingertips across display tables. He scanned the area and widened his sweep to the hotel lobby. He wasn't the only one who'd spied the alluring creature. He counted four men and two women tossing not-so-subtle glances toward the blonde. "Let me see you," he whispered. She couldn't have heard him. There was no way. Amidst the lively bar and lobby, at least fifty voices overlapped, drowning out any chance of his words reaching her ears.

But she stilled and glanced over her shoulder.

The breath caught in his throat.

He'd always had an eye for symmetry and balance. It was one of the reasons he'd connected with the outdoors. Nature made sense when the rest of the world became too much, too loud, too chaotic. When he longed for order and routine, he'd hike to one of the four hot springs on Starrycard Mountain. In the summer, he'd be on the lookout for perfectly symmetrical fauna and flora.

In that fleeting, peculiar instance, the clamor of the active hotel faded, and he focused on one aspect of the woman: her profile. His analytical mind went to work. Her nose had a delicate slope. Her chin, a soft roundness. The gentle contour of her cheek highlighted her prominent cheekbones and lent a refined grace to her features. He yearned to gaze at her straight on like a butterfly pinned to a display board. A new impulse surged within him, compelling and intense. But he couldn't give in. He diverted his gaze.

She was not part of the plan. Do not get distracted.

He caught the brunette's eye. She sat a little taller and arched her back, presenting her breasts. A sign her interest in him hadn't waned. He'd perfected the art of choosing a partner for a one-night stand. He did this by focusing on a set of behavioral cues. Between her body positioning and the back-and-forth eye contact, the brunette signaled she was up for a sexual encounter with a stranger. He also knew what he looked like. He understood how women reacted to his chiseled features and six-foot-five-inch muscled frame.

He schooled his features.

Sex would come later.

First, he had to meet with an old classmate and the man's wife.

They should have information for him.

"Kieran," a man called.

As if on cue, Kieran stood and greeted his guests. "Nelson, Amina, I appreciate you meeting with me tonight." He rose to his feet and pulled out Amina's chair for her. Disregarding his better judgment, he peered into the gift shop. A pudgy man in a rumpled shirt appeared to have initiated a conversation with the blonde. However, the blonde angled her body away from him, conveying she wasn't interested.

Good.

Good?

Why should he care? This woman was not his priority.

What was happening to him?

It had to be stress. He needed to work out this clawing, nagging energy. A night of hot, sweaty sex was what he needed to achieve a mindset shift. He didn't always seek out comfort when stressed. He wasn't the touchy-feely type—except when he fucked. And he would not be sleeping with that blonde. She was too much of a wildcard.

He set aside his carnal musings and attended to his guests. "I'm sorry. I was distracted. I thought I saw an acquaintance."

"No worries. It's always good to see you, Kieran," Nelson Abadi said. The rotund man with smooth, dark skin and bright eyes grinned.

Kieran relaxed a fraction. Nelson was always easy to decipher. The man wore his heart on his sleeve. He didn't joke around excessively, and he spoke clearly and to the point. Qualities Kieran appreciated. Nelson's wife was harder to decode. He assumed it was due to her work as a clinical psychologist and that he'd requested her help on a private medical matter. He nodded to Nelson's wife, not sure how to address her in this setting. He opted to go with a formal approach. "It's good to see you, Dr. Abadi."

"Amina," the woman supplied warmly, settling into the chair.

Time to get to business. Kieran Starrycard wasn't one to waste time. He returned to his seat and folded his hands on the table. "Nelson informed me via email that you've got another engagement to attend tonight." He glanced at the brunette, then flicked his gaze to the gift shop. *Focus.* He cleared his throat. "I promise not to take up too much of your time. I also have plans this evening."

"Our kids are home with Nelson's mother, and we've got tickets for a show at the performing arts center," Amina supplied.

"I appreciate you fitting me into your schedule," Kieran began, maintaining a neutral countenance. He had two objectives. Each individual at the table had information for him. It was time to collect this data and integrate it.

"I assume you were able to review the town charter I sent you," he said, directing the question to Nelson.

Nelson nodded. "I did. And I think it was a blessing in disguise that you missed the date to appoint yourself as land steward."

Every muscle in Kieran's body tightened. "Why would you say that? If anyone cares about developing the land on Starrycard Mountain, it's me. It's my home."

It was where he controlled nearly every day-in and day-out aspect of town life, which equated to his life. And thanks to—or despite—an obscure caveat in the town charter, there was a damned good chance that he wouldn't have the last say when it came to the one place he could relax. The one place where he could easily anticipate what was coming and react accordingly without assessing every minute detail. Navigating new situations and encountering unanticipated events were an exhausting brain drain. He could feel his body inching toward that running-on-empty, aggravated place. He detected his senses sharpening. Sounds that once blended into the hum of the hotel now competed for his attention. The flickering candles dotting the tables taunted him. The clink of glasses grated his nerves.

Maintain a neutral front. Eyes on Nelson.

"You believe I have no recourse?" he asked, his voice void of emotion.

Nelson offered a placating grin—not a good sign. "You're the best contract attorney I know, Kieran. I'm sure you pored over the charter line by line. You must have come to the same conclusion I did."

A muscle ticked on Kieran's jaw. A tiny ripple. A crack in his facade. *Pull it together.* He balled one hand into a fist beneath the table, channeling the negative emotions into his constricted fingers. "I hoped another pair of eyes might see something I missed."

"My professional opinion is to play nice with whoever the state sends in to assess the land," Nelson began. "The charter says that this individual will guide the town in developing the mountain. The position can be permanent or transferred to another individual after the initial environmental assessment. It's quite ingenious that your ancestors were forward-thinking enough to understand that the town may want to expand one day, and that expansion should consider the area's ecology. Not many contracts and charters I've reviewed from the eighteen hundreds contain such mindful stipulations."

Dammit! Kieran shifted in his seat. Mindful or not, it didn't help him. He was fucked. If anyone could have found a loophole or a workaround, it would have been Nelson.

"I understand," he answered, irritation flooding his system. "What I object to is that this *person* acting as land steward has no connection to the land in question. I've already collaborated with an architect and an engineer to create detailed plans. We need to begin the initial land work and construction as soon as possible while the weather is favorable. Over the last decade, I've watched Starrycard Creek lose vital revenue in the winter months. If we were allowed to develop parts of the mountain, that would bring a steady stream of income to our local economy. It would spark job creation, increase property values, and attract more tourists. Again, I have a strategy in place. I hadn't anticipated the need to clear it with an outsider—some so-called expert."

Nelson drummed his fingers on the table, then stilled. "Try looking at the situation from another angle. Perhaps it's a godsend you missed the date."

Had Nelson incurred head trauma?

"I cannot see how that statement is accurate or helpful."

The man raised his hands defensively. "Hear me out, Kier. Had you applied for the role of land steward, there's a good chance the state would have denied it. They could claim a conflict of interest thanks to your last name. And in another scenario . . ."

"Yes?" Kieran pressed.

"If someone else wanted to bid to develop the land, they could also cite your connection to the town and claim that made you biased. The issue could get stuck in court and—"

"And cause further delays," Kieran finished. A knot formed in his belly. This was his fear. This clawing concern was what had distracted him from meeting the deadline. There was no way in hell he'd permit anyone to ruin Starrycard Creek's charm and small-town feel. And there was no way in hell he'd capitulate to some stranger the state deemed qualified. Still, despite his dogged need for control, he had to admit the matter was no longer his alone to decide. His body went rigid. "I appreciate your guidance and advice, Nelson."

"Anytime," the good-humored man replied when his cell phone chimed. He removed the device from his pocket and eyed the screen. "It's my mother. She's trying to set up the projector for the boys to watch a movie. I need to step out and give her a call and tell her how to do it."

"I'll meet you outside, honey. I need a moment with Kieran," Amina said and patted her husband's arm.

Nelson rose from his seat. "We'll see you in a few weeks, Kier. We're bringing the kids to Starrycard Creek for the Fourth of July. We'll finally make it down to your neck of the woods."

"I look forward to seeing you then," Kieran answered and shook the man's hand.

"And good luck with the land steward. Who knows," Nelson called over his shoulder. "You might hit it off with the person."

Fucking doubtful.

Kieran exhaled an audible breath. One task completed, albeit not to his satisfaction. One task to go.

He turned to Nelson's wife. "Would you prefer I call you Dr. Abadi while we discuss my concerns?"

"No, Amina is fine," the woman replied, employing the same warm yet neutral expression she'd used during their previous telehealth video sessions.

"And you have the results?"

"I do."

"And?" he asked, mimicking the psychologist's facial appearance.

"Your aptitude tests show you're highly gifted. But you already knew that."

He nodded. This was not new information. "As I told you in our first online session, I was tested at school when I was a child. That's where we learned I'd scored in the gifted and talented range."

"And that correlates with what else I have to share with you," she continued.

"I'm on the autism spectrum, aren't I?" Kieran focused on the doctor's eyes, relying on a trick he'd taught himself years ago.

Amina narrowed her gaze. "You meet the criterion. I'm curious why you chose now to seek out the diagnosis."

"I required the information to solidify a decision."

She leaned in. "What decision would that be?"

He maintained a serene front. "I don't require psychological services. I simply wanted to garner the information. I conveyed this during our sessions."

"Humor me," Amina said, adding a warm grin to her attentive expression. It was a nice touch. He made a note to add this behavior combination to his repertoire.

"The decision to remain a bachelor," he replied, shifting his gaze over Amina's shoulder to look into the gift shop. The beguiling blonde stood next to a display of pastel-colored mugs. The man in a crinkled shirt he'd noticed earlier stood a few steps from her. Kieran clenched his jaw. *What was that fucker doing? She wasn't interested in him.*

Amina followed his line of sight.

Kieran snapped his attention back to the psychologist. "My apologies."

"Is your acquaintance in the gift shop?"

"No, I was mistaken."

Amina nodded. "May I pose another question?"

"You may."

"What if I told you that you hadn't met the criterion? Would you be trolling the internet for a wife?" The woman cracked a grin.

"No," he answered straight-faced. "My place in this world is to ensure the viability of Starrycard Creek. If I'm married to anything, it's my work. There's no room for anything else."

"There's always room, Kieran. And being on the spectrum doesn't mean you can't maintain a loving partnership. Autism doesn't prevent you from experiencing emotions, and that includes love and attraction. You love your family, don't you?"

"That's different. There are different expectations with my niece, siblings, parents, and grandparents. A partner—a wife would want more than I could give." He cleared his throat to distract himself from the peculiar hollowness in his chest.

Amina leaned in. "Are you sure that's your decision to make?"

He squared his shoulders. "I require control. I don't have the luxury of battling with romantic attachment dilemmas on a daily basis. The stress of anticipating the upcoming changes in Starrycard Creek is why I missed the deadline. I've been sidetracked. For this reason alone, I can't contemplate forging a long-term romantic relationship. It would distract me. Deplete me."

"Did you let anyone know about the deadline? Did you ask for help?" Amina asked, raising an eyebrow.

Again, he was confused by her question. "No, why would I?"

"Because you don't have to go it alone."

The doctor was wrong.

"I appreciate that you're trying to lead me to a eureka moment. I assume that behavior is part and parcel of being a clinical psychologist. However, I've made my decision. And it appears your husband has completed his call," he added, gesturing toward the lobby where Nelson stood. Kieran rose to his feet and helped Amina from her chair. "Our time is up."

"That's usually my line." She studied him. "Let me leave you with this, Kieran. There's always room for transformation and rebirth."

"You sound like you're describing a butterfly's lifecycle." He'd applied a skeptical bend to the words, but he was slightly intrigued.

"It applies to the human condition," Amina explained. "And here's what I'd like you to keep in mind. There's no one path to love. It's practicing a wide range of behaviors and seeing what works."

"That sounds like pretending, faking it, bullshitting to offer a crude term," he surmised.

"Whatever you call it, our reality comes down to what we believe about ourselves."

He watched the woman for a beat. This conversation had gone awry. He'd only required her assistance with a diagnosis. That information had been shared. Now, he needed to divert the conversation from himself and his shortcomings. He reviewed his choices and deemed that humor would be the best choice. He slapped Eliza's labor-of-love grin to his lips. "Will I be charged for this session, doc?"

"No, you won't. But you should know I work with people, on and off the spectrum, who want to be loving, supportive partners and build the communication skills that foster positive, fulfilling relationships."

Therapy? No way.

He maintained Eliza's vexed-yet-invested expression. "While I appreciate the offer, I can assure you that I will not be seeking those services."

"The door is always open. Don't underestimate yourself, Kieran. And if you meet someone, don't discard their feelings because they don't fit your *current* plan," Dr. Abadi offered.

Current plan? All his plans were current.

Conforming to etiquette, Kieran conceded with a nod, masking his dissent behind a cordial yet restrained smile as he bid farewell. Watching Amina reunite with her husband, he felt a surge of relief. He exhaled a slow breath and savored his final sip of whiskey, but he couldn't take his eyes off his friends. His gaze remained fixed. He studied the couple. They'd married when he and Nelson were second-year law students in Denver. He watched as Nelson reached for his wife's hand. He observed the pair. They smiled—no, they beamed at each other—as they left the hotel. A muscle ticked on Kieran's jaw as a covetous emotion threatened to overtake him. He pushed aside the irrational reaction. It was time to finalize his plans for the evening.

He scanned the bar and found the brunette eyeing him. The stool next to her was empty. All he had to do was walk over and sit down. He'd done this enough to know that in less than an hour, he could be clutching the brunette's ass as she rode his cock. The release he desperately desired was well within his grasp. But he didn't move. As if he'd adopted his mother and grandmother's unfounded sense of allowing the universe to mystically guide his behavior, he paused, and—quite remarkably—he was rewarded by his uncharacteristic actions when a woman's raised voice pierced the air.

"Listen, buddy, like I told you before, I'm not interested in getting a drink with you."

This wasn't any voice. Even though he'd never heard this voice before, he recognized it. No, he connected with it. Whatever it was, he knew what he had to do. As if he were a reprogrammed robot, he strode past the brunette and sized up the blonde and her unwelcome companion. The man wore a wrinkled baby blue collared shirt and creased khaki trousers. His cheeks were flushed. He clutched a beer. He staggered forward—a telltale sign he'd had one too many. Standing no more than five-nine, Kieran had a good six inches on him. The guy was doughy as hell. He probably hadn't lifted more than a stein of pale ale in years. In contrast, Kieran adhered to a strict exercise regimen, resulting in a mere three percent body fat and chiseled abs that could put elite athletes to shame.

His footsteps echoed crisply against the tile with each powerful step. He entered the gift shop and zeroed in on the pair. The blonde's back remained turned, her face just out of view.

The man gripped her wrist. "Come on, baby, have a drink with me. I'll make it worth your while."

White-hot anger tore through him.

This wasn't a common reaction. He prided himself on maintaining a steady countenance. But the sight of this Neanderthal with his meaty paw wrapped around his mystery blonde's wrist had him itching to land a punch that would leave this handsy drunk seeing stars for days.

No longer driven by logic and reason, he simply reacted. He came up behind the blonde and wrapped his arm around her waist. She inhaled a tight breath and flicked her gaze toward him. He could feel her eyes on him, and Christ, it sent a jolt of pure adrenaline surging through his veins. But he couldn't meet her eye. He had to deal with the intoxicated dough boy.

He glared at the man, utilizing a fierce expression he'd never employed. He caught his reflection in a mirror. Jaw lock. Eyes blazing. More beast than man, he tightened his hold on the blonde's hip. His protective posture matched the thrum of emotion pulsing through his body. He scrutinized the unwanted suitor. "If you want to make it out of this gift shop in one piece, I suggest you release my *girlfriend's* wrist, or I'll fucking break yours."

CHAPTER
Three

KIERAN

TENSION CRACKLED IN THE AIR. Kieran rarely raised his voice—especially in public. He'd never needed to employ the tactic until today. He studied the now white-faced wrist-gripper. The man's eyes looked ready to pop out of his head. *Excellent!* It appeared his beastly demeanor elicited the desired reaction: total fucking terror.

The doughy man's jaw dropped. "She's your girlfriend, dude?"

Dude? Anyone who added *dude* to the end of a sentence wasn't vying for Genius of the Year.

Pushing aside that observation, Kieran confronted the meathead. "She is. What kind of jackass harasses a woman while she's picking out a birthday card for her boyfriend?" He heard the words coming out of his mouth. Of course, he did. He'd said them. He just hadn't planned to say them.

No, that's not what was happening—not exactly.

He wasn't sure what he was doing, which was a departure from his usual behavior. Still, staking a claim to the woman by calling her his girlfriend—even if it wasn't true—was a swift and effective way to get the handsy man out of the picture. That being said, he'd cannonballed into uncharted territory. He wasn't one to lie or make up false claims, but something had shifted inside him the second the gift shop groper touched his golden-haired beauty. A call to action had overridden the orchestrated set of behaviors he'd meticulously practiced. These behaviors had served him well. They'd allowed him to maintain his composure and fit in socially. He'd recklessly tossed them aside, and it was . . . exhilarating.

"You heard what my *boyfriend* said. Are you going to let go, or should I tell him to break both your wrists? And what a shame that would be." She gestured with her free hand toward the man's drink. "How will you slurp your beer? I guess you'll have to use a straw," she cooed. It was a nice touch. It added a sweetness that functioned as a veiled threat. Once upon a time, those had been tricky for him to decipher. Fortunately, growing up with five snarky siblings had helped him decode these situations.

Still, he couldn't get mired in semantics because, holy hell, his blonde was going along with his story. She could have given him the same treatment she'd given the dough boy and told him to buzz off. She didn't. And she called him her boyfriend. Electricity zinged through his body. He'd never felt so alive, so connected.

"Don't break my wrists, dude. My fiancée would kill me. She thinks I'm stuck on my laptop in our room, tied up in a work meeting," the man slurred.

This guy had a fiancée and a job? There's a shocker.

Kieran shifted his gaze to where the drunk was still gripping the blonde's wrist. "I'll say this once more. *Let go of my girlfriend, or I'll break your fucking wrists.*"

Meaty Paws blinked. His frozen expression communicated that he hadn't realized he was still touching the woman. He released his grip, pulling back like he'd touched a hot stove. But that didn't stop him from resting his gaze on the woman's cleavage. "Sorry," he mumbled, "I thought you were giving me a signal."

Kieran scoffed. His neurological condition limited his ability to read social signals, but even he'd read the blonde's message loud and clear.

"Here's a signal," the blonde replied. She held her hand in the man's line of sight, which happened to be in front of her breasts, and flipped him off. "And a piece of advice. Don't hit on women when you've got a fiancée."

A vulgar gesture combined with a helpful tidbit of information was another nice touch. But the idiot didn't move. He required a more direct command.

"Fuck off," Kieran growled, lowering his voice for a menacing effect.

It worked.

The guy stumbled. Beer swished from his glass and soaked his shirt as he spun on his heel and hightailed it out of the gift shop.

Kieran peered at the blonde, feeling damned good. Hold on. She was no longer simply *the blonde*. Thanks to his choice of words, she was his girlfriend. By participating in his ruse and reciprocating by calling him her boyfriend, she'd become party to the deception. No, that wasn't it. She was his fake girlfriend. He was her fake boyfriend.

Fake.

He pondered the word.

When he'd pondered faking it, it sounded exhausting. Who knew pretending could be so thrilling?

But he had to move on if he wanted to navigate this encounter successfully. What behavior did this situation require? What would a boyfriend do after a drunken slob had manhandled his girlfriend?

The answer came in a flash.

She appeared unshaken, but he should inquire as to her mental state.

"Are you okay?" he asked, discarding his beastly behavior and employing a gentler tone.

She didn't look up to meet his gaze. Instead, she leaned into him. Her ass brushed against his thigh as she studied the rack of painted greeting cards. The contact reminded him of her gorgeous backside, stirring desire within him. However, that wasn't the only point of contact. His arm lingered around her waist—a novel experience for him outside the intimacy of sex. Surprisingly, he found the contact with his pretend girlfriend not just tolerable but pleasant. Her slender form complemented his own towering, well-defined physique.

She lifted her left hand and slid her fingertips across a card adorned with a painted midnight blue butterfly on the cover. His mind kicked into high gear while he waited for her reply to his question regarding her emotional state. Like a supercomputer analyzing a complex puzzle, he drank in her sensory cues and sifted through the data. She smelled like jasmine and vanilla—sweet and comfortingly familiar with a touch of sensuality. Her nails were cut short and unpainted. No wedding ring. From his vantage point, he eyed the crown of her head. She was a natural blonde—not that he had anything against hair dye. He flexed his free hand. It was all he could do to keep himself from twisting a golden lock around his finger. *What a peculiar urge.* He employed hair pulling during sex but had never yearned to feel a woman's hair to add another point of contact. And he still hadn't gazed at her straight on. His pulse kicked up at the prospect of simply looking at her, like that alone was what he wanted for his birthday. She was a gift—a wrapped birthday gift he craved to strip bare.

Strip bare.

The notion of this woman naked had him half-cocked.

"I'm fine," she purred. Her reply contained a playful, sassy note wrapped in a velvety warmth. "Thank you for asking, and . . ."

"And?" he repeated, hanging on her every word.

"And I know you've been watching me from your spot in the bar," she added, and he'd swear he detected a thread of amusement in her voice.

She liked having him watch her.

And she'd observed him.

They'd had each other in their sights. How tantalizingly intriguing.

This was valuable information, and it explained why she hadn't told him to get lost. Only one conclusion could be deduced. When she looked at him, she liked what she saw. As much as he would have enjoyed basking in this disclosure, he needed to formulate a reply.

"I'm relieved the encounter didn't rattle you. *And* to be precise, several people have been watching you," he continued, sticking to the facts—facts that would most likely pique her interest.

"My, my," she cooed, taking the bait. This utterance didn't have the saccharine-sweet knife-to-the-back quality she'd used with the beer-sloshing wrist-grabber. Like before, there was a sultry, amused quality to her tone. "Not only have you been watching me, you've been monitoring my admirers. I appear to be causing quite a ruckus with the gentlemen on my last night in Rocky Mountain City."

He processed her reply. By dropping that line about it being her last night in Rocky Mountain City, she'd insinuated that she wasn't from around here. She could have said her last night staying at The Pike, but she didn't. In addition, she didn't appear to have any companions with her—male or female. These assumptions, coupled with her admission of watching him, increased the likelihood that she'd be willing to engage in a night of carnal bliss. But there was more. He liked listening to her speak. Her tone was strong. It held an assuredness but with a soft edge. Her speech possessed a pleasing cadence.

As much as he'd love to mull over the agreeable nuances of her voice, he couldn't waste time on this endeavor.

"It wasn't only men who've been watching you. There were women. Two, to be exact," he offered.

"Only two women?" she mused.

She enjoyed whatever it was they were doing.

So did he.

"Two women. Four men," he answered, keeping his responses short and to the point. She seemed to like that.

"I must correct you," she countered. "The total is five men counting you. It's crucial to maintain an accurate count when collecting data."

And holy fuck! She sounded like him. He grinned—for another reason. It wasn't often people proved him wrong. "I stand corrected. Two women. *Five* men." She was highly intelligent. It was time to ask a few questions that would give him some insight into engaging in a one-night stand. He maintained a neutral front. "You don't seem bothered by the attention. Do you like being observed?"

She shifted, damn near close to rubbing her ass against his cock. "I like having your eyes on me."

What was he supposed to say to that?

"But it makes sense," she continued, taking the pressure off him to reply.

"How so?" He could hear the rasp in his voice.

"There's nothing nefarious about a *boyfriend* keeping an eye on his *girlfriend*. It's endearing. And, in our case, also a little naughty."

The probability of a one-night stand was increasing by the second.

"What makes it naughty?" he pressed. He had to keep up their titillating conversation. He'd learned long ago that questions kept interactions going.

"If a girlfriend was searching for the perfect birthday card for her boyfriend, it would imply that they cared deeply for each other. One wanting desperately to please the other, while the other's enthralled with observing their partner's process."

This woman!

The probability of sex peaked in the high nineties. In addition, he gained more information regarding her intelligence from her word choices and continued confident tone. Perhaps she was a scientist or a doctor.

"But," she continued, "that assertion would only apply to us if today was your birthday. Otherwise, there'd be no reason for me to select a card for you."

He'd never been happier to be born on this exact day.

He leaned forward, his lips mere inches from the shell of her ear. "Today is my birthday."

"Is it?" Again, he could hear the sultry thread of pleasure in her voice—and he liked it.

He glanced at his watch.

9:22 p.m.

"It's my birthday for the next two hours and thirty-eight minutes."

She plucked the card with the painted butterfly from the rack. "Have you made a birthday wish?"

He tightened his grip on her hip. "Not yet. But I know what I want." It was a bold statement. He deduced she'd read between the lines and deciphered his meaning.

"How do you know you want something if you haven't gotten a proper look at it?" Slowly, she turned, her body brushing against him as she maneuvered to look him in the eyes. A smirk graced her lips. "Hello, Birthday Card Boyfriend."

Birthday Card Boyfriend?

It was a mouthful, but it had an agreeable rolling cadence. Nevertheless, he couldn't fixate on the title. A flood of emotions swept over him. His eyes dilated as he focused on her. The breath caught in his throat. He'd never seen a face so aesthetically pleasing. Her profile had not prepared him for this level of perfection. And then he got to her eyes—her utterly beguiling eyes. He recognized this shade of icy blue. He'd known it his entire life. He flicked his gaze to the rack of cards, then back to her face. "Your appearance reminds me of the symmetry of butterfly wings."

Dammit! He should have held back his opinion. He watched

her, trying to decipher if his bizarre comparison had turned her off.

"I appreciate the observation. However, social norms would suggest you greet me in response to me greeting you." She wasn't being snarky or rude. Her statement was direct and without judgment. It was refreshing.

He frowned. "I don't know your name, nor do I have a nickname for you yet, like you have for me."

Yet? Why had he inserted that adverb into his response?

She shook her head. "We're not going to share our names."

Probability of sex: 99.99%

Her response made it even more likely she wouldn't want to maintain a connection after tonight. This information should have been a positive development. It was, and it wasn't. The conflicting emotions confused him. Try as he might, he couldn't pinpoint why it didn't feel like an encouraging advancement despite the pleasing probability.

Move on. Ask a question.

He admired the gentle curve of her bottom lip. "What should I call you?"

She tapped the card to her chin. "I haven't decided." She picked out a second card and corresponding envelope from the display, choosing one with a painted flower. She held up the items. "If you don't mind, I'd like to purchase these."

He gently removed the paper items from her grip. "Any particular reason you chose these two? The shop is filled with cards."

Her bottom lip trembled. He wasn't expecting that.

Was it something he'd said?

He felt a pang near his heart, a reaction to her distress. "Do you admire the starbloom flower and the starwing butterfly?" he asked, posing another question in hopes it would return the sly smirk to her lips.

She glanced at the cards. "You know your flora and fauna, Birthday Card Boyfriend." The smirk didn't return. Instead, she cocked her head to the side as a curious glint appeared in her eyes. That behavior was an improvement from the trembling lip.

"Allow your boyfriend to purchase these cards for you," he said and gestured to the clerk.

"Why would I allow that?" she asked. And there it was—the twist of her lips that made him want to press his body to hers.

He was inexorably drawn to her, captivated by the vivid allure of her ice-blue eyes. "Your birthday card boyfriend enjoys doing things for you."

It wasn't a lie.

She studied him and shrugged. "Who am I to constrain my boyfriend's joy?"

Permission granted.

"We'll take these," he said to the clerk. He pulled a bill from his pocket, paid, and then added the change to the botanic garden's donation jar.

"You're lucky you got them," the clerk crooned, placing the cards into a clear plastic bag. "We don't often get these in. They'll sell out in a matter of hours."

"Is that so?" he replied as he handed the slim bag to his fake girlfriend. "Shall we?" he said, directing the question to the blonde. This should be the moment he suggested they spend the night together. But he didn't gesture toward the lobby or the bar. He pointed to the door leading to the botanic gardens, which didn't fit his plans for tonight. The woman—his fake girlfriend— was interested in him sexually. He'd read the signs. And he was certainly attracted to her. His head understood this, but another part of him wanted more.

What was *more*? He couldn't define it.

His fake girlfriend gifted him with a grin, revealing dimples on her cheeks—symmetrical dimples. Jesus, her perfection only amplified.

"I love the botanic gardens at night." She entwined her arm with his—a behavior that would make sense if they were in a real relationship—not a fake one. The ruse didn't need to continue.

The drunk *dude* was gone. Still, it appeared she enjoyed pretending they were a couple, and he couldn't deny the more they extended the deception, the more curious he became. But he had experience with a situation somewhat like this. He understood what it was like to be utterly and completely fascinated with a subject. That's what his fake girlfriend was. A new subject. Identifying her in this way would allow him to respond accordingly.

The sliding doors to the gardens opened, and the gentle evening breeze caressed their cheeks as they followed the walkway past a row of towering juniper hedges. He couldn't tell if the jasmine and vanilla scent was coming from his fake girlfriend or the wide array of blooms lining the path.

They walked in silence, their footsteps in sync as they moved deeper into the foliage.

"I could have handled the guy in the gift shop," she said, tightening her hold on his arm. "But I must say. I haven't had fun like that since a pack of rabid alpacas chased me off a mountaintop." She offered this bizarre piece of information casually, as one would remark on the weather.

Was she messing with him?

He stopped near a trio of lilac bushes and studied her face in the light of one of the garden's ornate lamp posts. "You were recently chased by a pack of rabid alpacas?"

She shrugged. "Something like that."

There had to be more to it.

"Do you raise alpacas?"

"No, I'm . . ." She glanced away, then bit her lip as another smirk appeared. She gazed at him through her lashes. "You can't disclose what I'm about to tell you. Do I have your word?"

With that sultry look, she could have asked for his bank account password, and he'd be powerless to keep it from her.

"You do," he purred, utterly enchanted.

She looked from side to side, making sure the coast was clear, then waved him in. "You see, my birthday boyfriend, I'm an international spy. The rabid alpacas chased me after I infiltrated a supervillain's mountaintop lair in a remote part of Peru."

Yep, she was messing with him.

And he loved it.

He also felt he understood the rules of this interaction. It was like how he and his siblings spoke with one major difference. He and his fake girlfriend were playing a flirtatious game—a verbal foreplay he'd never engaged in before. Usually, interacting with a stranger drained him, but in this alternate universe, where he was a doting boyfriend and she was his girlfriend, the exchanges invigorated him.

"A spy?" he shot back. "I was going to guess you were a scientist or, more precisely, a naturalist?"

Her eyes widened. "Why would you say that?"

Interesting. She'd broken character.

He glanced at the bag. "The cards."

"Couldn't I simply be a fan of the artist who painted them, or perhaps I bought them for sentimental reasons?"

He tried to read her. She'd thrown out two random suppositions. Could one of them be true, or both? He wasn't sure. "Anything is possible," he answered. Add it to the list of odd utterances. He didn't like to leave anything to chance. Maybe it was him playing the part of a devoted boyfriend that prompted the reply.

"Do you believe that? Do you truly believe anything is possible?" she whispered, her bottom lip trembling again.

How should he reply? He racked his brain, and Goldie came to mind. "Anything is possible" was something his grandmother said. It wasn't often he looked to her for behavioral guidance. He loved the woman, but she was not one to advocate for pragmatic logic over emotion. She believed Starrycard Creek paper possessed a magical power. In her defense, most of the town felt this way. She adhered to the thinking that, as the locals say, love is always in the cards in Starrycard Creek. Still, Goldie's trust in love and fate, two topics he rarely entertained, might be his best guide as he played the part of a doting partner.

"It is my birthday," he began. "And birthdays are opportunities for making wishes. With that in mind, anything could be possible tonight."

Did he believe that?

It didn't matter. His words put a smile on his fake girlfriend's face. Why did knowing he'd done that make it feel like he'd won the lottery?

"Are you ready to make your birthday wish, Birthday Card Boyfriend?" Her voice brimmed with honey decadence, sweet deliciousness, and tasty pleasures.

The beast in him wanted to gobble her up like a slice of birthday cake.

He drank in her lips. He wasn't one for public acts of affection, but Christ, he wanted to kiss her.

"Wait, you'll have to hold that wish," she whisper-shouted, growing animated as she peered over his shoulder. She grabbed his hand and led him down the path.

"What is it? Did you see something?" he stammered, trying to interpret what had triggered her amped-up demeanor.

Breaking into a jog, she led him through the gardens, weaving around a myriad of hedges like she'd designed the place herself.

"You need cake," she replied, determination coating her words.

Had she read his mind?

It wasn't a bad suggestion. Still, something was off.

"Where are we going? We're not headed toward the restaurant," he replied. But he didn't stop her. Instead, he picked up his pace and tightened his grip on her hand.

"We're going on a cake-out," she whispered.

"A cake-out?" Had he read her wrong? Had her beauty and intelligence blinded him from noticing she was fucking delusional?

"It's a stakeout but for cake. A cake-out." She dragged him beneath the cover of a drooping willow tree.

"Ow!" he exclaimed, bumping his head on a branch. "We're off the path. That's against the rules. We'll get kicked out if—"

"*Shh!* Don't say a word," she whispered, pressing her index finger to his lips. "I just saw a guy through the bushes pushing a cart with the most decadent cake on it."

Cake-out was a clever way to describe cake surveillance. Eliza would give the word two thumbs up. But he required some clarification. "We're stalking a man with a cake? Do you intend to incapacitate him to steal the cake?"

She giggled. "No, International Spy Lesson 101. We're gathering intel. I bet that little old couple over there will remark on that gorgeous cake. Then we'll find out where it's headed."

That was a ridiculous assertion. He had to call bullshit. "I highly doubt the couple will ask about a—"

His fake girlfriend pressed her hand to his mouth, muffling his speech as the little old woman clapped her hands.

He knew what effusive clappers were like.

"Look at that cake!" the white-haired lady exclaimed to her elderly male companion.

Kieran glanced at his fake girlfriend. She tapped the tip of his nose with her index finger. A peculiar gesture he quite enjoyed. And he had to give her credit. It was as if she were pulling the old lady's strings like a puppet master.

"Doesn't that cake look delicious, dear! Is there a wedding in the botanic gardens tonight?" the old lady continued.

The employee with the cart stopped. "No, ma'am. I'm taking this to a sold-out cake-tasting event. It's being held near the butterfly pavilion beside the reflecting pool."

"How lovely!" the woman crooned.

"How lovely indeed," his fake girlfriend murmured, then turned to him. "It's your birthday. Cake is for special occasions like birthdays, engagements, and weddings. It's a rule."

He had to voice his objection. "I don't think it's an explicit rule."

"It is," she countered, clearly not taking no for an answer. "Come on, Birthday Card, I know where they're holding the event."

He didn't have a second to respond.

They were on the move again.

It's important to note that—like much of what was playing out —this activity was not typical for him.

Handholding was not his thing. Cloak and dagger antics in the bushes were utterly unbecoming of a town manager and prominent councilman. He'd never stalked anyone. But holy hell, it was fun. He glanced at their joined hands as she dragged his large frame down narrow, twisty paths. He was quite familiar with the gardens. This is where the major league baseball team Christian played for was based. And his family enjoyed vacations here during his child-hood. As an adult, he'd made dozens of trips to the city and always stayed at The Pike, but his gift shop girlfriend seemed intimately acquainted with the labyrinth of twists and turns.

"This isn't your first time visiting the gardens, is it?" he asked, looking to glean more information.

She glanced back at him. "International spies know the layout of all their hideout locations. And we're here. Get down."

He joined her and peeked through the hedge.

She closed her eyes, inhaled deeply, and then sighed a breathy, sexy rumble. He mentally noted it, starting a list of his fake girl-friend's utterances and expressions.

"Birthday Card Boyfriend, we've stumbled upon Cake Nirvana."

Her comparison was accurate. Twinkling lights lit the outdoor fairyland space. Fifteen decadently-decorated cakes lined a long table dotted with vases filled with an array of blooms. Attendants dressed in black jetted back and forth, shuttling slim slices of the sugary confection among two dozen circular tables as a harpist plucked the strings of his grand instrument, producing an angelic sound.

His fake girlfriend sighed again. "It's been ages since I've had cake. And do you smell that? I might be experiencing a sugar-rush orgasm from the scent alone."

Sugar-rush orgasm?

He'd never thought of pairing sugar and sexual release, but he sure as hell would consider the notion now.

"Each couple has a number on one of those metal table stands. The highest number I see is sixty-eight." She turned to him. "Want to sixty-nine?"

The double meaning was not lost on him.

"Hell, yes, but there is one problem."

She frowned. "There is?"

"The man pushing the cake cart said the event was sold out. And a rather smug-looking attendant is lording over the entrance with a clipboard. Do you have any spy tricks up your sleeve?" With the heady scent of cake, jasmine, and vanilla in the air, he fixated on her face and those lips.

She grinned, showcasing those adorable dimples. "I always have a trick up my sleeve. We're going to bullshit our way in. Watch and learn."

Watch and learn? That statement expressed a high level of confidence.

He kept his gaze locked on his fake girlfriend. It wasn't a difficult command to follow. He could watch her all night.

Moving like cat burglars—another first for him—they emerged from behind the foliage.

She smiled up at him. "Good thinking, boyfriend. The hands are a nice touch."

Hands?

He peered at their joined hands. "I did that?" He didn't recall reaching for her. No matter. He was playing a part. It was the ruse.

"Good evening, we're here for the cake tasting," his fake girlfriend crooned to the scowling man who gripped his clipboard like it was the last life preserver on a sinking ship.

Resembling a caffeinated lapdog, the little man jumped and emitted a high-pitched yip. "And you are?" he asked through pursed lips in a thick French accent.

"My boyfriend and I are couple sixty-nine."

Nice touch.

The clipboard attendant sneered. "I do not see a couple sixty-nine on the list." The man had a nasal voice and slick, mousy brown hair with deep frown lines carved into his cheeks. His expression and demeanor didn't bode well for them.

"I can explain," she continued in a fizzy champagne tone. "We were a late addition. The hotel concierge told us there was a spot for us, and I see two open seats at table two," she added in her singsong voice.

The man snapped his fingers, and another mousy man appeared. "Jeffrey," the clipboard guy hissed, "find the concierge and inquire about a late addition."

"*Oui!*" the young man yipped and skittered down the path.

Clipboard Man peered at his fake girlfriend's left hand. "This is an event for people planning a wedding in the next twelve months."

"And that's why we're here," his golden-haired maven answered, continuing to employ the sentiment of catching more flies with honey than vinegar.

The Frenchman glowered. "You're not wearing an engagement ring."

Kieran caught his fake girlfriend's eye. She tossed him a wink. A sign she wasn't deterred. He admired her gumption.

"And there's a reason for that," she answered smoothly. "I'm turning twenty-six in a few weeks. And somebody," she continued, smiling up at him, "has been hinting that he has a big question to ask me on my birthday. Here's the problem. We leave tomorrow for a month-long trip. We're volunteering at an alpaca sanctuary in Peru. This is our last night at The Pike. We'd love to choose our cake in this beautiful botanical setting."

He stared at the woman, blown away at how quickly she'd conjured up one humdinger of a lie.

"No, no!" the Frenchman barked. "I am the maître d'hôtel. I enforce the rules, and the rules are clear. You are not engaged. You cannot eat cake under the stars."

His fake girlfriend lost her sweet edge and stared down the cake cop. It didn't matter that he was on the spectrum. He could see from the set of her jaw that honey was out, and vinegar was in.

This maître d'hôtel was about to meet his match.

"Oh, I'm gonna eat cake under the stars," she fired back. "In fact, I'm going to eat all your *motherfucking* cake under the stars, *so help me, God!*"

Sweet Christ, he'd never encountered such resolve when it came to consuming sugar and frosting. It only made him want her more. He couldn't take his eyes off her.

"*Mademoiselle*, you will not eat cake," the mousy man hissed, standing his ground.

His fake girlfriend leaned in, nose to nose with the cake bouncer. "We're eating your cake. We're going to *devour* your cake."

As much as he enjoyed watching his fake girlfriend kick cake ass, the situation was close to dissolving into a cake catastrophe that could end up with his fake girlfriend in a jail cell instead of writhing in ecstasy beneath him. While she'd ordered him to *watch and learn,* now appeared to be the appropriate time for him to harness his skill set to *speak and act.*

"Excuse me, sir," he said calmly. "Give me a moment to rectify the situation."

"How will you do that?" the clipboard man asked in a huff.

The answer was simple.

Maintaining his serene demeanor, he turned to his cake-obsessed fake girlfriend. "Do you have a piece of paper? I need to make a paper hexagon."

"A paper hexagon?" she and the clipboard man repeated, both wide-eyed.

He held his fake girlfriend's gaze. "Yes, a paper hexagon."

Her brows knit together. "I have the cards. You can make a paper hexagon from an envelope. I only need one of them." She handed him the item and leaned in. "What are you doing?"

It was a good thing he'd grown up around paper. But he couldn't share that information.

"As I said. I'm rectifying the situation," he repeated, carefully tearing the shape from the envelope. He pocketed the excess paper, then proceeded to make a series of precise folds to the six-sided shape.

Her jaw dropped. "You know origami?"

"I know paper," he countered, carefully manipulating the scrap. After a tuck here and a fold there, he held up a paper ring. "May I have your left hand?"

"What is this? What are you doing?" she stammered but complied with his request.

"I'm doing something that would please my grandmother."

"Your grandmother?" she repeated. He could tell from her tone that she was questioning his mental fitness.

He studied her hand. He'd never pictured doing what he was about to do. But he'd never met anyone like his ice-blue-eyed fake girlfriend.

Fake. There was that word again.

He peered at the paper ring. It wasn't a real engagement ring. It was a prop. An object to further their ruse and get this woman some much-needed motherfucking cake.

He slipped the paper ring onto her ring finger. It fit like a glove and looked like it was supposed to be there. How interesting.

She peered at her left hand. "What does this mean?"

It meant he needed to continue faking it.

He glanced at the slack-jawed Frenchmen. He needed to say

something that would guarantee they'd met the cake-tasting event's requirement. The words to continue their evening of deception came to him like a grand revelation.

He was getting good at faking it.

Maintaining a neutral front, he ignored the yippy man. Using his index finger, he tipped up his fake girlfriend's chin. He paused. Drinking in the perfect symmetry of her face, a stirring in his chest intensified as he focused on the color of her eyes. He waited another two seconds. He'd orchestrated a buildup. Now, it was time to speak.

Unable to stop a subtle smile from pulling at the corners of his mouth, he brushed his thumb across the paper ring. "This ring means you're mine."

CHAPTER
Four

IZZY

YOU'RE MINE.

He'd said that. He'd really said it.

Izzy exhaled a shaky breath as she peered into her birthday card boyfriend's sage-green eyes.

He cupped her face in his hand—his enormous, steady hand. "Do you like your ring?" He'd spoken the words without a hint of irony or jest. He had to be going along with this crazy, birthday-inspired, fake couple cake quest they'd embarked upon. A quest he'd triggered when he swooped into the gift shop like a protective lover and claimed her as his girlfriend.

He'd started it, but she'd allowed the ruse to continue.

No, not *allowed*.

She wanted this electrifying role-play adventure to continue. It had been a long time since she'd felt so free, so light, so adored. She tried to read the man. He was selective with his emotions. Still, she could see curiosity welling in his gaze. She stroked the bit of folded paper as a wave of giddy energy pulsed within her. "I love the ring. It's perfect."

She wasn't lying. The paper ring was stunningly beautiful in its complex simplicity. Hands down, having a man origami his ass off to make her happy ranked as the most romantically touching act she'd ever experienced.

What was happening here?

She couldn't allow her imagination to take over. The ring-making was a stunt. A parlor trick.

Nothing between them was real.

But before she could utter another word, her birthday card boyfriend winked, stealing her move. He pulled back, removing his hand from her cheek, then lifted their joined hands in front of the snippy Frenchman's face like a boxing referee raising the limb of the newly crowned World Heavyweight Champion.

Her birthday card boyfriend gestured toward their linked hands. "I put a ring on it. We've met the event entrance criteria. Now, we'd like to eat some motherfucking cake."

Frenchie gasped.

Izzy pressed her lips into a hard line to stop herself from laughing. Heaven help her! Her fake boyfriend was not messing around. And what a turn-on. It wasn't only his colorfully creative use of profanity that was commendable. The deliberate cadence of his voice soothed her. From the moment her birthday card boyfriend encircled his arm around her waist, it was evident he desired her. She'd also noticed him checking out a brunette at the bar. She understood his game. She knew what he was looking for. She was looking for the same thing. And if anyone needed to be swept up by a night of sexual debauchery, it was her.

She'd been a damned mess since she'd arrived in Colorado.

Stuck in this boutique hotel without knowing her next assignment's location, she had to do something to avoid going stir-crazy. What was Pamela thinking? Why would she book her a room at The Pike? Her boss understood the significance of the place. It was a mind-fuck to send her there. With anger building in her chest, she was on the verge of calling Pam and telling her to take the Colorado job and shove it. But that's not what happened. When the gift shop clerk placed the cards on the rack, it was as if the universe didn't want her to leave—didn't want her to throw away her career. And now, she was masquerading as a sexy stranger's girlfriend as they bullshitted their way into an event to eat a shit-ton of cake.

Was this insane?

Yes.

The guy could be a serial killer.

What did she know about him?

A few things.

One: It might be his birthday.

Two: He'd come to her aid like a white knight.

Three: Her body tingled beneath his touch.

And four: This guy had the equipment to give her the release she desperately needed. When she'd brushed up against him, what she felt would put her Wham Bam to shame.

The Frenchman gasped again, rudely pulling her attention away from thoughts of her birthday card boyfriend's junk.

It was time to turn on the Isabelle A. Adaire charm. She offered him a shit-eating grin. "You heard the man. Give us our number so we can sample some motherfucking cake."

The little man scrunched his face like someone had just held a rotten head of lettuce beneath his nose. Despite his obvious displeasure, he whipped a card from his pocket and scribbled the numbers on the fibrous paper.

"*Monsieur*," the man hissed, ignoring her as he handed the paper to her fake boyfriend.

"Thank you." Mr. Birthday Card held the slip in his hand, then shook his head as he peered at it. "Look at that," he murmured.

Everything about the man was deliberate. She could sense that about him the second he touched her. It left her oddly comforted, but she couldn't figure out why he'd become entranced with a piece of speckled paper.

She patted his arm. "Everything okay?"

He brushed his thumb across the rectangle. "Yes. I apologize. I'm rarely surprised."

"The paper surprised you?" she asked, watching him examine the table number.

"Yes." A warmth overtook his features. And hot damn, with his chiseled jaw, full lips, and sparkling eyes, this man was beyond gorgeous.

The cake lord huffed, cutting into her ogling.

Couldn't he see they were having a moment?

"You are allowed to eat cake *until* I hear from Jeffrey. Proceed to table two . . . *for now*," he snipped.

Screw this asshat!

This haughty man was insufferable. She pegged him with her icy gaze, ready to knock him down a few pegs. "You know what, Cake Patrol, you and Jeffrey can shove your cake-eating rules right up your—"

"Table two, it is," her birthday card boyfriend said smoothly, unfazed by her outburst. He entwined his fingers with hers and led her into the event space. They'd made it a few steps out of the maître d'whatever's earshot when her fake boyfriend leaned toward her. "I predict we have ten, possibly fifteen minutes before Jeffrey returns. Will that be enough time to get your fill of motherfucking cake?"

She smiled as his steady, muted tone sparked a buzzy warmth in her chest. Cake would never be cake again. Thanks to her birthday card boyfriend, it would be motherfucking cake from that day forward. She gazed at the man. He'd become the calm to her storm. A slight grin pulled at the corners of his mouth. And damn, with those sharp cheekbones and green eyes that seemed to darken the more he looked at her, deciding to lose herself in this slice of tall, dark, and handsome might have been the best choice she'd made in ages.

She surveyed the line of cakes as they walked to table number two. "Don't you worry. When it comes to knocking back cake, I'm the master. And don't forget. You better eat some motherfucking cake, too. We're doing this to celebrate your *motherfucking* birthday. By the way," she added with a smirk. "I plan on making it one you'll remember."

He tightened his hold on her hand. "You've already made it unforgettable."

She studied his face. He'd delivered the line—the hella romantic line—so matter-of-factly, she wasn't sure if he meant it or if it was part of their game.

Did she want him to mean it?

Forget it. Go with the flow.

She glanced around. She was intimately acquainted with the layout of the gardens, but she needed to formulate an escape route. Her birthday card boyfriend was right. Once Jeffrey returned, the jig would be up. The cake tyrant would kick their cake-stealing asses to the curb—or worse, call security. They'd have to be ready to react at a moment's notice.

"If we have to eat and run, follow me. I know a secret way back to the hotel. The guardian of the cake table won't be able to catch us."

"More spy skills?" he asked, pulling out a chair for her.

She sat and set her plastic bag on the tabletop. "Something like that."

A cake delivery guy whooshed in. He placed two slices in front of them as another attendant removed a bottle of champagne from the ice bucket and poured them each a glass.

Now that's service.

"Here we have a slice of lemon blueberry cake with a Swiss meringue buttercream. Enjoy," the attendant rattled off before zipping back to the cake table.

"Blueberries?" she eked out. Was she ready for another brush with the fruit?

"You don't like them?" her birthday card boyfriend asked.

"I love them, but things got a little sticky with blueberries on my last assignment." She eyed the cake warily.

"Let me guess. It has something to do with the alpacas."

She stared at the man. A sly twist of a grin graced his lips. He thought she was bullshitting him again.

"Something like that," she replied, mirroring his expression.

He nodded, mulling over her reply. Without another word, he picked up his fork, sliced off a bite from his lemon blueberry cake, and held it in front of her mouth. "Eat the motherfucking cake." His commandingly beastly, steady voice and deliciously neutral countenance sent a rush of heat between her thighs, obliterating her blueberry hesitation.

She opened her mouth and allowed him to feed her. *And hello, deliciousness!* Wrapped in a velvety frosting, the tangy lemon cake seamlessly fused with the sweet blueberries and cream, crafting a delightful symphony of fruity flavors. She closed her eyes and hummed her satisfaction. "This cake tastes like . . ."

He leaned in. "A sugar-rush orgasm?"

She licked her lips, not about to let one morsel of motherfuckingly delicious cake go to waste. "Exactly," she answered as he loaded another forkful. She hummed again as he delivered the second helping of cake ecstasy.

"If you keep making that sound," the man said, his voice a low, dirty rasp, "I'll be the one dragging your pretty little ass out of here."

Eating cake had never been so hot.

And note to self. Make the sound.

But not quite yet.

She picked up her fork, loaded a bite of the delectable confection, and held it to his lips. "Is that your birthday wish? You want to listen as I eat cake. Are you sure that's all you want?" She rested her hand on his thigh. It was a bold move but not reckless. They clearly wanted the same thing out of tonight.

He mimicked her movement and rested his hand on her bare knee. "I want more."

She leaned in closer. "Let's hear it."

His gaze darkened. "I want to make you come on my tongue while you eat cake."

And . . . check, please.

But she couldn't speak as her birthday card boyfriend directed his laser focus on her as he devoured the bite of cake. Izzy trembled beneath his oh-so-watchful eyes. It was hard to think, hard to breathe. His blisteringly hot directness had her clenching her core muscles.

Could a vagina snap from extreme prolonged tension?

"That wasn't too forward, was it?" he asked, and while his tone remained neutral, she'd detected a thread of concern or possibly worry in his question.

That tingle returned. His need to ensure he hadn't crossed any boundaries was charming.

Luckily, she could put his mind at ease.

"I like forward. I like *all* the forward," she added, sliding her hand up his thigh and hoping he'd mimic her behavior. Go big or go home, right?

And the risk paid off.

His hand inched beneath her skirt as he dialed up the intensity of his gaze. "Your lips are perfectly symmetrical, and there's some cake on them."

In her normal life, if a guy told her she was rocking a food face, she'd have been embarrassed. But there was nothing judgmental about his words or his tone. The man's voice and touch had her nipples tightening into pearls.

He made circles on her inner thigh with his thumb. "I could help you with your cake situation."

She exhaled, feeling her breasts heave with each breath. "Be my guest."

His thumb grazed her lips, and the delicate caress left her spellbound and slightly dizzy.

"Excuse me, people who can't keep their hands off each other?" a woman blurted in a may-I-speak-to-the-manager tone.

But Izzy couldn't tear her gaze from her birthday card boyfriend.

"I believe a shrill-voiced woman at our table is attempting to get our attention," he said with a twitch of a grin.

Izzy blinked, then glanced across the table. She hadn't even noticed the two women sitting across from them.

In her defense, it was hard to notice anything besides the drop-dead gorgeous man beside her.

She steadied herself and took in the scene. Their table mates appeared to be mother and daughter. The two were dolled up with enough makeup to deliver the evening news. The pair shared the same bleached platinum-blonde hair and were weighted down in jewelry. But nothing stood out more than their puffed-up lips, nearly the size of inner tubes, and breasts large enough to inhabit their own solar system.

"We're trying to eat." The younger woman seethed, maneuvering around her giant orbs to pick up a crumb of cake with her fork. "If you need a room, get one. We're at a hotel."

Izzy held the woman's gaze. "That's the best you've got? Get a room?"

Inner-Tube Lips gasped like the Frenchman.

"Oh, Cordelia, honey," the older woman slurred. She knocked back a glass of champagne, refilled the flute, then downed another. "They're in love. And isn't that a *unique* ring you've got there." The older woman leaned forward, nearly knocking over her champagne flute, her jewelry clinking. "Is that ring made of paper, or have I had one too many glasses of bubbly?"

Izzy raised her hand. "It is."

"Mom, you don't need to talk to everyone," the young woman grumped as she stared at a giant diamond on her ring finger.

"I'm Brenda. This is my daughter, Cordelia," the woman chimed, ignoring her daughter's warning. "My Cordelia is getting married next summer. She's a little cranky tonight because her fiancé can't be here."

"He's a very important man, and he's very busy," Cordelia said with a smirk.

Izzy froze.

Was this awful woman the gift shop wrist-grabber's fiancée?

She shared a look with her birthday card boyfriend. He lifted his hand from her thigh and wrapped it around her wrist.

He was thinking the same thing she was.

"How nice that you're marrying such a catch," Izzy replied, watching as Cordelia couldn't help herself from throwing thirsty glances at Mr. Birthday Card.

Izzy plastered a placating grin on her lips. *Enjoy the view, bitch.*

"And you two are?" Brenda slurred, pouring herself another glass.

Izzy glanced at her fake boyfriend. "We call each other by pet names. I call him Birthday Card Boyfriend because . . ."

"Because we fell in love on my birthday," the man replied without missing a beat.

Wow! She wasn't expecting that. His answer made Cordelia frown. A win in Izzy's book. She glanced at him, and her silly heart skipped a beat. *Settle down!* He couldn't mean it. It was simply part of the ruse to stuff their faces with cake.

"And what does he call you?" Brenda pressed.

"He calls me . . ." she stammered. *Dammit!* Should she make up a nickname? Sweetie? Honeypie? She was drawing a blank. Had her brain hit its bullshitting limit? And her birthday card boyfriend wasn't helping either. The man stared at the cake table. He'd checked out of the conversation. *Ugh!* Now was not the time to perseverate on motherfucking cake!

He released her wrist and stood. "Excuse me."

"Where's he going?" Brenda asked, jewelry clanking and breasts taking a hard right as she angled her body to watch the towering man set off.

Izzy cocked her head to the side. "I'm not sure."

Cordelia smirked—or at least appeared to try to purse her voluminous lips. "Let him go, girl. Who wants a guy who thought a paper ring would do?"

"Cordelia, manners," Brenda crooned, nearly falling out of her chair.

Izzy held up her hand. "Cordelia, *girl*, this ring is environmentally friendly."

"How sad . . . and boring," Cordelia mumbled.

Oh, hell no!

Izzy picked up her fork and pointed it at the bleached grumbler. "Caring for the planet is boring? Are you a complete and total—"

"Starbloom," her birthday card boyfriend said in his steady tone.

She looked up. "Huh?" she got out. The rage in her veins dissipated as she held his gaze. She rested the utensil on the table. The man saved Cordelia from getting forked in her big, environmentally unfriendly lips.

But there was more.

He removed his hand from behind his back and presented her with a flower—the same flower painted on the card he'd purchased for her. "I call you Starbloom because of your eyes. They're the same color as the star-shaped blossom on our favorite flower."

Our favorite flower?

"Okay," she stammered, floored. The starbloom really was her favorite flower.

"I noticed one in the vase on the cake table and thought it would look lovely in your hair." He slipped the stem behind her ear, then peered down at her. "It does," he answered in his toe-curlingly hot, monotone cadence that was doing a damned good job of setting her body on fire.

"Isn't that sweet, Cordelia? He calls her Starbloom after a flower," Brenda chimed, going in for another sip of champagne.

Cordelia was back to pushing crumbs with her fork. "It's an *environmentally friendly* name, I guess," she huffed. She was trying to play it like she didn't care, but her flushed cheeks and a few more thirsty glances at Mr. Birthday Card gave away her feelings. The chick was crazy jealous.

"I also asked an attendant to prepare a cake to-go box for us," he continued, not even glancing Cordelia's way. As if on cue, an attendant placed a white pastry box on the table. "Thank you," he said and slipped the attendant a twenty.

She looked between the man and the box. "Why are we taking the cake to-go?"

"Jeffrey," the man answered, picking up the cake box and tucking it under his arm.

"Jeffrey?" she echoed.

He watched her closely. "Yes."

Izzy stared at the man and cocked her head to the side. She liked his muted veneer, but a little emotion from the guy would be helpful.

What was she missing?

"Number sixty-nine," the Frenchman yipped. "You do not get to eat cake!"

And then it clicked.

"Jeffrey's back? We're getting kicked out?" Izzy exclaimed, eyeing her cool-headed fake boyfriend.

"Yes," he answered succinctly. "I conveyed that piece of information."

"Fucking Jeffrey," she mumbled. She sprang to her feet, grabbed her plastic bag with the cards, and eyed her cake-stealing companion, Mr. Cool and Collected. She glared at the man. "How are you so calm?"

A crease formed between his brows. "We knew this was coming. Why do you think I got the cake?"

"Cake thieves! You did not fool me." The angry Frenchman zigzagged through the mess of tables with fucking Jeffrey in tow.

Cordelia balked. "You don't even have a real ring, and you lied your way into a cake tasting? Get a life, babe."

Izzy ignored the haughty woman and grabbed the ice bucket with an unopened bottle of champagne chilling inside. Might as well nick the bubbly. In for a penny, in for a pound.

She met her fake boyfriend's gaze. "Follow me."

He took the plastic bag from her hand.

"What are you doing?" she asked. They didn't have time to stand around.

He pocketed the cards, then took her hand in his. "I'll always be right behind you."

Damn, what a statement. Even if he'd uttered the words to maintain the ruse, it made her heartbeat flutter. But it wasn't only his words. She liked the warmth of his hand. The consistent pressure. The steadiness—like nothing could deter him when he set his sights on a goal.

"You might want to run. That little yipping man from the entrance is getting closer—or maybe it's the champagne," Brenda slurred, narrowing her gaze.

Izzy checked.

Brenda was right. Frenchie and Jeffrey were getting closer.

Izzy surveyed the scene. "Come on, Mr. Birthday Card, we have to go through the butterfly pavilion." Hand in hand, she led her fake boyfriend past the cake table and into the enclosed space. The structure was one of the largest butterfly pavilions in the United States. It featured leafy trees, lush greenery, wildflowers, and meandering walkways. And, of course, butterflies. The luminescent creatures peppered the air and painted the space with dancing flits and flutters. Under the moonlight filtering through the glass dome and replete with twinkling lights, the place resembled a magical fairyland.

"Are you sure this is the right way? It seems counterintuitive to go inside when we could take a more direct outdoor path," he offered.

"I'm sure. Remember, I'm an international spy. I know things others don't." It wasn't a complete lie. She did know about a hidden exit. Despite being chased by an irate cake lord, she smiled as a starwing butterfly landed on her forearm. She could almost hear her nana's voice.

There she is. There's our butterfly girl.

A door slammed, and she snapped out of it. "We have to go." She turned her wrist gently, and the creature joined its winged companions. She pulled on her birthday card boyfriend's hand, but he didn't move. He drank her in, wonder welling in his eyes.

She tugged again. "We've got like five seconds before the cake asshat and fucking Jeffrey catch us. Otherwise, we'll be mucho fucked."

Who knew she'd be mucho fucked for a second time in less than forty-eight hours?

Still, the man didn't budge. Instead, he narrowed his gaze as if he were engrossed in memorizing every detail of this moment. "You look like you were meant to be with the butterflies."

Jesus, this man!

Despite being on the brink of another mucho-fucked catastrophe, she pushed onto her tiptoes. But she didn't kiss him. She inhaled the sweetness of the cake and the warm bite of alcohol on his breath.

He concentrated on her mouth. "Your lips exhibit the highest degree of *kissability* I have ever observed."

She couldn't stop a stupid, sappy grin from blooming. "I'm not sure *kissability* is a scientific term."

A subtle twitch at the corner of his mouth revealed that he enjoyed their back-and-forth banter. "I believe it's a legal term regarding personal boundaries and consent. Lips like yours garner a high degree of *kissability* and are suitable for, or conducive to, consensual kissing."

Robot lawyer talk was crazy hot.

She raised an eyebrow. "You're bullshitting, right?"

The corners of his mouth curled upward a fraction more. "About the law, yes. About wanting to kiss you, no."

Cue an even sappier grin. "Do you know how romantic that sounds?"

He leaned in, his lips inches from hers. "I didn't intend for it to be romantic."

That silly, stupid grin slapped to her face must have stretched for a mile. "I kind of figured that." She closed her eyes, so ready to be kissed, surrounded by a kaleidoscope of butterflies.

"There you are," Captain Cake Patrol barked, shattering their *almost* first kiss.

She shrieked and nearly dropped the champagne ice bucket. "Dammit!" She scowled at her ridiculously handsome man. "Stop scrambling my brain with your sexy legalese."

He frowned. "I can't comply with that. I don't have control over your brain or its ability to be scrambled by speech."

Gah! They didn't have time to argue. The cake prick and his sidekick were headed straight for them.

"Which way?" her fake boyfriend pressed, finally seeming to sense the urgency of their situation.

"This way." She led him through a maze of trees and a sea of flitting butterflies toward a secluded alcove. "Here." She pressed her hands to the wall. "Our exit is one of these panels," she murmured, racking her brain. *Which one was it?* And then she saw a lone panel sticking out a quarter inch more than the others. To the naked eye, it looked like nothing more than a rectangle. But Izzy knew better. She felt along the side. Anticipation bubbled within her as she found the latch. She pressed it like her grand-parents, Nana Joan and Poppa James, had shown her, and the secret door opened.

"We're going down there?" he asked, pointing to the stairs leading into a darkened tunnel.

"It's an old route that the tradesmen and the builders used when the hotel and the butterfly pavilion were under construction. It's safe. Do you trust me?" she asked, not exactly sure what she was asking.

Trust was a sticky subject. Hell, she didn't even trust herself. Why did she want this man to put his faith in her?

He focused on her eyes. There was no way he could make out the color. It was too dark. But it was like he was caught up in them—in her. He tightened his hold on her hand. "I trust you."

A shiver passed through her as if she'd been touched by an invisible hand. She ignored the sensation and glanced over her shoulder. "Good, because this is our only hope, and the cake patrol is getting closer."

She and her birthday card boyfriend slipped inside and remained at the top of the narrow staircase. She had to release his hand to pull the lever to close the secret door behind them. And for a beat, they stood there, listening in the darkness.

"Where are they, Jeffrey? Do you see them?" the angry Frenchman bellowed.

"They just disappeared."

"*Merde*!" the cake ogre blurted as the beat of their footsteps faded.

Hooray! The cake patrol had moved on.

Score one for the cake thieves.

She took his hand. "This way."

She led him down the stairs into the tunnel. The sound of their footsteps on the compacted earth resonated within the concrete-walled space. It didn't take long before she spied light seeping through the gap beneath a door. She felt for the latch. *Click!* The hinges whined, and a puff of dust billowed as the old door creaked open, and they emerged into a passageway lit by glaring overhead fluorescent lights.

"Where are we?" he asked, scanning the space.

She led him down a hallway. "It's an underground mainte-nance corridor."

Ding!

"And there's our ride," she said and nodded toward the service elevator. "The cleaning staff uses this to get to the guest rooms."

He gestured for her to enter.

She leaned against the scuffed wood panel. "Your place or mine?" she asked with a flirty grin, her hand hovering over the buttons.

"Yours," he answered, and while his voice remained in that sexy monotone zone, there was something detached in his reply.

"Mine it is," she said, trying to read him and failing. She

pressed the button for the eighth floor and shifted the ice bucket in her arms.

He fiddled with the cake box. "I'm also on eight."

"We could jump from room to room. Might be fun," she chirped, hating that she could hear a desperate tinge to her air-headed reply.

Eyes forward and stone-faced, he nodded.

Where had his playful smirk gone? She glanced at her hand. Where was the man who'd made her this paper ring? Was he having second thoughts?

Ding!

The elevator doors opened to the eighth floor. She focused on the housekeeping carts lining the wall as she exited with her birthday card boyfriend a few steps behind her.

She hugged the ice bucket to her chest. "We have to exit through the doorway to get to our rooms."

"Your room. Not mine," he reiterated, his tone low and severe, like a wounded beast. His stern words hit her like a gut punch.

"Right, my room."

Why didn't he want her in his room?

Okay, there could be legitimate reasons. It could simply be messy—cluttered with work items. From their conversations, she'd deduced he had to be an attorney—or work in some profession related to the law.

She exhaled a slow breath. *Let it go.* This is a one-night stand.

They emerged from the service area, and she located the door to her room. She pulled her keycard from her pocket and inserted it into the card reader. The latch released with a sharp click. It pierced the silence between them that spanned across this perplexing, vast chasm of unspoken words. She couldn't pinpoint when their contagious excitement had given way to this heavy mix of uncertainty.

Where was the man whose eyes glinted with desire when he promised he'd make her come while she ate cake?

He held the door for her. Entering the dimly lit space, she

scanned the room. The light next to the turned-down bed was on. Housekeeping had been in. Awkwardly, she set the ice bucket on a table near the window overlooking Rocky Mountain City's twinkling lights. But she wasn't focused on the stunning mountain view. She watched her birthday card boyfriend in the reflection as he placed the cake box and her bag with the cards on the bureau. A shiver ran down her spine when he strode toward her, his long legs making short work of the space between them.

"I apologize for my lack of conversation in the elevator. I was working something out in my head."

She watched him. "Something about me?"

"Yes."

"You know you can leave if you've had a change of heart. There's nothing that binds us together." She flinched. Why did it hurt to say that? It was the truth.

He edged closer to her and twisted a lock of her hair around his finger. "Would you like me to leave?" He'd softened his tone like he'd made the modulation to reassure her. It was another one of his oddly romantic gestures.

"No," she whispered.

He released her hair and skimmed his hands down her torso. Gently, he drew her in, allowing her to feel the hard bulge in his pants. She inhaled a sharp breath.

"If it's not already evident," he said, resting his hands on her hips, his fingertips brushing against her most sensitive place. "I want to spend the night with you. But I won't be with you when you wake up. By agreeing to this, we're entering into an oral contract. Here are the terms."

More legalese—but with a helping of a hard-on. That was a first for her.

"The terms?" she replied, studying his expression as she swayed, brushing her ass against his cock.

He met her gaze in their reflection. His grip on her body tightened. "You cannot fall in love with me."

Whoa!

If any other man had spoken these words, she would have laughed her ass off. But her birthday card boyfriend wasn't kidding—not even a little bit. The firmness of his words and the set of his jaw confirmed it.

She mirrored his stoic demeanor. "I assume this agreement is reciprocal. Anything asked of me would be asked of you?"

"You assume correctly."

She turned and rested her hands on his chest. He tensed, but she didn't pull back. She got closer and pressed onto her tiptoes. "That means you, my birthday card boyfriend, cannot fall in love with me."

A muscle ticked on his jaw like he was holding back. "It does." He cupped her face in his hand and ran his thumb across her highly kissable lips. "I should warn you. I'm very good in bed. You may think you love me, but it's your body's reaction to mind-blowing, multi-orgasmic sex."

What a disclaimer!

"You're not joking, are you?" She had to confirm it.

He studied her mouth like he was mapping his every desire on her lips. "No."

She skimmed her hands down his hard torso, reveling in his beautiful body. "Then I should warn you that nobody's ever made me come as hard as my Wham Bam."

"I'm assuming that's a sexual gratification device."

"You assume correctly," she answered, borrowing his words.

He scanned the room. "Where is this device?"

She had to work overtime to keep from smiling. "It's stuck in a pile of alpaca shit on a mountaintop in Peru."

"Due to your role as a global operative?" Mischief glinted in his eyes.

The spark returned.

Butterflies erupted into flight in her belly, and heat built between her thighs. They'd returned to the place where they clicked, where she couldn't wait to hear what he'd say next.

"Something like that. Did you want to check out my Wham Bam? Maybe get a few pointers?" She smirked, goading him.

The corner of his mouth twitched, and she clenched her core.

"I don't need any pointers," he replied and stroked her cheek. "As I said, I'm well-versed in the art of lovemaking. I wanted to have you demonstrate what you considered a mind-blowing orgasm using said implement. Now, I'll have to rely on your honest assessment of my skills. But I can promise you one thing that I doubt a vibrator can."

"What's that?"

He leaned in. Ferocity glinted in his eyes as that maddeningly hot smirk played upon his lips.

That toe-curlingly muted expression might be the death of her.

"I'm a relentless lover," he continued. "My drive to make you come is unyielding."

"*Unyielding*?" she repeated, her voice a squeak of a sound.

"Unyielding," he confirmed.

She shivered.

He looked her over. "Are you all right?"

She chewed her lip. His gaze grew positively carnal at her slight movement. "I think I'm okay. This isn't a scientific statement, but my ovaries may be on the brink of exploding."

"Do you need medical assistance?" His smirk didn't disappear. He knew she was messing with him, and he liked it.

She shook her head. "No, keep talking."

Taking control, he walked her toward the bed. "I'll make you come so hard, so often, and with such enthusiasm, you may see stars permanently. But—and this part may enrage you," he cautioned.

"Oh, I'm ready to be enraged. Feel free to enrage me all night long," she purred.

"This is regarding the orgasms I'm promising."

"I'm listening," she whispered, on the verge of imploding.

He pressed his lips against the shell of her ear. "I'm going to make you beg for it."

CHAPTER
Five

IZZY

WOWZA!

"Beg for it?" Izzy repeated as her ovaries splattered across her pelvic cavity.

"That's right. I'll bring you so close to the edge that you'd sell your soul to taste one tiny, decadent morsel of sweet release. Could your Wham Bam do that for you?" her dirty-talking fake boyfriend pressed.

What the hell was any woman supposed to say to that?

"Um . . . no, and you're setting the bar awfully high. Are you sure you're up for the challenge?"

He unbuttoned her blouse and guided it off her shoulders. "Let me put it another way to convey my sentiments plainly while utilizing two words you've recently spoken."

"All right," she replied.

He removed his shirt, revealing a drool-worthy, ripped torso. The soft light accentuated the contours of his physique as he drank her in. "You are about to get *mucho fucked.*"

Now this was the kind of mucho fucked she needed.

"I am so ready to get mucho fucked." She brushed her fingertips across her lips. It was a miracle she wasn't drooling. Greek statues couldn't hold a candle to him. He was the living embodiment of masculine virility, and he wanted to direct all that sexual energy toward her, and, oh yeah, she was there for it.

She raised her hands into the air, then flopped onto the bed. "Let the *mucho* fucking commence!"

With a few flicks of his wrist, he knocked off her sandals and whipped off her skirt. And thank heaven for elastic waistbands.

He prowled the length of her body. The air crackled like the atoms around them were exploding due to sexual tension overload. And there was something else. That solid, steady feeling returned. It was the feeling she'd experienced the second he'd charged into the gift shop and pressed his hand to her back. Their connection was palpable, this unspoken bond she couldn't deny.

He kissed a hot trail from her navel to her collarbone, licking, sucking, and tasting. She arched her back as he settled between her thighs. Resting her arms above her head, she hummed, reveling beneath his touch. He slipped the flower from her hair and drew it across her cheek before kissing her neck. Slowly and oh-so deliberately, he dropped a kiss to her shoulder but froze when he got to her elbow.

"What the hell is this?" he growled.

Hello, beast!

Dizzy from his kisses, she blinked open her eyes. The first thing she saw was him. Bloody murder flashed in his gaze. She followed his line of sight and craned her neck, taking in the shades of blue, black, and purple covering her elbow. "It's a little bruise."

The explanation didn't pacify him.

A flush crept up his neck. "Did someone hurt you? Did that asshole in the gift shop do this when I wasn't looking? I should have broken his fucking wrists." He clenched his jaw. The man looked ready to bolt out of the room to serve justice and kick the gift shop creep's ass.

She had to put him at ease.

She stroked his cheek. "No, God, no! He didn't hurt me. I got this bruise diving into a helicopter."

"Bullshit! Who hurt you?" the man hissed. He rose to his feet and searched every inch of her body.

She sat up and leaned against the padded headboard. "It's not bullshit. It's the truth. I'm sure you've figured out that I'm not a spy, but my work sometimes requires me to ride in helicopters. I was clumsy getting into one recently. That's all."

"Dammit," he hissed and stormed into the bathroom.

What had gotten into him?

"It's just a little tender," she called after him.

What was he doing?

He returned from the bathroom with a plastic shower cap in his hand.

"What's going on, Birthday Card Boyfriend?" she asked, watching as he took a handful of ice cubes from the silver bucket, put them into the clear head covering, then twisted it into a little ice sack.

He sat on the corner of the bed and pressed the makeshift icepack to her elbow.

She inhaled a sharp breath.

"I can tell you haven't iced it," he said, disapproval coating his words.

"I've been busy."

A muscle ticked on his jaw. "You're sure some awful ex didn't do this to you?"

She sighed. "There's no awful ex. There hasn't been anyone in years. Well, there was one awful ex, but that was five years ago."

"Did he hurt you?" he asked through gritted teeth.

He looked like he'd tear this world apart to find the guy and rip him a new one, which her ex so richly deserved. But she couldn't, wouldn't, think about that awful, conniving man. Not now. Not when this night had been everything her battered heart desired.

Her fake boyfriend exhaled an audible breath and tenderly applied the icepack to her bruise like her pain was his.

Like her pain was his? Jesus, what was going on with her?

She pushed aside the thought. *Answer truthfully but succinctly.* "He did hurt me, but not the kind that leaves a physical mark. He tricked me. And I lost something very important." She looked up and met his gaze. His attention was trained on her chest. But he wasn't leering at her breasts. He focused on her hand donning the paper ring—her hand clutching her locket. She hadn't realized she'd reached for it. Releasing the cool metal, she lowered her hand.

They sat in silence. He didn't press her for more information or push her to keep talking. He adjusted the icepack, moving it so one spot didn't get too cold as he gingerly held her elbow in his strong, steady hand.

Maybe he was a father? He was certainly a caregiver.

Stop!

She couldn't help herself. Everything about this situation was like she'd fallen through a rip in time and landed in a world where she was a different version of herself. She was allowing him to care for her—which wasn't like her. She could take care of herself. No, she *had* to take care of herself. And why? The answer was simple. There was nobody else.

"There, that's enough. You should have iced it right away, but this should help with inflammation," he said, the anger burning in his eyes dissipating as he eyed her bruise.

"I'm fine. Truly, I am," she replied, then sneezed.

He felt her forehead. "Are you coming down with a cold?"

She waved him off. "No, it's a tiny sniffle. I'm okay."

He pegged her with his gaze for a beat and held up the makeshift icepack. "I need to take care of this." He strode into the bathroom, disposed of the ice, then opened the cake box. He sauntered over to the bed and presented her with a slice. "Now that we've addressed your bruise and you've assured me that you're not suffering from a respiratory ailment, it's time for you to eat this motherfucking cake," he ordered, the wisp of a smirk in place as he handed her a wedge of iced deliciousness. "It's the lemon blueberry you liked from the tasting event. We don't have any forks, so dive in."

She chuckled, grateful to have moved on from discussing her ex. She eyed the slice and took a monster bite. No need to be lady-like with a one-night stand. "Damn, this is good," she murmured, frowning as he stood and watched her. "Are you a cake-eating voyeur?"

"No."

She dusted a few crumbs off the comforter and onto the floor. "Are you going to eat?"

"Yes."

"Let me rephrase the question. What will you eat?" she pressed.

A muscle twitched on his jaw. "You."

Wow! This man wasn't wasting any time.

He leaned over and slipped his index fingers around the band of her panties. "Lift your ass, *Bloom*. These are coming off."

"Bloom?" she repeated, doing as she was told.

He set her panties on a chair. "You call me your birthday card boyfriend. I'll call you Bloom. It's short for—"

"Starbloom," she supplied. It was another romantic gesture she was sure he wouldn't perceive as such. As much as she liked the nickname, she had to give him a little shit. "How do you know I want you to call me that?"

"Because it kept you from being booked into the county jail."

"What?" She almost spit out her cake—cake that she was eating in only her bra. Another first for her. But like everything else about this upside-down world she inhabited with her birthday card boyfriend, there was a strange level of comfort, of ease, of not feeling self-conscious.

"I overheard your conversation with Cordelia," he continued. "I watched you pick up your fork in a menacing manner."

Izzy huffed at the thought of that moron. "That woman deserved to be menaced," she replied, taking an angry bite. "She was awful. Ill-informed, ignorant, and—"

"Jealous," he supplied.

She brushed a crumb from her lips. "Jealous? Of who?"

"Of you," he answered, not missing a beat.

She took a bite. "Because I was with you? You're probably right. Don't think I didn't notice her looking at you like she'd wished you were a slice she could order off the menu."

Confusion marred his expression. "I don't know anything about that. When I looked at her, it was to garner information. And to set the record straight, she was intimidated by you. Your poise. Your composure—at least until you wanted to stab her with a fork."

This man was an untapped well of perceptive surprises.

"How do you know that about Cordelia?" she pressed.

"I watched her."

She needed more. "We hardly spent any time with them."

"I excel at observation. For the majority of my life, I've worked to sharpen my skills of perception. It takes concentration and focused effort on my part. Let's leave it at that. And you'll allow me to call you Bloom," he added, his words taking on a gravelly edge.

She lifted her chin, not ready to give in. "And why is that?"

"It fits you. You're passionate about the environment. Your near brush with manslaughter exemplified that."

She rubbed her neck. "I might commit manslaughter if I have to keep looking up at the ceiling. Are you going to stand there all night like a sexy skyscraper?"

He gave her that sexy twitch of a grin. "I can sit."

"Wait, not quite yet." She pointed to his pants. "If I had to lose my skirt and panties, in the spirit of reciprocity, you need to lose everything below the waist, too."

Would he comply?

"I'd like to make a counterproposal," he replied evenly.

She took a bite of cake. "Counter away."

His gaze darkened. "Lose the bra, and then I'll strip."

She reached behind her back, undid the clasp, and rid herself of the lacy undergarment. "Done," she said and tossed the item at him like a cake-loving stripper.

He caught her undergarment, folded it neatly, and placed it on top of her panties. Turning to her, he raked his gaze over her body as he slipped off his shoes and then unbuttoned his trousers. With precise, measured movements, he removed them, folded them once, then twice, and rested them on the chair. Without an ounce of hesitation, he stepped out of his boxer briefs, revealing not only a gloriously naked body ripe with hard muscles and tanned skin but also an erect, ready-to-play cock that put her Wham Bam to shame.

Hello, Mr. Well-Hung Birthday Boy.

He settled beside her like getting buck naked and munching away on cake in bed was a routine they shared. "You can proceed with your questioning, Bloom," he said and folded his hands on his lap.

"What?" she stammered, her words stumbling from her lips like her thoughts were mired in mush. How could she maintain her train of thought with all this man candy beside her?

"We're debating why bloom is an appropriate nickname. I'm more than comfortable allowing you to stare at my cock if doing so helps you progress with your line of questioning."

She gasped. She was a Little Miss Cock-Gawker. She cleared her throat and flicked her gaze to his face. The exasperatingly attractive man had returned to his smirking ways.

"Putting aside the manslaughter," she said and broke off a bite of cake. "How else does bloom fit me?" She held the bite to his lips.

He tossed a furtive glance her way but allowed her to feed him. He swallowed the bite, leaned against the headboard, and crossed his ankles. "Flowers, or blooms, are radiant. They captivate the soul with their natural beauty. I'd argue that, like snowflakes, no one bloom is the same. Furthermore, though we haven't known each other for much more than an hour, I can't fathom the existence of another woman quite like you."

Who was this man?

The butterflies returned, flitting away in her belly as her heart leaped into her throat. All she could do was concentrate on his profile, the sharp cut of his jawline, and the tiny twist of a curl at the nape of his neck.

He pegged her with his gaze. "So, for tonight, you're my bloom. Can you agree to those terms?"

More terms—for one night only.

She nodded. It's what she wanted—one evening of passion to lose herself. But the twinge in her chest betrayed her better judgment. Better get to the mucho fucking.

She forgot about her heart and brushed her fingertips across her lips. "These lips, with a high degree of *kissability,* would like to be kissed now."

"Those lips will have to wait."

She cocked her head to the side. "Why?"

"Because there's an order to the evening."

"An order?" She wasn't expecting that.

He uncrossed his legs and got off the bed. Plucking a pillow from the stack against the headboard, he fluffed it in his hands, then directed his intense gaze at her. "Take a bite of mother-fucking cake and lift your ass, Bloom."

She didn't like orders—except, it appeared, when they were delivered in a commanding, robotic tone by a beast of a man rocking an impressive hard-on. Mimicking his neutral countenance, she complied.

He carefully slipped the pillow beneath her, and she sank into the softness. Excitement danced in her veins as he examined her with the precision of an eagle-eyed artisan.

He stood at the foot of the bed. "Spread your legs. Let me see you."

She permitted her legs to part like a bloom opening. Seconds stretched into millennia. Electric tension pulsed between them.

He licked his lips and held his cock, pumping his hard length. "Fucking gorgeous," he growled, drinking her in. He released his cock and prowled his way up her legs, drawing a hot line up her inner thigh with his tongue.

She clutched the comforter, her teeth sinking into her bottom lip as his warm breath against her delicate skin sent her senses into a whirlwind.

He gripped her elevated ass and settled between her thighs. She couldn't take her eyes off him. Raw need radiated off him in waves. He wasn't the only one raring to go. She was soaked, and he'd barely touched her.

He ran his tongue across her delicate folds and hummed a primal, guttural sound. Raising his gaze, he looked her square in the eyes. "Eat the rest of your motherfucking cake."

She raised the slice to her lips. "Are you going to watch?"

"You better believe it."

Trembling with desire, she took a bite.

He kissed her most sensitive spot, teasing her with his lips. "Is your motherfucking cake delicious?"

"Yes." The combination of lemon and blueberries ushered in a rush of sugary sweetness.

He worked her with his tongue, sucking and licking, then paused. "Now, take the last bite, Bloom. I want to watch you swallow it."

If her ovaries weren't completely decimated, they were now.

She slipped the morsel into her mouth and hummed a sultry, satisfied sound as her birthday card boyfriend nodded his head, slowly, rhythmically stroking her tight bundle of nerves. Her arousal swelled like a building storm. The air grew heavy with the scent of cake and sex as he hummed against her, dialing up the pressure.

It was almost too much to take—too many sensations, too much stimulation.

"Yes, yes," she murmured, threading her hand in his hair. She bucked her hips, marveling at this man's ability to please her.

Closer and closer, she edged toward release. Wet and hot, she was on the brink of a sexual eruption. He clenched her ass with one hand and teased her entrance with the other. Never breaking rhythm and never letting up, he increased the pressure. Moving his index finger in and out, he worked her into a heated frenzy.

The sensations lifted her until she'd become weightless. Soaring, she detonated into a burst of flickering light and all-consuming lust. A supernova outshining the sun. It was too much and not enough. It was the decadence of hoarding everything and the ease of letting go. He held her there, suspended in time, wrapped in the glow of desire.

Teetering on the edge, she gritted her teeth and begged, "Please, please, make me come."

He growled against her, and the vibration was her salvation. The frenzied flood of her release severed her connection to her body. Waves of pleasure lifted her higher and higher. The man responsible for her state of rapture didn't let up, didn't slow down. He worked her like he'd been born to make her come. Gasping, she floated in the airy darkness lit by tiny bursts of light. *Stars.* That's what they were. She could taste them, like sweet whispers of time, as the spark of their celestial fire coursed through her veins.

Slowly, she returned to her body. Trying to catch her breath, she gazed down at her birthday card boyfriend. He was watching her, his sage-green eyes glinting with carnal victory as he zeroed in on her from between her legs.

"I told you you'd beg for it," he said with a cocky twist to his lips.

She couldn't even deny it. But he needed to know that she could dish it out, too.

"I need a little space. Could you remove your giant-ass body from between my legs?"

He pulled back, and she rose from the bed.

"Going somewhere, *Bloom*?" he asked, coming up behind her as she eyed the cake box.

Bloom.

A delicious tingle ran down her spine. "Snack break. Get on the bed, Birthday Card Boyfriend."

"Is that an order?" He sounded like he hoped it was.

The note of gravelly desire in his voice stoked her cocky side. She suppressed a grin. Two could play at this beg-for-it game.

She looked over her shoulder at him through her lashes. "It's not just an order. It's a *motherfucking* order."

She eyed the slivers of cake, listening as the bed creaked under the weight of his massive frame. *Good! He could follow directions.* She stared into the cake box. It was too dim to make out the different flavors. She dipped her hand into the box. "Eenie, meenie, miney, mo," she chanted, then glanced at her fake boyfriend. "Those are scientific terms, by the way."

"Utilized to make high-stakes decisions, I'm sure," he replied.

She smiled, liking his quirky yet buttoned-up sense of humor.

She chose a piece and sauntered to the bed. "Absolutely," she answered and took a monster bite. "Oh my God." She was rewarded with the same decadent icing from the lemon blueberry cake, but this piece didn't feature fruit. Nope, an explosion of chocolate with a caramel filling tantalized her tastebuds.

She broke off a piece. "Open your mouth, Birthday Card. You've got to try this."

"What flavor is it?"

"You'll see," she purred.

He took the bite and hummed his satisfaction. "Fuck, that's good cake." He pinned her with his sage-green gaze. "Or perhaps I just like having you naked while you feed it to me."

She studied the man. That face. The tiny curve at the corners of his mouth. Not to mention his beautiful cock. And that gave her an idea.

"If you like that, you'll love what's about to happen."

"And what's about to happen?"

She took another bite, then plucked a few tissues from the box. She placed them on the bedside table and set the rest of the slice on it, using the sheets as an improvised plate.

She settled herself between his thighs. "You, Birthday Card Boyfriend, are getting a chocolate birthday blow job. Has anyone hit you up with one of those today?"

"No, today I've only received a short display of gymnastics prowess accompanied by fruit consumption."

What?

She chuckled. "I'm not sure what I expected you to say, but it wasn't that." But now was not the time to press him on whatever the hell gymnastics prowess accompanied by fruit consumption was. He'd gone downtown, and she was ready to reciprocate to make this man lose control. She wrapped her hand around his hard length, then circled her tongue around the tip.

He inhaled a sharp breath, then slipped his hand in her hair, twisting the blond locks in his fist. "I love your tongue on my cock."

All right! It had been freaking ages since she'd been with a man and even longer since she'd rocked a BJ. It appeared she still had some skills in the seduction department. She worked him with her hand and mouth, taking as much as she could. He was big, like big-big—another pseudo-scientific term.

"Bloom, yes," he hissed, tightening his grip on her hair. But he didn't try to take control. He allowed her to set the pace.

His low, guttural groans drove her to crank it up. She hummed as she sucked, treating him to what he'd given her.

His breaths grew audible. "Wait, Bloom, stop."

She gasped and popped up. "Did I hurt you? Did I do something wrong?"

Had she used her teeth? The last thing she wanted to do was cop to being a total novice in the BJ delivery department.

"No, not even close. It felt good—too good. You're a master with that mouth. But that's not how I want to have you."

"How do you want me?"

Lust glinted in his eyes. "Shall I show you?"

"Okay."

She should have braced herself. For a big guy, he could move.

She'd barely taken a breath before he had her on her back and hovered over her body.

"This is how I want you." His cock nudged against her entrance. He glanced at the chair bearing their discarded clothes. "Wait. We require protection. I have condoms in—"

"I get this shot," she said, cutting him off as her mouth overrode her brain. "It's a birth control shot. And I get other shots, like a flu shot, but for sure, I get a shot that prevents me from getting pregnant."

"I'm clean," he said evenly. "I get tested every year before my birthday. Of course, I have condoms. They're in my pocket."

"Me too," she replied, her renegade mouth still in control.

"You have condoms?"

"No."

He frowned. "You also get tested before your birthday? Is your birthday coming up?"

"It is, and that's when I usually get an annual lady bits checkup with the stirrups and the speculum. But I did it earlier this year because of my work schedule. Never too soon to have one's pelvic cavity probed." *Stop!* She clamped her mouth shut. She didn't have to explain the female examination. *Start over. Use your brain—and real science—to sound reasonable.* She exhaled a slow breath. "I do not currently carry any sexually transmitted diseases or infections." She shook her head. "I don't know why I added *currently*. I have never harbored a sexually acquired infection." She chewed her lip. "Am I making sense? Because I hear the words, but my brain doesn't seem able to regulate what's coming out of my mouth. But I did like having your cock and the cake in there—my mouth, that is." She closed her eyes. This had to be the part of the evening where her birthday card boyfriend grabbed his clothes and ran out the door to escape the word-salad-spewing crazy lady.

"You can look at me," he said softly. "I acknowledge and fully comprehend your statements."

She opened her eyes and stared at the man. "You do?"

"Yes, I appreciate your candor, and I also enjoy having my cock in your mouth."

He spoke these words plainly, as one would comment on the progress of a local sports team. No judgment. No mockery. Just acceptance and perhaps a bit of gratitude.

"You're saying that it's safe for us to engage in sexual activity without the use of condoms," he continued.

He understood, and he was still here.

"Yes, and on the matter of sexual health disclosures, you'd have to trust me, and I'd have to trust you," she added.

What was she doing? Was this insane?

A muscle twitched on his jaw as his body tensed like a predator on the brink of pouncing. "Trust is imperative. And in that vein of thinking, under the current circumstances, I feel obligated to make another disclosure."

Her body ached. The very thought of his cock filling her to the hilt sent a shiver of anticipation down her spine. And it wasn't just the allure of sleeping with this man. She wanted him to believe her.

When no one else trusted her, would he?

She steadied herself. "Disclose away, Birthday Card."

He hovered above her, a bow on the brink of snapping. "In about ten seconds, I won't be able to stop myself from kissing you. And after I kiss you, I believe there's a high probability I won't be able to stop myself from making love to you until you swear you can see—"

"Stars," she whispered, awash in a fluttering current of exhilaration. If he could make her see and taste stars with his mouth, there was an excellent chance he'd get her there with his magnificent cock.

"Yes, stars," he affirmed and flicked his gaze to her left hand. She flexed her fingers, observing a tenderness in his demeanor as he studied the paper ring.

Why did he choose this moment to examine her hand, and why did his action spark a buzzy warmth in her chest?

She cleared her throat. "Regarding the kissing?"

"Yes?" he replied.

"I've been told my lips exhibit a high degree of kissability."

"They do," he answered, devouring her with his gaze. "And a kiss would be an excellent way to signal we agree to forgo the use of condoms and enter into an understanding that you've spoken the truth, and so have I."

He did trust her.

She smiled up at him. "Then you better kiss me."

He lowered himself. His hard body pressed against hers. Every nerve ending came to life. It was as if a magnetic force drew them together. An intoxicating zing traveled through her, and damn, she liked being pinned to the bed by this man. She let out a gentle, breathy sigh, savoring his body's reassuring weight and the sensation of being grounded while simultaneously feeling as if she could float away to join her beloved butterflies.

He drew closer. "My bloom," he whispered, his heated breath caressing her lips.

She needed to be cautious. She liked having him call her that more than she should. But the notion evaporated when his lips met hers. He kissed her gently, carefully. She hadn't expected such tenderness, but perhaps she should have. He kissed her methodically like he was forging a map or painting a picture in his head. Exploring and tasting, he deepened the kiss. Lightheaded, she wrapped her arms around him, anchoring herself to this profound moment. A kiss had never left her feeling so seen, so desired. There was no Earthwise, no professional screw-ups, no dead relatives, no dwelling on her greatest mistake. There was only this man, kissing her like she made up his entire world, trusting her like she could do no wrong.

And she wanted to fall deeper into this fairy tale.

She arched her back and rubbed against the tip of his rock-hard cock. The titillating sensation rippled through her core, now dripping with raw need. "I want to feel you. All of you," she said between kisses.

"I'll go slow," he replied, a tightness overtook his tone. "I don't want to hurt you."

He was on the edge of losing control. She could feel it.

"I don't want to go slow with you. I want everything. And I want it now. And keep calling me Bloom," she demanded, her voice shaking with a bone-deep yearning.

He thrust forward in a blisteringly powerful move and filled her, stretched her. "Christ, you feel so damned good, *Bloom*."

He concentrated on her eyes, like he longed to lose himself in the pools of ice blue, and made love to her in long, languid, and deliciously tormenting strokes. She met each pump of his hips with a breathy exhale. Relishing in the velvety slide of his cock, she bit her lip, trying to contain the clawing need to escape herself.

"I know what you want," he growled.

He straightened his arms, altering the angle of penetration. She inhaled a sharp breath as pleasure and the sweet bite of pain knit together in the slap of skin meeting skin. He reached for her hand. Entwining his right hand with her left, he dialed up his pace. His biceps flexed, and his abdominal muscles tightened into a chiseled wall as he thrust his hips, taking her hard and fast. Sweat coated their bodies as he lowered himself and captured her mouth. Her mind emptied. There was no thinking, only moving, thrusting, kissing, and writhing. Their bodies came together like jagged bolts of electricity, illuminating the night sky in a violent blast of crackling light.

And God help her. The man hadn't lied about his skills.

With every thrust, he caressed her most sensitive place, working her into a frothy fervor. He possessed an innate sense of her needs. Riling her up, then allowing her to unravel. Again and again, he played her body like a sexual virtuoso.

But a woman could only take so much.

"Stop teasing me. I want to come so badly I can taste it. Give me what I need," she breathed.

Was she begging again?

Oh, hell yeah, she was.

He pressed his lips to the shell of her ear. "I'm not teasing you. You like this game. You want to be pursued. You live for the chase. And Bloom, just so we're clear, I'm giving you the fuck you deserve."

Holy hell!

But she couldn't let him have the last word.

"Here's another game. Your game. You don't think anyone can catch you—could understand you. But you've never met anyone like me." She tightened her core, gripping his cock, then dug her nails into his taut ass with her free hand. And now came the kicker. "Happy birthday to you," she got out in a sultry singsong rasp as her body shook with each thrust of this man's glorious cock.

Carnal delight glittered in his eyes as he pistoned his hips, amping up his pace. She could barely catch her breath. The friction between them hovered on the brink of igniting. But she had to continue—had to show him their attraction was mutual. She knew how badly he wanted her.

"Happy birthday, Birthday Card Boyfriend," she continued, then moaned a deep wantonness sound.

"Where did you come from?" he asked, curiosity coating his words. He gripped her hand, and the paper ring's delicate imprint pressed into their skin as he squeezed.

But she couldn't answer his question. The words wouldn't come. She existed in a world of swirling sensations, thrusting bodies, and heated kisses. And she could almost taste those stars and the promise of sweet release.

"I'm there. I'm close," she breathed.

"I'm with you," he bit out. "I'll follow. I'm always right behind you." He was holding back, denying himself, waiting for her.

She gasped. His words unlocked a revelation. The notion pierced the haze of lust and longing and struck the chords of her heart. She wasn't alone. Not tonight.

He kissed her hard. "Stay with me. Don't hold back. I want you to come now, *Bloom*."

His gruff tone was her undoing.

Each kiss was another invitation to surrender. And heaven help her, she did. Letting go of the bullshit, she catapulted into the sweet abyss. Pleasure rippled through her core, a wave swallowing her whole. But she wasn't alone. Her birthday card boyfriend held her close, losing himself right behind her, just as he'd promised.

How could two strangers be so in tune with each other?

How could she feel like she knew both nothing and everything about him?

He pulled back, but she tightened her hold on him. "Don't go. Not yet," she whispered, her throat growing thick with emotion when her cell chimed.

"That's not mine," he said, brushing a few errant strands from her forehead.

"It's mine."

"Do you need to check it? I understand if you do."

She shook her head. "It's probably work. My next assignment."

"Your next international spy caper?"

"Something like that," she answered, manufacturing a slip of a grin.

"Bloom, if you have to get it, get it. Work comes first for me, too."

What a curious thing to say.

"I don't. Unless you need to go. Maybe you have work to get to."

Was that it?

He watched her again like he was studying her, memorizing her expression. Could he see the doubt in her eyes? The worry? The confusion about who she was and what she was supposed to be in this world?

"I can't leave you, Bloom."

"You can't?"

"I'm not through with you. Not even close."

"We should collect more data for the—"

"Wham Bam comparison," he finished.

"Yes. One bout of life-altering sex could be a fluke."

Delectable mischief glittered in his eyes. "You'd label our copulation as life-altering?"

She scrunched her face. "*Ew!* I love science dirty talk, but never say *copulation* again."

"Understood. Now," he continued, gently rising from the bed. But he didn't walk away. He lifted her into his arms like she weighed nothing, set her ass on the edge of the table, then zeroed in on her lips. "Here's the order of events, Bloom."

"Like a meeting agenda, right?" she teased. She loved his verbal quirks.

"Yes, like a meeting agenda. May I proceed?"

"By all means."

"I'm going to kiss you deeply. After a sufficient amount of kissing, I'll make you come on this table."

"Using your cock, mouth, or hands? I'm asking for the data collection," she tossed back, trying to play it cool, but her lady parts were on the verge of combusting.

"This round, I'll utilize digital stimulation."

Fingers for the win.

She peered up at him through her lashes. "Will I need to beg for it?"

He pursed his lips. "I haven't decided."

She cupped his face in her hand. "That's okay. A girl likes a little mystery."

He rested his hand on hers and gently stroked her paper ring. "I'm not usually one for mystery. However, I enjoy it with you."

She clenched her core. Welcome back, belly butterflies.

"And then," he continued, "after I've kissed you adequately, then made you come with my hands, in the spirit of data collection, I'd like to let the words of a wise woman guide the rest of the evening."

Izzy's jaw dropped.

The words of a wise woman? She pictured Elder Pachamama.

Big dick make you smile. Get some boom-boom action, and all will be good.

"Just out of curiosity," she stammered, "are you acquainted with a Peruvian wool witch? Is that the wise woman you're referencing?"

She sounded insane.

But her birthday card boyfriend was unfazed. He didn't even flinch. "I am not acquainted with a Peruvian wool witch. The wise woman I'm referencing is you."

"Me? What wise words did I impart?"

He slipped his hand between her thighs and kissed the corner of her mouth. "You said it quite effusively." He pulled back as a devilish grin graced his lips.

"Do you have something against *effusive* displays?"

His expression grew positively carnal as he worked her tight bundle of nerves. "Not with you, Bloom."

"Well, let's hear it, birthday boy," she said through heated breaths. "What wise words did I deliver *effusively*?"

He pressed his lips to the shell of her ear and picked up the tempo between her legs. "These wise words. Let the *mucho* fucking commence."

CHAPTER
Six

IZZY

OH, what a *mucho-fuckingly* beautiful day!

Izzy drank in the golden rays of sunshine, painting the mountainous terrain in vivid shades of green. A playful summer breeze teased stray tendrils of her hair as she cruised along the winding interstate. Each mile she covered brought her closer to a new challenge, a fresh start. Yes, that's what this next job had to be. And she'd set her sights on not fucking up. The *no-mucho-fucking-up* chapter of her life would unfold the second she reported to her post.

But not yet.

She'd given herself the drive to live in the not-so-distant past for a little longer.

Warmth radiated through her body that had nothing to do with the summer air flooding her rental. Here, in the limbo of travel, she had time to replay the events of last night. She sighed and glanced at her left hand, still adorned with the paper ring. A sated smile pulled at the corners of her lips. *What a boom-boom of a night!* She clenched her core—her deliciously tender core. Unlike her poor elbow, she welcomed this souvenir from a night of *mucho, mucho* fucking. Oh yes, double-*mucho*. From one to ten on the mucho-fucked scale, she was a certified two bazillion. That was her professional and highly scientific opinion.

She tapped her hands against the car's steering wheel and hummed the "Happy Birthday" tune. She couldn't help it. It had been stuck in her head like thoughts of her birthday card boyfriend. True to his word, he'd left before she'd woken up. The starbloom he'd given her was gone, too, but he hadn't disappeared without a trace. The man had penned a note on a piece of the same paper envelope he'd used to make her origami ring. She'd found the cream-colored scrap on the pillow beside her. Steering with one hand, she reached into her pack and felt the fibrous paper. He'd written to her while she'd slept, and the notion of him recording the sentiments as he watched her sleep set the butterflies—that had been working overtime in her belly for the last twenty-four hours—into flight. She didn't have to remove the note from her bag to know what it said. She'd memorized it— not that it took much work to recall. It was only a few lines.

Dear Bloom,

Thank you for making this my most unforgettable birthday.

If birthday wishes came true, I'd wish for you.

And please ice your elbow once a day for the next three days. Just fucking do it.

-Your Birthday Card Boyfriend

It was just like him: unwaveringly honest, a little beastly, unintentionally romantic, and endearingly protective.

"Oh, Mr. Birthday Card Boyfriend," she cooed and rolled her head from side to side, feeling loose, light, and lusciously limber.

Perhaps Elder Pachamama was right. A night of big-dick boom-boom sure did a world of good for her body. But those weren't the old woman's only words.

The lone bearer of burdens shall find their own demise.

That proclamation shut down the butterfly flit-fest and sent an icy tremor through her body.

But they were just words.

Even if the violet poncho-clad wool witch was right about the sex part, it didn't mean she was right about everything. Isabelle A. Adaire was doing fine on her own. If an outside observer pulled back the curtain and sneaked a peek into her life, they wouldn't assume she was hurtling toward her own demise, would they?

Damn.

Okay, maybe they would come to that conclusion due to her past actions, but she was on the cusp of moving forward.

Onward and upward—but again, not quite yet.

She pictured sage-green eyes and hands that ignited her body while steadying her. Unable to stop herself, she glanced at the paper ring for what had to be the fiftieth time since she'd gotten in the zippy sedan two hours ago.

Was it silly that she was wearing it?

Yes, of course it was.

Had she taken it off to shower this morning, then carefully put it on after she thoroughly dried her body?

Also, yes.

Did she want to be with someone? A certain tall, dark, and handsome cake-loving someone whose even tone, magnificent cock, and restrained grin left her swooning? Was she better off alone, or would her demise be like the old lady predicted?

Stop!

"Come on, Isabelle. Get back to the *mucho* fucking. Think of when he pressed your body against the floor-to-ceiling window, fed you cake, and banged your brains out," she whispered, her words carrying in the mountain breeze.

But attempting to block out the elder's foreboding prophesy was easier said than done. Like the birthday song stuck in her head, she couldn't stop toying with a notion—a hypothesis. If love—or the perception of love—hadn't clouded her judgment and led her to make an unforgivable mistake, would it have been possible for her to build a life with someone? And if so, could her birthday card boyfriend have been that certain someone?

A hollow ache carved a jagged space in her chest. No, he couldn't be hers. That was never an option.

Even if she'd wanted to get to know him better, he didn't want to pursue anything with her. He could have asked for her name and number. He didn't. Still, from the moment she'd woken up, she inhabited a state of uncertainty. Her heart and head had been playing a game of tug-of-war since she'd read the note. She didn't regret any part of their one-night stand, but whispers of what might have been lingered in the back of her mind.

What was that ache? Lust? Love?

No, it couldn't be love. It was simply . . . science.

Yes, science.

Neurochemicals and hormones released during sexual intercourse contributed to feelings of bonding and connection. This had to be why he'd cautioned her not to fall in love with him. He must have also understood the physiological connection between two people who clicked in the *mucho*-fucking department.

But it wasn't just the sex.

It was the man coming to her aid and threatening to break a dude's wrists. It was stalking a cake cart and bullshitting their way into the dessert tasting. It was his undivided attention, his sage-green eyes mapping her every smile, every move, even the shade of her blue eyes. That sly semblance smirk. His comforting, neutral tone. And his words. *I'll always be right behind you.*

And Bloom.

The mere thought of hearing him utter the nickname set her aflame.

Then again, he could invent a nickname for every nameless woman he'd slept with. That could be his schtick—his game, his act. Rescue a damsel in distress, get into some shenanigans, then go at it like sex maniacs. She chewed her lip. While that was possible, it didn't feel like he was faking it when he slipped the ring on her finger.

Enough of the goddamned head versus heart tug-of-war.

The rush would wear off. The pie-in-the-sky, true-love-did-exist musings would fade. And she sure as hell couldn't forget what happened the last time she'd trusted a man with her heart.

In two miles, take the Starrycard Creek Exit.

The voice of the car's navigation jolted her from her thoughts. It was a timely diversion. She had to forget about her one-night stand and get her head in the game. Luckily, she had a little over two hours until she was due at the land management hearing. Plenty of time to prep—and to poke around a bit. This wasn't the first time she'd heard of the small mountain town. In fact, when she'd checked her email this morning, she could barely believe her eyes. Her best friend, Hailey Higgins, had inherited a cabin in Starrycard Creek and had fallen in love with Finnegan Starrycard, the local handyman, who also helped run his family's artisan papermaking business. Unfortunately, she only knew the basics of the whirlwind love affair that had led to Hailey and Finn's engagement. Her crazy work schedule and limited access to Wi-Fi meant they'd been sharing life updates through disjointed emails, texts, and voice messages. Going by Hailey's latest email, she understood that the engaged couple wouldn't be in Starrycard Creek when she arrived. The pair were camping in a remote part of Arizona. It was unclear if her stay in Starrycard Creek would extend long enough to catch up with her bestie and her beau. Still, Izzy was excited to visit the town her bestie now called home.

The case brief from Pamela estimated the time on site would be minimal—a few days at the most.

And what exactly would she be doing in Starrycard Creek?

Acting as a proxy for the State as a land steward.

In a nutshell, her job was to confirm the environmental fitness of a plan to build on a large parcel of mountain terrain recently sanctioned for development by the town's charter. She would have loved to get Hailey's input. But it wasn't necessary. She'd earned her master's degree in Colorado and understood the ecological landscape. She'd make her assessment, file a report, and move on—unless the town had plans to decimate this untouched mountain acreage and disturb the wildlife and migration corridors. She simply wouldn't and couldn't tolerate that. However, she wasn't the only nod of approval required by the charter. The townspeople had a role, too. They would vote either in favor of or against the plan or multiple plans if several were presented. However, Pamela noted in the brief that one plan had been submitted to date by the town's manager.

It sounded cut and dry.

But it wasn't.

That town manager part set off alarm bells in her mind. She'd spent a fair share of her time in small towns. She knew the games they played. She wouldn't yield to some backwoods bloated bureaucrat. She'd observed several of these so-called public servants. Most were more interested in fast cash over responsible development.

Responsible development.

She knew a thing or two about that and a hell of a lot more about *irresponsible development.*

The comforting warmth that had enveloped her moments before evaporated, replaced by a scalding heat radiating from her hardened heart. *Dammit!* She couldn't spiral into that dark place. She hadn't even started her assignment and was already itching for a fight. She shifted her attention from the mountain scenery, her knuckles whitening on the steering wheel as she exited the interstate, her eyes narrowing and jaw set.

Calm down. Do something, anything.

She tapped the phone button on the steering wheel. "Call Hailey," she barked. The call went to voicemail, but her sweet friend's cheery greeting helped alleviate the pressure building inside her.

Beep!

What was she supposed to say? *Work's been like walking a tightrope, and I needed a bit of Hailey-sunshine to avoid turning another town against me and requiring an emergency extraction?*

No, she couldn't say that.

"Hails, hey, babe," she blathered, her head spinning. "I had a mind-blowing one-night stand. No, it was more than that. It was an adventure—a madcap, magical, cake-stealing adventure. I don't even know his name. But he was . . ." She paused and glanced at the paper ring. "He was unforgettable." She paused. Why the heck had she mentioned her birthday card boyfriend? Before she could untangle the word salad she'd unleashed on her bestie's voicemail, her nose tingled. She sneezed a series of explosive *achoos*, blinked her now watery eyes, and cleared her scratchy throat. "Sorry, Hails, I've got the sniffles—nothing to worry about." She cleared her throat. "And there's more. You'll never believe where I'm headed. Starrycard Creek. Yes, your Starrycard Creek. I've got an assignment as a land—"

Bloop, bloop.

She glanced at her cell on the console. An incoming call from Earthwise flashed on the screen. "Work's calling. I have to get it. We'll connect when you're back on the grid. I want to know everything about your engagement and your new teaching position. I love you, Hails."

She tapped the phone button, ending her call to Hailey and picking up Earthwise. "This is Isabelle Adaire."

"Izzy, it's Pam. My assistant just caught a typo on the Starrycard Creek Case Brief."

Izzy checked the time on the car's dash. "No worries. I have plenty of time until the hearing."

"No, you don't. The hearing is in seven minutes."

"What?" Izzy exclaimed.

"The time zones on our scheduling software glitched."

Dammit!

"It's an initial hearing," Izzy said, wishing like hell she'd prepped more before leaving Rocky Mountain City. "It'll probably be a meeting to set dates. No real substance."

"No, Izzy, that's not correct. Today, you'll evaluate the environmental viability of the town's proposals and give your approval."

What? She hadn't even set foot on the mountain.

"Only as long as they're ecologically sound," Izzy countered.

"You're familiar with the case, aren't you?"

Izzy cleared her throat. "Yes, absolutely."

"What am I saying?" Pamela mused. "I'm sure you dove in the second it hit your email last night. Didn't miss an inch."

At the mention of inches, Izzy clenched the tender muscles between her thighs. "Oh, I got all the inches last night."

"Excuse me?" Pam barked.

Do not think of Mr. Birthday Card Boyfriend's cock.

"I'm saying that I took all the inches, down and dirty, hard-core inches," she blurted, digging that hole deeper.

"Are you okay?" Pam pressed.

Izzy busted out a prom queen smile, which was pointless because this wasn't a video call. "I'm terrific. Loose as a goose. Feeling easy-breezy apple-squeezy," she sang, her voice rising a disturbing octave.

"Why are you talking like a deranged preschool teacher?"

Gah! That was a valid question.

"I'm pumped for this assignment. Rah, rah, hooray for the Earth!"

Stop talking.

"If this goes sideways, I have to let you go," Pamela fumed.

A knot formed in Izzy's belly. "It won't go sideways. I know what's on the line."

Fortunately, she'd read the brief and knew the basics. She could bullshit the rest.

"It better go smoothly. I'll be out of the office for the next couple of weeks on a family vacation. I don't want to get a call that you've been run out of town—again."

"I understand," Izzy replied, doing her best *not* to sound like a deranged preschool teacher as a weight lifted from her shoulders. At least Pamela wouldn't be breathing down her neck. "You don't have to worry about me."

"Bullshit," the woman answered, a weariness creeping into her tone. "No crusading. Don't lose your cool. Be a professional.

Think of your parents and grandparents. It would have broken their hearts to see you like this."

"I know." Izzy swallowed past the lump in her throat. "Will your daughter be vacationing with you?"

"Yes."

"How is she?" Izzy asked, hating the shake in her voice.

Pamela waited for a beat and then another. Her silence spoke volumes. "She misses what your family built. Everyone who'd worked for them does. You know that."

Izzy nodded, anger and shame settling in her chest.

"You tried, kid. You tried to fix it. There's nothing more to be done. He won," Pamela said softly. And dammit, a gentle Pam was a hell of a lot harder to take than a stern one. The pity and disappointment in her voice cut like a dagger to the heart.

"I'm sorry. Let her know that—"

"It's been years, Izzy," Pam interjected, regaining her bulldog tone. "Move on. Do your job. No screw-ups. Am I clear?"

"Yes," Izzy lied. There was no moving on, but she needed this job.

The line went dead.

She rolled her head from side to side. Tension had crept into her muscles, leaving her stressed and teetering on the edge of losing control.

In one mile, turn left on Main Street.

A wave of clawing humiliation washed over her. "Pull it together," she admonished and eyed the navigation screen. Fortunately, she was headed to the hearing. Her *initial* plan had been simple: identify the town hall designated for the hearing, pull over, pore over the case's specifics, and sift through the ecological databases.

So much for that.

She'd have to wing it.

Turn left.

Izzy rounded the bend and gasped. She'd traveled the world. She was no stranger to natural beauty. But what lay before her soothed her tormented soul. Starrycard Creek unveiled itself like a page from a fairy tale. Mountains stood as guardians around a valley town, their peaks piercing the blue sky. A rushing creek carved a path through what appeared to be the town center as a series of bridges connected the sides of the quaint town like delicate stitches. She rolled down her window as the GPS supplied directions to the Town Hall. She followed the driving commands, but her focus was on the alluring soundscape and the rush of the cascading creek beckoning her closer, like this place had a secret it wanted her to uncover.

What the hell did that mean?

She didn't have time to wax poetic about this place. This was nothing more than an assignment. Period.

You have arrived.

She parked on the street and studied the quaint red brick building with arched windows offering views of the babbling creek. Fluttering aspens and stoic evergreens dotted the perimeter as a rock wall followed the line of the flowing waters leading toward the town's library.

Welcome to the freaking Mayberry of the West. No wonder Hailey liked this place.

It still didn't mean they understood responsible ecological practices. This would be their first expansion in over a hundred years. There was an excellent chance they didn't know the first thing about an environmental impact assessment. They could also have contracted to work with an unscrupulous builder. She was keenly aware of what drove those greedy wolves to don sheep's clothing. She pictured a sugar-sweet used car salesman smile. Anger built in her chest. There it was again. The snarling feeling that sustained her. The clawing ache of betrayal was what remained of her legacy. Fueled by fiery fury, she grabbed her bag and squared her jaw. Storming out of her car, she narrowed her gaze on the ridiculously adorable town hall. But she wouldn't be fooled. This was no picturesque municipal building. This was a battleground. A battle between greed and preservation. She glared at the building's entrance. "Bring it on, town manager. This badass, Earth-loving bitch is ready to rumble."

"My, my, that's quite a pep talk."

Izzy spun on her heel and took in an attractive older woman with a silver braid trailing past her shoulder. She carried a platter covered in tinfoil. *Who the hell was this?* A sly twitch of a grin pulled at the corners of the woman's mouth as she glanced at the paper ring.

Shit! She still had it on.

"Ma'am, I didn't see you there," Izzy blathered, feeling her cheeks burn with the intensity of a thousand suns.

The woman looked her over and pursed her lips. "You're in dire need of a muffin, dear."

"A muffin?" Izzy repeated, but before she could respectfully decline, she turned away from the muffin lady and exploded into a contagion of sneezes. *Achoo, achoo, achoo!*

"And it appears you could also use some lemon ginger tea. You're coming down with something," the senior citizen added.

Izzy blinked her itchy eyes and sniffled. "I'm fine," she rasped as her stomach released a visceral, churning grumble. *Come on, body. Give a girl a break.*

The woman peeled back the platter's covering and handed Izzy a muffin. "My grandson requested lemon blueberry. An interesting choice for him. You'll need energy if you're fighting a cold. And everyone knows badass, Earth-loving bitches can't rumble on an empty stomach."

This old gal had sass in spades. She and Pachamama would be besties.

Izzy stared at the muffin. So much for rolling into town like a professional. She looked up to find the woman watching her with a curious glint in her eyes when chimes denoting the time echoed in the warm mountain air.

Two chimes. Two o'clock. She was late!

Izzy gasped and held the woman's gaze. "I need to go. I'm expected inside. Thank you for the muffin, ma'am."

"It's Goldie."

Whatever. Izzy offered the woman a placating smile, then burst into the town hall. She scanned the space and eyed a kiosk. The mayor's office was to the left. The town council meeting room to the right. That had to be the place.

A grandfather clock ticked away the seconds in the corner of the vestibule.

2:01 p.m.

She was officially late.

With the same enthusiasm as she'd used at the entrance, she flung open the door. The place was packed. She strode up the aisle when a piece of paper sailed into her path.

"Lady, could you get my picture for me?" A little girl with caramel-colored pigtails waved as she sat in an aisle seat, swinging her legs.

Izzy plucked the drawing from the floor. She stroked her thumb across the fibrous, cream-colored paper. An odd sense of déjà vu overtook her. She turned over the sheet and did a double take as she studied a drawing of a butterfly—and not just any butterfly. With the words *Papilio stellata* printed at the top in a child's wobbly letters, this butterfly had deep violet wings and silvery markings.

"Pretty, huh?" the girl chimed.

Izzy snapped out of her butterfly stupor and returned the picture to the child. "Yes."

"This is my favorite butterfly," the gap-toothed girl continued, kicking her feet.

Izzy's roiling fury waned. "Mine, too."

"You got a muffin," the girl chirped.

"Um . . . yes." She eyed the baked good.

The child pursed her lips. "Don't let my Uncle Kieran see it. He ate three, and then I saw him sneak a fourth muffin."

She chuckled. This kid was a piece of work. "Thanks for the tip."

"Nice ring," the girl continued, shooting the breeze. "I know how to make those, too."

Izzy peered at her hand and smiled. "It is a nice ring, isn't it?"

"Miss, we've got a hearing in progress. It's an hour's drive for me to get here from the county seat. I don't appreciate interruptions, and I don't tolerate delays," a man boomed from a table near the front of the room.

That had to be the judge.

Izzy flicked her gaze from her hand and winked at the girl. "Gotta go, kid. Nice butterfly drawing. Excellent attention to detail." She tapped the sheet, then hurried down the aisle, eyes trained on the scowling judge. "Sir," she said and made a beeline to the empty table across from the austere man.

"It's Judge Ironside or Your Honor," he snarled.

Stone-faced with salt-and-pepper colored cropped hair, thin lips, and dark appraising eyes, the name Ironside fit this guy to a T.

"My apologies, Judge Ironside. I'm Isabelle A. Adaire from Earthwise Consulting. I've been contracted by the State of Colorado to serve as the land steward regarding the development of mountain acreage in Starrycard Creek, Colorado." She could feel the intense gaze of whoever was sitting at the table on the adjacent side—her opposition and surely the town manager, aka the bloated bureaucrat. She didn't acknowledge the person. She wasn't there to make friends. She went in ice-cold.

"Ms. Adaire, my hearings start promptly," the judge admonished.

"I understand and apologize."

"Have you reviewed the plan put forth?" the gruff man pressed. "Are you ready to provide your expert opinion?"

Shit!

"Sir, I've reviewed the materials provided to Earthwise. However, I cannot sign off on any plan or proposal without conducting an onsite ecological assessment of the area."

It wasn't a lie. Could she have signed off, sight unseen? Yes. Would she? Oh, hell no. Would Pamela be pissed? Probably.

The judge peered at a file. "The town manager, who also holds a seat on the town council, has assured me that he's completed this step."

Cue the familiar flair of anger in her chest. She released a hollow, mirthless laugh. "The *town manager* has assured you, has he? Does this person hold a degree in environmental sciences, or does this person—*and this town, for that matter*—care about profit over the protection of their lands? That's the only justification I can see for bypassing an expert's opinion."

A gasp echoed from the audience, filling the room with whispers and palpable tension.

Izzy lifted her chin defiantly. Oh, yeah, Isabelle A. Adaire wasn't here to play games.

A man's booming laughter caught her attention, quite a contrast to the hissing whispers.

She peered over her shoulder. While the rest of the townspeople glared at her, an older gentleman, a row back in a ball cap with an unlit cigar pressed between his lips, let out another hearty chuckle, his eyes dancing with merriment. A woman's amused cackle joined his low snickering. *Oh my God!* It was the muffin lady.

"Settle down," Judge Ironside snapped. "Mr. Town Manager," the judge bellowed as the room quieted, "the State's environmental expert posed a question. Would you like to respond?"

"On behalf of myself and the town, I would, Your Honor," came a man's even gravelly, deliciously robotic reply.

Goose bumps peppered Izzy's skin. Her nipples tightened into sharp peaks. Her downtown lady parts quivered. *No, no, no. It couldn't be.* She turned toward the table and met the gaze of the man who'd rescued her from the smarmy gift shop wrist-grabber, made her a paper ring, fed her stolen cake, and *mucho*-fucked her brains out last night.

The judge folded his hands on the table. "Mr. Town Manager, please proceed."

"My academic credentials in law are impeccable. In addition, I'm keenly aware of the ecological implications involved in developing the land in question, *Ms. Isabelle A. Adaire.*" He narrowed his muted gaze, focusing on her like a heat-seeking missile. A muscle ticked on his jaw like he was doing everything to keep from pouncing.

She should take a page from his playbook. His android intonation added to her body's inappropriate response to his presence— a presence she'd never expected to encounter again. She swallowed hard, which freaking hurt, thanks to her scratchy throat.

The universe had thrown her one hell of a curve ball.

"Ms. Adaire, your response to Mr. Starrycard," the judge said dryly.

"Starrycard?" Izzy eked out.

This guy had to be related to her best friend's fiancé, Finnegan Starrycard.

"Yes, my name is Kieran Starrycard," her sugar-rush, orgasm-granting birthday card boyfriend replied, his voice low and deadly. "It's Starrycard after the creek, the mountain, and the town. *My town,*" he growled. *The beast!*

Oh, that's how he wanted to play it? Act like adversaries. Pretend he was an expert while attempting to intimidate her. No matter of *mucho*-fucking could save him now. The titillating warmth surging through her transformed into an ice bath. It didn't matter how many times he'd made her come last night. That was a cake-laden, butterfly-infused fantasy land. This was real life with real implications, and she ate puffed-up town managers for breakfast.

She faced the judge. "The town manager's response lacks substance. While he may hold an *impeccable* degree, it is in a field unrelated to ecology. In addition, anyone can claim to care, but only a trained expert can offer an informed opinion. If this court respects the environment, I'd discount the town manager's *envi-*

ronmental musings. He's not qualified, nor is he an objective observer."

"Excuse me?" Kieran Starrycard balked, a slight shake to his voice like he was on the edge of losing control. The man rose and strode toward her table. "You believe to possess more insight into this land than I do? Nobody knows it better. I've dedicated my life to this town."

Izzy sighed.

Blah, blah, blah.

She'd heard it before.

Her footsteps echoed in the large room as she closed in on him. She held his gaze. The sun streamed through the windows lining the room. All dark hair, stone-cold eyes, and cheekbones that could cut glass; he was more beautiful in the daylight, which didn't even seem possible.

Dammit! This man was the enemy. Don't forget that.

Kieran turned to the judge. "May I have a moment to confer with the State's expert?"

"You may, Mr. Starrycard."

Kieran took another step toward her and lowered his head. "What the hell are you doing here?"

Going right for the jugular. She could respect that.

A smirk played on her lips, the prelude to a verbal spar she was certain to win. "I'm saving the environment from greed and misuse. *What the hell are you doing here?*" she tossed back, dishing it out like the Earth-loving bitch she was.

"I live here," he seethed, his breath warm against her lips.

A tingle settled between her thighs.

Ignore it. Do not think about that breath on your neck, lips, between your thighs.

Stop!

"Well, I work here now, and I don't answer to you, Mr. Birthday Card Boy . . ." She gasped, cutting off her use of the nickname. And God help her. Pulse thumping, her breaths ragged, she'd never been this turned on in her entire life.

"Do you two need a room?" the judge snapped.

"For what?" she squeaked, her voice doing that crazy-lady octave jump. "What do you think we need to do in a room, Your Honor? I can't think of anything I'd do in a room with the town manager." *Shut your damned mouth.*

"To hammer out your differences so you don't waste any more of my time. It was my understanding this land management issue would be handled quickly. Why else would you need a room, Ms. Adaire?"

Her cheeks were on fire. "Oh, sure, right."

"Your Honor, we do not need a room," Kieran said smoothly. He stepped back, but he didn't look away. Instead, his gaze flicked to her hand. Her left hand. The ring. The corners of his mouth tilted upward in that beguiling, butterfly-inducing, almost imperceptible grin.

Had he missed her? Had he thought about her?

His words returned like a sweet lemon blueberry serenade wrapping around her heart.

If birthday wishes came true, I'd wish for you.

The door slammed, jolting her from her birthday card boyfriend La La Land.

"You know who does need a room?" boomed a man's syrupy voice she'd wished never to hear again. "Thousands of tourists who want to visit Starrycard Creek and spend their hard-earned cash in this town but can't because there's not enough available lodging."

Oh, no!

Izzy's stomach dropped. Loathing and a tumultuous tornado of regret raged like a whirlwind inside her.

"What is it, Bloom?" Kieran asked softly, losing the killer-lawyer vibe.

She peered up at him. A fierce protectiveness flashed in his eyes. In the space of a breath, he was hers again. She parted her lips, not sure where to start.

"Who are you, sir?" Ironside barked before she could utter a word.

"Regis Greenstone, green-build developer, Your Honor. I apologize for my tardiness. I was volunteering at a forest reserve, assisting with their tree-planting efforts. You see, I care about the environment, and that's why I'm here." Regis slapped a slick smile to his lips and gave her a leering once-over as he sauntered to the front of the room. "Do you mind if I steal a little table space, Iz?" he said, lowering his voice as he removed the satchel looped over his shoulder and took over her table. "Nah, you don't mind giving it up—the table and, well, you know, everything else."

This jackass.

Her skin crawled as she glared at the blond, sun-kissed conman. In a flashy ensemble of brand-name outdoor gear and a leather bag most likely made from the hide of some poor endangered creature, the slippery snake who'd taken everything from her strolled in like he owned the town. What was unsettling was the very real possibility that he intended to do just that.

A hand pressed to her back. A steady warmth emitted from the touch.

"Come with me," Kieran said, picking up her pack as he guided her to his table. "You know him, don't you?"

"He's . . ." Her bottom lip trembled.

His jaw clenched, a visible effort to restrain the anger simmering beneath the surface. "That's your ex. The one that hurt you."

She nodded, trembling like a shaking leaf. *Dammit!* She hated that Regis Greenstone could render her a pathetic mess.

"What's your business in Starrycard Creek, Mr. Greenstone?" the judge asked.

"It's simple, Your Honor. I have a proposal from my company, Ashbourne Building and Development. And . . ." He turned to the townspeople. "I want to give every small business owner in this community ten thousand dollars."

The crowd responded with another gasp, followed by a smattering of applause.

The knot in Izzy's belly tightened. These people didn't know what they were clapping for.

"It's my understanding that today is the deadline for proposal submissions regarding the development of the newly accessible land on Starrycard Mountain," Regis crooned.

"It is," the judge answered.

Her asshole ex reached into his bag, produced a folder, and brought it to the judge. "My ecologically friendly construction and development company is extremely interested in winning the contract to build on this land. I'd like to submit a proposal for the town's consideration."

Izzy glanced over her shoulder. Unlike when the townspeople whispered about her, they now grinned, hopeful gazes locked on what they thought was salvation. "No," she murmured. This is how it started. This is how communities lost everything. She had to think of something, anything. She needed more time. She needed . . . She glanced at her birthday card boyfriend—*the attorney*. And it clicked. She needed the law.

"I'm proposing a sprawling residential village with a luxury ski resort," Regis continued.

"How would business owners get ten thousand dollars?" a man called from the back of the room.

Izzy could see dollar signs in Regis's beady gray eyes.

"Just sign on to be an Ashbourne partner and agree to support the *Ashbourne* project," he answered, tossing an arrogant glance her way as he accentuated a name that once was the leader in green building and development.

As Regis droned on, spoon-feeding ecological buzzwords to the crowd, she touched her birthday card boyfriend's arm. "Regis is lying. Don't let him submit his proposal to the town."

Concern creased Kieran's brow. "I can't stop him. Anyone is allowed to submit. It's in the town charter."

Her heart raced. She scanned the townspeople. Over half

appeared to be buying it. The other half of the room eyed the man skeptically. That was a good sign. It meant she had time. She had to act—had to present a legal challenge. *Think, think, think!* Her gaze settled on the little girl with the butterfly drawing.

Butterflies.

"Residents of Starrycard Creek," Regis continued, mock sincerity oozing from every pore, "my humble belief is that we can prosper, protect the land, and the—"

"Butterflies!" Izzy exclaimed, finding her voice.

"Sure, we'll protect the butterflies," Regis echoed, but his sugar-sweet tone had soured.

"No, Your Honor," she continued and rushed to the center of the room. "As the State's expert, I request six weeks to complete my assessment because of butterflies."

"Six weeks?" the judge repeated, raising an eyebrow. "What's so special about butterflies?"

Izzy tossed another glance at the little girl, then focused on the judge. "Your Honor, the presence of the threatened starwing butterfly has been documented within the development zone authorized by the charter. The unique environmental features of this locale, including Starrycard Falls and the geothermal springs, render it a possible corridor for the species' migratory patterns."

"I see," the judge replied without an ounce of annoyance.

She'd won him over. Her argument was sound. This could work.

She held her birthday card boyfriend's gaze for a beat, drawing strength from his steady countenance, then returned her attention to Ironside. "In accordance with the provisions of the Colorado Butterfly Migration Protection Act, land developers are obligated to adhere to stringent regulatory measures and facilitate an evaluation by a qualified expert. I'm the expert."

Boom! This Earth-loving bitch was back.

Now, had she framed the situation accurately? Yes, the law existed. What wasn't clear was whether the rare butterfly had been sighted. A child's drawing might not be the best evidence.

But it was evidence, nonetheless. And it was all she had to buy some time.

"As much as I love butterflies," Regis said, feigning earnestness, "starwings haven't migrated through this part of Colorado for the past few years. We investigated this matter."

Oh, he was a crafty swindler, but he was also a liar. She could use that to her advantage.

She bit back a grin. "Your Honor, is Mr. Greenstone ready to submit this investigation data?"

Regis pursed his thin lips.

She had him.

"I ask because the State is ready to provide the documentation from an observer." Lies, lies, lies. She was playing with fire, and he could still call her bluff. Would he? Her heart was ready to beat itself out of her chest until her birthday card boyfriend took a step closer, his arm brushing against hers.

"Breathe," he whispered.

Yes, stand firm and breathe.

Regis shifted his stance. "*My company* wouldn't want to hurt a single butterfly." His tone was light, but his eyes burned with irritation.

"Is this sighting true?" Kieran asked softly, wonder coating his words.

She mustered a grin. "From what I understand." Her reply wasn't exactly the truth, but it wasn't a full-blown lie either.

"We're losing too much revenue over the winter," a woman called from the center of the room. "We need to build. We need to expand. The town needs to vote, and I sure could put ten thousand dollars to good use."

A chorus of "yeses" and "we need to act now" erupted.

"They're not wrong," Kieran said. "Costs are up. The town needs to increase its revenue."

An icy chill ran down Izzy's spine. "If we don't do something, and the people of Starrycard Creek vote for Regis's plan, they're . . ." She trailed off. "It won't be beneficial for them. I know what I'm talking about, but I can't say more. Please, help me buy some time."

Would he help her?

"Judge," he said calmly, "I understand the urgency expressed by members of my community, but the law is the law. As town manager, I agree with the expert's request for six weeks to finalize her assessment."

Oh, thank God.

"Well, I don't agree to that time frame," the judge blasted.

She froze, the rush of relief obliterated by the judge's bark.

Ironside pegged her with his gaze. "You've got three weeks from today, Ms. Adaire."

"Three weeks?" she stammered. "That's my . . ."

It was her twenty-sixth birthday.

"Your what?" he snarled.

She cleared her throat. "Nothing of consequence, Judge. I can complete my work in that time frame."

"That's what I like to hear." He raised his gavel. "In accordance with the charter, the proposals from Mr. Starrycard and Mr. Greenstone will be posted inside the Town Hall. We'll return in three weeks to vote. The hearing is adjourned." The judge banged his gavel.

Regis hooked his bag over his shoulder. The man's gaze darted between her and Kieran. A slimy smile twisted his lips. "Aren't you two something."

What the hell did that mean?

She looked her asshat ex square in the eyes, cold disdain coming off her in waves. "You won't win, Regis. Move on. Find another town to screw over."

His eyes glittered with greed. "I'm not going anywhere. You know how I work. *It's just business, baby.*"

She bristled. He used the same line after he'd tricked her.

"You understand," Regis continued. "Then again, of course, you do. You entrusted me with your family's legacy and let me take your V-card. I'll always own a piece of you, *baby.*"

Forget this guy. Forget her reputation. Forget Pamela's warnings.

"And you best keep your lips sealed. You signed on that dotted line," he continued, slippery as a snake. "You know what happened last time you started squawking and poking around my business. Keep your mouth shut unless you like forking over your money and making a fool of yourself."

She balled her left hand into a tight fist, ready to punch the smarmy smirk clean off his face. "You are a piece of—" A steady warmth cut off her tirade. She peered at her fist engulfed in Kieran's large hand.

She focused on the man. He appeared serene and in command, yet the tension in his jaw revealed a different tale. There he was, playing the white knight once more, but she could see what was brewing below his muted countenance. The man was ready for a fight.

"If you would, Ms. Adaire." He squeezed her fist, gaze locked on Regis as a foreboding hollowness threaded through his words. "Allow me to offer Mr. Greenstone some parting sentiments."

The room pulsed with anticipation, the air crackling with tension. What was he about to do?

CHAPTER

Seven

KIERAN

KIERAN NARROWED HIS GAZE, zeroing in on Regis Greenstone. *And God help him.* He was working overtime to refrain from punching this smug fucker into next week.

Sweet Christ, what a shift to the afternoon.

He'd entered the town hall, walking on sunshine.

When prompted by Goldie's text about which type of muffins to bake earlier that morning, he'd joyfully, yes, joyfully, suggested lemon blueberry with a smiling face emoji.

Why?

Because they reminded him of the best damned night of his life. Then, when the State's land steward seemed to be a no-show, he'd tasted victory, only to have his world turned upside down by a pair of ice-blue eyes.

The lights in the meeting room hummed a buzzy, irritating thrum. The sun he'd been walking on now streamed in through the windows like high-wattage spotlights. The intoxicating scent of jasmine and vanilla threatened to overtake him. The tiny, balled fist adorned with a paper ring in his grip anchored him to the moment, granting him a measure of restraint. The owner of this fist trembled as anger and humiliation rolled off her in turbulent waves.

Not *her*. His Bloom. His stunning, symmetrically perfect, endearingly effusive, slightly reckless, cake-devouring goddess had a name.

Isabelle A. Adaire.

And she had a job: Starrycard Creek Land Steward.

Fucking hell.

He couldn't deal with that revelation. A five-foot-ten blond douchebag wearing a pair of pristine hiking boots that he'd bet his last cent had never touched a trail required his immediate attention. He tightened his grip on Isabelle. His behavior served two purposes. It kept the town's current land steward from committing simple assault, and it allowed him to take a beat. This tactic often threw people off. He studied the shifty-eyed Regis Greenstone. The guy wouldn't look him in the eyes. Regis adjusted his stance, his gaze darting around the room. Beneath his arrogant demeanor, the developer wasn't as confident as he'd like to project. *Good!* Kieran knew his type. A fast talker. A promise breaker. A fucking liar.

And one more thing that made his blood boil.

Regis Greenstone was Isabelle's ex who'd taken her virginity and screwed her over.

He shouldn't allow that factor to cloud his judgment, but the thought of this scumbag touching *his bloom* sent his pulse skyrocketing. His protective instincts kicked in. His heart pounded like a war drum. Time slowed as if the universe itself paused to witness the raw, unbridled fury pumping through his veins. He yearned to unleash his wrath. It was a visceral rage, an animalistic response. This guy deserved to have his ass handed to him, but a display of physical aggression inside the town hall wasn't the answer.

At least not yet.

He fought every impulse to inflict bodily harm and extended his right hand. "Mr. Greenstone," he said coolly.

A stiff smile spread across Regis's face like two slender slices of rotten cantaloupe. "Mr. Starrycard," he replied, accepting the handshake.

Kieran's fingers, strengthened by years of crafting handmade paper, effortlessly asserted dominance over the developer's baby-soft hand, damn near crushing it.

Regis flinched.

There was no way this guy had spent the morning planting trees. These hands had never done an hour's worth of manual labor.

He leaned in toward the man. He might not be able to punch him, but he could issue a warning. "This handshake will be my last act of civility toward you, Mr. Greenstone. In addition, under no circumstances are you to speak to Ms. Adaire in that manner again. If you do, you'll answer to me, and I guarantee you will not enjoy the consequences."

"Anything else?" the little man hissed.

Kieran pulled the developer in an inch closer. "One final sentiment. Take your boots that you sure as hell didn't wear to plant trees and get the hell out of my town hall."

Well, so much for civility. He couldn't help it like he couldn't help his outburst in the gift shop. He had to play this smart. He couldn't allow himself to lose focus. But all he could concentrate on was Isabelle—and keeping her safe.

He released the man's hand.

"We're on the same side, Mr. Starrycard," Regis clucked like an overstuffed hen. "We both want to develop that land and prosper. What's standing in the way is Little Miss Butterfly. I know who you are, *Kieran Starrycard*. I know you want your town to prosper."

"Congratulations, you found my name on the town's webpage," Kieran replied smoothly, but he couldn't help catching a strange lilt in the man's voice. *Had they met before? He couldn't recall.*

A saccharine-sweet smirk played across Regis's lips as if he were the keeper of a delicious secret. "Let's just say I've done my homework. You're a smart man. You know Isabelle is stalling."

That might be true, but Kieran wasn't about to agree with the man.

And the developer was wrong about his allegiances.

"We are not on the same side, Mr. Greenstone. I'm only on one side, and that is with my town, my home. Nothing else matters to me besides protecting the small business community and preserving Starrycard Creek." A disconcerting shiver traveled down his spine. The town was what mattered to him. He hadn't lied, yet the statement didn't ring as true as it used to. *What the hell?*

"We'll see," Regis replied, then eyed Isabelle. "You look a little tired, Iz."

"Is that so?" she shot back.

Regis glanced between them, then shifted his attention to where Kieran held Isabelle's clenched fist, but he couldn't let go. She could take a swing at the slimeball. The woman had a reckless side—a reckless side he quite enjoyed last night. But this was not last night.

"You look a little worn out, too, Mr. Starrycard," Regis continued, his voice taking on an unnerving serpentine quality.

Kieran squared his jaw and stared down the man.

Regis waggled his finger at them. "You guys may want to get some rest before the next hearing. I might bring my fiancée with me when I return. She'd like it here. Well, she'll like it after I put the Greenstone stamp on it, and I will. I get what I want. Good luck chasing butterflies." The man plastered a smarmy smirk to his thin lips and strode down the aisle.

Good riddance. Fucking finally.

Kieran pressed his thumb to Isabelle's wrist as Regis left the room. Her pulse pounded. Her fist trembled. He had to reassure her she was safe. Yes, there was a chance she was lying about the butterflies. If anyone could track the elusive starwing butterfly in Starrycard Creek, it would have been him. And it had been years since he'd seen the ethereal creatures that migrated beneath the moonlight. And yes, she was the land steward who'd accused the town of putting profit over the environment, and holy shit, that was one hell of a mischaracterization of a community that treasured its natural surroundings. Still, she didn't deserve to be blindsided and degraded by anyone. He pictured her sleeping. He visualized her kiss-swollen lips, and her hair swept across her pink cheeks. She'd drifted off in his arms, tracing her fingertips down his jawline, a sensation he'd never thought much of until last night. And that's how they'd stayed, nose to nose, legs tangled as she slept in his embrace. Another first for him. Perhaps the scent of cake on her breath made it tolerable. He couldn't quite puzzle out what had made the sleeping arrangement pleasurable.

A smile lingered in his mind. It was her expression after their final kiss when she was still asleep. A serene smile, enhanced by the playful dance of her dimples, had graced her lips. He'd added the expression to the *Bloom List* in his notebook. Yes, he'd started one. He even had a bookmark of sorts for the page. He'd never wanted to keep a piece of a one-night stand with him until last night. That expression had driven him to write the note before slipping out of her room at dawn.

Stop dwelling on last night. He was losing precious seconds, getting lost in his head.

The paper ring pressed into his palm as he stroked the delicate skin on the back of her wrist.

This situation required him to formulate a reassuring response.

"Greenstone is gone. You didn't break any assault and battery laws, and you're with me now." *What the hell was that last part?* It came out like when he'd told her she was his.

You're mine.

A warmth spread through him.

Dammit, don't overthink it.

He was playing a part. Faking it. That's what he was doing with the fist-holding business. That was it.

Her thrumming pulse slowed, but it remained elevated.

She pulled her hand from his grasp and stepped back.

He checked the room. The last of the townspeople had filed out the door, leaving them alone.

"How are you the town manager? I figured you were some lawyer," she bit out, shaking her head.

What kind of question and assumption was that?

"They're not mutually exclusive. I'm both. In fact, I hold many positions of leadership in Starrycard Creek."

"Yeah, I figured that part out." She stared at him, her ice-blue eyes awash in wonder. "And you should know I stand by my words at the hearing," she said, her bottom lip trembling. "But . . . I'm grateful for what you said to Regis. I froze. He knows how to hit me where it hurts."

Kieran pursed his lips. Dammit, he hated to hear the shake in her voice. It took every ounce of self-control to refrain from sprinting from the meeting room and beating the living hell out of Regis Greenstone.

He schooled his features. Violence wasn't appropriate *yet*. And he wanted desperately to take away her pain, which wouldn't be accomplished through a show of force. *What could he do?* She enjoyed his short, concise responses and his use of profanity. That was his next move.

"Regis Greenstone is a fuckwad. It wasn't hard to come to your defense. A man of honor wouldn't speak to a woman in a degrading fashion."

She chuckled, the color returning to her cheeks. "You're making it hard for me to dislike you."

"Why should you dislike me?"

She squared her jaw. He recognized this fearless stance. She'd used it with the French cake warden. "I'm the obstacle in the path of your intentions for this town. I'm your opponent, and I'm not one to back down from a challenge."

He drank her in. "I'm aware. I've already witnessed your determination. Look at the lengths you went to for a few slices of motherfucking cake."

The ghost of a grin tickled the corners of her mouth. Her dimples winked on her cheeks, and damn, he'd spent the morning replaying this expression in his mind.

His pulse kicked up as he relished the ability to make her smile. He shouldn't be fascinated with her. She was telling the truth. She was an obstacle. She and Regis Greenstone presented dire complications for him. Each could eviscerate his control and derail the town he'd sworn to protect.

She glanced into the empty meeting room. "I got your note. It was very . . . you," she said and met his gaze.

The note.

He studied her. This expression was new. A subtle meekness in her smile hinted at a vulnerable side. The tenderness in her countenance drew him in. She didn't show this side to many people. Yes, that was speculation, yet he was oddly confident in his assumption. And he was pleased he could elicit this reaction from her.

But he had to draw a line. He had to separate what happened last night from who he had to be today and every day moving forward. With that in mind, how was he supposed to explain what he'd written? He didn't even understand it himself. Inspired by her serene expression, the part of him faking it wanted to leave something for her, wanted to share one last piece of the man he'd pretended to be. So, he'd done it. He just hadn't expected to discuss it with her. That was it. That was the angle. He schooled his features into a carefully practiced blank slate. "I left the note because I thought I'd never see you again. And you need to ice your elbow if you want the swelling to go down."

She studied him. "You didn't mean what you wrote about the birthday wish?"

He concentrated on the symmetry of her face, which left him breathless. What was wrong with his throat? He cleared it, but it didn't help.

"Birthday Card—" She shook her head. "*Kieran*, answer my question."

Hearing her say his name left him . . . lighter. That wasn't possible. Words couldn't decrease one's body mass. But she was right. He needed to reply.

"The person who was with you last night meant it."

Her brows knit together. "And that's not who I'm looking at today?"

How could he make her understand?

"Last night, we agreed to a level of anonymity and entered into a verbal agreement to participate in a one-night stand. The parameters of that agreement allowed me to behave in ways I normally wouldn't."

"And no falling in love," she added.

His fingers ached to caress the soft curve of her cheek. And Christ, he wanted to kiss her. He tensed, willing himself to calm the hell down. But he couldn't help himself. He had to touch her. Gently, he brushed his knuckles down her jawline. Longing swelled within him. "Correct, no falling in love." Under her spell, he couldn't look away. "I do have an observation. Shall I share it?"

"Okay," she whispered.

"Your lips aren't as symmetrical as they were yesterday. They're slightly swollen."

She nodded, a slight bob of her head. "It's a physiological response due to prolonged use, friction, and suction, all of which increase blood flow."

"I prefer them like this." She was a bloom, and like the flower, ever-changing and ever-captivating, he was enthralled with each infinitesimal deviation.

"From your perspective, would you say they exhibited a high degree of *kissability*?" she asked, eyes sparkling.

"The highest degree," he replied, enthralled as a yearning sensation building in his chest intensified. He'd trained himself to pull back, to not give in to his natural inclination to ruminate and obsess. But try as he might, he couldn't move on.

She closed her eyes and leaned into his touch. "The way to maintain the appearance is by—"

"More prolonged use, friction, and suction," he supplied.

She opened her eyes. "Yes."

"Time seems to lose all meaning when I look into your eyes," he confessed, unable to control what he said to her. The weight of his obligations and responsibilities melted away. Christ, he wanted to keep faking it and continue with the ruse they'd started last night. What was the harm in quietly reliving those brief, sinfully delightful moments once more?

"You did it again," she said softly.

"Did what?"

"Made me want to believe that anything was possible."

He tipped up her chin and focused on her kissable lips when a creak and slam yanked him from his Isabelle infatuation.

"Uncle Kier, Uncle Kier, I need to talk to you," McKenzie called, charging into the room with Goldie's phone in her hand.

What the hell was wrong with him? He could not allow himself to fall under Isabelle's spell. Too much was on the line.

He could not kiss this woman.

The thought barely materialized when his niece hurled her flailing body toward him. He stepped away from Isabelle, snapped the girl out of the air, and held her to his hip.

"What is it, McKenzie?" he asked, his voice a low rasp.

She cocked her head to the side. "Why are you talking like that?"

"Like what? This is my voice."

"It's growly and low like you're an angry beast, and you really, really, really want something," she replied, mimicking his gruff tone. "Can I make a video of you talking?"

The kid had no idea how right she was. But he could not go there. He had to divert her attention. "No videos. What did you need to tell me?"

The child inhaled an audible breath, which did not bode well for him. It signaled she was gearing up for an info dump.

Focus.

"Okay," she began, "I told everybody I'd come to get you two because I know Isabelle A. Adaire. And Mommy said, 'No, you don't, Kenz.' And I said, 'Oh, boy, I sure do, but I'm not telling anybody how I know her until I tell Isabelle I know who she is.' So, Goldie said, 'Just go get them and meet us over in the mayor's suite.'" McKenzie eyed Isabelle. "We're having a snack and watching Christian and the Rattlers baseball game in there. That's my grandma Maeve's office because she's the mayor. And my uncle Christian is a big, famous baseball player, and he's on TV at a game in Chicago. That's a town in Illinois." She turned to him. "Illinois has an S at the end, but you don't hear it in the word. Did you know that, Uncle Kier?"

How the hell did she say all that in one breath?

"Hello, Uncle Kier? Isabelle A. Adaire? Can you hear my words, or should I talk louder, or should I make a video of me talking and play it for you?" McKenzie pressed.

He turned to Isabelle. Wide-eyed with her lips parted, the newly appointed land steward didn't make a sound.

He could record this as her gobsmacked-by-McKenzie face. Everyone in the family had one.

He sifted through the child's word salad and zeroed in on the most pertinent information. "Yes, we can hear you. Did you say that you know Isabelle?"

"Yup," the kid replied and glanced at the muffin Isabelle had brought into the meeting. He hadn't given it much attention, but she must have gotten it from Goldie.

"Your niece dropped her butterfly drawing. I picked it up for her. That's how we know each other, right?" Isabelle asked, looking him over with warmth in her gaze like she'd solved a mystery.

What mystery could that be? Nothing had changed in his appearance aside from the addition of Kenzie on his hip. Nevertheless, her expression softened.

"No, that's not it," McKenzie countered with a giggle. The child employed her widest, toothiest grin, eyes sparkling with glee.

She appeared to know something he didn't.

"How do you know me?" Isabelle asked.

McKenzie pointed to the table. "Split that muffin with me, and I'll tell you."

"Kenzie," he chided, using the tone Eliza employed when the child made an outlandish request, which happened a hell of a lot.

The girl lifted her chin. "It's a contract negotiation. A verbal muffin contract. I'm *lawyering* like you and Grandma Maeve."

While he was pleased with the child's legal prowess, this was not the time to quibble over a muffin.

"It's fine. I'm happy to share." Isabelle picked up the treat, removed the paper liner, and then handed half to McKenzie. "There you go. I've complied with your terms."

"Take a bite," McKenzie instructed. "We're splitting it. Fifty-fifty. Fair and square."

Isabelle looked from him to his niece and suppressed a grin. "You're a bossy bunch."

"Nope, I'm McKenzie Fiona Starrycard-Dunleavy," the kid announced.

Isabelle chuckled, then held up her half. "Here we go. Are you watching, McKenzie Fiona Starrycard-Dunleavy?"

"Yup," his niece replied, a toothy grin in place as she recorded the event on her phone.

Isabelle took a bite, closed her eyes, and hummed. "Wow, that's one delicious muffin."

God help him. He loved that sound.

"You like watching Isabelle eat, don't ya, Uncle Kier?" the child mused, watching him like a little hawk.

Fuck!

"No, McKenzie, of course not. That's . . ."

"Creepy?" the kid offered.

"Yes, and stop recording," he said.

She tapped the red square. "Your face looks like you like it. Now watch me eat." McKenzie jammed the muffin into her mouth. "Not the same face," she mumbled through the bite as muffin crumbs rained onto his chest.

He wiped the spongy morsels from his clothing. "You're lucky you're my favorite Starrycard, Kenz."

The girl beamed. "I'm everybody's favorite Starrycard."

Isabelle beamed right back at the girl. "All right, McKenzie," she said, eyeing his niece. "I ate my half, and you ate yours. The contract is complete. It's time to fess up. How do you know me?"

McKenzie wiggled with excitement. "Miss Higgins' phone. I have to call her Miss Higgins at school. She's gonna be my second-grade teacher when I go back to school in September, and then she'll be my aunt after she marries Uncle Finn. So, she's my almost-aunt Hailey and my almost-second-grade teacher."

"You know Hailey Higgins?" Isabelle asked, wide-eyed.

"Yeah, we have sleepovers and everything. She shows me stuff on her phone, like pictures of her kitties. I saw her email, and now that I'm a great speller and a super-good reader, I can read the names, and your name was in there. *A-D-A-I-R-E.* I asked her, 'Who's that person sending you so many emails?' Hailey says you're her best friend, and she calls you Izzy. That sounds like dizzy. But Hailey's not here. She's with my uncle Finn camping. I'm taking care of their cats."

Holy fuck! He stared at Isabelle. This woman was his brother's fiancée's best friend. There's a mouthful.

"You're right. Hailey is my best friend. I've known her since I was a girl. And I might be dizzy and Izzy," Isabelle replied, again exhibiting her gobsmacked-by-McKenzie expression.

He could relate. "Dizziness is a normal reaction to McKenzie. I experience bouts of lightheadedness a few times a week after she speaks at length."

Isabelle looked him up and down. "So that makes you . . ."

"Finn's older brother."

Isabelle chewed her lip. "Did I offend your entire family, who will soon be my best friend's family?"

"Does *offend* mean to make people mad so they really, really,

really don't like you? Because when you were talking, people looked like this." McKenzie contorted her face into a deep, jowly scowl.

"That's the gist of the word," Isabelle answered warily.

"Then, yeah, everybody probably doesn't like you," his niece mused. "But not Goldie and Great-Grandpa Rex. They were laughing when you talked. But Mommy says that can happen when attitude adjustment hour happens at lunchtime."

Isabelle turned to him. "Attitude adjustment hour?"

"Cocktail hour," he translated.

"I could use one," she said under her breath.

"You're not the only one." He'd had the one-night stand of his life with his soon-to-be sister-in-law's best friend, who also happened to be the land steward in control of his town's fate. This might be the very definition of a mind fuck. He set down his niece. He needed a moment alone with Isabelle. "Head to the mayor's suite, Kenz. Tell everyone we're on our way."

"You got it, Uncle Kier," the child replied, skipping down the aisle. *What the hell did his sister feed that child? Espresso-laced fruit snacks?*

"We?" Isabelle said, worry creasing her brow. "That's not a good idea. I never socialize with clients—or eat cake with them or sleep with them." She cringed. "Talk about being *mucho, mucho* fucked."

Oh, he *mucho, mucho* fucking understood.

"Like you, I've always maintained a clear boundary between my public and personal lives. Nevertheless, it appears that line has been crossed."

She sighed. "We *mucho* crossed it. And crossed it. And crossed it. Then crossed it some more. And more."

The words *crossed, mucho, and more* never had him so turned on.

"A surplus of *mucho crossings*. Let's leave it at that." He could not allow himself to get hot and bothered.

Isabelle released a shaky breath. "Our history and connection to Hailey is quite problematic now that I'm Starrycard Creek's land steward and you're the town manager. I should consider stepping down."

His heart leaped into his throat. It's what he wanted, wasn't it?

She shook her head. "But I can't. I won't."

"You can't?" he repeated, struggling to make sense of the conflicting emotions roiling inside him.

"I can't because what Regis has planned will be catastrophic for Starrycard Creek, and I'm the only one who can stand up to him. The one who knows what he's truly capable of." She sniffled and rubbed her eyes. "I should go. I have research to do, and I have to get out into the field."

"You can't leave," he said, knowing what was coming, and it brought him relief.

She frowned. "Why not?"

"My family will insist on meeting with you." He gestured toward the doors. "Let me countdown."

"Countdown?" she echoed.

"Three, two, one."

"Hey, everybody," McKenzie called on cue, her voice echoing through the hall loud enough to penetrate the meeting room. "Isabelle A. Adaire, *A-D-A-I-R-E*, the lady everybody in town doesn't like, is Hailey Higgins' best friend, and I got to eat half her muffin, and Uncle Kier watched her eat the other half."

"Wow," Isabelle muttered.

"I should warn you." He had to give her a quick tutorial.

She cocked her head to the side. "Warn me?"

"My family can be *effusive*. There may be clapping and cheering. Then again, this situation may simply warrant raised voices. There's also an excellent chance my sister, Eliza, McKenzie's mother, will have taken to heart your comments about our townspeople wanting to decimate our treasured lands for a few dollars. My brother Owen, who is an artist and oversees the creative side of our family's artisan papermaking business, will glare and stew. My brother-in-law, Eliza's husband, Jack, is the local veterinarian.

Think of him like a good-natured golden retriever. He'll be on standby if Eliza gets carried away."

"Yikes," Isabelle murmured.

"Eliza is outspoken and opinionated—much like every Starrycard woman. Alongside my mother and grandmother, she takes pleasure in strategizing and frequently crafts schemes to influence the lives of our family members."

"Um . . . okay. Anyone else I need to know about before a Starrycard onslaught?"

"Yes. My mother will take a kill-them-with-kindness approach, and there's a good chance my father will suggest we listen to nineties hip-hop to invite *good vibrations* into the gathering. He may also mention a recording artist named Marky Mark."

Isabelle's mouth opened and closed like a flummoxed goldfish. "I don't know what to say to that."

"Try not to say anything," he cautioned. "My siblings and I do our best to discourage my dad's behavior. Unfortunately, my mother gets a kick out of it. That's why I believe my father continues."

The concern etched on her face melted away, and her dimples returned. "It's sweet. He'll do whatever it takes to make your mother happy. My parents and grandparents were like that."

Were?

Past tense.

Isabelle looked away and blinked a few times. "Any other Starrycards to be on the lookout for? Wayward cousins? An eccentric aunt?"

Talk of her family made her emotional. His best course of action was to press on.

"No," he answered. "My youngest sister is living abroad, and as McKenzie explained, my brother Christian is in Chicago."

Isabelle rubbed her temples, worry etched on her face. "I don't want to mess anything up for Hailey. She's happy here. I don't want my actions to reflect poorly on her."

He couldn't comprehend her concerns. "I don't understand."

"I care about her. She's . . ."

"She's what?" he pressed.

Isabelle ran her hands through her hair and stared out the window at the creek. "She's all I've got. And to think, this was supposed to be the start of me not screwing up everything I touch."

He understood that sentiment. The entire reason she was here was because he screwed up. A question formed. *What had she screwed up?* His legal, linear thinking expanded. Did Isabelle have a checkered past? Had it impacted her work? How much did he know about her? Before he could press her for answers, she gasped.

She held her locket in her trembling hand. "Did you tell anyone in your family about what we did last night?"

He abandoned thoughts of interrogating her. It killed him to see her tied up in knots.

What could he do to help?

It came to him in a flash.

He'd lean into his robotic, acerbic humor. She liked that.

He donned his best placid expression. "My family knows about us. I make a point of informing them anytime I engage in sexual activity. It went out in the Starrycard newsletter this morning."

He waited for a beat, then received his reward.

The fear and worry subsided, and the intelligent, playful, and utterly enchanting woman returned.

There she was. His Bloom.

She grinned up at him, her dimples drawing him in. "Let me guess. The announcement was followed by the recipe for the lemon blueberry cake we ate while engaging in the aforementioned sexual activity?"

He chuckled. "Even if there was a newsletter, which there is not, I didn't know your name until you walked into the meeting."

She sniffled again and rubbed her eyes. "Right. I'm a bit light-headed and clearly scatterbrained."

And she looked it.

"You've gone from pale to flushed in a matter of minutes. You need to rest. Did you ice your elbow this morning?"

"I haven't iced it, and I'm just jet lagged."

Why didn't this woman take care of herself?

He frowned. "It's not jet lag."

"I don't need to be fawned over or lectured. I can take care of myself." She grabbed her pack and charged down the aisle.

He followed a few steps behind.

She stopped in the empty vestibule, glanced from side to side, then turned on her heel. She pegged him with her gaze. "In less than an hour, Mr. Birthday Card Boyfriend," she whisper-shouted, "I've come face-to-face with the man who made me come seven times in one night and the ex who tricked me into ruining my family's legacy." She swished her hair over her shoulder. "I must apologize for not appearing as fresh as a daisy."

He detected the sarcasm in her final statement. She was also incorrect regarding the statistic she'd rattled off. "It's eight."

"What?" she quipped, sizing him up.

"I made you come eight times."

"You did?"

"Yes."

"I was guessing, making up a number. You kept count?" She surveyed him with a keen eye.

"Didn't you say accurate data was important?"

"I did."

He took her hand and peered at the ivory-colored paper ring. "Every detail of our evening is etched in my memory."

She shook her head. "Dammit, do you know how romantic that sounds?"

He knew how to answer. "It's a statement of fact, not meant to be romantic or otherwise." Okay, that was a lie. He'd meant it to be romantic. He'd allowed the part of him that enjoyed faking it to formulate the answer. She appeared to enjoy it when he didn't acknowledge romantic statements. When he did this, she made him feel as if anything was possible.

Anything was possible.

But as quickly as the expression bloomed, it withered away. She slipped her hand from his grasp and stared at the ceiling. "We can't . . . You and I shouldn't . . ." She closed her eyes. "Am I losing my mind? What am I doing here?"

"I asked myself the same question when I stepped foot in this town. For starters, have a cup of tea with a touch of honey in this environmentally friendly reusable metal tumbler with the town logo," his mother chimed, presenting the cup like a trophy.

Christ! When did his mom show up?

Isabelle's eyes fluttered open. She shrieked and staggered backward. He caught her around the waist and pulled her into his chest, steadying her.

She clung to him. "I'm going to have a heart attack in this town. First, the muffin lady snuck up on me, and now this tea pusher. What's going on? Does everyone in Starrycard Creek eavesdrop on people's private musings, then pop out of nowhere with snacks and beverages? Does this happen every day here? Is there something in the water?"

He studied the new land steward. Maybe she was losing her mind.

Regrettably, the news he had to deliver wouldn't offer her any solace, help with her frazzled psyche—or win her any points with his family.

"Oh, honey, there's definitely something in the water," his mother replied.

"And you are?" Isabelle pressed.

His mother smirked.

He had a very good feeling Isabelle was about to enter a new level of *mucho-fucked-dom.*

"Isabelle Adaire," he said, bracing for impact, "may I intro-duce my mother, Starrycard Creek's mayor, Maeve O'Leary-Starrycard."

CHAPTER
Eight

IZZY

EVERY MUSCLE in Izzy's body tensed. "The mayor?"

"Indeed, I am," the woman replied with a grin as she held the Starrycard Creek tumbler. "Have some tea."

Izzy accepted the metal cup and took a sip. The hot, spiced liquid soothed her scratchy throat. "Is this lemon and ginger?"

"It is. It's my mother-in-law's specialty. She makes it herself."

And then it clicked.

"Your mother-in-law is the muffin lady? The badass Earth-loving bitch?" Isabelle plastered a nervous grin on her lips. *What was going on with her mouth?*

Amusement danced in the mayor's eyes. "We call her Goldie, but yes, she was handing out muffins earlier, and characterizing her as a badass Earth-loving bitch is quite on the mark."

Isabelle felt her cheeks heat. *What must these people think of her?* She usually didn't care, but she was wading into uncharted territory in Starrycard Creek. She took another sip of the soothing drink, buying herself a few seconds to get it together and assess the mayor. With hair resembling the caramel brown hue of Kieran's niece but with a subtle silver glint running through her strands, the elegant woman sported a sly grin. That smile must be a family trait.

Okay, now she had to speak and sound professional and not psychotic.

"I didn't mean to be rude, ma'am. I mean, Madame Mayor. You startled me. And I seem to be . . ." She peered at her left hand —a hand that gripped Kieran's crisp white button-up. *And no, no, no!* She was still in his arms. "Mr. Starrycard," she said, wide-eyed, "I must apologize for—"

"For wrapping yourself around my big brother like a pretzel?"

Izzy gasped. *Who the hell was that?* She wasn't overreacting. These people did pop out of the woodwork. She tightened her pretzel grip on Kieran as a young woman bearing a striking resemblance to Maeve O'Leary-Starrycard emerged from the mayor's suite and strolled over.

That had to be the opinionated sister, Eliza.

"Nice ring," the woman offered coolly.

The ring! And another piece of the puzzle clicked into place. Kieran had said that he knew paper when he'd *origami-ed* his ass off and cranked out the ring. And, of course, he did. He came from a papermaking family. And so did his sister. The woman peered at the ring with a curious glint in her eyes.

Izzy surveyed the paper jewelry. "Oh, this? It's just . . ." She released Kieran's shirt and stepped away from the man, trying to get her oatmeal brain to generate a believable response.

"Something you picked up in a gift shop, correct? Isn't that what you told me when I inquired about the unique piece?" Kieran supplied.

This man was good.

Then again, this was his family, and he understood the Starrycard playbook. She, on the other hand, was floundering. Damn, she wished Hailey was there. Her best friend could reassure these people that she wasn't a lunatic.

"Correct, Ms. Adaire? It came from a hotel gift shop?" Kieran repeated with a subtle lilt of *are-you-currently-mucho-fucked-in-the-brain* resonating in his tone.

She met his gaze. Her oatmeal, mucho-fucked brain was growing thicker by the second. "What?"

"The paper ring we're discussing with my sister and mother." His voice was subdued yet laced with a hint of worry.

A thin beam of clarity pierced her muddled mind. "Yes, it found me in a gift shop."

"It found you?" Eliza repeated.

So much for clarity.

"No, I found it." Izzy's gaze bounced from the ring to Kieran. "Actually, we found each other." *What a time for her mind and mouth to mutiny!* Maybe she had lost it. It would make sense. Between incurring the wrath of a wool witch, nearly dying by alpaca, followed by eight sugar-rush orgasms, then learning the orgasm master was her opponent, only to—minutes later—encounter an even greater foe, a gal might experience a break with reality.

Eliza moved closer. "Your ring looks like it's made from Starrycard Creek paper."

Izzy dropped her hand to her side. "I wouldn't know."

"I would. So would you, Kier," the woman said, eyeing her brother.

Izzy studied the paper ring. Kieran must have suspected the paper had come from his family's shop. Not that he would have told her. And that wasn't all. The cards from The Pike's gift shop were similar to the birthday card she carried everywhere. Could that card also have been made from Starrycard Creek paper?

"Isabelle?" Eliza said.

"It's just Izzy," she replied, snapping back.

"Izzy, may I inquire which gift shop you discovered the ring in? While we don't sell paper rings, artists purchase our handmade, eco-friendly paper and sell their creations worldwide. We enjoy learning about how our environmentally responsible company, which would never put profit over protecting our treasured lands, helps others, don't we, Mom?" Eliza cooed.

Yep, the sister was upset about the profit-over-preservation comment, and she was digging for info to boot.

Izzy took another sip from the tumbler. She might as well tell the truth. "It's from the gift shop at The Pike in Rocky Mountain City."

"Was it a recent purchase?" Maeve asked warmly, then shared a look with Eliza.

What was going on between these women?

Izzy glanced at her hand. "I got the ring yesterday." Not a lie—exactly.

"Yesterday!" Eliza remarked. "Kieran was at The Pike yesterday. He had a meeting and stayed overnight."

"It was his birthday as well," Maeve added and patted the man's cheek.

Izzy met Kieran's gaze. "Happy belated birthday. I hope it was everything you wanted it to be." She couldn't help herself. The reckless streak that lived in her heart couldn't resist.

"Thank you," he offered coolly, but the upward tip of the corners of his mouth proved he enjoyed playing this game.

"Did you notice Izzy at The Pike, dear? My son is quite perceptive," Maeve offered.

Hell, yes, the man was perceptive. He knew how to make her beg for sweet release.

"Did you notice me?" Izzy asked, anticipation bubbling in her chest.

That sexy, barely there twitch of a grin bloomed on his lips. He studied her face. "You do look familiar. I may have passed you in the botanic gardens when I was admiring the . . . blooms."

Oh, that was a good one.

"Or perhaps you saw me inside the butterfly pavilion. I was there, too." Damn, with his unassuming air, her birthday card boyfriend made it so easy to fall into this elusive banter, this under-the-radar, titillating verbal back-and-forth. Was this a wise decision? No way. Engaging in this furtive flirtation in front of his sister and mother was risky. Still, it sent a delicious zing through her body.

He drank her in. And thank God nobody could tell she was clenching her tender, *mucho-fucked* lady parts under his penetrating gaze.

"That's it," he said robotically. "You were with the butterflies."

And cue her butterflies.

"What a coincidence," Eliza commented, her voice laden with undertones that suggested it was anything but. Still, there was no way she could have known what had occurred.

The doors to the mayor's suite creaked open, and McKenzie stuck her head out. "We're almost ready. Everybody, except for Uncle Kier, can come in." The child giggled, then shut the doors.

"Mom," Kieran said, keeping his voice low, "today is not my birthday."

"Play along, sweetheart. McKenzie found a box of birthday candles in my office and wants to surprise you with a muffin party." She paused, and a sly, knowing grin appeared. "Izzy," the woman continued.

"Yes?"

"As our Starrycard Creek land steward, who will be working closely with my darling Kieran, our very own town manager, could I ask a favor of you, dear?" Maeve purred.

Wow, with a tee-up like that, this woman was probably one hell of a mayor.

"Sure, if I can help, I will."

"Stay with my son and make sure he acts surprised for his niece."

Izzy glanced at the man who had donned a placid mask. "I can do that."

"And wait a few minutes before coming in," Maeve continued, then shared another glance with Eliza before entering the mayor's suite.

"Sure thing," Izzy answered as the door closed.

Alone, the ticking clock in the corner was their only companion. Kieran didn't speak, which gave her a moment to reflect on the strange conversation with the Starrycard women. "Whatever that was with your mother and sister, it wasn't what I was expecting," she said, breaking the bout of silence. "Given our combative exchange, Regis's ten-thousand-dollar proposal, and my revelation that a rare butterfly had been sighted, which could impact the development, I'm surprised they didn't ask about any of that. Or even Hailey, for that matter. They know I'm her best friend. Your niece told them. But they seemed more interested in you and me."

A muscle twitched on his jaw. "Don't worry. They'll ask about everything you stated. This is their way."

"And what way is that?"

He shifted his stance. "The way my grandmother thinks. Well, the way every Starrycard woman thinks. Scratch that. That statement is incorrect. My father, grandfather, and Finn also subscribe to this fanciful view."

She cocked her head to the side. "I don't understand."

"They don't believe in coincidences. Instead, they work to decipher some grand design behind every twist of fate. Our proximity to Starrycard Creek paper piqued their interest."

She frowned. That didn't make sense. "Why would they care about us being close to paper?"

He gestured to a portrait of a man who strongly resembled the Starrycard men, holding the hand of an elegant, fair-complected woman with flowing auburn hair. "Since the town was founded by my ancestors, William Starrycard and his wife Fiona Donnelly-Starrycard, people have believed that the paper made using Starrycard Creek water contains a quality or essence, if you will, that can lead one toward their destiny."

She studied the painting. "What sparked that belief?"

"Fiona's father, a rancher named Brian Donnelly, had turned down every suitor who'd come calling for her. It's said he was an exceptionally protective man who loved his daughter dearly. William and Fiona met and fell in love on the day William arrived in this part of Colorado, which also happened to be William's birthday. That day was yesterday, back in 1880."

"You and William share the same birthday?"

"We do."

She noted the way the couple gazed at each other. "They met and fell in love on the same day?"

"It's said they fell in love after one glance," Kieran corrected.

Her gaze snapped to him. "One glance, like they fell in love instantly. Love at first sight?"

"Yes, and quite to William's surprise."

"What do you mean?"

"William Starrycard wasn't looking for love," Kieran explained. "He was the second son of a prosperous English paper-maker. He understood that his older brother would inherit the family business. Consequently, he decided to depart England and embark on building his own business in America. His journal entries reveal his intention to remain a bachelor, dedicate his life to his work, and do everything in his power to prove to his family that he didn't need their help to succeed."

She drank in the portrait. "The lone bearer of burdens shall find their own demise."

He zeroed in on her. "Excuse me? What was that?"

"Nothing," she said, tossing him a glance, then returned her attention to the portrait. "But his intentions changed when he saw Fiona?"

"That's how the story goes."

"What did William say to Fiona's father that made him give his blessing to their marriage?"

"It wasn't what he said. It was the paper he'd used to write a letter to Brian Donnelly. He'd made it using water from the creek, now called Starrycard Creek, and botanicals, seeds, and blooms from the lands around the Donnelly Ranch. The myth of Star-rycard Creek is woven around a special kind of paper, said to have the mystical power to bring to life the innermost hopes and dreams of anyone who holds it, granting what many refer to as the heart's deepest wish. People come from across the globe to write these wishes on a piece of our paper and tuck it into a crevice or crack on the rock wishing wall that follows the line of the creek through town. However, there is a caveat."

"Which is?" she pressed.

"Whatever you wish for must be meant for you."

Her scientist mind kicked in. "How do you know if something is meant for you?"

"You don't."

"So, it's a leap of faith—trusting yourself to make the right wish?"

His intense gaze stirred the butterflies in her belly. "That's what some say."

She held up her left hand. "This ring is made from Starrycard Creek paper, isn't it? An artisan or painter must use it to create cards to sell in the gift shop. That's how it must have gotten there, right?"

He fixed his gaze on the clock. "That appears to be the case."

"Do you believe the legend? Do you think Starrycard Creek paper can shape your destiny and grant you your heart's wish?" she asked, immediately recalling what he'd written on the scrap of paper he'd left beside her.

If birthday wishes came true, I'd wish for you.

Her pulse kicked up as another revelation came to light.

He'd written the note on Starrycard Creek paper—and he had to have known it.

His neutral demeanor hardened. "Perhaps for others, it's true. Not for me. *Never for me.*"

A shiver ran down her spine as a lead weight settled in her chest. His reply hit like a punch to the gut. But she wouldn't allow him to see that. She followed his lead and projected cool composure. And honestly, what was she expecting him to say—that he'd slipped the ring on her finger, yearning for the legend to be true? That he hoped she was meant for him? That he wanted to live a life of rainbows, butterflies, and sugar-rush orgasms? She was a scientist. She knew creek water didn't hold a magical ability to guide one's fate. Still, she found herself captivated by the romantic allure of the legend—a leap of faith for love grounded in trusting one's heart. Then again, like him, she was also out of the running for enchanted interventions. She would never trust herself. And that's what she needed to remember when fanciful thoughts of Kieran Starrycard popped into her head. She was here to do her job and protect the land—and this town—from Regis Greenstone.

"We've waited for six minutes," he said robotically. "We should enter the suite, or my niece may combust from extended anticipation."

"Yes, sure. Remember to act surprised." She adjusted her pack on her shoulder, putting ideas of legends and love out of her head.

"I know the drill, Isabelle. I don't require a reminder. And I should convey that my mother asked you to wait with me because she believes we have a connection."

"The paper proximity thing. I know. But she doesn't know about what we did last night. As far as they're concerned, we simply passed each other at a location teeming with people. And wait . . ." She recalled another instance of Starrycard Creek paper. "The paper on the tables at the cake tasting was similar to Starrycard Creek paper."

"You're correct. I believe it was my family's paper."

"Does that mean you have a connection with everyone at the event?" she pressed.

He shook his head. "Those extraneous factors are inconsequential. I know my mother. She's focused on a specific set of facts. One: How I admitted to noticing you on my birthday, which coincides with William Starrycard's and the day he fell in love with Fiona Donnelly. Two: The presence of the Starrycard Creek paper added to her suspicions that there's some cosmic force at play. Three: You're Hailey's best friend. My mother regards herself as Hailey and Finn's matchmaker because she included my brother's business card in the letter informing Hailey of her inheritance of her great-uncle's cabin. And four: My mother wants more grandchildren. Every Starrycard couple for the last four generations had only one child, starting with William and Fiona. One son. Until my mother and father knocked out six of us. They see my generation of Starrycards as the way to ensure the health and longevity of the town and business—to bolster the Starrycard legacy if you will. I'm certain my mother and sister have shared their beliefs with my grandmother, who will assure them that their observations point to me falling in love with you."

Izzy cocked her head to the side, again feeling dizzy. "That's quite a rundown. An alarmingly specific conclusion."

"As my mother said, I've always been a keen observer. It's how I function. I know my family. I know how each of them thinks and reacts. But I know myself even better. I can't allow myself to fall in love with you or anyone. Here, the locals say love is in the cards in Starrycard Creek. It's written on every piece of tourism literature. However, love is not in the cards for me. I don't understand romantic love. I'm not the man from The Pike." He gestured to a large map of the town adorning the wall beside the portrait. "Starrycard Creek is where I live my *real life* in *my town*. This is who I am. It's how I'm built. I never expected or wanted to see you again. Having you here is a disturbance in my carefully crafted life." He paused and clenched his jaw as if battling to restrain a deluge of emotions.

So much for how he'd come to her rescue when Regis tore her apart. This guy didn't want anything to do with her.

"And I will protect the livelihood of Starrycard Creek at all costs—from Regis Greenstone and even from you, if that's what I have to do," he continued, his words taking on a hollow quality like he was speaking more to himself than to her.

Maybe the guy was conflicted—but that didn't mean he had to be such an asshole. The fiery anger within her ignited.

She poked him in his broad, hard chest. "You have some nerve. This is my real life, too. My career. My job. My dedication to protecting and preserving the creatures and lands that can't protect themselves is what *I must do*, even if that means going up against a brick wall of an arrogant town manager like you."

He watched her for a beat, then glanced over her shoulder. "I'd advise you to refrain from adding any more to your outburst."

Outburst?

Oh, she'd show him an outburst.

"You suggest I refrain from proceeding?" she roared, her voice echoing through the cavernous vestibule. "I don't agree with the *oh-so-esteemed* town manager. I will proceed. I have another issue to address." She poked him again, adrenaline fueling her tirade. "It wouldn't matter if you fell ass-over-elbow in love with me. I'm not built for love, either. Why do you think I told you we couldn't share our real names last night before I let you put a paper ring on it, feed me lemon blueberry wedding cake, and bang my brains out? I'm not looking for the one. I'll never be looking for *the one*. Not ever again. Work is my companion. Love isn't in the cards for me either, Mr. Birthday Card Boyfriend," she finished, breathless, chest heaving.

The man didn't speak, didn't make a peep.

"Nothing to add to that *outburst*?" she asked sweetly.

"Wow, this video is gonna be great," a child chirped. "But I have a question. Why would you let my uncle bang on your brain, Izzy? I don't think you should be banging on Izzy's brain, Uncle Kier. She needs it. Right, Goldie. People need brains to think."

Izzy cringed. Her stupid mouth strikes again. *Shit, shit, shit . . .*

CHAPTER
Nine

IZZY

. . . and shit, shit, shit! All the shit! Every shit that had ever been shitted!

She met Kieran's gaze. "That's McKenzie, isn't it? She's recording us."

"Correct," Kieran answered robotically.

"And Goldie is with her?"

"Also correct."

This was bad. This was very bad.

"Anyone else?" she asked through a nervous grin, coming off her *I-sure-as-hell-don't-need-a-man* high horse.

"Yes. A total of eight individuals."

She held the tumbler to her chest and chewed her lip. This would be an excellent moment for the earth to crack open and swallow her whole. "And are these eight individuals observing us?" she asked, lowering her voice—not that it mattered now.

"Their attention is directed toward you," he reported, accurate and precise as always. "McKenzie, please stop recording," he added.

"Aw," the child whined, "it was getting good, Uncle Kier."

"Kenz," he chided.

"Okay," the girl moped.

Izzy took a breath. "Is everyone still looking at me?"

"Yes," he replied.

It made sense. Who wouldn't gawk at a self-proclaimed cake-loving, paper-ring-wearing sex maniac?

She eyed the exit. She could make a run for it. She could start driving and never return—well, until Hailey's wedding. Oh, and probably the wedding shower before the nuptials. And anytime she wanted to visit her best friend. Oh God, of course, she'd be there if Hailey and Finn had kids. *Double damn!* She couldn't bolt. And there was another reason besides her best friend. Thanks to Regis, she couldn't go anywhere. She was the only one who understood what this town was up against. She had to set the record straight with the eight people standing behind her. Slowly, like a woman about to walk the plank, she turned toward Kieran's family. Yep, every pair of eyes was zeroed in on her like heat-seeking missiles. She parted her lips, but nothing came out. Blast her banged-to-the-max oatmeal brain!

"Isabelle Adaire," Kieran offered smoothly, coming to her side, "you've met my mother, my sister, my niece, and I'm sure you recognize my grandmother, Goldie. She offered you a lemon blueberry muffin."

"Yes," Izzy answered, going for breezy but sounding like a strangled frog. And, oh my God, how could Kieran remain so poised? She'd outed him as a cake-devouring sex maniac, and the man exhibited Mr. Darcy-level cool composure. Still, what was he supposed to do? Press her body to the wall next to the portrait of the town founders, rip off her panties, then bang her brains out for all to see? A tingle settled between her thighs. *Oh, hell no!* This was no time to daydream about orgasm number nine, which he would not be giving her. It was best to ride the manners train with the town manager and emanate an amiable, non-horny vibe.

Kieran stepped toward her and gestured to a man with sage-green eyes and a sharp jawline. It was clear the guy was a Starrycard brother. However, instead of being put together like the coiffed town manager, this guy had a tumble of dark hair and desperately needed a shave. "May I introduce my brother, Owen Starrycard. To his right is my brother-in-law, Eliza's husband, Jack Dunleavy. Next, we've got my father, Hank Starrycard, and my grandfather, Rex Starrycard," he continued, channeling the formal Mr. Darcy like they'd slipped into the eighteenth century.

She eyed the group, then . . . curtsied.

Dammit!

"What was that?" Kieran asked under his breath.

"Nothing," she whisper-hissed through a smile that would put a debutant to shame. "I thought I dropped something. But I didn't."

"Was that a curtsy?" Eliza shared a look with her mother and grandmother.

Izzy took a monster gulp of tea. *How was she supposed to answer?*

She'd have to bullshit her way out of it.

"Yes, it was a curtsy. You caught me," she said with a disconcerting, feathery laugh. "I did it out of habit because, at my last assignment in a Peruvian mountaintop village, it was considered a sign of respect to curtsy for the . . ." *Think, think, think . . .* "for the alpacas," she blathered like a lunatic.

"Alpacas?" Maeve repeated, confusion marring her features.

Izzy widened her grin, her lips on the brink of snapping.

Why did she say alpacas? Those berry-loving beasts were seared into her brain.

Say something to sound less crazy.

"And the elders," she offered. "Yes, in this village, it's customary to curtsy for alpacas and the village elders."

In for a penny, in for a pound. She couldn't turn back now.

"My mother visited Peru," Hank offered, nodding to Goldie. "She studied horticulture and traveled quite extensively in that corner of the world."

"Did you?" Izzy replied, relief coating the question. Talk of Peru was a hell of a lot better than discussing how she and Kieran banged while binging on cake.

"Yes, I love South America—the land, the culture, the languages, the people. Peru was my favorite place to visit. I had a bit of an epiphany there." She pressed a kiss to Rex's cheek. "That was many moons ago when I was a student. I also spent time in a mountain village, but it couldn't have been the same place as you, Izzy. It wasn't customary to curtsy to elders or alpacas during my time there," she finished with a sly twist of her lips.

Kieran turned and coughed, but it wasn't a cough. Was the man stifling laughter? Oh, the audacity.

"Is your brain gonna be okay, Izzy?" McKenzie asked, worry creasing her brow.

And . . . they were back to brain-banging.

"Maybe you're curtsying because Uncle Kieran banged your brain up too much, and you forgot you weren't supposed to curtsy anymore because this isn't Peru, and we're not alpacas. It's kind of weird," the child mused. "I've never seen Uncle Kier bang pots or trash can lids or brains. Is that what you do when you leave Starrycard Creek? Bang and bang and bang?"

Izzy peered at her banging birthday card boyfriend. The man stood rooted to the floor, a blush creeping up his neck as McKenzie's innocent bombshell left him gobsmacked, a six-foot-five deer caught in the headlights.

Welcome to the mortification melee. It served him right for laughing at her.

For what seemed like a century, no one spoke. Time ticked away, the grandfather clock recording each excruciating second.

Izzy took a sip of tea and cleared her throat. She had to say something. She surveyed the group. Start with the little girl. She needed to put her at ease. "McKenzie, my brain is . . ." Is obviously about to explode and ooze out of my ear. No, she couldn't say that. "My brain is . . ." *Stick to science.* "It's intact and inside my skull."

Wowza!

McKenzie pulled on her pigtails and tapped the top of her head. "Mine, too."

Okay, everybody's brain was where it was supposed to be.

"That being said," Izzy continued, "I'm glad you're all here. Well, glad probably isn't the right word." *Her mouth was at it again.* "You're here, and so am I, and I'd like to take this opportunity to address you as your land steward and—"

"And my brother's girlfriend?" Eliza offered, raising an eyebrow.

It was Izzy's turn to grow wide-eyed. "No, no, no, no! I'm not his girlfriend."

"You called him your birthday card boyfriend," Maeve offered in her honey tone.

Izzy met Kieran's gaze. "I did?"

"You did, and if I were your attorney, I'd urge you not to say another word or . . . curtsy. You may end up feeling," he leaned in and lowered his voice, "mucho fucked." There was that twitch of a grin.

Ugh! This man. Again, trying to tell her what she can and can't do and throwing a *mucho-fucked* at her. Infuriating!

"Well, Birthday Card Boyfriend, you're not my attorney. You're—"

"The birthday card boyfriend," a chorus of Starrycards called.

Izzy gasped.

"You keep saying it," Kieran murmured with that sexy, stupid smirk slapped on his face.

Perhaps she should have taken the advice of counsel. Oh, who was she kidding? She was well beyond the point of no return.

"I'd like to level with you," she said, her heart pounding as she spoke to the Starrycards. "Things are not as they seem." She glanced at McKenzie, not sure how to word what she needed to say. She had to acknowledge her connection to Kieran. But more than that, she had to let Kieran's family know what they were up against with Regis Greenstone, and none of it was appropriate for a child to hear. She scanned the group and caught Goldie's eye.

The woman nodded, seeming to read her mind like she recognized something in her, then patted the child's shoulder. "McKenzie, my little star, I left my favorite shawl on the bench by the creek. You know the spot I like. Can you retrieve it for me?"

"Yeah, okay, Goldie. I'll find it for you." The girl waved to the group. "Glad your brain is okay, Izzy. We can do birthday muffins later, Uncle Kier," she called and skipped out the door.

Izzy glanced at her birthday card boyfriend—no, *Kieran*. And speaking of *Kieran*, that name was far too sexy. *What was she supposed to call him?* Mr. Town Manager. No, it had too much of an eighteenth-century formality to it. If she used it, she might fall back into curtsying.

"The floor is yours. Say what you need to say," Kieran said with a peculiar undertone.

Was that relief she'd noted? She wasn't sure. She exhaled a heavy breath. "Thank you, Birth—" *Dammit!* "Thank you, Kieran." *Focus, woman.* "Kieran and I met yesterday and spent the evening together at The Pike. At that time, we didn't know each other's identity. We didn't intend for our connection to last more than the night. But I can assure you, what transpired between us won't impact my ability to serve as Starrycard Creek's land steward. Also, this is a temporary position, so my time here is limited."

"Not necessarily," Maeve chimed.

Izzy frowned. "I'm sorry?"

"The charter allows for the position to become permanent. But the town must vote on it," Hank explained.

"Which won't be necessary. As town manager, I can take on the responsibilities. That option is also allowed and does not have to be brought to a vote," Kieran interjected, his voice low and commanding.

"And I have no plans to stay," Izzy fired back. *Take that, Mr. Town Manager.* The flutter in her belly signaled he was watching her. No, devouring her with his gaze. *Enjoy the view, buddy. Isabelle A. Adaire didn't need a man.* She lifted her chin. "The past is the past. Kieran and I are moving forward and will maintain a strictly professional relationship during my time here." She caught his eye. "Correct?" Her heartbeat quickened as his gaze lingered on her lips.

"Correct," he replied, his voice a low purr.

Her core clenched. So much for not needing a man. That gravelly, beastly tone set her ablaze. And she was back to this place—this flurry of fizzy, all-consuming attraction to a man she could not be with and who did not want to be with her. End of story. But she couldn't look away from him, couldn't stop from observing the hard set of his jaw like his mouth hadn't wanted to agree with her.

"I have a question," Eliza chimed.

And thank goodness! The last thing Izzy should do is moon over this man in front of his family. She nodded to the woman. "Go ahead. Ask away."

"Why do you call my brother your birthday card boyfriend?"

Izzy shared another look with her . . . birthday card boyfriend. He offered a slight nod—an okay for her to proceed.

And the story was innocent enough.

"It's a bit of an inside joke. When I was in The Pike's gift shop, a man was coming on quite strong and wouldn't leave me alone while I was near a display of cards."

"Were you looking for a card for Kieran—for his birthday?" Jack asked.

"No, and come to think of it, I only got the idea to buy the cards when I noticed a clerk stocking some unique ones on a display. They caught my eye because they were similar to the one my family gave me."

"Interesting," Goldie purred.

"I noticed the interaction," Kieran continued. "The man appeared intoxicated and wouldn't comply with Isabelle's requests. That's when I intervened and told the man to refrain from engaging with my *girlfriend*, utilizing that terminology for effect."

"Did it work?" Rex asked, clearly intrigued.

"He banged her brains out, dear. I'd say it worked beautiful-ly," Goldie replied.

Holy horny seniors alert!

"When you're right, you're right, my star," Rex answered as the pair giggled like a couple of teenagers in love.

"Grandpa! Goldie!" Owen exclaimed, looking ready to lose his lunch.

The elder Starrycards ignored their grumpy grandson.

"You know, Owen," Hank mused, bright-eyed like he'd stumbled upon something.

Kieran leaned toward her. "Here it comes."

What was he talking about?

"Marky Mark and the Funky Bunch teach us that good vibrations and sweet sensations are hard to ignore," Hank finished.

Izzy pressed her lips into a hard line and glanced at Kieran. His reaction was muted, but there was a tenderness to how he watched his parents.

"Good vibrations and sweet sensations are how we ended up with six children," Maeve cooed, starry-eyed, as she gazed at her husband.

"Mom! Dad!" Eliza exclaimed, wide-eyed, as Jack patted his wife's back and laughed his ass off.

This family was something else.

"I cannot go there." Owen huffed and pinched the bridge of his nose. "Can we discuss what happened in the meeting? I have some thoughts," the grumpy artist continued.

"Yes, the meeting. Please, go ahead," Izzy said, grateful to shift gears.

"From your presentation, it seems as if you're intent on preventing development on Starrycard Mountain because of one butterfly sighting." Owen crossed his arms and donned a dour expression. "That's not an option. Our company might not be hurting, but plenty of other businesses are."

"My brother's assessment is accurate," Kieran elaborated. "My family's business isn't as severely affected by economic fluctuations as other local small businesses that rely on pedestrian patronage, such as eateries, coffee shops, and galleries. The winter season poses significant challenges for these establishments due to increased operating costs and the decline in tourism post-autumn. Developing the land on the mountain would stimulate commerce, especially in the winter months, with ski facilities, lodging, and access to the hot springs."

"Everything is connected," Eliza added. "I'm the principal at Starrycard Creek Elementary, where your best friend will join the faculty as our full-time second-grade teacher. Our funds are tied to tax income. To draw in educators, substitutes, teaching aides, nurses, maintenance managers, and cafeteria staff, we need to offer a good, livable wage. My staff deserves it."

"Expansion opportunities are rare. This area is the only piece of land our charter allows us to develop. It's the one shot we've got, and it feels like you've already made your decision," Owen added.

"Have you already decided?" Eliza pressed.

Izzy looked between the angry brother and sister. They were out for blood.

"Let's give our new land steward the benefit of the doubt. I have a feeling I know what you're made of, Izzy, and you'll do what's right," Rex offered.

She latched on to the elder Starrycard's gaze for a beat. He was almost as unreadable as Kieran, but something intriguing flashed in his eyes. An odd flicker of recognition, a quiet acknowledgment that seemed out of place.

What would he know about her?

Still, it didn't hurt to have a Starrycard in her corner.

"We need to expand," Kieran said, pulling her attention from Rex. "And as the town manager, it's my responsibility to protect our town's legacy."

"It's *our* responsibility," Maeve interjected.

Kieran shifted his stance. "Of course, I misspoke. The bottom line is that we're an artisan paper town that champions small business, as our founders intended. And we'll continue the tradition."

Izzy nodded. This wasn't lost on her. "I understand. I simply want to ensure that the environment isn't harmed."

Eliza crossed her arms. "What does that mean? How do you decide?"

"I investigate."

"What if you find the butterflies have returned? Is development off the table?" Owen asked. "And don't get me wrong. My family understands the importance of protecting the starwing butterfly. Hell, William and Fiona's daughter-in-law, Delilah, was the naturalist who identified the new species and named the creature *Papilio stellata*. But there must be a way forward."

This was where it got sticky, where Izzy usually veered toward throwing the weight of her opinion on the side of the environment like she'd done days ago in Encanto de las Alturas, Peru. But she'd never had a connection to any of the places she'd been sent on assignment like she now had to Starrycard Creek—at least not to her knowledge. She'd never taken a middle-of-the-road stance because she couldn't trust that her recommendations would be followed. Could she trust these people? She gathered her thoughts. "If the butterfly is spotted here," she began slowly, wading into uncharted territory, "there are stringent safeguards the town must follow to ensure the species' migration corridor remains intact."

"If? I thought you said there was a sighting?" Hank asked, watching her closely with those Starrycard sage-green eyes.

"I meant that I have to verify the sighting."

Maeve shared a look with her husband. "So, there really was one?"

"Yes," Izzy mustered.

Hank nodded. "Do you know who reported it?"

Izzy resurrected her debutant mega-watt smile. His granddaughter had knocked the likeness out with a couple of crayons.

But she couldn't say that. "That information isn't made public." It wasn't a lie, nor was it the whole truth.

Goldie studied the painted map of Starrycard Creek and Starrycard Mountain that adorned the far wall. "My eyes aren't what they used to be, but I thought I might have seen a starwing butterfly when I was up on the mountain with McKenzie a week ago. It was around dusk."

"It's possible," Izzy answered, a wave of relief washing over her. Could she count this as a second sighting? Not officially, but it was better than nothing. "Starwing butterflies migrate in the evening. Dusk would be an optimal time for a sighting."

"Where were you on the mountain, Mom?" Hank asked.

Goldie approached the mural, her silhouette outlined against the cascade of sunlight that draped the detailed map in a warm glow. "We were near Fiona's cabin, close to the falls and the hot spring."

"Spotting the butterfly near a hot spring is highly possible," Izzy replied, going into ecologist mode. "The starwing butterfly is attracted to the starbloom flowers that grow predominantly near the geothermal pools. They feed on starbloom nectar around dusk. The flower's bioluminescent quality draws them in when the petals emit a gentle glow. I believe Starrycard Creek has four hot springs near Starrycard Falls that feed the creek and keep your waters flowing year-round. Since the starblooms grow around hot springs, that leaves a limited number of corridors for the starwing's migration." She joined Goldie near the mural. "All of which are located in the area the charter set out for development."

"That's what you shared with the judge during the meeting," Goldie offered.

"Yes, ma'am. That's the situation and why I need to investigate."

"You know quite a bit about our region. Have you been to Starrycard Creek before?" Rex asked, joining them.

"No, but I earned my master's in environmental studies at

Rocky Mountain College. Many of the case studies presented to us focused on Colorado's diverse ecological landscape. From extreme heat to glaciers to erosion, the mountains here were formed from a diverse combination of geological processes. I was also fascinated to learn that the creek in Starrycard Creek doesn't freeze. Even in the harshest of Colorado winters, the veins from the hot springs up on the mountain keep it flowing. It's quite a feat at this elevation."

"Quite true, but I do have to correct you, Izzy. There are *five* hot springs," Rex said with a glint in his eyes.

Izzy studied the map. "Five? I only know of four. And the mural depicts four."

"That's because the fifth hot spring is a legend," Kieran answered and crossed his arms, mimicking his scowling brother's posture.

Rex led her to a drawing on the wall near the clock. "My grandmother, Delilah Starrycard, painted a watercolor landscape of a hot spring that doesn't resemble the four known geothermal pools. She titled it *Only Known to the Stars*. My father told me the painting was with her when she passed away."

Izzy drank in the twilight shades and billowy strokes of gray, midnight blue, and emerald-green foliage. A jagged rocky outcropping with water trailing down the sides and a sky alight with a sea of stars added an otherworldly touch to the hot spring. "It's enchanting," she said, her voice barely a whisper.

"If you look close enough," Rex said, lowering his voice, "you can see it's shrouded by the dense thicket and veiled in mist. And see that right there. The tiny strokes of ice blue on the water."

"Yes."

"It could be the stars reflecting off the pool or the ice-blue markings on the wings of starwing butterflies," the man offered.

"That would be quite a few starwings. Their migration patterns aren't well known. Some say they migrate in small clusters. Others think the number could be greater."

"I guess anything is possible," Rex replied.

"Perhaps," she said, intrigued by her strange connection to the elder Starrycard.

"It doesn't matter what it is," Kieran growled, irritation coming off him in waves. "Like I said, the fifth hot spring is a myth. There's no proof."

The guy was seriously not a fan of his town's legends.

"It could be out there," the older man replied, a touch of wonder in his voice. "The terrain gets rough and unforgiving. There are plenty of parts of the mountain nobody's explored. Anything is possible, my boy. Isn't that right, Goldie?"

He'd used the phrase again.

"Indeed, it is," Goldie replied, taking the man's hand and leading him to where the family members stood conversing outside the mayor's suite.

Anything is possible.

Izzy couldn't help but smile, recalling the words from last night. However, her birthday card boyfriend had the opposite reaction.

His posture stiffened as if he remembered the words, but not warmly. "Again, Delilah's painting could be anything. Something she made up. An improvisation on another spring. There's talk that she drank quite a bit. She could have been intoxicated when she'd created the painting."

Izzy concentrated on the landscape and the stars dotting the midnight-blue sky.

Her throat grew thick with emotion.

Rex and Goldie's talk of possibilities and fairy tales triggered a cascade of memories of her parents and grandparents. Their marriages blossomed with love, respect, and tenderness. The little stolen moments. The lingering gazes. The gentle touches. The snippets of time when she'd catch her father gazing at her mother or her grandfather observing her grandmother with such devotion, she'd tried to absorb the emotions like a flower soaking in sunshine. And the laughter. There had been so much laughter. And then, it was gone, replaced by a slice of deafening silence and regret, so much damned regret. She tightened her grip on the tumbler. Her throat constricted as she swallowed, her vision grew glassy as the starry picture blurred, and the voices of Kieran's family melted into a low murmur.

Kieran took a step toward her. "What is it, Bloom? You're holding your locket."

Was she? She brushed her thumb across the cool metal. Maybe it was the sound of Kieran's voice, even and reassuring. Maybe it was how he called her Bloom. Whatever it was, she couldn't help but answer. "Sometimes, it becomes too much, the weight of it. It's a lot to carry."

"I know," he whispered, pain infused in his reply.

She looked up at him. He drank her in, taking in every detail, studying her in that way that made her feel seen, like he could read her mind. Or was it her heart? The air between them echoed of when he'd discovered her black-and-blue elbow. He hadn't spoken the words, but she'd known he wanted to take away her pain just like she believed he wanted to at this very moment. And for the space of a breath, she'd almost let him.

Kieran shifted his stance. Nothing overt, but the movement allowed his arm to brush against hers. She released the locket and lowered her arm to her side.

He hooked his little finger around hers like two halves of a whole coming together. From the angle of his hulking body, no one could see what they were doing. They were two people admiring a painting of a magical hot spring beneath the sparkling heavens.

"I'd like to offer you words of comfort, but navigating emotions isn't one of my strong points," he said, lowering his voice.

She dropped her gaze to their hands. He stroked the paper ring with his finger. Damn, this was nice, comforting. The storm raging beneath the surface calmed when he touched her. No, she couldn't think like that. *What was she doing?* She had to get him out of her head and do her job. "It was a strong point for you last night. But that wasn't you, was it?"

There it was. That's what he'd said—and she'd be smart to believe him. She'd already ignored warning signals with Regis, and look where that had gotten her.

Kieran focused on her mouth. "Correct, it was not the real me."

There was the answer. Again. He wouldn't have to tell her a third time. Still, she couldn't muster the strength to pull away from him.

"I know Kier has consulted with a local civil engineer and architect. He's had plans drawn up, but I think we should consider Regis Greenstone's proposal. It sounds like he has the means to do it all. And wouldn't that make things easier and faster?" Owen proposed, his voice carrying across the vestibule.

Izzy gasped, recoiling from Kieran's touch as Owen's words snapped her back.

"Ten thousand dollars to each business is quite an incentive. And the shopkeepers could use it. After the meeting, I spoke with Mr. Perry and Mrs. Brimbles. The bookstore and the deli take a hit when the tourists disappear," Hank replied.

Izzy strode toward them, her heart pounding and the storm welling inside her intensifying as Kieran followed a step behind. "No, no, you can't do that," she exclaimed, her voice echoing through the chamber.

Eliza held up her phone. "I googled Ashbourne Building and Development. It's labeled as a green business. It has a bunch of certifications and everything. I know you're Hailey's best friend. We love her. She's family, and because of that, I'll give you the benefit of the doubt. But I must ask, are you simply hellbent on stopping us from helping our town? Is that how you operate? It's certainly what you project, and the town knows it."

"Go easy, Eliza," Kieran growled, his voice taking on a hard edge.

"It's okay, Kieran," Izzy said softly, but talk of trusting Regis had her on the cusp of losing control. And she could not do that. She made a fist, directing all the rage and humiliation to her clenched hand. But this time, it was different, thanks to the ring around her finger. She rested the pad of her thumb against the fibrous paper and found her breath. "I can't fault your sister for caring about her town and her home." She turned her attention to Eliza and the rest of the family. She had to say something to the Starrycards, but a nondisclosure agreement with her name on it limited her ability to warn them. "I'm unable to elaborate, but I promise you, Regis Greenstone is not what he seems, and neither is Ashbourne Building and Development." She cringed. It never ceased to hurt when she spoke the words.

"How would you know that? What do you know about him?" Owen pressed. "What do you mean you can't elaborate?"

Where to begin?

Scratch that. Where to begin without violating the nondisclosure agreement . . . again.

Her breath hitched. The anger and frustration that lived in her heart were on the brink of bursting like a swollen storm cloud seconds before a fierce downpour. She focused on the feel of the ring against her skin. "Starrycard Creek could lose everything if you choose to partner with him."

"That's quite an accusation," Maeve said, her hand pressed to her chest.

"It's one I can make whole-heartedly, ma'am."

"Why? What happened?" Goldie asked, worry creasing her brow.

"I'm limited on what I can say. There's a nondisclosure agreement."

Kieran's muted mask cracked, and the man's jaw dropped. "You have a nondisclosure agreement with Regis Greenstone?"

She held his gaze. "And an asset purchase agreement."

"What did you sell to him?" he pressed.

"My family's business."

"You signed a contract and sold your family's business to

Regis without an attorney?" Kieran asked, his tone remained even. There was no judgment in the question, just a man gathering information.

Her throat thickened. The bitter bite of humiliation and regret invaded her mouth. "I worked with his attorney. I thought Regis had my best interests at heart. He didn't."

"I see."

She took a breath and surveyed his family. "What I can tell you is that my parents and grandparents were passionate about protecting the environment. I lost them in an accident five years ago. Their hearts would shatter into a million pieces if they saw what I'd let become of their life's work. I spent every penny I had trying to get back what Regis took from me and trying to right the wrongs I've caused."

"What's the name of your family's company?" Eliza asked.

Izzy released a joyless chuckle. "It's my name."

The woman cocked her head to the side. "Adaire?"

"No. My name is Isabelle A. Adaire. The *A* stands for my mother's maiden name. That's the name of our company."

"Ashbourne Building and Development," Kieran supplied, putting it together.

"Yes, it was once one of the top green-build firms in the country," she repeated. "Now, it's . . ."

A sham.

A lie.

A company perverting a good name to do bad business.

She wanted to say that but couldn't.

"All I can do to honor my family is dedicate my life to protecting and preserving. I won't let Starrycard Mountain get ravaged or ruined."

"Even if that means stopping us—the people of Starrycard Creek. People who'd never hurt the land we love?" Kieran asked, the intensity of his gaze strong enough to melt steel.

A lead weight settled in her chest. "People talk a good talk, but most choose profit over preservation."

Was her position unreasonable?

Maybe.

But it was all she had.

Tears pricked her eyes. She had to get out of there. She could not cry in front of the Starrycards. But she was dangerously close to letting her emotions overtake her. There was a good chance Pamela would fire her. Hailey would question her extreme motives. Still, she couldn't worry about that. Fueled by her resolve, she zeroed in on the town manager. "I'll stop anyone in my way. I'll do whatever it takes." She lifted her chin as a traitorous tear rolled down her cheek. *"Watch and learn."*

CHAPTER
Ten

KIERAN

"ISABELLE, stop! Do you even know where you're going?" Kieran broke out into a sprint. Jesus Christ, the woman could move.

"You don't have to follow me," she called over her shoulder.

But he did. Dammit, he couldn't stop himself. He hadn't paused to process the information when she'd bolted from the town hall. He saw that damned tear trail down her cheek and charged after her.

Her blond hair swished against her canvas backpack as she speed-stomped down Main Street.

"What are you doing?" he called, his heart hammering. Sure, his reaction could be attributed to strenuous movement. No, it wasn't the exercise causing his pulse to skyrocket.

It was Isabelle.

She was pure, unbridled emotion. Despite knowing her for less than twenty-four hours, he couldn't allow her to be alone. She'd fight him tooth and nail, but he had to persevere. He wasn't certain how he knew this. He just did.

"Not that it's any of your business," she called. "I'm looking for a hotel. I have to get to work. There's so much to do and so little time to do it."

He could save her the trouble, but it would certainly add to her stomping rage-fest.

He quickened his pace. "You won't find a hotel in Starrycard Creek."

She skidded to a stop and spun to face him, nearly taking him out with her pack.

"Careful," he called, jumping out of the way to dodge the canvas wrecking ball.

"What do you mean I won't find a hotel?" she shot back, then rubbed the back of her hand across her cheek.

"Are you still crying?" The muscles in his chest tightened. Tears shimmered in her ice-blue eyes, turning them into pools that mimicked starlight. "You are," he whispered. The ache in his chest intensified. He reached out to touch her cheek.

She batted away his hand. "I'm not crying. I'm producing tears, which is a response to . . . stress." She sniffled. "I'm mimicking the *Mimosa pudica*."

What the hell was that?

"Mimosa, what? That sounds like how my grandparents start their day," he replied.

She huffed. "It's not an alcoholic beverage. The *Mimosa pudica* is a plant found in tropical and subtropical regions. It responds to stress by folding its leaves, closing itself off, and releasing droplets. It's a defensive mechanism to deter predators."

He analyzed her explanation. "That's plant science for crying."

She brushed her hand across her cheek, wiping away another reaction to stress that produced droplets, which was crying, but he wouldn't dwell on that point.

"Dammit," she hissed, pain slicing through the word. "I need to—"

"Work," he supplied.

She peered up at him, all red cheeks, shining eyes, and those trembling lips. "Yes, work. It's what I've got. It's everything I've got."

He tensed. *What the hell was happening in his chest?* He did his best to school his features. "I understand. I also need to get to work."

"I need a room and Wi-Fi." She gasped, hope edging out the anguish etched on her face. "Wait! I can stay at Hailey's cabin."

He braced for impact. He'd have to deny her again. And despite it being out of his control, the task grated him. But that didn't change the answer. He worked to maintain a placid demeanor, usually an easy task, but now, it took every ounce of strength he possessed. "No, Isabelle, you can't stay at Hailey's cabin."

"*Gah!*" she exclaimed and poked him in the chest. "You may be in charge of a lot of things in this town, *Birthday Card Boyfriend*, but I know my best friend would be happy to let me stay in her cabin."

"I agree. She would," he answered, biting back a grin. She'd done it again. She'd used the nickname. Most likely, it slipped out because she was in the grip of strong emotions. That fact only brought him more . . . More what? Enjoyment? No, he didn't like seeing her upset. Still, he couldn't label his reaction. Again, he had to move on. He knew from experience he only had seven seconds to reply before the person he was conversing with would note his peculiar behavior. "You can't stay in the cabin because it's occupied."

"Who's there?" she pressed, sounding ready to challenge the current occupants to a duel for the right to reside in the mountain abode.

"Friends of Hailey and Finn. One of my brother's college professors and her family are using both Hailey's cabin and the cabin next door, my family's cabin, aptly named Starrycard Cabin. I believe they're using both for much of the summer."

Isabelle fiddled with the tumbler. "What about their house in town? They just bought a cute brick bungalow to be closer to work. She sent me a picture of it."

He shifted his stance and stepped backward. She may want to

claw his eyes out after he answered her question. "You can't stay there either."

"Says who?" she exclaimed, poking him in the chest again, which was better than having his eyes dislodged from his head.

"The floors have been torn out of their new home."

"The floors? All of them?" she exclaimed.

"Most of them. It's a surprise for Hailey."

"I've known my best friend since we were girls. Hailey has no issue with . . . floors. Who doesn't like floors? Why would he have the floors torn out for her? I thought he was a handyman. Why isn't he doing the work? Are you bullshitting me, Mr. Birthday Card Boyfriend?" The words rushed from her perfect, slightly swollen, and oh-so-kissable lips like a raging river.

Do not fixate on her mouth!

He couldn't help it. She'd done it again. She'd called him Birthday Card Boyfriend but with a mister added for emphasis. He maintained his muted demeanor, but on the inside, he fizzed like a shaken soda can, ready to burst. The sensation was both oddly comforting and whole-heartedly disconcerting.

He had to get out of his head and reply.

He held her fiery gaze. "Finn tells me that Hailey likes heated floors. He learned this fact when she stayed with him at Starrycard Cabin, which offers this feature. While they're gone, he's having them installed, so when they return, she won't have to prepare to teach a summer school enrichment session in a construction zone."

"Goddamn it!" Isabelle roared.

"This angers you?" He wasn't expecting that reaction, but perhaps he should have. This woman did nothing but surprise him.

"Yes!" she exclaimed, then shook her head. "I mean . . . no. It's a very considerate gesture on Finn's part."

"Finnegan is enamored with your best friend. I've never seen my brother so happy. And, as you know, my entire family cares deeply for Hailey. Me included."

"I know," Isabelle said softly, losing steam. "And as someone who loves her dearly, I'm grateful. However, I'm in no state to discuss anything. If it isn't painfully obvious, I need to get a room. I must decompress and—"

"Work," he finished, understanding her state of mind. While he might not emote, it didn't mean that overwhelming emotions didn't take a toll on him. "I understand. You've clarified your goal. I apologize if our conversation increases your distress."

She sighed, then turned in a circle, taking in her surroundings. He observed her closely as one watches an active volcano. She'd headed toward the business district but hadn't quite made it. The creek that carved its way through the town gurgled and splashed not far from where they stood. Tourists and locals strolled down the path that followed the waterway's gentle curves. Between the stoic evergreens and vibrant wildflowers, she fit in here. It was as if the very landscape had been crafted for her.

Jesus, what was going on in his head?

She stilled and met his gaze. "If there are no hotels, what lodging facilities do you have in this place?"

That was an easy question to answer.

"A bed-and-breakfast and an inn."

She exhaled an irritated huff. Eliza and McKenzie made similar utterances when they were precariously close to a loss of self-restraint. Knowing Isabelle was growing increasingly irritated, he needed to proceed with extreme caution.

Isabelle took a sip from the tumbler. "Okay, either of those options will work. Point me in the direction of the inn or the B-and-B."

"You can't stay at the inn or the bed-and-breakfast."

The woman growled, a low primal sound.

Then again, she moved like a lynx through the gift shop the first time he'd laid eyes on her.

"Birthday Card Boyfriend," she blasted, "you're worse than the French cake ogre at The Pike."

Wide-eyed, he replayed the interaction. Should he have softened his reply, but how? There were no rooms available. It was the truth.

"What are you? Starrycard Creek's one-man *anti-tourism* bureau?" she continued, formidable as hell.

"No, we don't have one of those. My mother and Goldie are involved with the tourism information distribution with other merchants and town employees. The room shortage is because this is our high summer season. The B-and-B and the inn are sold out. The rental cabins, too."

"Did I hear someone is looking for a place to stay in Starrycard Creek?" came the voice of a man with a thick Italian accent.

Of all the times for this guy to pop up.

"Fuck my life," Kieran mumbled under his breath.

Isabelle pivoted like a caffeinated squirrel. "Who the hell are you, and what the hell are you wearing?"

"I'm Nico Romano," the man purred. "And these are my activewear clothes," he explained, pointing to the very short shorts the man was famous for sporting in even the most frigid weather, which baffled the mind. "I wear this form-fitting athletic apparel to sprint down the trails and battle the creek in my kayak. Picture it. A man. The land. The water. The ultimate challenge. And I know who you are, *bella.*"

"You do?" Isabelle replied, eyeing the man warily.

"You are *Isabella*, the beautiful bringer of doom!"

"That's quite a name," she said, still watching Nico like she wasn't quite sure she was still on planet Earth, which was an understandable response to a grown man with bulging quads and biceps squeezed into tiny neon yellow spandex shorts and matching tank top.

"That is what the town is saying," Nico continued, "but I say, how can a beautiful flower like *Isabella* ignite anything but *amor* and passion in a man, woman, or child."

"Birthday Card Boyfriend," Isabelle murmured, head cocked to the side as she took in the town's watersports expert. The man achieved a level of effusiveness that went well beyond any Starrycard, even McKenzie.

"Yes?"

"Am I hallucinating?" She pointed to Nico. "Is he real?"

Kieran eyed the man. Nico had never bothered him until he caught the beefcake of a kayak instructor devouring Isabelle with his gaze. Still, he had to rely on his manners. "Isabelle Adaire, Nico works at the outdoor outfitter shop and runs the water sports programs for the town. He is, in fact, real."

"And it is a *real* pleasure to feast my eyes on you, *Isabella*," the handsome Italian crooned.

A muscle ticked on Kieran's jaw. *Fuck manners.* "What the hell do you need, Nico?" he barked.

Nico stepped back. A wide grin stretched across his perfectly tanned face. "Kieran Starrycard! You are quite worked up. Would you like to accompany me on a riveting run along the creek to work out your frustration? As I am a student of passion, I can see you are suffering from sexual frustration. The most taxing passion of all."

Oh, for fuck's sake.

"No, Nico. I'm not suffering from sexual frustration, nor do I require physical exercise," he replied, absolutely suffering from the condition and requiring some means to expel the restless energy Isabelle had ignited. It gushed through him like Starrycard Falls. But he sure as hell wasn't about to admit this.

"Do you know of a room for rent?" Isabelle pressed.

Nico's grin widened. "I do, *bella*."

"Perfect. Where is it?"

"My home."

"Your home?" she echoed.

What was this fuckery?

Kieran steadied himself. Christ, he was the one on the brink of explosion.

"You are welcome to stay with me, *Isabella*. I have a spare bedroom. I promise, any woman who visits my *casa* always leaves satisfied."

Isabelle's jaw dropped. "Wow."

"What the hell did you say, Nico?" Kieran asked, his voice taking on an uncharacteristically homicidal lilt.

"It is because of my cooking, of course," the man explained. "My mama taught me everything she knows back in my village in Italy."

Isabelle shrugged. "I'm not one to turn down a meal. And if there's nowhere else to stay, my answer is—"

"No," Kieran growled. "She says no, Nico. She's declining your offer for lodging, pasta, and whatever the hell else you're offering."

Holy fuck! What the hell did he just say?

"No?" Isabelle shot back, staring him down.

"It's the town manager's job to arrange accommodations for the land steward. It's my responsibility. *You're mine, Isabelle.*"

Fuck! Fuckity, fuck, fuck, fuck!

He'd trained himself to remain calm, collected, and observant. He prided himself on maintaining a subtle air of detachment. He appreciated McKenzie's remark about his robotic-like composure. *Where was that man?* It was as if he'd short-circuited, his head no longer in charge of his reactions.

Isabelle and Nico stared at him wide-eyed.

Dammit, this wasn't the time to assess his dysfunction. He cleared his throat. "Your accommodations are my responsibility. Excuse me, I misspoke."

Better.

"Such passion, Kieran Starrycard! You need that run. Many runs. Perhaps a run followed by strenuous kayaking and a very cold shower," Nico replied.

Kieran eyed the beefy Spandex-clad man. Perhaps there was some merit to his suggestion. "How far of a run do you suggest?"

Jesus, what was he doing?

"This has to stop!" Isabelle exclaimed. "If you'll excuse me, gentlemen. This day, which I didn't think could get any crazier, just hit absolutely freaking bonkers. I cannot be held responsible for my actions if I have to endure another second of whatever this is. Good day, fine sirs." She curtsied. "Fuck!" she whisper-shouted, then speed-stomped toward the business district.

"Fuck!" Kieran repeated and took off after her.

"Another time for the run, my passion-filled friend," Nico called.

Kieran couldn't deal with the man. His focus was Isabelle.

"Now, where are you going?" he called.

"I'll sleep in my car." She skidded to a stop.

He plowed into her pack and wrapped his arms around her to keep her upright.

"What are you doing?" she shrieked, peering over her shoulder.

"I have no fucking clue," he answered, tightening his hold on her. "Why did you stop?"

"I'm going in the wrong direction. I left my rental parked near the Town Hall. I can work in there and live there."

"In your car?"

"Yes."

"What is it with you and Hailey and cars?" he muttered.

"Excuse me?" She pulled away and spun to face him.

"Finn told me Hailey suggested doing the same thing when she showed up in Starrycard Creek."

Isabelle waved him off. "It doesn't surprise me. Hailey and I are tough as nails. We do what we have to do. You have to be strong when no family is looking out for you. We share that in common."

The peculiar pang in his chest returned. "Hailey's not alone anymore, Isabelle. She's with Finn. She's a Starrycard—or at least she will be soon. And like my family says, everyone in town is quite fond of her."

"And everyone in Starrycard Creek hates me. Well, everyone but your grandparents and the Spandex guy. A gal's got to start somewhere." Isabelle huffed and stormed from the sidewalk toward the path that followed the creek.

"Where the hell are you going now?" he called, losing his damned mind. *Christ! Could she not stay still for ten seconds?*

"I don't know!" she shrieked, waving her arms and splashing tea from the tumbler. She spun around, nearly taking him out with her pack again. "Maybe there's a hollowed-out tree. I can take shelter with a family of yellow warblers. Warblers prey on the starwing butterfly. Maybe they'll lead me to a starwing butterfly orgy where the insects gorge on starblooms until they pass out, only to be gobbled up by a family of blood-thirsty birds. Could that be how I find the butterflies and save the land?" she cried like she was practicing environmentally friendly witchcraft.

Kieran scanned the walkway. His irate land steward was causing quite a spectacle. "You'll stay at my house," he said, lowering his voice and hoping, no, praying, she'd follow his cue to dial it down a few notches.

"Your house?" she called for the folks two hundred miles away in Denver to hear. "You want me to live with you? Your entire family knows what happened between us last night. If I stay at your place, everyone will assume we're sleeping together —which we are not. You, Birthday Card Boyfriend, will not be supplying me with a ninth orgasm."

Sharp intakes of breath pierced the air. A slack-jawed family by the creek gawked at them. Joggers halted mid-stride. Wide-eyed parents cupped their hands over their children's ears. It was as if someone had hit the pause button on Starrycard Creek, and the world stood still.

Isabelle's cheeks burned crimson. "I said that loudly, didn't I?"

"Yes."

"And people are looking at us?" she whispered, lowering her voice.

"They're looking at you." He surveyed the area. "There are nineteen adults, eleven children, and three dogs observing you. No, four dogs. It's important to be—"

"Precise with data. Yes, I know." She rubbed her eyes.

He watched her like one observes a pot about to boil over. "Are you going to mimic the crying flower?"

"No, I'm pondering why I keep ruining everything. I don't set out to. I've always tried to do the right thing. It was never this hard until . . ." She choked up. "And now," she exclaimed, "everyone in this town thinks I'm a sex-obsessed bringer of doom."

Another round of gasps peppered the air.

The woman was imploding. He had to do something.

"Isabelle Adaire, our land steward, is not obsessed with sexual pursuits or intent on doom," he called at the top of his lungs. "She's suffering from altitude sickness. Yes, you're new to Starrycard Creek, and the altitude is getting to you. And it's known that altitude sickness can often induce temporary psychosis, causing a person to spout irrational content."

Was that true? Could altitude sickness bring on a psychotic break? Probably not, but it was the best he could muster.

"What are you doing?" she whispered, eyeing him like he was the one on the brink of a psychotic break. And dammit, perhaps he was.

"I'm giving an excuse for your irrational behavior," he whispered, scanning the area. "Nothing to worry about, everyone. Enjoy the day," he called, then surveyed the scene again. "Why is everyone still frozen? I provided an explanation for your behavior."

She shook her head. "Because now, we both look crazy."

"Shit," he murmured, taking her hand and leading her down the trail. He had two pressing objectives. He needed to remove them from the situation and ease his companion's mind. "Listen to me, Bloom, you haven't ruined anything," he said softly and threaded his fingers with hers. "I'll stay at my parents' place. You can have my bungalow to yourself."

"It still seems improper," she said, not screaming at the top of her lungs. An improvement.

"There's no other choice," he continued. He didn't have to worry about modulating his voice. The tenderness arose spontaneously.

Isabelle pulled her hand from his grip and leaned against the trunk of a great oak. The sun-dappled light lit her in a radiant glow. "I don't know, Kieran," she said, weariness edging out the fury.

He caged her in, needing her to listen to him. "Look at me."

She met his gaze, her ice-blue eyes shining.

He leaned in, inhaling her jasmine-vanilla scent. "You're not sleeping in your car. You're staying at my house."

She lifted her chin defiantly as a lock of hair brushed her cheek. *Christ, how was there still sass in her tank?* "I have a tent. I could camp in the woods."

This woman would drive him insane.

"There's no way you're sleeping in a tent when I can have you in my bed." He'd raised his voice again. He wasn't sure how much because he couldn't focus on anything besides this infuriating woman.

She parted her highly kissable lips, but nothing came out. He cupped her face in his hand and brushed his thumb across her slightly swollen lips. Lips he'd sucked and bitten. Her mouth had him behaving like a madman. A madman who desperately wanted to kiss those perfect lips.

"Well, hello," came a voice he'd know anywhere. "We meet again. And look, my star. The town manager and land steward appear to be getting along famously."

Kieran grimaced. *Goddammit! Could they not catch a break?*

CHAPTER
Eleven

KIERAN

STARTLED by his grandmother's voice, Kieran's eyes widened. "Goldie, Grandpa, what are you doing here?" he stammered at the unexpected visitors.

"We're walking home. What are you doing against that tree?" his grandfather tossed back with a sly expression, relaying that the old man was quite aware of what was going on against the tree.

Shit!

Kieran schooled his features. "We're discussing . . . housing options." He needed to divert his grandparents' attention from his questionable tree-trunk antics. Unable to come up with a better solution, he met Isabelle's gaze. "Hand me your rental's key fob."

Just do it, woman.

She reached into her pack and handed them over, which was a miracle. He'd expected a fight. Fortunately, the mortification written on her face appeared to render her mute and compliant. He glanced at the keychain and read the make and model of the car.

"Could you drive Isabelle's rental car to my place? It's a white sedan parked near Town Hall. The plate is written on the keychain. Due to the shortage of rentable rooms, she'll stay at my bungalow while I bunk at Starrycard House with my parents. We're unable to complete the task of procuring the car because we need . . ." Nico popped into his head. "We require physical exercise to expel energy and prefer to walk." *He was sounding unhinged again.*

"We're happy to help," his grandfather replied and presented his open palm.

Kieran exhaled a relieved breath. "Thank you." He tossed the man the keys, then took Isabelle's hand. "Come on. Let's . . . expel energy," he urged, guiding her down the path.

Her gaze widened in sheer astonishment as she glanced over her shoulder. "Your grandmother . . . Look at her. What is she wearing?" she uttered, struggling to articulate. A bazaar reaction. She'd spent time with his grandmother. She knew what Goldie looked like and what she was wearing. *Oh, fucking forget it.* Chalk it up to this insane day. And they couldn't dawdle. He couldn't chance another public outburst.

"I don't know, Isabelle. She's wearing clothes. But we shouldn't let ourselves . . ." He couldn't finish the thought.

What shouldn't they be doing?

Plenty of damned things.

Kissing.

Touching.

He should not be thinking about having her in his bed, beneath him, writhing, moaning, her breath hot against his lips.

He tightened his grip on her hand. "We *should* keep moving. We *should* get in some cardio by walking to my home to expel energy," he replied, wishing he could expel the torrent of pressure building in his chest.

"You think I'll stay at your house? You've got to be mucho-fucked in the head to believe I'd agree to that. I should find the tiny-shorts guy and take him up on his offer," she barked, squaring her shoulders and rooting herself to the trail.

Dammit! They were back to this? Perhaps his brain was mucho fucked, but he wasn't about to let her stay with Nico.

He recalled his mother's expression from his childhood—those moments when she had to lay down the law with her wild pack of Starrycard mischief-makers. Copying her expression, he narrowed his gaze and pursed his lips, mimicking not having one last ounce of patience remaining because he was well and truly fresh out of fucks when it came to Isabelle A. Adaire. "We're going to my house, Bloom, which, thank Christ, isn't far from here. You can walk beside me, or I'm throwing you over my shoulder."

She yanked her hand from his grip and stared him down. "You wouldn't dare."

"Shoulder it is." He hoisted her into his arms and maneuvered her over his left shoulder. This was a position McKenzie enjoyed. He'd also done this with Caroline when she was a girl. He knew to be firm but gentle.

"Kieran, my pack, my tea, and I'm wearing a skirt!" she yelped.

Fuck, fuck, and triple fuck!

The second he gripped her bare ass, a sea of items and a trickling of tea rained onto the trail.

"Cover my butt!" she called again, for everyone in a two-hundred-mile radius to hear.

He gasped. "You're not wearing underwear?"

"I am, but it's a G-string."

He shifted his hand and felt the strip of lace. "Okay, now I feel it. You're correct. You are wearing undergarments."

"Kieran, pull down my skirt!" she shrieked.

Dammit!

"An excellent suggestion," he blathered. *What the hell was wrong with his brain?*

"Just put me down," she roared.

He sure as hell couldn't do that. "No, God only knows what you'll do."

"What *I'll* do?" she bellowed as he carefully lowered himself to retrieve the items that fell from her pack. He gathered a trio of cards and a thick, worn envelope that looked like it had seen better days. He eyed the writing.

Ashbourne Building and Development Sales Contract

He placed the items into her bag, secured it with the zipper, and set off. They walked silently, and while it gave him a moment to collect his thoughts, he knew it wouldn't last. He left the trail, crossed over the creek on one of the wooden bridges that connected the two sides of the town, and breathed a sigh of relief when his bungalow came into view.

"I didn't take you for *this* kind of man," she snarled.

"And what kind of man is that?" he replied, knowing it wouldn't be a positive association.

"A Neanderthal. A caveman."

"You bring out an entirely different side to me, Bloom," he replied, exhausted yet strangely invigorated as he ascended the three steps to his covered porch.

"Where are we?" she demanded.

"My house."

"I can't see it. All I can see is your big, muscly back."

He sighed. Here was the moment of truth. "If I agree to put you down, you must give me your word you won't run. Keep in mind, I will follow you, Isabelle. And I'll catch you. I'm fast as hell. I'm the oldest of six. I spent a decent chunk of my childhood corralling and collecting Starrycards while my parents and grandparents ran the town and the paper company. Christian was hard to catch, but he's a professional athlete. He doesn't count. When Caroline was four, I held her like this for fifty percent of an entire summer. She was a handful. Still is." It wasn't like him to spill personal details. However, he wasn't himself when he was with this infuriating woman. "Do we have a deal? Do you agree to my terms?"

"Another verbal agreement?" she asked with a curious lilt.

"Yes."

"Like not falling in love?"

His throat tightened. "Correct."

"Fine," she hissed. "I agree—but under duress."

This woman.

"Duly noted." He maneuvered her from his shoulder and set her beside him. "Don't run."

She smoothed her blouse. "Does it look like I'm going anywhere?"

Surprisingly, it did not.

He unlocked the door and held it open. "After you."

She stormed past him. At least, she'd complied.

He observed as she entered the space. The bungalow had an open, square floor plan. A living room that led into the kitchen. A full bathroom separated the bedrooms on the opposite side. He didn't entertain many guests here. Family get-togethers occurred at Starrycard House, Goldie's restaurant, or the patio off the back of the paper company's building.

She eyed a bookshelf in his living room. "You have quite a few pictures of McKenzie."

"She is everyone's favorite Starrycard," he said, using the child's words.

"I can see why. She's smart, vivacious, and hilarious." She glanced at him, her gaze softening. "You're good with her. You know that, don't you?"

He nodded politely, finding it hard to discuss his niece. No, he found it difficult to focus on anything other than the strong-willed land steward. It was as if his mind needed to record every detail of this moment.

She left the living room and sauntered into the kitchen. Resting her pack on one of the chairs at the table, she went to the sink and set the tumbler on the counter. There was nothing unusual about her movements, yet he couldn't take his eyes off her. *What would she do next? What would she say?*

She leaned against the counter and pegged him with her gaze. "Last night, I wondered if you were a father."

Every muscle in his body clenched. "I'm an uncle. That's what I'm capable of being."

"What does that mean?"

Dammit! He wasn't going there. Not now. He eyed the refrigerator. "Let's get something to eat."

She raised an eyebrow. He recognized this movement. Would she ask why he couldn't be anything more than an uncle? The arch of her brows told him she was contemplating the question. He shouldn't have mentioned the *capable* part. As an attorney, he adhered to an economy of words, never saying more than he needed and never giving away too much. A rule he'd rarely broken until this golden-haired, cake-eating environmentalist crashed into his life.

She sneezed, then rubbed her eyes. "I'm not hungry."

He should be relieved that her poor health had diverted the conversation. But he wasn't. He was too concerned with her physical condition. She was rundown. Anyone could see that.

He opened the refrigerator and removed a container. "You will eat. I won't take no for an answer."

She came to his side and eyed the container's label. "What's Goldie's on the Creek?"

"My grandmother's restaurant. This is some of her chicken noodle soup."

Isabelle sniffled. "I told you. I'm not—"

"Get the baguette," he ordered, not putting up with her shit. He gestured toward the door to the pantry. "We can do this the easy way or the hard way. You will eat—even if I have to lift the spoon to your lips and shovel it down your throat."

"Now there's a visual. I guess I'm eating—and fetching baguettes from pantries." She huffed.

She was angry, yet warmth spread through him as he heated the soup on the stove, listening as she opened and closed the drawers, rifling through his kitchen. Seconds later, a serrated knife rhythmically crackled through the bread's crust as she sliced the loaf. It was a pleasing sound. He relaxed a fraction as the savory scents of fresh crusty bread and homemade chicken broth hung in the air.

"Bowls?" she asked softly.

"Cabinet to the left of the sink," he answered, drinking in the clinks and clanks of having a companion in the kitchen. She collected the utensils and tableware, set them beside the stove, and then padded into the living room.

"Is this accurate?" she asked, peering at a framed topographical map of the Starrycard lands that hung on the wall next to the bookshelf.

"It is. But there are some parts still left uncharted. The terrain gets steep and rugged on the other side of the falls."

She lifted her hand and traced a line an inch above the map's surface. "Is Fiona's cabin close to the largest hot spring?"

"Yes." He turned off the burner. "Is that the location where the novice observer noted the presence of a starwing butterfly?" he asked, distributing the soup into the bowls. He paused, counting to seven—a duration he had learned was long enough to await a response, but Isabelle remained silent. "Bloom?" he said, knowing he shouldn't use the nickname, but it seemed appropriate in this situation. He watched her as she stared at the map, then flinched. A curious reaction.

"Sorry, yes, I believe it was sighted near there," she stammered, not meeting his eye.

He opened the fridge, going through the motions of meal prep. He attempted to focus on his task, but he couldn't. Something was off with Isabelle. "Would you like lemonade or something stronger?"

That got her attention.

She raised an eyebrow. It didn't matter that he had a condition that made it tricky for him to read people. Her expression screamed, *what do you think, Mr. Birthday Card Boyfriend? Absolutely, I want something stronger. This day demands it.*

"Hard lemonade it is," he replied, assembling the drink Goldie had perfected: fresh-squeezed lemonade, Vodka, ice, and a few mint sprigs. It took a couple of trips to get the cups, bowls, bread, napkins, and utensils to the table, but Isabelle didn't seem to notice their meal was ready. She stood in front of the map as if she were mesmerized—or troubled—by something hidden in the topographical landscape.

What was his next move?

He'd draw her out through conversation.

"That's interesting that the sighting was in that location," he offered.

The color drained from her face. "Why would you say that?"

Another odd reaction.

"There's a gate that leads to the cabin. It's for family use only. We don't allow tourists up there. There are other ways to access the property, but those are unmarked trails."

She returned her attention to the map. "People disregard gates. They abandon the beaten paths. They don't always follow the rules. Sometimes, they can't." Her voice had taken on a faraway quality.

"That appears to be the case regarding the sighting." He kept her in his peripheral view as he prepared the drinks, wishing he could decipher what was going on inside her head. He combed through her expressions. They were written in his notebook, but he didn't need to check it. He'd memorized them, but perhaps not this one.

What was she exhibiting now?

It wasn't fear. It wasn't anger. Sure, she was tired and probably hadn't eaten a decent meal in days, but something inside him didn't believe her behavior was due to hunger or fatigue. "Please, join me," he said and gestured to the table. He'd continue his assessment after they ate. He peered at the place settings. A peculiar unsureness gripped him. His table sat six, and he'd placed their bowls side-by-side. He'd purchased a large table to occupy the space. All six chairs had never been used at once. He ate alone or with McKenzie, on occasion, when he'd watch her for Eliza and Jack. Should he have put Isabelle's bowl across from him? Was this too intimate?

He cleared his throat. "Is this eating arrangement suitable?"

She sat, took a sip of her hard lemonade, then looked up at him. The vexing expression he couldn't decode melted away. She looked up at him through her lashes—a look that made his cock twitch. She patted the seat beside her. "You can sit next to me. I don't bite."

Sweet Christ!

He focused on her lips, wet with the drink. "That's not an accurate statement. You do bite," he replied, lowering into the chair.

Her ice-blue eyes darkened. "I guess you'll have to take your chances."

There it was—her sultry side. The purr in her reply sent a pulse of lust through his veins. He stared at her glass, hoping the object would assist him in ignoring how much he liked having her teeth graze his cock. The sweet bite of pain and desire overlapped like tumultuous, pleasure-laden waves. They ushered in a flood of memories from last night.

"Are you okay?" Isabelle asked, cutting short his X-rated musings.

He sprang to his feet. "I forgot the blueberries."

"What?"

He needed to complete an action to get his mind off his cock. "Don't take another sip. The drink needs another element." He went to the fridge and returned with a tin. He sprinkled four plump berries into her glass.

"Nice touch," she said, her voice retaining the sultry cadence.

Dammit, her tone had his heart hammering.

Reply with a factual statement.

"I know what you like, and I'm acting on that information." Focusing on his task, he added four blueberries to his glass and returned to his spot.

She took a sip and hummed. "You do, Birthday Card Boyfriend." She shook her head. "I shouldn't keep calling you that, should I?"

He pondered the question. "I don't mind. McKenzie calls me her old-man uncle. Birthday Card Boyfriend is an improvement from that moniker."

Isabelle chuckled and traced the rim of her glass with the tip of her index finger. "I can picture her saying that."

"Perhaps we could use our pet names for each other in private," he offered, studying her eyes. They'd deepened to periwinkle, mirroring the color of starbloom flower petals before the sunset.

"Okay," she whispered.

And he was back to this place—a lighter place where he wanted to lose himself in her pools of dreamy blue.

Dreamy blue? Get a grip, man.

He snapped his gaze to her bowl of steaming soup. "Please, eat."

"Do you want me to eat the *motherfucking* soup, Birthday Card Boyfriend?"

He maintained a neutral countenance, but the surge of excitement that sparked within him when she uttered his nickname coursed through his veins. He handed her the spoon. Might as well go with it. He leaned toward her. "I insist you eat the *motherfucking* soup."

She complied and hummed more sexy little sighs after each mouthful. He couldn't blame her. Given Goldie's comprehensive horticulture expertise, she was skilled at cultivating herbs and spices. Her soups were legendary.

With that curious fizz pulsing through his veins, he tucked into his bowl but couldn't focus on the flavors. Distracted, he watched Isabelle out of the corner of his eye. The simple act of observing her consume soup, bread, and an alcoholic beverage left him mesmerized.

She cast aside the spoon and drank the last few sips straight from the bowl. Sinking into the chair, she sighed. "Oh my God, that was out of this world delicious. The seasoning. The touch of heat. It was exactly what I needed."

"My grandfather says Goldie's soup is a salve for the soul," he replied, again, surprised to find himself sharing intimate family information.

"He's right." She watched him for a beat, then took another sip of hard lemonade. "Do you mind if I get a map from my bag? Earthwise sent me enhanced satellite imagery of the land I've been sent to evaluate. I printed it out at the hotel. I've reviewed it and made some notes, but I have a few questions. Maybe you can answer them for me?"

He dipped a piece of bread into his soup. "Are you asking me to work with you?"

A muscle twitched along her jawline. He'd struck a nerve and reveled in the effect. It was out of character for him. Then again, his every reaction to Isabelle was atypical. His pulse quickened as he waited for her reply.

"Your *land steward* is asking the town manager to assist and provide counsel," she clarified.

"*Temporary land steward*," he corrected, making his own clarification. But the phrase felt misplaced. Misaligned. Inaccurate.

"I wonder if your grandparents have returned my car. I could work in there," she mused in the deceptively sweet voice she'd utilized when speaking to the gift shop wrist grabber regarding the difficulty of drinking beer with two broken appendages. She rose to her feet, but he wasn't about to let her leave.

"Sit your perfect ass down," he said, gripping her hips. "Show me the motherfucking map."

"There's the beast." She gifted him with a smirk, then reached into her pack and grumbled.

He watched her. "What is it?"

"It's a mess in here." She glanced at him. "That's your fault because of the caveman maneuver."

He stayed quiet. Experience had taught him that replying to

anything murmured, whispered, or snapped often intensified feel-ings—and passionate Isabelle seemed to live on the cusp of ignition.

She pulled the cards, the envelope, and a snippet of paper he recognized from her bag and set them on the table as she sifted through the contents.

He peered at his handwriting.

Dear Bloom,

Thank you for making this my most unforgettable birthday.

If birthday wishes came true, I'd wish for you.

And please ice your elbow once a day for the next three days. Just fucking do it.

-Your Birthday Card Boyfriend

"Here it is," she said and placed the map beside the other items. She eyed the pile and zeroed in on the note. She touched the corner of the paper. "I . . . um . . . I probably shouldn't have kept it, but . . ."

He had to put her at ease.

"There's nothing wrong with retaining a souvenir after an enjoyable experience." He produced a slip of paper from his pocket with *69* scribbled in the center.

"Is that all you kept?" she asked, gaze locked on the cake table number.

"Why do you ask?"

"I couldn't find the starbloom you gave me. I wondered if you took it with you."

He could have easily removed his slim notebook from his pocket and shown her the flower pressed between the pages, but he didn't. He wasn't ready. *Wasn't ready?* He couldn't decode this reaction. Instead, he shifted his attention to the thick envelope. "Is that the contract from the sale of your family's company?"

"It is."

"You keep it with you?"

She traced a worn crease across the length of the paper. "It provides an incentive to do what needs to be done."

"May I see it?"

She rested her hand on the envelope and glared at it before sliding it toward him. "It's a bunch of legal contract gobbledy-gook and different ways of penalizing me if I say anything negative about the company or Regis."

"The nondisclosure clause?"

"Yes."

"You could speak to your counsel."

She shook her head. "I've tried that route and got burned."

"My specialty is legal contract gobbledygook. I practice contract law."

"It's over thirty pages, Kieran. It's ironclad at that length."

He removed the packet from the envelope. "Longer contracts aren't necessarily stronger. Often, they provide more chances to find loopholes. And I'm the master at finding them."

"You couldn't find a loophole to circumvent the state assigning a land steward," she tossed back with a twinkle in her eyes.

That challenging glint elicited a further quickening of his pulse. "I tried like hell. That was one of the reasons I went to Rocky Mountain City. A friend from law school lives there and practices contract law. I sought legal advice from—"

"Were they the couple you were with?" she pressed, cutting him off.

She'd been more attentive to his activities than he'd perceived.

"Yes. Nelson and Amina. They married while we were in law school."

"Which one was the lawyer? You spoke to both. Let me guess." Isabelle took a sip of hard lemonade. "The woman. You had an intense conversation with her when her husband left the table."

Quite perceptive.

"No, Nelson is the attorney. His wife is a psychologist." He drank her in, needing to collect more information. "I had no idea you'd taken such a keen interest in my activities prior to our unorthodox introduction."

She smiled the same smile she'd given him during the cake-out. "I'm stealthy like that, Birthday Card. By the way. Who was the brunette at the bar?"

Dammit!

"You don't miss much."

Isabelle propped her chin on her hand and pegged him with her captivating gaze. "Was she supposed to be your birthday gift?"

He was not prepared for that discussion. Time to pivot. He gestured toward the pile of cards. "Is that the birthday card your family gave you?"

She observed him intently, clearly aware he'd avoided her question. "Yes."

"Do you carry it with you wherever you go?"

"I do."

"Why?"

She took a sip of her drink. "More incentive. But a happier reminder. My family loved this card. Well, all the cards with nature scenes. We noticed this one on a trip to The Pike. My grandmother mentioned she'd recognized the paper."

"It's possible," he confirmed. "Our paper has been around since the late eighteen hundreds. Did you often visit The Pike?"

She smiled, but it didn't reach her eyes. "My family's company built the hotel, the butterfly pavilion, and the infrastructure for the gardens. That's how I knew about the secret tunnel." She peered at the three cards, then turned to him, wide-eyed. "Your brother Owen is an artist."

"Yes."

"And these cards are made from Starrycard Creek Paper. Even this one, the birthday card my family gave me that's several years old."

He studied the paper. "Correct."

"Did your brother paint these cards?"

He took a sip of his hard lemonade. "No."

"Are you sure?"

Oh, he was sure.

"Kieran?" she said softly.

"He's not the artist. Owen's not interested in painting nature scenes. He prefers to create portraits."

She drummed her fingers on the table. "There must be some other artist that uses Starrycard Creek paper."

He couldn't take his eyes off her. "What's special about this card?"

"It was the last birthday card I received from my family. We were environmentally friendly to a tee. They would sign one card for birthdays to cut down on paper waste. They gave it to me when they dropped me off to start my master's program at Rocky Mountain College. I was admitted to the summer session and was eager to get a jumpstart on my studies. The coursework started the day after my birthday."

"You have a summer birthday?"

She nodded. "It's the same day as the hearing."

"In three weeks?"

"Yes."

"May I?" He gestured to the card.

"Go ahead."

He carefully opened it as if he were handling a fragile butterfly and not simply a painted image of the creature. "To our butterfly girl," he read aloud. "We know you'll spread your wings and fly. We can't wait until you join us at Ashbourne. Love, Poppa James, Nana Joan, Mom, and Dad." He closed the card and returned it to the table. "Butterfly girl?"

"That's what they called me."

"Let me guess—because you liked butterflies growing up."

She chuckled. "Not much of a head-scratcher, is it?"

"Were you going to work for your family?" he pressed. He'd never wanted to know about the women he'd been with until her.

She relaxed into her chair. "After I earned my degree, I was supposed to join the business and shadow my mother and grand-mother. They ran the day-to-day operations while my dad and grandfather focused on design. The plan was for me to one day run the company. But they died in a plane crash not long after they gave me this."

Jesus.

"I'm sorry, Isabelle. That's truly awful."

"My grandfather was flying the plane, but the crash wasn't his fault. It was deemed a mechanical failure. They were surveying a building site on Colorado's Western Slope, and . . . well . . . here I am not running Ashbourne Building and Development." Her bottom lip trembled as she reached for her locket.

"What were they like?" He'd asked this question before. As a small-town attorney, he often assisted families with legal issues when a loved one passed. While he knew almost everyone in town, this question often lightened what was often a somber conversation.

Isabelle smiled at him, and Christ, it was like rays of sunlight slicing through a sea of gray. She opened her locket and revealed two couples, one on each side. His mind went to work, analyzing her family. Isabelle and her mother shared the same blond hair. She must have gotten the ice-blue eyes from her grandmother. He studied the men. Her father was also fair-haired. Kieran turned his attention to her grandfather, who appeared to be the group's outlier. The man wasn't looking ahead in the photo like the others. His gaze was trained on his wife.

Isabelle peered at the images, sighed, then closed the locket. "You ask what they were like? They were glorious. Intelligent. In sync. In love. People doing work that mattered. People driven to protect and preserve the planet. They were true partners." She touched the paper ring, methodically rotating it around her slim finger as she spoke. *Did she realize what she was doing?* She stopped twisting the paper but didn't release the makeshift ring. "The funny thing is, Ashbourne Building and Development almost didn't happen."

"How did it come to be?"

"It's quite a story," she began. "My grandmother inherited her father's construction company, Wilcox Construction, in Arizona. That's where I'm from. My nana Joan was twenty-three with a degree in ecology and no interest in owning a construction company when her father passed away. Her mother died not long after she was born, so it was just my grandmother and her father. The family attorney set up interviews for her to sell the business. She met with several men—it was all men back then. After she thought she'd had her last meeting, a young man, who would become my grandfather, walked in."

"Did he own a construction company?"

"No, he worked in an architecture office across the hall. He walked into the lawyer's office and, in front of the attorney, told my grandmother that his name was James Ashbourne and that he'd heard the men she'd met with that day disparage her for asking questions about being mindful of the environment when building. He said even her attorney had spoken poorly of her and made fun of her for caring about preserving bees and butterflies."

"Sounds like a shit attorney," Kieran mused.

"Don't worry. He got what he deserved."

"What happened next?"

Isabelle's expression warmed. "Right there, in the asshat lawyer's office, my grandfather told my grandmother he'd never seen anyone quite like her. He said the second he saw her enter the building at eight sixteen a.m., he knew he'd marry her. Then he told her that she shouldn't sell—that they should build the business into something they believed in. And then he told her she was an absolute knockout, and her curves were ingrained in his mind. He wasn't wrong. My nana was a hot little number."

"She didn't mind his comments on her appearance?"

Isabelle shrugged. "Oddly, no. I believe she appreciated his unfiltered honesty and searing directness."

"Still," he pressed, "that's quite a leap of faith on your grand-father's part."

"It was—a huge leap of faith on both their parts," she agreed. "A week later, on her birthday, they filed to make Ashbourne

Building and Development a company, sent in a formal complaint to the Arizona bar about the lawyer, and got married."

He reared back. "They got married after a week?"

"Yes, my poppa James was an interesting man. He didn't worry about social conventions or doing things the way others did. He could seem aloof and spoke with a bit of a mechanical cadence."

"Like a robot?" he asked, thinking of how McKenzie described his speech.

"Yes, but it wasn't a hollow sound. It was frank and truthful. He was perceptive and purposeful. His speech and behaviors were precise. It's what made him a gifted architect. He said he'd chosen the field because it taught him to look for details that others didn't see. And when he knew what he wanted, he went after it with no reservations." She smiled. "When it was just family, he let his quirky side shine. He showed his affection in the most endearing ways."

"How was he quirky?" Kieran asked, unable to ignore that he shared similarities with her grandfather.

"With his out-of-the-box musings, especially with design and time."

"Time?" he echoed.

Her eyes brightened as she grew more animated. "Out of nowhere, he'd say things to my nana like, 'At two twenty-six, the light struck your hair and reminded me of the sun dancing in a wheat field.' And then, as if he hadn't rattled off the most romantic thing, he'd go back to doing whatever he was doing. It was unexpected, sure, but the smile it put on my grandmother's face spoke volumes. They were smitten with each other."

"Could your grandfather have suffered from a neurological condition that made him *quirky*?"

He shouldn't have introduced the topic. Still, he couldn't help himself. Another out-of-character action. Add it to the list.

She shrugged. "Suffered? No. He was *Poppa*. Whatever he was or wasn't, he was okay with it. It wouldn't have affected how he lived his life."

"How do you know that?" he pressed, tension building in his shoulders.

"He had my grandmother. They'd built a successful business and were crazy about each other. He had a daughter and a son-in-law who adored him. And he had me, his butterfly girl. And he didn't give a damn what anyone thought—well, besides my grandmother." She chuckled.

"What is it?"

"I just remembered an interview he did with some fancy green-build design magazine. I had to have been around fifteen or sixteen years old. Hailey and I tiptoed into my grandparents' house and hid in the hallway, eavesdropping. The interviewer asked my poppa the secret of his success."

"Did he answer?"

"My grandfather looks at my nana as she walked past him to put a tray of biscuits on the table, then says, 'Find yourself a great ass to follow in this life, and you'll never be led astray.'"

Kieran scrutinized her words and expression, unable to tell if she was serious. "Ass, like the posterior pelvic region?"

Isabelle giggled, and the sound sparkled in the air. "Yes, ass, like the posterior pelvic region. He said the secret to his success was following my grandmother's perfect ass. Then he said he'd been happily following my grandmother for the better part of his life, letting her guide the direction of the company. The interviewer asked if he minded the dynamic, and my poppa said, 'Hell, no. Have you seen my wife's ass? It's a masterpiece. If she jumped, I'd follow that woman straight off a cliff. That ass is what grabbed my attention the day we met. I owe damn near everything to that spectacular ass.'" She pressed her hand to her heart. "He was simply marvelous, fearless, and one of my favorite people."

The breath caught in Kieran's throat. "I couldn't take my eyes off of your . . ." he mumbled as a tremor passed through him.

She leaned in. "What did you say? You went pale. Are you okay?"

It was a good question.

And the answer was no.

This woman threatened to upend his entire damned life.

He had to act quickly. And what he was about to do—no, what he *had* to do—would be unforgivable and move him to the top spot on her shit list.

CHAPTER
Twelve

KIERAN

KIERAN TUGGED AT HIS COLLAR, cursing the damn thing for constricting his breathing. His pants twisted against his legs. His heart hammered. He peered out the window, looking for something to distract him and provide an ounce of respite from the building turmoil. He noted the setting sun's amber glow. It usually soothed his soul. But the tranquil light couldn't help him regulate his emotions. Quite the opposite. It pierced his pupils with an unbearable intensity. And the creek? The continuous rush and dance of the water calmed him for as long as he could remember, but today, it couldn't quell the storm brewing inside.

Of all the times to lose control.

Get. Out. Of. The. House. Now.

"Excuse me," he sputtered, rising from his seat. He bolted from the kitchen, pulsing urgency fueling his stride as he headed for his bedroom. Moving like the place was on fire, he yanked a duffel bag from the closet with such force that an old paint-speckled tin followed, crashing onto the hardwood. Brushes fanned out like fallen leaves. He froze in the throes of a near breakdown as a soft, rhythmic tapping joined the calamitous backdrop.

Footsteps.

Isabelle's footsteps.

He kicked the brushes into the closet and shut the door.

"What's going on with you?" He could detect threads of anger and disbelief in her tone—and he deserved it. He'd behaved atrociously. "You completely disconnected while I was sharing something . . . something real with you," she continued.

Yeah, that's what he did when the uncertainty of a situation and the inability to maintain control collided.

"I apologize for my rudeness." He could feel her gaze burning into his back. But he couldn't look at her, couldn't get drawn in by her hauntingly beautiful eyes. He placed the bag on his bed and peered into its hollow depths. "I should pack and leave for my parents' house."

"You're taking off now? I haven't asked you about the land and the map. I have questions, Kieran." The anger in her voice had intensified—or was that disappointment or disillusionment? *Dammit!* He didn't know. He'd upset her, and the guilt of causing her pain ate at him as if it were gnawing at his soul. He had to go before he did something he couldn't undo.

"I'll answer your questions tomorrow at the town hall during business hours," he rattled off, his voice muted and robotic.

"*During business hours?*" Her voice jumped an irate, highly effusive octave. "I'd like them answered now, *Mr. Birthday Card Boyfriend.* Can you please look at me?"

It was as if his mind was at war, one part longing to absorb her presence, the other desperate to shut her out.

Rely on practiced social conventions.

Behave rationally.

Exhibit a muted demeanor.

He peered over his shoulder and assessed his hostile houseguest as she stood her ground inside the doorway, arms crossed, jaw set, ready for a fight. He should have concentrated on deescalating the tension crackling through the bungalow, but her presence hijacked his thoughts. He'd never encountered a lover in his bedroom. That part of his life played out under the veil of anonymity in hotels. A separation he required, and that had gone to shit. The storm inside him intensified. He had to say something, give her something. But what?

"Kieran?" she snapped.

Fuck!

"I'm experiencing an abundance of energy that needs to be *expelled*. And . . ." *Fuck, fuck, fuck!*

"And what?" she demanded.

The storm raged. He was holding on by a thread. "And I'm having difficulty being near you."

She moved toward him. Five steps. *Tap, tap, tap, tap, tap.* Close enough to inhale her vanilla jasmine sweetness. "What kind of difficulty?"

Was that pain in her voice? Was she conflicted? Was she frightened?

"Just look at me. I want you to see me," she added softly.

What did that even mean?

He didn't have time to process the situation or a second to assess her expression. He did as she asked and concentrated on her face. *"Dammit!"* he cursed under his breath. She was so fucking symmetrical, so maddeningly intriguing. She smelled so damned good. He was drawn to her as if she were a sensory siren, and he was powerless to resist. "I'm holding back an impulse. I'm keenly aware that if I give into it, I won't be able to control it. That's why I must leave."

She rested her hand on his wrist. The paper ring grazed his skin, threatening to obliterate his whisper-thin composure.

"Isabelle," he rasped, a beast caught in a trap.

She gazed at him, and her pools of blue drew him in. "I don't want you to leave. And I don't think you want to go."

His restraint was waning by the second. "Do you understand what you're asking of me? I'm limited by what I am capable of offering."

She narrowed her gaze. He knew this look. She was formulating a plan. "Then we negotiate. What can you offer? What's on the table?"

She was serious. The tilt of her head told him that.

But how was he supposed to answer? What could he offer?

Was he entertaining this line of conversation? He should relay that her proposition was unadvisable—or he could treat this situation no differently than any other negotiation.

It took everything he had to maintain a calm facade. "While you weren't able to elaborate, I gleaned that Regis Greenstone doesn't have the town's best interests at heart. Therefore, we share the same aim: to stop the developer from harming the people of Starrycard Creek."

"And harming the environment," she added.

"And harming the environment," he repeated, amending his statement. "And we agree to work together."

"You *want* to work with me?" She dropped her hands to her sides, severing their connection.

He could not react. He remained still, exerting every ounce of will to mask the hollow ache at the loss of her touch. "As town manager, it's my job to stay appraised of your activities, which requires granting me close proximity."

"I'm not used to that."

"Neither am I."

She chewed her lip.

"Shall we proceed to the second phase of the negotiation? The physical aspect of the arrangement," he continued, relying on legalese.

"Go on," she replied, watching him, studying him, and the woman seemed damn close to looking into his soul.

He had to keep her out. *Stick to the law.* "Any conduct or interaction that transpires outside of designated business hours will be maintained in strictest confidence, existing solely as a private matter between the two parties. This arrangement will last the duration of your tenure in the capacity of land steward. Upon the cessation of said tenure, this arrangement will be deemed null and void, with no plans to perpetuate the arrangement beyond the stipulated term. Do you understand?"

"When it's over, it's over," she said, not missing a beat as she succinctly summarized his legal word salad.

"Correct," he rasped, but he couldn't concentrate on the law or the town's dire situation. All he wanted was to touch her—a need so strong it bypassed his defenses. He captured her left hand with predatory speed and peered at the paper ring. "Why are you still wearing this?"

She trembled but didn't look away, didn't pull away. "I like it. And it felt wrong when I took it off to shower. I know it's paper. I know it won't last."

"It won't," he growled. *Dammit, dial it down.* He exhaled a shaky breath. "It can't last." He went through his usual scripts and lists of social conventions. But nothing fit this situation. *Wait! There was hope. This was a negotiation. Follow that framework.* "We need to agree to a set of parameters regarding our behavior when—"

"When expelling energy?" she offered.

"Yes."

"No explanation of your parameters is necessary. I'm already familiar with them. No falling in love, right?"

"Correct."

"I'm not at risk of doing that. You've met the last man I fell in love with. A man who told me he loved me, then took a wrecking ball to my heart. I won't allow that to happen again." Tears shined in her eyes. "Your conditions are clear, Mr. Town Manager. I accept them. Can you?"

The thought of Regis Greenstone touching her and taking—no, stealing—her virginity was the final straw. The dam of his restraint burst, flooding his body with raw need. His pulse quickened as he drew her into his embrace. With the hunger of deep, heart-wrenching longing, he kissed her hard. With every caress of his tongue meeting hers, every brush of their lips, and each heated breath, he worked to erase Regis Greenstone from her mind—wipe the fucker clean out of her head and replace it with . . . He froze.

"Kieran," she whispered, the syllables wrapped around him, tethering him to her with an invisible thread.

Had she read his mind? Had he meant to suggest himself as a substitute? Before he could give the musing consideration, she pressed her left hand to his cheek, cutting off all rational thought.

"I need you to do something for me," she said, her voice a wisp of a sound.

"Yes?"

She stroked his cheek. "Get out of your head and continue your assessment of my lips' degree of kissability."

And just like that, his focus shifted from conventions and returned to her. "You know how I feel about your mouth."

"Show me."

He ran his tongue across the seam of her lips, tasting the bite of vodka, the tartness of lemon, and the lush, velvety sweetness of blueberries. Christ, he wanted to go slowly and savor each sensation, but a torrent of lust took over.

He edged up her skirt, slipped his hand between her thighs, and was duly rewarded. So warm. So wet. He stroked her most sensitive place as he kissed a trail to her earlobe. "I'm going to toss you on my bed, peel off your panties, and fuck you until you can't see straight. And one more thing."

"You'll make me beg for it?" she offered.

He shook his head. "Not this time. This time, you'll let me do whatever I want. You'll take each hard inch of my cock like a good girl who loves to be bad."

She trembled in his arms, moaning as she rocked her hips against his hand. "My God, your dirty talk game is on point."

He knew how to respond.

"My intent wasn't to engage in dirty talk. I'm simply verbalizing my plans to make your body writhe with pleasure."

The truth? Indisputably, he'd engaged in dirty talk. But she liked it when he took a robotic approach. He tipped up her chin and ran his thumb across her bottom lip as he formulated the perfect companion statement to his previous remarks. "And after I render you breathless and starry-eyed with my cock, I'm going to fuck that gorgeous mouth of yours."

"Wow," she breathed, her pupils dilating.

Precisely the reaction he'd aimed for.

Before she could utter another word, he scooped her into his arms and rested her in the center of his bed. Christ, she was a delectable sight. Making good on his claim, he slid her G-string down her thighs, rested her panties on his dresser, then admired her glistening center. Raw animal need gripped him. The side of him that adhered to rational, methodical principles disappeared.

He was a beast who ran on pure lust now.

It roared through him.

He removed his belt and shoes and lowered his pants while keeping his gaze locked on her wet, blushing perfection. "You are so beautiful. So goddamned symmetrical."

She pushed onto her elbows. "From beg for it to good girl to mooning over my anatomy."

"Your symmetrical anatomy," he corrected.

"You are one fascinating man, Kieran Starrycard."

He hiked up her skirt and covered her body with his. "How about this? I'm about to fascinate the fuck out of your body," he rasped, lining up his cock with her entrance. "I'll etch my fingerprints into your skin." He frowned. "Except for your black-and-blue elbow—which we will be icing," he continued as he rocked his hips and entered her.

She arched her back and opened for him, welcoming his hard length. "Keep talking, *Birthday Card Boyfriend*."

He didn't have to ignore the warmth surging through his veins or suppress the twist of a grin pulling at the corners of his mouth at the sound of her using his nickname. That's who he could be in this space. Under these conditions, he resumed the role of the man from last night. The person ready and willing to follow her perfect ass into whatever crazy adventure she could muster.

Resting the bulk of his weight on his knees and forearms, he pumped his hips, making love to her in long, languid strokes. "When you're in this bed, *Bloom*, every part of you belongs to me," he bit out, using the name he'd created for her. And fuck, it felt good, owning it, treasuring the word, cherishing the woman without an inkling of worry.

She threaded her fingers through his hair. "Don't forget. I insist on reciprocity. If I'm yours, that means you're mine. Does counsel agree?"

Lust, longing, and unrestrained jubilation consumed him as he worked her body. "Counsel concurs fucking completely, and now . . ."

"Yes?"

"I'm going to request you shut that *motherfuckingly* perfect mouth and allow me to deliver orgasm number nine."

Desire and carnal delight danced in her gaze.

His lips met hers, and he put every ounce of this version of himself into the kiss. Electricity coursed through him. He was flying, light as air, absorbing every sensation without strategizing or analyzing the correct response. He simply did what his body commanded. Pistoning his hips, he pulled back and devoured her with his gaze, taking in every detail unabashedly.

And she let him.

She let him make love to her relentlessly.

She let him drown in her beauty.

She radiated energy—a force that insulated them from the outside world's expectations. Here, it was Bloom and Birthday Card, giving in to what their bodies craved.

She rolled her hips, meeting him thrust for thrust, their bodies in sync. Her choppy breaths and feathery moans told him she was close. That knowledge spurred him on, heightening his need to be the one—the only one—to make her body tremble with pulsing pleasure.

He threaded his hand with hers, and his hammering pulse quickened as the paper pressed into his skin.

"Me, on top," she got out between heated breaths.

She could have said, "Me, on the moon" and he would have scoured the planet for an available rocket.

Giving her what she wanted, he shifted onto his back as she lost the skirt and straddled him. He caressed her curves as she lowered onto his weeping cock. She gazed down at him. Mischief glimmered in her eyes.

He rocked his hips, savoring the moment. "What do you have up your sleeve, Bloom?"

"Interesting you mention sleeves," she replied, eyeing his button-up.

"Bloom?"

With a wicked grin, she tore open his shirt. Buttons went flying and danced a popping tune against the wood floor.

Now, who was the beast?

"Oops, look what we have here. A big, strong, strapping Birthday Card Boyfriend," she cooed, her voice a dirty little purr as she traced his pectoral muscles. "Hope that wasn't one of your favorites."

Damn, he loved being ogled by this woman. "It wasn't. I don't have a favorite shirt."

She rocked her hips, taking him deeper. "Do you have a favorite anything?" She smiled a coy, beguiling smile. He knew this one. It was in his notebook under the heading *seductive dimples*.

He gripped her thighs, digging his fingertips into her soft skin. He took in her mussed hair and wet ruby lips. "Yes."

"I believe I know one of your favorites." She undid her blouse, slipped it off her shoulders, and removed her bra. "Could this be your favorite view?"

While this view was magnificent, it was his *second* favorite. Fortunately, his brain was still sufficiently oxygenated for him to realize that this piece of information was better kept to himself. "It's certainly in the top five."

"You're keeping track?" she asked, closing her eyes. She

swayed her hips, taking him deeper, inching up, then sinking onto his hard length like her body was custom made to take his cock.

He looked up at her, watching as the final rays of the sun filtered through the curtains, bathing her tanned, smooth skin in a golden glow as she rode him hard and fast. "I always keep track," he bit out, finding it harder and harder to speak.

She pressed her hands to his bare chest. He palmed the globes of her ass—that fucking beautiful ass—and delighted in the slap of skin meeting skin. She leaned forward, her breasts grazing his chest. With one hand clenching her ass, guiding her, supporting her, he slid his other hand into her hair. With those two points of contact, he held her close, drilling into her, applying pressure just how she liked it.

Her breath hitched as their mouths met in a melee of lips, teeth, and tongues. Kissing, nipping, sucking. He lost himself in a tangle of moans and thrusts. He clutched her body, holding her close as they hovered on the edge of oblivion.

"I'm there . . . I'm . . ." she rasped between kisses.

"Let go," he gritted. "I'll follow you. I'll always be right behind you."

Her eyes fluttered open.

"Always," he got out, giving in to this version of himself, surrendering to this extraordinary woman.

Her lips parted, and her body shuddered as she crashed into her release.

He'd experienced splendor his entire life. He'd grown up surrounded by the wonders of nature, but watching Isabelle come with his cock buried inside her ignited a roaring passion within him.

And there was no holding back.

"*So. Fucking. Beautiful.* You open for me like a starbloom welcoming nightfall. You're my Bloom, all mine," he whispered against the corner of her mouth, the words tumbling from his lips.

But if he were free to do and say as he desired, he had to give her more. He needed to wring out every drop of pleasure and leave her deliciously sated.

Changing their position, he sat up, keeping her in his lap. He wrapped his muscled arms around her delicate frame, her softness meeting his hard angles. This primal need to protect and please her gripped him, wrapped around him like a ribbon threaded with searing devotion. Eye to eye, he allowed gravity to heighten her arousal and lengthen her release. He slipped his hand beneath her, feeling his cock thrust into her wet heat, and reveled in her arousal.

She circled her arms around his shoulders, anchoring herself to him. "Kieran," she rasped as raw, unfiltered desire echoed in the syllables.

It was his undoing.

His orgasm hit like a freight train colliding with a tanker truck hauling gasoline. He exploded, spilling into her. Primal and heated, he groaned, letting go and letting Isabelle in. A buzzy burst of elation zinged through him as she watched him surrender to the rhythm of their bodies. Wonder and wanton lust welled in her gaze. And damn, he loved holding her complete and total attention.

Loose and heavy-limbed, they collapsed onto the bed. She shivered, and he drew the quilt from the foot of his bed. Covering their bodies, he wrapped his arms around her, holding her close as he dropped kisses to her eyelids, soaking in the sensations. There was no sifting through sensory data. No prioritizing. There was only Isabelle, her body in his arms, her silky hair fanned out on his arm.

She hummed a lazy, honey-warm sound that fed his soul. "So much for fucking my *motherfuckingly* perfect mouth," she said, her voice gravelly and her eyes closed as she nuzzled into him.

He twisted a lock of her hair around his finger. "We'll get to that."

"Will we?"

"Yes, but we'll stay like this for a while."

"Kieran Starrycard," she murmured, "town manager, my birthday card boyfriend, and a cuddler on the down low."

He chuckled and pulled the quilt over her shoulders. A serene stillness settled over the space. He focused on Isabelle. The sun had set, and the moon's silver light traced the contour of her chin, casting her in a dreamlike radiance. He drew his fingertips down her jawline, admiring this view and drinking in the hazy blue hue.

"Remember the map I wanted to look over with you," she said, drawing lazy circles on his chest.

He stilled. "After an earth-shattering ninth orgasm, you'd like to discuss work?"

She smiled, a dimple emerging in the moonlight. "Not exactly. I want you to tell me about the land. Specifically, the land to the west of Fiona's cabin. Closer to the falls. I can only get so much from maps, photographs, and ecological reports. And yes, I'll be in the field collecting data to complete my assessment. But I'm curious. What do you love about it?"

Where to start?

He returned to caressing her cheek. "Starrycard Mountain isn't just a place on a map. It's a living canvas. The wildflowers cover the mountainside in splashes of blue, red, violet, and yellow in a sea of green. With every breath, you breathe in the starblooms, vanilla, and jasmine. There are other blooms, hundreds of them, but the starbloom always calls to me. And the nights," he paused, drawing her in closer. "The soundscape is alive beneath an ocean of stars. You feel so close to them, you'd swear you could reach out and stir them with your hand."

"You sound like an artist," she said, her words heavy with the pull of slumber.

He observed her, noting the calmness within him. He dusted a few wisps of hair from her forehead. "And you sound sleepy."

She yawned. "I'm not sleepy."

Christ, she was something else.

"Not even a little?" he pressed as a wide grin bloomed on his lips.

"Nope," she replied on the sleepiest of exhales.

"If you say so." He watched her, content to let his gaze linger on her until the sun rose. But when he stroked her cheek, his grin disappeared. She'd gone ice-cold in a matter of seconds. "Isabelle, are you warm enough?"

"Mm-hmm."

He tightened his hold on her. He was a furnace. If anyone could warm her up, it was him. He rubbed her arm, his thoughts drifting to the mountain and the scene he'd described. "Tonight, we'll rest. We'll figure out how to stop Regis Greenstone and find a way forward for the town. We'll do this together. You and me. But I know you. Don't do anything foolish or ill-advised. Keep me in the loop." He waited for her to reply, but his words were met with her rhythmic breathing. "Bloom?" Nothing. He touched the paper ring, his eyelids growing heavy as her sleeping breath lured him toward slumber. Still, he wouldn't give in to sleep—not yet. He couldn't stop himself from memorizing how she looked, asleep in his arms. Was he fixated, or was he enchanted? It didn't matter. Right now, she was his. With that knowledge, he closed his eyes and recalled the line he'd written when he'd last watched her sleep. That stupid grin returned to his lips. "If birthday wishes came true, I'd wish for you," he whispered into the darkness before surrendering to sleep.

———

Kieran stretched, his movements unhurried as the babbling creek and the bird's morning chatter drifted through the window. With his eyes still closed, he rolled his head from side to side as a rare, contented sigh escaped his lips. He'd nodded off minutes after Isabelle. With her in his arms, he'd slept like the dead. The echoes of a restful night's embrace lingered in his bones. A feeling so unique, as if he'd discovered a new part of himself.

No, not a new part. He got to play this exact part when he was alone with Isabelle, his Bloom.

With that in mind, he had a question to answer.

How could they start the day?

Tangled in the bedsheets sounded perfect.

He could draw her in close and make love to her from behind, slowly, languidly. He'd slip his hand between her thighs and rub her sweet bud, making those little circles that made her breath hitch. And he could not forget about her breasts. Perfect C-cups. Symmetrical, like the rest of her. Oh, yeah, he should pay special attention to them. Licking, sucking, and biting—but he had to be somewhat gentle. She bruised easily.

Look at that! He was a man with a sexually explicit plan.

He exhaled a heated breath, desire welling below his belly. His cock was onboard—always a good sign. Side note, slight addition to the sex plan: After he delivered orgasm number ten, he would fuck her gorgeous mouth, then make her pancakes. A wicked grin pulled at the corners of *his mouth.* He would make lemon blueberry pancakes and feed each bite to her in bed, which could lead to more fucking. *To Be Determined Fucking.* Holy hell, he was terrific at boyfriend bullshitting.

He reached for Isabelle and felt . . . a piece of paper. No, not just paper. A card made from Starrycard Creek paper.

Why would there be a card on her pillow?

Dammit, he knew why.

It was for the same reason he'd left her a note yesterday.

She'd left him.

She was gone.

CHAPTER
Thirteen

KIERAN

SO MUCH FOR easing into the day with *TBD* screwing.

Kieran bolted upright and glared at the painted starbloom card, resting where Isabelle should have been sleeping.

Kieran,

I had to leave. I have to stop Regis. And I must do this myself.

Don't be mucho-fucking mad.

-Isabelle

"Don't be *mucho-fucking* mad?" he grumbled. Was she trying to inject humor? He thought they'd come to an understanding, especially after everything that transpired between them. He threw the quilt onto a chair and banged the hell out of his drawers as he dressed. He wouldn't be wearing slacks and a button-up today. And he wouldn't be gracing City Hall with his presence. He checked his appearance in the mirror. Khaki hiking pants. Trail shoes. Wool socks. Dry-wicking shirt. Hat and sunscreen. He grabbed the outer shell of his jacket. It was June, but the weather was unpredictable at twelve thousand feet. He worked the lotion onto his face and neck—his red-from-anger face and neck.

Why would she do this?

Wait! He could answer that.

Regis Greenstone had hurt her beyond measure. That fact

alone had him itching to punch the smug fucker in the face for what he'd done. Still, he couldn't lose his head. Isabelle wasn't exactly on team Starrycard. She might not be his main adversary, but she did not understand nor sympathize with how badly the town needed to grow.

And she didn't know the mountain. Hell, there were parts he didn't know, and he'd been hiking the terrain for years.

The anger boiling inside him crystallized into jagged shards of ice.

She shouldn't be out there alone. Yes, as an environmental scientist who assessed land for a living, he assumed she knew how to take care of herself in the wild, but that didn't mean she had to put herself at an unnecessary risk.

And there could be risks on Starrycard Mountain. Plenty of them, especially in early summer.

Some areas still had snow and ice, and the melting snow increased the risk of flash flooding. Sudden weather changes could also occur. Mountain lions and bears were active, particularly in remote corners of the rough terrain. And that's exactly where she'd be. There was no way she'd stick to the trails. She'd want to explore the most isolated, dangerous locations. This terrain could tax even the most conditioned athlete. And while Isabelle was fit, she'd been sneezing, and her voice sounded scratchy.

"Dammit!" he hissed as a revelation hit like a punch to the gut. *How could he have not connected the dots?*

She was ill. She'd felt warm last night. He'd attributed it to their rigorous sex, but then she'd gone cold.

He had to get to her.

He finished rubbing the sunscreen onto his skin when a muscle twitched on his cheek. "Bloom," he growled. But as he gritted out the word, a knock echoed through his bungalow.

Someone was at his front door.

Thank Christ! It had to be Isabelle.

He breathed a sigh of relief. She'd recognized her error. She'd been momentarily caught up in crusading for the environment, but she'd come to her senses and realized they'd be more effective if they worked together. He could understand her folly. While he was pragmatic, she ran on passion. It was one of the things, besides her great ass, her whip-smart humor, and her symmetrical face, he found so intriguing.

He strode through the bungalow, exhaled his restless energy, and schooled his features. He reviewed the sequence of events most likely to play out. Isabelle would begin by begging for his forgiveness. Of course, he'd ease her mind and grant her that kindness. Then, they could discuss a rational course of action, followed by lemon-blueberry-pancake sex.

His pulse evened out as he regained control. He opened the door. "Isa—"

"Good morning, my star. You must be on your way to meet Izzy."

"Goldie," he stammered, "what are you doing here? And what do you mean I must be on my way to meet Izzy?" He worked his ass off to maintain a neutral expression. But once more, the stability he craved crumbled thanks to Isabelle A. Adaire.

"Your grandfather saw Izzy in that little white sedan when he was out for his morning walk. We left the keys on the porch last night. We knocked, but no one answered."

Shit! He couldn't tell Goldie he'd missed her because he'd been balls-deep in the town's appointed land steward.

"We must not have heard you," he said, his pulse back to skyrocketing.

Goldie watched him for a beat. "Your grandfather said she was headed toward Starrycard Mountain."

"When did he mention this?" That damned muscle on his jaw twitched. *Don't lose control!* But it was impossible to keep his emotions in check.

Goldie continued her hawkish assessment of his face. "About an hour ago."

Dammit, Isabelle had one hell of a head start.

He had to play this cool. *Find an object. Focus on it.* He concentrated on the giant oak across the street, just beyond Goldie's shoulder. "And Grandpa said she was alone?"

"Yes, she was alone. You appear preoccupied, dear."

That was an understatement.

Pull. It. Together.

"It's my job to be concerned. I apologize for my behavior. May I ask why you've stopped by?"

She held up a basket with a dish towel covering the contents. "I thought I'd drop off some muffins for Izzy. But on my way here, I bumped into your father."

Kieran concentrated on the oak. "Is that so?"

"He tells me you didn't make it to Starrycard House last night. I assume you stayed here."

He could read her mind. It would only be a matter of minutes before she mentioned some Starrycard Creek legend, some prophecy of love and happily ever afters.

He eyed his grandmother, who, like every Starrycard woman, was excellent at procuring information. He needed to tread cautiously.

"There's a simple explanation, Goldie. Isabelle and I were . . . working." He glanced at the table. The thick envelope was still there, but the card from her family and the map were gone. She must have been in one hell of a hurry this morning—or out of her mind, half-delirious with fever.

"I'm sure you were *working*," she replied with a deceptively serene smile. He also recognized this expression and understood what was being insinuated. He opted to remain silent.

She peered past him into the bungalow, then moved the dishcloth to the side, revealing the muffins and a pouch of dried herbs. "I also wanted to leave some tea for Izzy. How long do you think you'll be up on the mountain?"

"I'm not sure."

She drummed her fingertips on the side of the basket. "I fear our land steward might be coming down with something. She appeared a bit flushed yesterday. The same thing happened to me after I left Peru years ago. I had one heck of a cold. Luckily, I had your grandfather to nurse me through it."

He glanced at his watch.

"I'm keeping you from her, aren't I? You need to be on your way."

Shit! It was rude to check the time when conversing. He knew this. But this Isabelle situation had left him off balance and unable to regulate his behavior.

"No, I have a moment. Come in, Goldie, please. We can finish our chat while I inspect my pack."

He moved aside and allowed the woman to enter.

Goldie gestured to the basket. "I'll put these in a container."

He nodded and went to the closet, where he stored his gear. Thank Christ, his pack was ready to go. He'd prepped it so he could spend a few days hiking and hiding treasures for McKenzie to find on their next adventure. He opened the pack and checked the items. Extra clothing. A knife and waterproof matches. Emergency shelter. Dried fruit. A water purifier. First aid kit. Bear canister. He had more supplies in his car. He could survive for a couple of weeks if he had to.

"Are you okay, Kieran?" Goldie called from the kitchen.

"Yes, I've got everything under control." He glanced at his grandmother. "And I'll take the tea with me."

If Isabelle was as sick as he suspected, she'd need it.

"It would be all right if you didn't have everything under control," Goldie chimed.

He carried his pack into the kitchen and added the bag of herbs. "We don't have to worry about that because I always do." He scanned the items once more. Did he have everything he needed? Hell if he knew. He could barely focus. And she'd better be okay. If she was hurt or lost, he'd lose his fucking mind. *Calm down!* That was easier said than done. He could hear the blood whooshing through his veins. His heart pounded like a marching band had taken up residence in his chest.

"Would you like to take the muffins, Kieran?" Goldie asked softly.

"Muffins?" he repeated. Jesus, he nearly forgot he was standing beside his grandmother.

"You need to go, dear. You thrive when taking action. We both know that."

He focused on the woman and nodded.

She handed him the tin. "I'll lock up here."

"Thank you. You are correct. I do need to get on the road. Isabelle needs me." *Shit!* "Forgive me. I misspoke. Isabelle is . . . expecting me." A lie, but he didn't want Goldie to know his head was about to explode from frustration and worry. He added his wallet, keys, and notebook to the pack.

"Are you heading up to Fiona's cabin? Izzy seemed quite interested in it. And she said the starwing sighting was near there."

Where the hell was he heading?

"Kieran?" Goldie called from the kitchen.

"Yes, we'll be in that area," he answered, falling into his robotic cadence. It was easier when he had a million thoughts racing through his head. And Fiona's cabin was as good a starting point as any. Okay, Goldie had provided the basics for a plan to catch up with his infuriating land steward. He rested his hand on the doorknob.

"Kieran, dear, one last thing."

Here it comes. The legends and mystical Starrycard musings.

He had to dissuade her from continuing.

"Are you about to remind me of the town saying, 'love is always in the cards in Starrycard Creek'?" he pressed. "Or do you believe Isabelle's destined to be mine because I made a ring out of Starrycard Creek paper for her? Or would you like to refresh my recollection regarding the date I met Isabelle—my birthday—the same day William Starrycard met Fiona and fell in love with her?"

His grandmother strolled out of the kitchen. The corners of her mouth curved upward. "I was simply going to let you know that the lemons in the bowl on your counter are a day or two from going bad. You should use them."

God help him! Talk about stepping in it.

Be polite. Remain calm.

"I'll address the lemon situation as soon as I'm able. Thank you for locking up, Goldie." Best to get the hell out of there. He threw open the door. Leaping off the porch, he bypassed the steps, loaded his SUV, and gunned it out of town.

Was he losing his mind?

Should the town manager haul ass down Main Street? Hell no, but he wasn't acting in the capacity of the town manager. He was . . . *Dammit!* He didn't know who the hell he was supposed to be.

With the town behind him, he headed up the mountain road. It was still early. In a few hours, tourists and day-trippers with their pets and picnic lunches would pack the trails. But Isabelle wouldn't venture on those routes. She had a satellite imagery map —and a damned good one at that. The maps they sold in town didn't include the back roads or the unmarked trails. She'd head that way. He knew it. He slowed the SUV as he approached the first unmarked route. And look at that. Fresh tire tracks were carved into the dirt. Yep, she'd come this way. Round and round, he maneuvered through the hairpin turns, hugging the mountain-side. After forty-five minutes, he was rewarded with a flash of white through the sea of evergreens.

Isabelle's car.

"Watch and learn," he whispered.

He parked behind her rental and spotted her footprints. There were no official trails in these parts. But that hadn't stopped him from scouting this land when he was a kid. He could get to Fiona's cabin from here. That had to be where she was headed. He followed her tracks as the sun peeked through the clouds. "Where are you, Isabelle?" he said, the question mingling with the rhythmic pat of his footsteps. Goldie had taught him to walk softly so he wouldn't frighten the wildlife. He paced himself, staying vigilant. He pushed aside a few prickly evergreen limbs and then stilled. A tan jacket rested on a rock. He picked it up. He took a few more steps and spied a hiking boot a few feet away.

But that wasn't all.

He kicked up his pace, collecting socks, a shirt, a pair of hiking pants, and a wide-brimmed hat. The woman had left a bread-crumb trail of clothing. Still, there was no sign of her. And he had to find her. Her life may depend on it. The evidence scattered along the ground pointed to a single truth. She wasn't in her right mind. Illness and extreme exhaustion could cause hallucinations. She probably still had a fever. That's why she discarded her cloth-ing. She better not have gone into the hot springs—not in her condition. She could drown.

"Isabelle, clap your hands, stomp your feet. Make a sound—any sound—so I can find you," he yelled. *Stay calm. Be smart.* He scanned the area. He didn't see her, but he'd spied another breadcrumb.

Her canvas backpack was open and lurched on its side. Nearby, a brush and a few hair elastics were scattered among the low foliage. He placed the items in the pack and zipped it, urgency coursing through his veins. She had to be close.

A flutter caught his eye—a winged insect or perhaps a bird—something quick and fleeting in his peripheral vision. He spun, turning ninety degrees. Relief flooded his system as he peered past a cluster of boulders and locked in on a swish of blond hair.

"Isabelle, Isabelle!" he called, racing toward her. He dropped to his knees, leaving her clothing in a pile beside them. He held her face in his hands. She was burning up. "Are you awake? Can you hear me?"

"Mm-hmm, I'm resting," she murmured, her eyes closed as she slumped against a rock like a rag doll.

"You're in your underwear," he said, gathering her into his arms. He looked her over and spied a few scrapes on her knees and dirt on her cheeks. He almost breathed a sigh of relief until he noticed what was missing. She wasn't wearing her locket.

"I've got my ring. I didn't take off my ring." She kept her eyes closed as she lifted and then lowered her hand, collapsing into him. "It got hot . . . so, so hot, which is an abnormal temperature shift for this region of . . . Colorado. I mean, *Rado-colo*? No, *Colo-rita*?"

He rested his chin on the crown of her head, tightening his hold on her. "You had it right the first time, Bloom."

"Mr. Birthday Card Boyfriend?" she asked on a wisp of a breath.

"Yes?"

She licked her parched lips. "Do you have any motherfucking cake?"

Jesus. A chuckle escaped his mouth, the sound tinged with relief. "No, I don't have any motherfucking cake with me."

"Any alpacas around?"

"Nope."

She sighed. "I found the cabin, but it was locked. I didn't have a key."

He stroked her hair, removing bits of leaves and twigs. "Obviously, you don't have a key. You're not a Starrycard yet."

Yet? What the hell was that?

A reaction to stress. Nothing more.

"I decided to head back to my car, but I got sleepy. So sleepy. And it got hot. And . . ." She opened her eyes a sliver, and the slice of ice blue pierced his soul.

"Did you fall? Can you walk? Did you twist your ankle?" he rattled off, hating to interrupt her but compelled to confirm her well-being. He scanned her body again and eyed her ankles. Thank Christ, they showed no signs of swelling.

"You followed me," she said, her feather-light words floating in the breeze as she hovered on the brink of unconsciousness.

A faint smile touched his lips. "I'll always follow you."

"It's my symmetrical ass, right?"

This woman! Even teetering on the edge of collapse, she retained her spirited spark.

"Yes," he said softly, "along with two other qualities that

caught my attention the first time I saw you. Your golden hair and the way you moved."

She shivered. "It's important to be precise when recording data."

"It is." He peered at the cabin, then eyed the sky. Clouds were gathering. "Let's get you inside and settled."

She shook her head, a loose, drunken movement like her muscles were made of jelly. "Wait . . . I have to tell you something."

"Bloom, some weather is about to move in, and—"

"And . . ." she whispered as a faint grin graced her cracked lips, "if birthday wishes came true, I'd wish for you."

"I wrote that to you," he replied, his words touched with an emotion he couldn't identify.

"But wishes do come true, and it doesn't even have to be your birthday," she continued, her lids fluttering like she was fighting to stay conscious.

Utterly captivated, he found himself lost in her bewitching allure. "How do you know that?"

She closed her eyes and hummed a contented sigh. "Because you're my wish, and you're here."

CHAPTER

Fourteen

IZZY

IZZY HUMMED SOFTLY. Had she ever felt so safe, so cherished, so utterly and completely at peace? A warm breeze kissed the apples of her cheeks. The gentle blend of jasmine, vanilla, and honeysuckle bathed her in aromatic bliss. Birds chattered, a lyrical fusion of chirps and warbling trills. As she lingered in the soft, hazy boundary between slumber and wakefulness, her breaths came slowly, deeply.

Had she ever been so effortlessly attuned to her surroundings?

Had she ever known such pure contentment?

The answer was yes.

Swinging in a hammock, cuddled next to her nana, her little legs dangled over the side as her eyes grew heavy, listening to her nana's voice, rich with wisdom, as the woman narrated the twilight's secrets.

"Watch the butterflies, Isabelle. No two are alike. Each wing is intricately etched with a star pattern mimicking the night sky. Notice how a few butterflies have left their perch and stopped feeding on starbloom nectar. Observe as they fly in a lazy arc, then stretch into a wide loop. Note how a few more join the circling celestial dance. And now they're all in flight. They're communicating it's time to go, time to continue their migration like the generations before them. Round and around, they

align themselves with the Earth's magnetic field, this invisible naviga-
tion tool that led them from Nevada to Colorado and now to Arizona, to
us. They're headed to the hot springs in the valleys in the south of
Mexico. That's their final stop. It's a long, strenuous trip, but they don't
do it alone. They rely on each other to thrive and survive. When it
storms and the air grows cool, they'll pull together to conserve heat. But
tonight, there's not a cloud in the sky. The moon is full, and the stars will
help guide them home. Now, Isabelle, my sweet butterfly girl, say
goodbye to our winged friends. Wish them safe travels. We must go
inside. We cannot interrupt the dance. When you wake up tomorrow,
they'll be gone."

"Goodbye, butterflies. You're stronger together," Izzy spoke the words as the hammock's wooden, rhythmic creak faded. She shifted, suddenly unable to feel her nana's embrace. The light changed, brightening as if she were emerging from a tunnel. She inhaled and detected another scent—an earthy, metallic scent.

Linseed. Turpentine.

Was that paint?

"Isabelle," came a voice—a voice that didn't belong to Nana Joan.

She strained to open her eyes. It was as if they'd been glued shut. Slowly, she cracked them open and detected a thread of golden light. She peered between her eyelashes, and a blurry face appeared. She blinked, coming back to herself, coming back to her body, and leaving the sweet embrace of the in-between place. The image came into focus. "Birthday Card?" she rasped, her voice a strained croak of a sound. She stared at him—unsure if she could believe her eyes. He looked different—younger. His dark hair was disheveled, giving him a carefree air, and the stubble on his cheeks and chin had filled in. He had a blue smudge just below his left eye. That must have been why she'd smelled paint. *Why would he be painting?* Her muddled mind couldn't connect the dots. She attempted to touch his face, to wipe away the periwinkle splotch, but raising her arm felt like lifting a boulder.

A boulder.

Streaks of rocky terrain flickered in her mind. More images surfaced. She saw a cabin, a staircase, a waterfall, and a pool of crystal waters with edges kissed by sleeping starbloom buds. She arched her back, then winced, inhaling a tight breath at the sharp twist of pain. Had she cut herself? Bruised herself?

The pieces didn't fit together.

She relaxed into the softness and stared at Kieran. Concern welled in his sage-green gaze.

She swallowed, her throat straining to complete the movement. "Where am I?" she whispered.

"I'll tell you everything. Please, drink some water first." He eased her up and propped a few pillows behind her back.

Her eyes adjusted to the light as she drank in her surroundings. She was in a bed covered with a faded blue quilt. She raised her gaze, not sure if she was still dreaming. It was as if she'd fallen back in time. She was inside a log cabin. She eyed the knotty timber encasing the space. Light filtered through the dust-speckled windows, casting a glow on a rustic wooden table across from an old iron stove. Embers crackled in its belly. She turned her head. An easel sat by the far window with an array of paint tubes and sheets of oatmeal-colored paper scattered on the windowsill and spilling onto a small table beside a stool.

"Drink," Kieran said, cutting short her visual field trip. He held the metal water bottle to her lips.

She sipped, then gulped. *Damn, she was thirsty.* She held the bottle with trembling hands and downed every drop.

"Better?" he asked gently, taking the bottle from her shaky grip.

She melted into the pillows and sighed. "Yes, thank you."

He sat on the edge of the bed and faced her. "We're in Fiona's cabin. You've been in and out of consciousness for the last fifty-eight hours and . . ." He checked his watch. "Eight minutes."

She gasped. Reality hit like an adrenaline-infused wrecking ball as the events of the last few days tore through her groggy haze.

The Pike with her birthday card boyfriend.

Kieran holding her in his arms as she drifted off to sleep in his bed.

And Regis Greenstone. She clenched her trembling fist. Fury spiked within her adrenaline-filled veins. Regis wanted to get his smarmy, greedy hands on the town, and she was the only one who could stop him.

What the hell was she doing in bed?

"Breathe," Kieran coaxed, his voice soothing, like when he'd said the word after her asshole ex crashed the hearing.

She followed his advice, taking a few breaths to steady herself, still too weak to do much more. She cleared her throat. "I've been asleep for over two days?"

He watched her—no, he evaluated her as if he were gauging her pain.

She mustered a grin. "I'm okay, Kieran. Just a little shaky. Please, tell me what's going on."

He looked her over and nodded, more to himself than to her. "You're correct about the duration, but you haven't been asleep for the entire time. You were up long enough five times for me to help you have a few sips of water, and you used the restroom twice."

She watched him. "You've been with me the whole time?"

"Yes."

"Only you?"

He smoothed a wrinkle in the quilt. "Only me."

She shifted, feeling her cheeks heat. "And you helped me pee?"

"I did."

She rubbed her eyes. "Sorry about that."

He frowned. "Why are you sorry? Urination is the body's way of excreting waste. I'd be more concerned if you didn't urinate over fifty-eight hours. It was no hardship on my part. I have experience with female urination."

She had to be dreaming.

Now, she was the one assessing him. "What experience do you have with female urination?"

"I helped with McKenzie's potty training when she was a toddler. In the beginning, she'd never make it to the bathroom in time. She'd urinate everywhere—usually mere steps from a toilet."

This man never ceased to surprise her.

"I hope I didn't pee all over the place," she murmured, a thread of sarcasm in her tone.

"You did. But only once."

Wait . . . what? She'd peed her pants.

Cue the flush of heat racing back to her cheeks. She sighed and hung her head. "How embarrassing."

"You shouldn't be embarrassed. It was your first attempt after sleeping for seventeen hours and twenty-six minutes. You could barely walk. I carried you most of the way. Like McKenzie, you were a few feet from the toilet when . . ."

"When I peed on myself."

"Correct. After you voided, I helped you clean up. Thankfully, you didn't squirm as much as a two-year-old."

There was one hell of an accomplishment. Better at pissing oneself than a toddler.

She scanned the cabin. "This place has a bathroom?"

He nodded toward a side door. "Not in the modern sense. There isn't plumbing or running water. We have a composting toilet."

"That's very environmentally friendly."

"Starrycards care about the environment."

She wasn't ready to have that fight. Instead, she peered out the window. "Can we never talk about me missing the toilet again?"

"Too late. It's gone out in the Starrycard Newsletter. But you're in good company with McKenzie."

She swept her gaze back to him. His lips curved into a twitch of a smile. Jesus, it was hard to know what to feel for him when he gifted her with that expression. She mirrored the hint of a grin. "I hear McKenzie is everyone's favorite Starrycard."

He nodded, but his expression grew hauntingly neutral. "Now that you're more alert, we need to talk about what you did."

She wasn't ready to go there either. "No, I have another question."

A muscle ticked on his jaw. His tell. "No more questions, Isabelle. You could have—"

"Why do you have paint on your face?" she pressed, cutting him off. "You've got a smudge of blue oil paint on your left cheek."

He rubbed the area—that muscle on his cheek was working overtime. He schooled his features. "The paint's not important. Why did you sneak out of my house and come here on your own?"

She twisted the quilt around her index finger, her mind racing. Here's what she knew. She'd woken up beside Kieran, feeling like death warmed over. But she'd decided to push through it. She'd done it before, but her health took a nosedive thirty minutes into her hike. The last thing she recalled was wanting desperately to cool off and sit for a spell. She'd found a spot. She'd only meant to rest for a few minutes, but Kieran had to have found her there, unconscious. Undoubtedly, her actions were reckless, but she couldn't help herself.

"I thought we had an understanding," he continued, his tone softening.

She wound another layer of the quilt around her index finger, then gasped. "Ow," she hissed, studying her hand.

"You had a few splinters. I removed them."

She ignored the pain and pegged him with her gaze. "This is my fight, Kieran."

He pressed his hand on hers, stopping her restless movements. The tenderness in his gaze shifted to fury. "Your fight? How many times do I have to say this? This is my town. My home. My legacy," he said through his clenched jaw, his eyes burning with intensity.

She'd never seen him this worked up, this furious.

Welcome to the club, Birthday Card.

She leaned forward and squared her shoulders. "How many times do I have to tell you that Ashbourne Building and Development is my legacy?"

"What do you think you're going to do? Stop Regis and somehow get your family's company back?" There was no neutral countenance. No robotic cadence to his voice. Along with his new outdoorsy, disheveled look, his voice had taken on an unrestrained cadence.

It fed her fury.

"I don't want it back," she exclaimed, shaking but not with weakness. Determination coursed through her. "I don't know the first thing about running a building and development company. I want the employees to have it—the people who worked for my parents and grandparents. They cared about it as much as my family did. I don't know how I'll make that happen—or even if it's possible. So, I'll do what I can. And what I can do right now is stop Regis and the people of Starrycard Creek from developing the mountain acreage. It's like the universe meant for me to be assigned to this case."

He held her face in his hands. "Forget about the fucking mountain! Don't you get it? You could have died, Isabelle. I found you in your underwear, slumped against a rock, burning with fever."

She closed her eyes, trying to shut him out. "I would have been okay. I would have come out of it."

"Come out of it?" he snarled, pulling away and breaking their connection.

She opened her eyes. "Yes."

"You've got to know better," he continued, wild-eyed. "The temperature can drop below freezing at this elevation at night. There's wildlife that would be happy to call you supper, and you weren't far from one of the hot springs. You could have drowned. If I hadn't come along—with meds to bring down your fever and a place to care for you, you might have died. Can you not get that through your head? Nothing matters without . . ." He shook his head like the words were stuck. "Can you not understand what that would have done to—"

"To who?" she shot back. "It can't be you. No falling in love for the birthday card boyfriend. Bachelor life or bust for Kieran Starrycard." She lifted her chin and willed her voice not to shake, but she needed him to be aware, painfully aware, of who she was. "I have no family. Nobody. Who would miss me? Wait! There's one person. Hailey, she'd show up at my funeral if I keeled over. Hallelujah! There's one!" She was spiraling, a ball of trembling, angry, heartbroken energy.

"It was dangerous behavior, Isabelle."

She shrugged—might as well give him what he wanted. "Fine, you're right. Are you happy? It was reckless of me to set off alone when I knew I was getting sick. It was shitty of me to sneak away." She tapped her chest, instinctively reaching for her locket. *Where the hell was it?* She patted her neck, then pegged Kieran with her gaze. "Where's my locket? Did you take it off?"

"No," he said, his anger receding.

That wasn't a good sign.

She glanced around. "Is it in the cabin?"

"No, I've been looking for it. Every couple of hours, when I knew you were in a deep sleep, I'd comb the area where you'd shed your clothes. I checked your pack. It wasn't in there, but when I found you, your bag was open, and items were strewn around."

Her broken heart cracked, opening a gaping abyss of agony.

"What about the card from my family?" she said, trembling. "I grabbed it off the table with the map. They were in my pack."

The muscles in his throat contracted as if he wanted to swallow the answer to her question. "The map was there. But there was no card."

A knot formed in her belly, twisting like it was being pulled by a strong man. "What?" she eked out, barely able to breathe. She pushed him away and staggered from the bed as unsteady as a fawn taking its first steps. "The locket and the card were the last things my family gave to me. They can't be gone. I can't have lost them. They have to be here." Tears pricked her eyes, but she blinked them away. She could not fall apart. She had to search the area.

"Isabelle, slow down. Your fever barely broke. You'll pass out if you push yourself," Kieran warned.

He couldn't stop her. No one could.

She spied her boots by the table. "You can come with me, or you can stay behind. It's your choice, but I've got to look. I can't lose them again," she sobbed. The thought of misplacing the locket gutted her. She couldn't even trust herself with a damned card and a piece of jewelry. She grabbed her shoe, collapsed into a chair, and wrestled with trembling hands, unable to get the damn thing onto her stupid foot.

"Christ, Bloom!" he exclaimed, exasperation coating the words. "Don't even think of reaching for your other mother-fucking boot. You'll fall over and get a motherfucking concussion. Just sit on the—"

"Motherfucking chair," she finished, unable to stop her sharp tongue as treacherous tears trailed down her cheek.

He picked up a bowl near the easel and set it beside her. Kneeling before her, he removed the shoe from her grip and exhaled a tight breath. "I'm coming with you. There's no way I'm letting you out of my sight. There are berries in the bowl. Eat them. You need the energy. Just fucking do it."

Just fucking do it.

She sighed, wiped her tears away, and eyed the plump blue-berries. "Did you bring them from your house?"

"No, they grow wild on the mountain," he replied, catching his breath. "Goldie planted them years ago. They're safe to eat. You had them in the muffin and the lemonade."

She picked up a berry and placed it in her mouth. She recognized the taste. "Alpacas," she whispered.

"Nope, we don't serve alpaca in Starrycard Creek. They're blueberries. And Christ, eat more than one," he chided, irritation woven into command. "It's been days since you've had anything besides sips of water."

Was he correct?

Sure, but she was too much of a basket case to put up with his beastly shit.

She pushed aside the bowl. "I don't need your help. I don't want your berries or your company."

Was she a giant, trembling mess?

Yes.

If anyone on the planet required assistance—or food or a boat-sized helping of common sense, for that matter—it was her.

Obviously, she should accept any help this man could offer, but that wasn't an option.

"You know I'll follow you. I will always follow you," he growled, deftly slipping the boot on her foot like a master cobbler compared to her shaky, butterfingers attempt.

She stared at him. His words triggered a . . . She couldn't quite put her finger on it. A swirl of questions and snippets of words tossed around in her mind like her brain was on the spin cycle. Had she made a wish, or was that a dream?

"Do you want to change into your clothes?" he asked, pulling her from her muddled thoughts.

She looked down at what she was wearing. She hadn't even noticed the T-shirt tented around her. "Is this yours?"

"It is," he replied, stone-faced, back in robot mode.

She peered out the window. The sun hung low in the sky. She had an hour, maybe two, until sunset, and she had to take advantage of every last ray of light. "It's fine. I don't need to change. I need to move." She edged forward.

"Slow down," he cautioned, holding her thighs with his warm hands to keep her still. "You need your other boot. It's one thing to be out in a T-shirt—at least it's got SPF protection, and it's dry-wicking. But you sure as hell aren't taking one step outside this cabin without appropriate foot protection." He lifted her left foot. "Now point your toe like a fucking ballerina."

It was an odd command.

She complied, and he slipped the boot on. He tightened the laces, working methodically.

The anger and frustration building in her chest ebbed a bit. "Do you say that to McKenzie when you help her with her shoes?"

"Yes, but without the *fucking* part. She still has trouble getting on her hiking boots. They're stiffer than her sneakers."

Izzy focused on the sensation of his capable hands cradling her foot. "You take her hiking?"

He finished up, double knotting the laces. "I make her little maps and hide treasures for her to find. I teach her about outdoor safety—about not exploring unknown terrain alone." His expression darkened. "She can't drive a car or complete multiplication, yet she's able to follow simple mountain safety protocols."

This man! Dammit, just when she was trying to be civil, he had to go and piss her off again.

"I know what you're doing. I caught that little dig loud and clear, but I'm not alone, am I, Birthday Card?" She glared at him, trying to make sense of the turmoil inside her, trying to stabilize her reactions to this place, this person who made her feel things she couldn't allow herself to feel. One minute, she was ready to jump into his arms. The next, she was a ball of spark-spitting fire, prepared to burn it all down and go out in a blaze of glory.

He stood and offered her his hand.

She batted it away. "I don't want your help."

"You'll hold my *fucking* hand, *Bloom*. The last thing I need is to have you twist your ankle or tumble down the mountain," he growled.

Mr. Birthday Card Potty Mouth wasn't playing around. And he called her Bloom, something she should not want to continue.

"All right, all right," she mumbled, ignoring the butterflies in her belly. She extended her left hand, and her breath hitched. The paper ring was still on her finger. Kieran had locked on to it the second she reached for him. But it looked different. The top edge was frayed. More rounded, it had lost its sharp definition. It was bound to happen. It wasn't made to last. The thought sent a shudder through her, echoing in the hollowness of her broken heart. She flicked her gaze to the unshaven mountain man in front of her. A storm flashed in his eyes, intense and probing. But when he blinked, the emotion disappeared.

He wrapped his hand around hers and gently helped her up. A methodically practiced motion. She knew it. She watched him as he guided her out the door and down the porch steps. She'd noticed similar, methodical qualities in her grandfather. When her poppa was in a group, he'd observe others as if he were making a list or evaluating people's responses.

"This is how you hold McKenzie's hand, isn't it, or how you'd guide a child?" she asked, intrigued to see if he'd confirm her prediction.

"I'm the oldest of six. I've spent most of my childhood guiding children."

"But you practiced the behavior. You thought about it," she pressed.

"Do you consider repetition, followed by evaluating one's progress and fine-tuning their response as practicing a behavior?"

"I do."

"Then yes, for the sake of this argument, it's practiced. Nearly everything I do is. It's how I operate."

"I like that about you." She shook her head. "I don't know why I said that."

The storm returned to his eyes, but like before, he suppressed the emotion. He scanned the rocky terrain and pointed due east. "I found you down there by a large boulder. I've searched the area around it. It would be pointless to retrace my steps." He glanced at his watch. "Do you remember where else you were before you ended up at the rock? We've got an hour and nine minutes before the sun sets."

"Sixty-nine minutes?" she tossed back.

"It appears you're able to complete simple addition."

"That was our number."

He kept his attention on a point in the distance. "For the cake tasting. I'm aware."

She sighed. He'd fallen back into muted mode—his safe place, but she couldn't let her thoughts linger on this man. She had a locket and a card to find. She scanned the landscape, and her nature-loving side drank in the views. This place was nothing short of a mountain paradise. Not far from the cabin, just up the slope, a rush of water flowed over Starrycard Falls into the hot spring below, creating a calming, rhythmic white noise. It provided a serene backdrop to the birds' chatter and the breeze rustling through the smattering of low, scruffy shrubs and pops of wildflowers brightening the terrain. Under nature's spell, she closed her eyes and inhaled, allowing the surroundings to soothe her and ground her, like nature always did. Out of habit, she felt for her locket. But before a pang of anxiety could wipe out her contentment, Kieran squeezed her hand.

"The jasmine-vanilla scent in the air is from the starblooms. They're beginning to open," he reported, his tone still muted, as he pressed the pad of his index finger to her wrist, monitoring her pulse. He was trying to distract her from her missing keepsakes, trying to keep her pain at bay. She sensed it from his touch and his attention to her movements and breath.

And it worked.

His words eased her heartache. She nodded. "They're preparing to greet the moon."

"Yes."

She opened her eyes and found him observing her. The intensity left her breathless.

Steady yourself, woman. Start searching for the locket and card. A trustworthy person wouldn't have lost them.

She glanced over her shoulder at the cabin and noticed the steps going down into the root cellar. "That's where we start looking. I went down there. The door's unlocked."

"Are you sure? We don't usually leave anything open."

"I went down there after I made it to the cabin. I know I did. I was looking for a way in. I recall the coolness."

They followed a dirt path to the rock and earth stairwell. They'd need a flashlight.

She patted where she usually kept her cell in her pocket. "My phone. We need light. It's got to be dark down there."

"It's out of energy."

"Do you have yours? There's no way we can search without a light."

"My phone is also at zero charge. In my haste to leave, I forgot to pack a charger. But don't worry. My family knows we're here. My grandmother stopped by before I left the house. She mentioned that my grandfather saw you leaving town. I let them know we'd be spending time on the mountain."

"Together?" she pressed.

"Yes."

"Did she say anything about us?" Izzy chewed her lip. After her performance at the hearing, blurting out details of her sex life, and then her near make-out session against a tree with the town manager, the Starrycards—and likely the majority of Starrycard Creek's population—must have thought she was a few slices short of a loaf.

"Goldie brought tea for you. She was concerned you might be coming down with something, and she didn't have to say anything about us." The muscle on his cheek twitched. "I did that for her."

"I don't understand."

He reached into his side pocket. "It's of no consequence. Here, I have a flashlight." He clicked it on and shined the light on the weather-beaten wooden door at the bottom of the staircase.

"I remember this. I'm certain I went inside. Come on," she

said, tugging on his arm, but the man didn't budge. And why would he? He was the size of a linebacker. She huffed. "What is it?"

"We do this together. Slow and steady."

"Forget calling you Birthday Card Boyfriend. You should be the Safety Card Boyfriend."

He frowned. "What's a safety card?"

"Like on an airplane or directions for how to proceed safely with . . ." Dammit, she was talking out of her ass. "With an unstable object," she blathered.

"Unstable object?" he repeated with that barely there smirk. "Perhaps we should switch your nickname to that."

"Oh, so now you're funny?" she fired back.

"I'm not trying to be funny," he replied, definitely trying to be funny.

She stared at this freaking handsome mountain man who kept her on her toes.

He held her gaze. "I prefer Birthday Card Boyfriend for me and Bloom for you. Now, do you consent to the safety protocols?"

"Yes, I consent to the binding requirements of this bullshit oral safety agreement. Does that work for you, Mr. Birthday Card Boyfriend?"

That slight twitch of a grin pulled at the corners of his mouth. "It does."

Damn him and that stupid, sexy scruff.

"Let's go," she said, gesturing with her chin.

Step by step, the light faded as they descended the rocky staircase. She turned the doorknob. *Creak.* The hinges groaned as she opened the door, and they entered the chilled space. The scent of wood and earth filled her nostrils as their steps kicked up plumes of dirt, the specks hovering in the flashlight's golden beam.

The old door creaked shut behind them, and she shivered in the darkness.

"Here." He slipped off his jacket and placed it over her shoulders.

She didn't fight him on it. "Thanks, and I promise I'll take it slow."

"I just want to keep you safe." His tender words floated in the darkness.

"I know," she whispered, her throat thickening with emotion.

When it came to this man, she couldn't figure out up from down.

Focus. Find the card and the locket.

With cautious steps, she surveyed the room, her fingers tracing the snugly arranged stones on the walls. "I recall feeling the rock beneath my touch—the chill, the coarse surface. I was here."

As if being led by an unseeable force, she took a few steps, then dropped to her knees. Methodically, she ran her hands across the packed earth. Kieran joined her, patting the ground with one hand while holding the light with the other.

"Isabelle."

Izzy paused. Had someone whispered her name? Was it the breeze whispering through a few thin gaps in the rock? Or was she on the brink of another round of fevered delusions?

No, the voice—or whatever it was—came from a few feet away. She inched further into the darkened chamber, then gasped when she curled her fingers around something cool and solid.

"Are you okay?" Kieran asked, coming to her side with the light.

"Yes." She traced the object, but it wasn't her locket. It wasn't the right shape. She scraped away at the dirt, then pulled on the bit of metal—metal secured to the ground. A rusty whine cut through the inky silence as she moved the object from side to side.

"What is that?" Kieran asked.

"It's a handle. Feel for yourself." She took the flashlight from him and pointed it at the exposed arc of tarnished metal.

Kieran pulled on it, but it wouldn't budge. "It's attached to a door or a hatch."

She watched as he strained to open it. "Did you know it was there?"

"No," he answered, wonder coating the word.

"No?" Her heartbeat kicked up. *This was a good sign.* "Maybe there's a crack in the ground," she stammered. "My locket might be in there. It might lead to a chamber."

"I don't think so. The lid doesn't look big enough for a person to fit through." He pulled again and grunted. "There's movement. I don't think it's locked. It may be weighed down by the hardened dirt."

She studied the tarnished metal. "What a curious find. Could it be for food storage? Whatever it is, we need to get in there."

He stood and brushed his hands against his thighs. "Don't move. I know what we need." He turned and bounded up the rock steps. Seconds later, he returned with a shovel. He chipped away at the half-inch of dirt crusted across what turned out to be a compact door about the size of a record album with a hammered iron handle mounted in the center. "That should do it." He rested the shovel against the wall, then knelt and grasped the handle. But before he opened it, he swiveled toward her, a scowl etched to his face.

"What? Why that face?" she exclaimed. "I'm adhering to your safety protocols."

"Don't dive in. Don't be impulsive. Give me a second to make sure it's—"

"Safe," she supplied. "Kieran, I graduated summa cum laude. Top of my class in environmental studies. I have the capacity to understand what you're asking of me." She shined the light around the darkened room. "We're team safety around here. Now, come on, Birthday Card, please. I need to see what's inside." She swallowed past the lump in her throat. "I have this strange feeling that whatever's in there, it's meant for me."

Despite their dim surroundings, she could feel his gaze locked on her. She shouldn't have spoken that last part aloud. She sounded insane.

"What did you say?" he asked, his voice tinged with concern.

Oh no! He sure as hell better not throw her over his shoulder and cart her back to bed. There'd be hell to pay if he tried that stunt again.

Think, woman!

She had to figure out some way—any way—to stay in the cellar. Every cell in her body was telling her one thing.

There was something down there, something whispering in the dark, and she couldn't leave this place without it.

CHAPTER

Fifteen

IZZY

IZZY AIMED the beam of light at the handle, trying like hell to concentrate on what was right in front of her. "Let's get the show on the road and open her up. Time's a-wasting," she crooned, going for casual but sounding more like a casually psychotic country music singer. She cleared her throat, took a page from Mr. Birthday Card's playbook, and sealed her lips.

Just don't curtsy.

"You think whatever's in there is for you?" Kieran asked.

Of course, her hyper-detail-oriented, attuned-to-her-every-word-and-move birthday card boyfriend wouldn't let it go. This was what she'd dreaded when the statement jabber-jawed out of her mouth.

"This is your first time in Starrycard Creek, Isabelle. Why would you assume anything in here would be for you? Are you feeling all right? Are you spiking a fever again?" He cupped her face in his giant man hand.

Come on, oatmeal brain. Generate a non-psychotic response.

"I meant my locket. My locket might be in there." She shined the light on a crack between the outer wooden frame and the slats, making up the bulk of the covering. "See that. The wood's dried out. There's a groove and slim slit. It's possible my locket fell through."

That was a perfectly reasonable response. She sure wasn't about to tell the man, who already thought she should be in bed resting, that she'd heard a voice on the wind whisper her name and that she knew something was hidden beneath the earth. If she did that, she had no doubt their locket treasure hunt would end. And she had to find out what was tucked away in this hidden spot.

"I just feel . . . hopeful," she said, and it was the truth.

She could feel his eyes on her. He was analyzing her words and preparing his reply. But his attention didn't scare her. Quite the opposite. It solidified their unspoken connection.

"Let's open it. I'm experiencing a similar sense of urgency and hopefulness."

"Okay," she replied on a relieved breath as anticipation bubbled in her chest. She couldn't decipher what was happening to her, but it was profound, and Kieran understood.

"Take a step back and keep the light trained on the spot," he said, adjusting his grip.

"Got it," she answered, maintaining her cool, but that fizzy anticipation had swelled into a rush of excitement. *What was going on with her?*

Kieran pulled, tugging once, then twice. With a *pop* and *poof,* he removed the lid from its resting place. A plume of musty air escaped, peppering the beam of light with an earthy cloud of dusty confetti. Moving with caution, he set the wooden covering aside.

This was it!

She aimed the light into the darkened hole. No, not a hole. They'd uncovered a buried wooden crate like the kind once used for milk delivery years ago. And she was correct. Something was hidden beneath the mud-caked covering. She studied the object. "Is that leather?"

"It appears to be a bag with a strap. Keep the light on it.

There's something etched into it." Kieran leaned closer. "*D.G.S.* Those are Delilah Gable-Starrycard's initials. Give me a second. I don't want to reach in with my bare hands." Kieran retrieved the shovel. Carefully, he fished the object from its hiding place. "Check if there's anything else inside. I felt like I bumped something. And make sure to look for your locket."

She swept the light around the square space. "No bugs or rodents. Just a bit of dirt and a few empty glass bottles." She plucked one from the bottom of the crate. "Starrycard Creek Stumble Juice. *Stumble Juice?*" she repeated, reading the embossed label.

Kieran chuckled. "It's moonshine. Bathtub brews. It was Nathan and Delilah's *hobby* during prohibition. It's my understanding that they had quite a good time back in the day and enjoyed their drink. We have their old moonshine and bathtub brew recipes. Christian got into recreating them a few years ago. He does it at the Donnelly compound—Fiona's family's home. He turned it into his training compound. But Delilah shouldn't have been drinking later in life. She developed a heart condition. That's what took her."

Izzy removed two more empty bottles of Stumble Juice from the crate. "We know why Delilah enjoyed spending time up here."

"But no sign of your locket?" he pressed.

She set the bottles to the side and did another sweep. "No."

"I'm sorry, Bloom."

Bloom.

The evenness of his tone and the effortlessness he used when speaking her nickname washed over her like the mountain's jasmine-vanilla breeze.

"It was a long shot." She gave the area another once-over with the flashlight, then trained the beam on the leather bag. "Is it heavy? Is there something in there? I'm quite curious."

Kieran shifted his grip on the handle, assessing the blade's weight. "It feels like it. Do you want to do another sweep of the cellar floor for your locket?"

"It's not here," she said, a sureness in her tone. "We can leave the root cellar."

"Are you sure? I know the locket and card mean quite a bit to you. We can keep looking. I won't stop."

He wouldn't, and she should want to press on searching for her treasured items, but that damned bag held something—for her. She just knew it. In fact, the need to ascertain its contents built inside her like a child excitedly eyeing their wrapped birthday presents. "I have a feeling the locket and card will turn up. They've got to be out there," she answered, that hopeful edge nudging her to keep going.

What was happening?

Hope had become a rare visitor in her life since she'd lost everything. Perhaps it was this place. She hadn't felt this alive in years. With each passing minute, she grew stronger. A fierce, vibrant energy lit her from within. A drive to follow her instincts —to trust her instincts.

Could she trust herself again?

She caught a movement in the darkness out of the corner of her eye. It was Kieran observing her, again, calculating what he needed to do . . . for her.

"Isabelle?"

"Yes?"

"This moment feels significant."

She smiled as that little seed of hope in her chest sprouted. "It does."

She followed a step behind him as they ascended the stairs, her curiosity growing with each step. She inhaled the fresh air as the sun kissed her cheeks. She blinked, allowing her eyes to adjust to the late-day summer light. Kieran carried the bag on the shovel's blade, then eased it onto the top of an old barrel tucked along the side of the cabin.

He rested the shovel against the wall. "I think there's a book inside."

"A book?" She studied the buried find. An array of scuffs and scratches were etched into the well-worn brown leather bag bearing her initials. It was a well-used item. The leather was darkened in places where Delilah must have gripped it and worn it smooth, but it still appeared tough and ready for adventure.

"It's just a guess," Kieran continued. "But whatever's in there is in one piece and solid."

She reached for the bag and then froze. "Sorry, you should do the honors. Whatever is in there belongs to your family."

He stood there for a beat and glanced away. It wasn't an aloof behavior. The wheels in his head were turning. Her grandfather used to do the same thing when he needed a second to gather his thoughts.

"No, you open it," he said and crossed his arms. It wasn't a combative movement—more of a permissive, trusting gesture.

She stroked the worn leather the way one would approach a skittish animal, trying to convey she was a friend, a kindred soul. Was it a strange behavior? Yes, but at least she didn't curtsy to show her respect. Carefully, she loosened the strap, removing the prong from the well-worn notch. Lifting the flap, she peered inside. "You're right. It is a book." She could only view the spine —a muted, neutral khaki with no printing on it. She jiggled the flap. "I don't see any bugs or debris. It seems safe to retrieve."

Kieran stepped closer. "Go ahead."

She slipped her hand inside the cool pouch and removed the item.

Isabelle.

There it was again. Her name murmured in the wind. She glanced at Kieran. Had he heard it? It didn't seem like it. His gaze was locked on the book.

"I know what that is," he said, his voice barely a whisper.

She turned it over and read the two words embossed on the center of the cover. "*Papilio stellata.*" She met Kieran's gaze. "That's Latin for starwing butterfly." Her breath hitched with eager anticipation. She opened the cover, taking in handmade paper with starbloom petals pressed into the page. "Delilah

Gable-Starrycard. Naturalist. 1953," she said, reading the penned line of text.

"I'll be damned," Kieran murmured, shaking his head. "It's one of Delilah's journals. They're housed in the library. But this one clearly didn't make it."

"Delilah was the daughter-in-law of the founders, William and Fiona, right?" Izzy asked, recalling the conversation with Goldie and Rex.

"Yes, and she passed away here."

Izzy eyed the log structure. "She died inside the cabin?"

"They found her on the porch. She'd been painting."

"Who found her?"

"Tristan and Lavinia, her son and daughter-in-law."

They should distribute a family tree cheat sheet at Town Hall.

"Tristan's your . . . ?"

"My great-grandfather," Kieran supplied. "I never met him. He passed before I was born. It goes William, Nathan, Tristan, Rex, then my dad, and . . ."

"And then you. You're the firstborn Starrycard son of your generation."

He glanced away. "I'm one of four sons and one of six siblings. I'm nothing special. It's not like how it was for the others—the only sons. Those who ensured the Starrycard legacy."

She watched him. He downplayed his role, but she knew three things for sure about this man. Family was important to him. He was entirely dedicated to his town, and he did carry the weight of being the firstborn.

"Still, you are who you are," she offered, feeling the weight of Starrycard Creek's history in her hands.

"I am," he added, a touch of melancholy in his reply. He touched the page with Delilah's name. "I wonder why this was hidden. She must have put it here without telling anyone."

"Why do you say that?"

"Tristan—or any Starrycard, for that matter—would have added it to the collection in the library."

Izzy turned the page. "It's dated June first, nineteen fifty-three."

"She died in early July of that year. These would have been her last entries. She was quite prolific. There are nearly a hundred journals in the collection. She didn't hold back when she noted her observations."

Izzy flipped through the pages. "It's only half used," she said, leafing through the blank sheets until she came to the final entry. She skimmed the first few lines and gasped.

Kieran wrapped his arm around her waist and gripped her hip. "What is it? Are you feeling off balance? Do you need to sit?"

"No, I'm all right. I can hardly believe my eyes." She rested the journal on the top of the barrel. "Delilah was concerned about the tourists on Starrycard Mountain impacting the starwing butterflies' migration corridor. She also mentioned miners *skulking*—her words—around Starrycard Creek. This part of Colorado wasn't affected by the gold rush and silver mining, was it?"

"No."

Isabelle returned to the journal. "Delilah writes that she's grateful for the town's charter but fears for the future. She put together a summary of the last fifty years of the starwings' migration patterns in the region. She noted the butterflies appeared to bypass Starrycard Creek when tourism increased, but there's a note. It looks like it was penciled in at a later date, saying her initial observations regarding the matter were inaccurate."

"Inaccurate? Where did the butterflies go?" Kieran pressed.

Izzy skimmed through several entries and stopped on a sketch of a mountaintop with a distinct feature. "A summit crater," she whispered, tracing the lines of the drawing with the tip of her index finger.

Kieran eyed the page. "What is that?"

"It's a depression near the top of a mountain."

"A depression, like an indentation?"

She pointed to the area on the sketch. "Yes, they can form a valley in volcanic regions. They often go undetected, especially in remote areas or terrain that's difficult to access."

Kieran read the passage, then frowned. "But Starrycard Mountain was never a volcano."

She chuckled. "Actually, Birthday Card, you and your impeccable credentials are wrong about that."

"I would know, Isabelle. I grew up here," he answered.

She leaned into him. "How about this? We're both correct."

That hint of a grin curled his lips. His arm was still wrapped around her waist, and he drew her in a fraction closer. "That cannot be true."

"It can. You're correct. Starrycard Mountain was never a volcano. But I'm also correct because its formation was due to a *volcanic intrusion*."

He frowned. "I've never even heard of that."

"I geeked out on these back in college. Starrycard Mountain's makeup is like the Spanish Peaks in southern Colorado. Millions of years ago, magma blasted into the rock layers. There's no eruption activity. Starrycard Mountain isn't comparable to Pompeii or Mount Saint Helens, but a volcanic process created it. It also explains the geothermal events here—your hot springs."

"Where is this summit crater?"

"That's a good question." She picked up the journal, flipped through the pages, and then stopped when a loose sheet slipped out. She pulled it from between the pages and studied the image. The lines were drawn with a shaky hand, but it was still legible.

"That's the falls," Kieran said, eyeing the drawing. "Delilah made quite a few sketches. She also painted oil and watercolor scenes on squares of Starrycard Creek paper and tucked them between the pages. Her journals are teeming with them."

"And she painted the picture in Town Hall, correct? *Only Known to the Stars*?"

"Correct," he confirmed.

Isabelle studied the drawing. "Kieran, it's not a sketch. It's a map. Look at this notation. She writes that entry to the summit crater is behind the waterfall. And that's where . . ."

Kieran took the sheet from her, turned it over, and skimmed his great-grandmother's wobbly notes next to another sketch—a sketch of a sea of butterflies flitting about a hot spring.

She touched the page. "This is where the starwing butterflies went. It's an alternate resting place. A hidden away oasis. I recognize it."

"Holy shit," he whispered as they gazed at a rough pencil drawing—a near replica of the framed watercolor painting in the Town Hall next to the grandfather clock.

"Only Known to the Stars," she said, wonder coating her words as she peered at the faded sketch. "It's real. There's got to be a hot spring in the summit crater. And if there's a hot spring, there will be starblooms." Effervescent excitement hummed in her veins. She recalled her conversation with Pamela. Her boss had mentioned her granddaughter had been disappointed they'd missed the starwing butterflies when they'd visited Nevada.

A realization hit. The elusive butterflies had an ace up their sleeves. If her hypothesis was correct, these fluttering beauties had one hell of an ability to alter their migration routes and departure dates as well as the size of the swarm. Most thought they migrated in small groups, but that might have changed. She needed more information. She paged through the journal, scanning for dates and temperature readings.

"What are you looking for?" Kieran asked softly.

"Hold on. I need a second to put this together." She was in the zone, recalling everything she knew about the species. She flipped to the section of the journal denoting when the elusive creatures arrived and departed and the years when Delilah thought the butterflies had bypassed Colorado. She analyzed another two lines of data. One titled *Summer Tourism Revenue.* The other, *Population.* Years when the number of visitors increased, the butterflies appeared to bypass Starrycard Creek. *Fascinating!* Izzy turned to the next page and spied a few faintly printed words jotted in an unsteady hand at the bottom of the page in ice-blue colored pencil.

They were here all along, hidden and only known to the stars.

"The butterflies altered their patterns and behavior. They adapted to survive. They found ways to do it together. Delilah believed there could be large waves of migration, days or even a few weeks apart. They were here all along, hidden and only known to the stars," she said, running her index finger below the naturalist's words, feeling Delilah's spirit.

"The butterflies have always been visiting Starrycard Creek?" Kieran echoed as if he couldn't quite believe it. "Even these last five to ten years when we've barely seen them?"

"Delilah would say yes and that they've come in large waves."

"And they've been stopping at this summit crater hot spring?"

She smiled up at him. "That's it in a nutshell, according to your great-great-grandmother." She turned back to the journal and eyed the observation dates. The thrum of excitement flowing through her exploded into an all-out eruption of exhilaration. "And there's a chance that the butterflies are there now. We have to go."

"How do we get there?"

"Look at the drawing," she explained. "There's a passage in the mountain behind where the water rushes over the cliff against the rock face. Delilah must have found it before she passed away. She's been to the secret resting site. She's seen the fifth hot spring."

Kieran flicked his gaze to the waterfall. "I want to go, but I'm concerned about your health. You're barely over your fever."

She shook her head. "I've never felt more . . . more . . ."

"What?" he asked, looking her over.

She inhaled the vanilla-jasmine-scented air. "More like myself. More like the old me. I'm okay. Actually, I'm better than okay." She laughed. "We can do it, Kieran. Delilah Starrycard was an old lady, days away from dying of heart failure, and she made it. And if the butterflies are there, that means there's a migration corridor not impacted by your plan to expand. Not to mention, it's ground-breaking science if we discover the starwing's ability to alter its behaviors and swarm size."

"In the past, there were times when only a few starwings were spotted. No large swarm."

"It's not uncommon for a few to break off from the group due to a pheromone anomaly, where they read the wrong signals in their environment. The yellow warblers often consume the stragglers."

"I have noticed more warblers," Kieran confirmed.

She nodded and peered at the falls. Resolute determination flowed through her veins. "I have to listen to my gut. You can stay here, Mr. Birthday Card Boyfriend, but I need to go." She started to pull away, but he tightened his grip.

"When will you understand?" he said with a boyish grin. "You're not going anywhere without me, Bloom. I'm not trying to deter you. I simply need more information. It's important to be precise."

"Yes."

"Explain why we can't wait until tomorrow."

She stared at the sky, recalling the time she'd witnessed the starwings' dusk departure—the evening she'd fallen asleep in the hammock with Nana Joan narrating the butterflies' celestial dance.

The conditions were identical.

"Isabelle?" he said, drawing her into his embrace.

"It's perfectly clear. Not a cloud in the sky. It's temperate—the starwing Goldie Locks' zone, not too hot and not too cool. Not to mention, we'll be losing light soon."

"I'm concerned about the sunset. That's why I'd like to wait until tomorrow."

No, they couldn't afford to wait.

She had to make him understand, but she also had to be careful with her words. McKenzie's sighting, confirmed by Goldie, was a week ago. While it wasn't official, it was something. Given that time frame, if the butterflies were still here, it wouldn't be for much longer. But she couldn't tell him that—couldn't let him know she'd lied about the *official* amateur observation.

There was something else.

If the butterflies were there, she didn't want to go alone. She wanted him by her side, wanted to experience this with him.

Okay, how could she convince him?

Data.

If he needed data, she'd give him data.

She steadied herself. "Based on the conditions and from what I can glean from Delilah's reporting, and . . ." She paused and swallowed past the lump in her throat. "And from the information I've obtained regarding the recent siting, it's my opinion that tomorrow may be too late."

"You think the butterflies are there now? You believe they may leave tonight?"

She held his gaze. His sage-green eyes bloomed into the world around her.

Bloom.

Everything that had been askew in her life was clicking into place. Her purpose. Her drive. Her excitement. Her heart's ability to open and to receive . . . love.

The breeze picked up, and the answer to his question drifted in the wind.

When you wake up tomorrow, they'll be gone.

"Based on the data and what I know about this region and the butterflies, I believe they're there. I believe it with my whole heart, and I need you to believe it, too."

He watched her, his gaze piercing and expectant, as if he could sense the unspoken words she needed to say.

He was right. There was more.

Summoning her strength, she steadied herself. "And I need something else from you." Her heart pounded. Her throat tightened. This was not a man who blindly followed others. Yet, she had to speak the words that had kept her in a state of perpetual doubt and self-loathing. She had to have a little faith.

"Name it," he replied, his words intertwining with the whispering wind.

She peered at the paper ring, then drank in her birthday card boyfriend's tousled hair and scruffy cheeks. My God, this man had become her world. "Kieran Starrycard, I need you to trust me."

He schooled his features, but mischief danced in his eyes. "Put on some motherfucking pants, take two motherfucking ibuprofen tablets, and grab your motherfucking backpack. We're going to track down some motherfucking butterflies."

CHAPTER
Sixteen

IZZY

IZZY peered into the split carved into the damp rock wall. She surveyed the scene and laughed a girlish, giddy sound. "This has to be it," she said to Kieran over the rush of the falls, but he didn't hear her. He was preoccupied. She beamed at the man, watching as he raised his hand to allow the waterfall's spray to rain down upon his palm like a child delighting in nature.

He wasn't the only one.

A lightness had taken over her—a buzzy, blissful fluffiness like walking on puffs of vanilla-jasmine clouds.

He must have sensed her observing him. He turned toward her and directed that piercing intensity her way. But there was something else hidden beneath the surface. Wonder and pure awe. It came off the man in waves. *What a shift!* It was as if finding the journal and setting off to explore the summit crater had granted them a new lens to view the world.

She'd donned her motherfucking gear. And boom! A few motherfucking minutes later, they were off.

"This is the entrance," she called over the thrum of the falls.

He studied her mouth and mirrored her expression, his smile slicing a toothy grin through his scruff as a curtain of water flooded the tight space with a cool mist like something out of a fairytale. He glanced past her. "What makes you think it's this one? I see another crack ten feet in front of us. Should we check both?"

She shook her head. "No need. I've got evidence."

"Evidence? Let's see it," he replied, edging toward her on the rocky outcropping.

She knelt and plucked an object from inside the darkened opening. The label had worn off, but the vessel's shape matched the ones they'd found in the hidden crate. She passed him the empty bottle. "Delilah left us a breadcrumb."

"I'll be damned. This must have been here for almost seventy years," he said, slipping it into a side pocket on his pack. "We're doing this, huh?"

She wiped the droplets of water from his cheeks. "You left a note in the cabin detailing our whereabouts. Your family will be able to find our bodies if we don't make it."

He watched her, and that sexy twitch of a grin—made even sexier by his disheveled mountain man appearance—curled the corners of his mouth.

"We have something else in our favor," she added.

"Which is?"

"If a drunk senior citizen days away from heart failure could make it to the summit crater, we have a decent chance of getting there and back in one piece. Don't worry, you're in good hands. I'm a seasoned explorer. I've been across the globe. I'm an ace in the field."

"And don't forget, you've curtsied for blood-thirsty alpacas in Peru."

This man.

She glanced at the flashlight in his hand. "Just turn that on, point it in front of you, and follow my ass."

He tipped up her chin. "You do have one hell of an ass, and we both know how good I am at following you."

Electricity thrummed between them. And yes, the attraction was off the charts, but the charged air held something else, something both heavy, like the weight of a warm woven blanket, and light, like a butterfly wing brushing against her cheek. And that special something was time. The journal discovery anchored them to this moment and this place—a moment that would always be theirs. It was as if a glimmering, invisible thread connected them, and that thread was made of hope. A feeling she'd barred herself from experiencing until this moment with this man. It sent a rush of possibilities carouseling through her mind. Perhaps there was a way to safeguard this land while still allowing the town's development and keep Regis' wolf-in-sheep's-clothing plan from deceiving the residents.

Would it be okay? Would she be okay?

But now she had to focus and treat this expedition like an environmental expert.

"Now that you're adequately motivated by my backside, let's go." She turned to enter the darkened space, but Kieran grasped her hand, keeping her in place.

He surveyed the rocky passageway. "I'm not sure how long we'll have to walk. We're cutting through a mountain. I want you to take it slow. If you get lightheaded or need to rest, tell me. We'll stop."

His concern for her well-being was unwavering. And while she didn't need to be doted upon, she couldn't deny it was a welcome respite from the years of going it alone.

A warmth spread through her chest. "I will. I promise."

She pulled her flashlight from her pack's side pocket, clicked on the beam, and moved into the darkened cavity. Step by step, they followed the rocky route as the beat of the waterfall dulled to a distant thrum. The corridor narrowed, and the air grew thick and ripe with minerals. She shined her light against the side of the rock enclosure. Streaks of green were embedded in the rough gray walls. As they traversed deeper into the mountainside, the mood shifted from giddy to somber—but not in sadness. Quite the opposite. It was reverence in appreciation of this mountain and the ecosystem it supported. Neither spoke. It wasn't necessary.

The tap of their footsteps and the ease of their quiet closeness wrapped them in a timeless cocoon. In this rhythmic zone, family memories came flooding back to her, but this time, the recollections weren't paired with a thread of sorrow. She recalled magical nights camping under the stars. The crackle of fire and the scent of roasted marshmallows. Her mother and grandmother liked them crispy and burnt. Her father and grandfather demanded precision and relied on timing to get a perfectly even light brown toasting to their treat. The sounds came back to her. The hum of insects. The call of the frogs and toads. The stirring of wildlife rustling in the brush. And oh, the sweet buffet of scents. Air perfumed with flowers, berries, and earth carried her away to sweet slumber beneath the stars.

"Isabelle," Kieran said, bringing her back, "I think we're almost to the summit crater. This air is different. Do you notice it?"

She inhaled notes of vanilla and jasmine. "I smell starblooms, but there's something else. Blueberries?"

"I agree. Goldie planted her special mountain blueberries around Fiona's cabin. It would make sense they'd be here. And I should caution you."

"About what?"

He held the flashlight to his watch. "We might not have much light. There's only half an hour until sunset."

"We'll have a full moon. Don't worry. We won't lose our way. I've got glow sticks in my pack. We can leave a few by the entrance." She edged forward, then stilled when she stepped on something slim and cylindrical. She trained the light on the ground. "We've got another breadcrumb. A colored pencil." She picked up the drawing implement, glanced over her shoulder, and held it for Kieran to see.

"When a person consumes their weight in moonshine, they're bound to drop something," he said, then cocked his head to the side. "Do you hear that? It sounds like water."

It did. They continued, and the murmur of water cascading

over stones became more distinct, blending into the sensory symphony with the earthy aroma and the heady fragrance of ripe blueberries and aromatic starblooms. She took a few more steps and slowed her pace. The stone trail had maintained a consistent grade, alternating between gentle ascents and descents, but that changed. She pressed her hand against the rocky wall and pointed her light a foot or so in front of her feet as she encountered a pronounced plunging slope. She navigated the steep grade, one step at a time, then stilled when Kieran's footsteps paused. She peered back at him. "Are you okay?"

"Look," he said, training his flashlight's beam above her head.

She followed the light and spied a pair of midnight blue wings —slightly muted from the male's more iridescent sheen. Her heart leaped into her throat at the splendor of a female starwing butterfly. "Hello, lovely," she said, greeting the creature. "I do hope you're not alone."

"She's not," Kieran replied.

The female starwing flitted. She burst into a jagged flight and led them out of the corridor, passing scores of her companions resting on the rocks. Izzy exited the passageway and inhaled a breath of fresh air as she peered up at the sky. In the waning light, violet bands adorned the horizon, stretching as far as the eye could see. The moon, at the ready, waited for the sun's final goodbye. She lowered her gaze to the hot spring at the base of the shallow crater and gasped. "I've never seen anything like it."

Kieran laced his fingers with hers. "Breathe, Bloom, breathe. You were right. They're here. Hundreds, maybe thousands," he said, his words floating in the sweet mountain air.

She surveyed the utterly breathtaking scene. Years ago, when she'd observed the starwings with Nana Joan, it had been a small swarm. What she witnessed tonight was what naturalists would call a super generation, a glorious kaleidoscope of butterflies. Scores of starwings fluttered from starbloom to starbloom and even stopped to partake in blueberries—a new behavior. The flowers circled the hot spring at the crater's base, fanning out and dotting the bowl of mineral-scented water in a hazy blue glow as low, hardy clumps of mountain blueberries were scattered throughout the wildflowers. The mist from the heated pool mingled with the soft glow of the starblooms' bioluminescent light. Water streamed down the sloped sides, gurgling into the vast expanse of the hot spring as tufts of low mountain foliage atop the boulders reached into the shimmering water, resembling rocky tentacles.

She set down her pack, removed the glow stick, rested it against the entrance, and reached back into her pack, searching for her notebook, which wasn't there. *Shit!* "I need to count them. I should also assess the habitat and make a few behavioral observations. Do you have a notebook or paper on you? Mine must be lost in the woods."

He nodded. "I have one."

"May I use a page or two? I need to get this down." She surveyed the landscape. The place was humming with activity. "Do you see that? There's some intense nectaring going on. And see the group near that small puddle?" She pointed to the hot spring. "The butterflies are ingesting salts and minerals from the water. Damn, I wish we had our phones to record this."

He pulled a slim spiral with a pen slipped inside the coils from his pocket and stared at it. "There are a few empty pages at the end."

"That's okay. It'll work." She presented her palm.

He glanced at her hand, then opened the notebook, treating the well-worn object like an old friend. "There's something tucked inside the pages. It's of value to me."

"I'll be careful," she said, gently taking the notebook. "Thank you." She drank in the mountain paradise teeming with starwings, the silver spots on their iridescent midnight-blue wings glinting among the berries and blooms like earth-bound stars. Emotion built in her chest. She glanced at the blank page, then back to the butterflies. "There's so much to do, but I'm not sure where to start."

"Perhaps we simply observe," he replied with a crack to his voice, his gaze locked on her.

He had tears in his eyes. "What is it?"

"It appears my body has chosen to mimic the *Mimosa pudica* flower as a reaction to the stunning view."

In her haste to record data, she'd glossed over how rare it was to encounter the elusive creatures—especially in this quantity.

Tears brimmed in her eyes as the enormity of this moment swelled inside her. "My body appears to have made the same choice."

He exhaled a slow breath. "Nature has always been my refuge. It's where I go when the noise and the stimulation become too much. I've spent much of my life on this mountain. I've taken in its splendor countless times, but I've never seen anything as beautiful as . . ."

She understood. "As this. The butterflies. The flowers. The berries. The crater hot spring. It's breathtaking."

He concentrated on her face. "No, as beautiful as you. You belong with the butterflies, Isabelle."

"I do?" she replied, recalling when he'd said the same thing as they evaded the French cake patrol in the butterfly pavilion.

He swept his gaze over her. "Look at your shoulders."

She glanced from side to side. Two starwings perched on her left shoulder. One rested on her right. "What do we have here?" she said softly to her companions, then met Kieran's gaze. "You're sweet, but I must look a mess. I passed out against a rock and haven't showered in days. Yellow warblers could have built a bird nest in my hair, and I wouldn't know it."

He stroked her cheek with that coy Starrycard grin on his lips. "I wouldn't allow birds to nest in your hair while you slept. But that's not what I'm looking at."

She tried to read him but couldn't. "What are you looking at?"

He pursed his lips, his brow furrowing as if he were searching for the words. After a few seconds, his expression smoothed. "I'm looking at you."

"I got that part, Birthday Card. I need a little more information."

He nodded. "It helps me when you're explicit with your needs. Let me explain. I'm doing more than merely recognizing your presence and beauty."

"Keep going," she said, noting a new vulnerability in the man.

"You asked me to look at you when you found me packing in my bedroom. You wanted something more than my acknowledgment of your physical presence."

"I did."

"I didn't understand what you were asking of me then. I do now." He paused and drank her in, an easy, boyish countenance taking over. "I see you, Isabelle. I only see you and butterflies. I see your different smiles, the way your dimples dent your cheeks, every curve and slope on your face. I see those lips that make me forget what I'm supposed to do and focus on what I want to do. I see each strand of your hair, the way a few wisps kiss the apples of your cheeks. And I have this fierce urge to keep *seeing* you."

Good God! This man.

She fell back on her usual response when he dropped one of his adoringly poetic observations. "Do you know how romantic that sounds?"

Bathed in twilight's purple light, he looked so at peace. "It's simply a statement of fact, not meant to be—"

"Romantic or otherwise," she finished as the butterflies on her shoulders flitted their wings and landed on Kieran's arm. "And look at that. It appears the butterflies believe you belong with them, too."

"I've had a few run-ins with the species over the years, but nothing like this. You're always welcome in Starrycard Creek, my friends," he said to the creatures. His gaze was intent, absorbing every meticulous detail as if committing each butterfly to memory. After a few seconds, the butterflies left their post and zigzagged to a nearby cluster of starblooms. "When we get back to town, I'll begin the paperwork to have this area designated under protective status. I'll need a reputable environmental expert to sign the document. Could you recommend one?"

She chuckled. "I could. But this summit crater isn't on the map. Wouldn't that exclude it from the zone designated to be developed?"

He shook his head. "It's not on any map, which puts it in a gray area. But there's an excellent chance it could be included if it were. And we can't have that. It deserves every protection. This place can't be spoiled. It's for the butterflies."

She watched him closely. "You think the town will back you up?"

"I know they will. They'll demand it."

They would. The Starrycards would make sure of it. And while this comforted her, she couldn't escape the pang of regret. She reached for her missing locket.

"What is it?" Kieran asked, his attention trained on her hand pressed to her chest where her locket usually rested.

"I was wrong. I characterized you and your town as money-hungry nature-haters who'd do anything to make a buck. I seem to think the worst of people when it comes to my work."

"You're driven to protect the things you care about. I believe those feelings stem from what Regis Greenstone did to you and your family's company."

She nodded, her gaze growing glassy. "I want to tell you what happened. I want you to know everything, but . . ."

But she couldn't.

A tear trailed down her cheek.

Without a word, Kieran brushed it from her cheek. He took her hand and led her down the gentle slope to a flat boulder streaked with green near the edge of the hot spring. Slipping off his pack, he removed a wool blanket. As if he were tucking the rock in for bed, he spread the colorful throw and gestured for her to sit.

She eyed his impromptu office. "That is not the blanket I'd expect you to carry, Birthday Card," she said, mustering a weak grin.

"It belongs to my grandparents. Take a seat," he replied, shifting into lawyer mode.

Taking comfort in his even, reassuring tone, she removed her pack, settled herself, and rested Kieran's slim spiral notebook on her lap.

"You could share the details with your attorney without fear of retribution," he offered.

She sighed. "Attorneys are expensive."

A trace of a smile played across his lips. "Not all of them. Attorneys are allowed to set their fee schedule."

"Like you, for example, Mr. Small-Town Lawyer?" she asked, playfully raising an eyebrow.

"Correct." He glanced around theatrically—a behavior that seemed like something McKenzie would do. "It appears my next client is a no-show. I'd be willing to provide counsel. A financial contribution of any amount is all that's needed to retain my services."

A financial contribution?

And then it clicked.

While she didn't have US cash, she did have another form of currency. She reached into her pack, feeling for the cool metal. "Bingo," she whispered and removed the one-sol coin minted with the image of an alpaca—the parting gift from Elder Pachamama. She held up the coin. "Do you accept Peruvian currency?"

He looked her over appraisingly—another McKenzie-like movement—then nodded. "I do." He accepted the coin and placed the item in a small exterior pocket of his pack. "Ms. Adaire, you have successfully retained counsel." He took her hand in his, his expression softening. "What happened, Isabelle? Who is Regis Greenstone, and what exactly has he done to you?" His words came out in a low, protective rasp.

She concentrated on his strong and steady hand. It was so much larger than hers. She wanted to shrink down and take refuge there, hide from the painful truths, and give herself a second to catch her breath.

He brushed his thumb across her knuckles. "This will be difficult, but I need to know everything. Just breathe. Take it one word at a time."

Izzy focused on the butterflies, sipping nectar from the star-blooms and dancing between the dense mats of mountain blueberries. "Days after I buried my parents and grandparents, I booked a room at The Pike. Hailey didn't want me to go. She wanted me to stay with her in Arizona. It was her first year teaching, and she couldn't get away. But I had to leave. I wanted to feel close to my family, and we loved The Pike. I was at the bar when Regis sat next to me and introduced himself. In retrospect, I'm sure he knew who I was. He was charming and funny. I was in a bad place and welcomed the distraction. I even wondered if, through some cosmic, beyond-the-grave force, my family might have sent him to me to ease my pain. We spent a week together. I told him everything. I thought he was a good listener. When I told him I had to return to Arizona to figure out what to do with the company—my company now—he said that he was from Arizona as well and that he could help me. That connection—being from the same state really stuck with me. He seemed kind, trustworthy, and knowledgeable. He agreed with my environmental viewpoints. He said that while we hadn't known each other very long, he'd fallen in love with me. That night, I told him I loved him. I slept with him and lost my virginity."

Kieran tightened his hold on her hand. "The thought of him touching you makes me want to punch him in his smug face."

"That makes two of us," she replied with a mirthless chuckle. "It infuriates me that I thought he was like my grandfather. Remember how I told you about how my poppa helped my nana?"

"I do. They built Ashbourne together."

"I couldn't fathom running a company on my own. I was still in grad school. My parents and grandparents had assured me they'd teach me the nuts and bolts of the business after my education was complete, but, as we know, a plane crash made that impossible. I thought I was doing the right thing when I entrusted the business to Regis. He said, for legal reasons, it would be better if I sold it to him outright. He also said I'd be a part of it again once my education was complete and we were married, but he didn't want to rush that because I was still grieving. I should have seen the red flags. His words were hollow. He never loved me. I didn't understand what I was giving up, and, in the process, I ruined everything. He fired the employees, and the man couldn't give a damn about protecting the environment. I didn't realize the extent of the NDA. After he'd taken everything, I asked him why he'd done it. Hate burned in his eyes. And then he smirked and said, 'It's just business, baby.'" She cringed as a coppery taste invaded her mouth. "Those words haunt me."

"He said that to you at the hearing," Kieran noted.

"He knows it hurts me."

Kieran's expression hardened. "That jackass. I should have punched him when I had the chance."

"No, it would have only diminished your standing in the community and helped him."

He nodded, his demeanor softening. "I hate that he did this to you and your family, Isabelle," he continued in his even, reassuring tone, returning to attorney mode. "You were targeted and manipulated. I'll comb through the contract. What I need for you to do now is to tell me about specific misdeeds you believe he's committed. Locations of these acts. Outcomes. An overview of how he operates would help, too."

She searched his face in the waning light. "Can you do anything—legally?"

"I don't have enough information to answer that question. Tell me what you know."

She sighed, an exhausted huff of a sound. "Where to start? He purchases respectable building and development businesses and uses their reputation to score contracts. Once he ruins their name, he casts the companies aside, buys another, and continues building his fortune by wrecking lives and the environment. He lures desperate towns in with cash advances. He doesn't care about building up local communities. He'll either turn a town into a pricy resort, where the locals can't afford to stay because his friends will come in with their high-end shops and stores and multimillion-dollar housing developments. Or, if he can squeeze more profits by stripping a place of its natural resources, he's got friends who'll help him go that route and give him a cut. By the time the towns catch on, it's too late. Want to challenge him in court? It's futile. He's wealthy enough to outlast any legal battle. For most, it's easier to move on and start over. That happened in two small towns I know of, first in Texas and then in Utah. I spoke out when I saw what he'd done, and he sued me. He won. He took nearly every penny I had. My inheritance, what I got for the company, it was all eaten up by legal fees and the judgment." She steadied herself. "Regis cannot win the Starrycard Creek development contract. But I can't speak out."

"Then we have to prove to the town that we know what's best for Starrycard Creek."

"We?" she echoed.

"Yes. You and me."

"And, in your opinion, what do *we* define as best?" she pressed.

"*We* believe in smart, ethical development that protects the starwing butterflies and allows the town to remain a vibrant place to live and work. Do you agree?"

Once upon a time, she would have yelled, "*No development on my watch!*"

But not anymore.

"I do agree. And you trust me to do this with you?" She whispered the question but wasn't sure if it was directed at Kieran—or herself. *Could she trust herself? Trust her judgment? Trust she wouldn't screw it up?*

"Yes."

"Why? What changed?" she pressed.

"You've been let down and left to fend for yourself. It makes sense you'd be wary of others' intentions. I believe you'll be fair and honest in your assessment. But I also trust my town. I can promise you that Starrycard Creek will not let you down. The people love the mountain. They care about their home. They treasure the creek and the wonders it affords us in the valley. And more than that. I won't let you down. You're too important to me, Isabelle. You can trust me. Can you do that?" He searched her face, and the raw sincerity of his words caused her breath to hitch.

Emotion welled in her chest. "Yes, I trust you." She ran her fingers over the texture of the woven blanket as vivid recollections of Peru surfaced. But it didn't stop there. She recalled the flurry of her past assignments. Her prejudices against development had jaded her perspective—and her scathing reports reflected this bias.

He cupped her cheek in his hand. "What is it? I know you're hurting when your bottom lip quivers or when you reach for your locket. What are you thinking about?"

"The wool witches," she whispered. "I did them a disservice. I was unfair. I need to amend my report. They deserve to expand their business. I'll have other assessments to change as well, but I should start with them."

"Wool witches?" Kieran repeated, looking her over with an appraising eye.

"Yes, the ones who slathered me in berries and sent the alpacas after me."

He felt her forehead and cheeks. "You don't appear flushed."

"What are you doing?" she asked as he continued his patting and prodding.

"I'm checking for fever."

"I don't have a fever, Birthday Card."

"Are you hallucinating?"

"No," she shot back. *What had gotten into him?*

"You said you needed to amend a report for alpaca wool witches. *Wool witches*, Isabelle," he restated.

She gave him a half-shrug. "That does sound a little strange."

"A little?" he countered.

Okay, her language could be misconstrued as the ramblings of a mad woman.

"They're not witches," she explained. "That's what I call them. Well, honestly, that's debatable. They move like a coven, especially when they're commanding alpacas. Let's just say the elder in charge was *witchy*."

"Witchy wool people who command alpacas?" Kieran summarized, pressing his palm to her forehead again.

Damn, she needed to drop the witch talk.

"I can see how you might be concerned. It does sound—"

"Like the musings of a person on the cusp of delirium," he supplied.

She huffed. It was time to put this issue to rest.

"They're the indigenous Peruvian elders from my last assignment. They wanted to expand their alpaca wool-making business. They required an environmental impact assessment to build a new facility. I told them they couldn't due to the presence of an endangered bird. That wasn't completely true. I was wrong to deny them. I didn't trust they'd do right by their land. I took the most severe position, and it was the wrong call. I saw how they lived, how they cared for the environment and the creatures who lived there. I don't want to believe the worst of people. And I don't want to believe the worst about myself. If I do, Regis wins." She paused as the elder's translated words returned. "The lone bearer of burdens shall find their own demise," she whispered.

"What's that?" Kieran asked.

"Something a Peruvian elder said to me. Something I'm still trying to figure out. But that's my issue."

"Why is it your issue?"

She stared at the butterflies. What was she supposed to say? She feared she was a fly in the ointment—the wrecked one, the one with terrible judgment, the one who could not be trusted, that she protected others by staying away, staying apart, remaining alone.

A question surfaced.

Kieran trusted her. But would she let him down, too?

She pushed the thought aside and stroked his scruffy cheek. "As my mountain man attorney on retainer, please remind me that I need to revise my report for the wool witches?"

"I can. The request is locked in my brain."

"I believe it. I imagine there's quite a bit locked in there." She brushed an errant curl from his forehead, needing to move on and get out of *her head* and ignore the demons whispering in the darkest corners of her heart.

He studied her, doing that thing where he mapped every inch of her face and focused on her lips. "Could I share something with you about my brain?"

She smiled at him. "Let me guess. It wants you to kiss me."

"It always wants that, but it . . ." He shook his head. "No, not *it*. I want you to know something about me."

Whatever it was, it weighed on him. The tightness in his expression relayed that in spades.

"I'm listening."

"One other person knows what I'm about to tell you, and she's bound by doctor-patient confidentiality. You witnessed when I obtained this information from Nelson's wife, the woman you saw me speaking with at The Pike."

"The psychologist?"

"Yes, and I never planned on sharing this information—not even with my family. I'd sought it solely to confirm a choice, but . . ." He peered at the notebook on her lap. "For reasons I don't quite understand, I'm compelled to tell you."

"Okay," she murmured, her voice barely a whisper.

He looked up from the notebook. The muscles in his throat constricted as he swallowed. "I have a neurological condition."

"What condition?"

His jaw clenched. His tell. The subtle twitch signaled a crack in his neutral facade. But there was more. She could sense the chaos churning beneath his calm exterior.

"You can tell me, Kieran."

"It's what causes me to be different."

"Just say it. I'm not going anywhere."

He held her gaze, his eyes clouded with turmoil. "I'm autistic."

CHAPTER
Seventeen

IZZY

WAS Kieran trying to shock her? Scare her? Autism sure as hell wouldn't do that. Nevertheless, the diagnosis had shaped his view of himself and who he could be. Still, she couldn't let him think his news was earth-shattering. *How to proceed?* Like a scientist. She'd go with the facts. "Based on the cadence of your voice and your reactions and non-reactions to certain stimuli, I figured you were on the spectrum."

"You did?" he stammered, his jaw dropping—a lapse in his polished demeanor.

"Sure, like I assume my poppa probably was. You share similar qualities. Not to mention, testing wasn't as prevalent when my grandfather was younger. Regarding your situation, testing wasn't as robust even twenty or thirty years ago. I would assume there are many undiagnosed people your age."

"I'm not like other people, Isabelle."

"Yeah, neither were Mozart, Isaac Newton, Albert Einstein, and Frank Lloyd Wright—all thought to have possessed traits that would have landed them on the autism spectrum. It's how your brain works. People live, work, and thrive with it."

He clenched his jaw.

Dammit, that mouth of hers.

His diagnosis had a profound effect on him.

What could she do to help him?

He didn't require a lecture on neurodiversity.

Think!

And then it came to her.

Whenever her painful past bubbled up, he'd distract her to help her move on.

Now, it was her turn to offer the same comfort.

She tapped the tip of his nose. "I can understand why you weren't diagnosed until adulthood. Was testing even around when you were a kid? You are McKenzie's *old-man* uncle. Did your parents bring you home from the hospital in a horse and buggy after you were born?"

He watched her for a few seconds before his coy smirk returned. "I gather that inaccurate historical example is your attempt at inferring I'm of an advanced age—at thirty-three."

She shrugged, playing it cool. "You're eight years older than me. You were old enough to drive, and I was in third grade playing with dolls. That's hella old."

"*Hella old?*" he repeated like someone *hella old*.

"That's how the cool kids say it. Get with the lingo, Grandpa Birthday Card Boyfriend. Oh, and if it makes you feel better, let's be precise. You're only seven years and a few weeks older than me. So, I was starting sixth grade when you were in college, pursuing that *impeccable degree*. Feel less old?"

"Jesus fucking Christ, Bloom," he muttered, shaking his head and chuckling.

And *Jesus fucking Christ*, knowing she'd lightened his mood filled the void in her chest.

He twisted a lock of her hair around his finger. "It doesn't bother you?"

"You being old?" she teased, but he wasn't having it.

He released the strands and sat back. "Me being autistic. I'm telling you this because it's why I can't love you."

Now, she was the one profoundly affected by a piece of information.

Love?

"You want to love me, but you can't because you're autistic?" she stammered, trying to wrap her head around his statement.

"You deserve to be loved by someone who can project those emotions and declare their love for you."

"Why are you saying this, Kieran?"

"Because you're like no one I've ever met. When I found you against that rock, I'd never been so scared. And then, when your fever broke, I'd never been so relieved. It's hard to recall what my life was like before you. There's just you. I don't know how to proceed. While you slept, I turned the question over hundreds, perhaps thousands of times, trying to decode my responses. They confused me."

Her heart hammered. All his talk of *not* falling in love and then dropping an *L*-bomb had her pretty damned confused, too. "A man once proclaimed his love for me. That didn't work out so well. Maybe I require something different."

"An alternative to love?" He pursed his lips and drummed his fingertips on the blanket. "Still, even an alternative to love would require reciprocation."

"Kieran, your autism doesn't make you any less deserving of happiness. It also doesn't change how I feel. How I think I might be . . ." She froze. *Was she falling in love with this man? No. No? Oh, God.*

"It wouldn't matter how someone felt about me. My condition precludes me from fulfilling the role of a long-term partner," he continued, his words tumbling out in a robotic cadence. "But . . ."

But?

She sat there, stock-still. He had more to say, which was good because she didn't know how to respond.

Kieran's brows arched inward as if he were wrestling with a mental conundrum. "You see, I live with limitations. I rely on lists and practiced behaviors."

"What kind of lists?"

He gestured to the spiral on her lap. "I've had that notebook since I was a kid. It's my secret. It's how I taught myself to read people—to behave normally. It doesn't come naturally to me."

She pulled out her flashlight, opened to the first page, and skimmed a sheet crammed with behavioral cues.

Wait no longer than seven seconds to reply to a question.

To look someone in the eye, focus on the color. Do not maintain for longer than seven seconds. Blink, glance away, then maintain another round of eye contact. Include nodding after speaker makes a point.

Mirror the speaker's expression when discussing lively matters. Note —with McKenzie and most Starrycards, due to their effusive nature, reduce by fifty percent.

"The next several pages catalog my family and friends' different expressions and behaviors, what they mean, and how I should react."

She met his gaze as an invisible thread of jealousy tightened around her heart. "Are there pages for the women you've been with?"

"No, I simply adhere to practiced behaviors with the women I've slept with."

She glanced away, willing herself not to wince.

"But there's a page for you. Two, actually. They're marked with a pressed flower," he said, lovingly touching the corner of the notebook.

Cue the butterflies—the ones in her belly.

She turned to the page with a slight bump between the sheets. "The starbloom. My starbloom. You keep it here?" she asked, tracing the delicate petals with the tip of her finger.

He touched the flower, his finger brushing against hers. "Yes, as a reminder of the first time I wished birthday wishes could come true."

This man.

"May I skim my pages?" she asked and gestured to the notes.

He mustered a boyish grin. "Don't laugh."

"I'd never laugh at something that helps you."

"Go ahead."

She scanned the sheet. He'd filled the pages with her mannerisms, her expressions. He'd even sketched her face and a star-bloom bud in the margin.

She nudged him with her shoulder. "You're an artist and a lawyer?"

"It's just a drawing." He toyed with the wool blanket. "Now that you've seen my notes, what are your thoughts?"

"It's a bit overwhelming, but not in a negative way. It's touching. I'm impressed with your observation skills, especially these notes on my peak arousal expression."

"It's not creepy?"

She turned off the flashlight and slipped it into her pocket. "Not to me. I like it when you look at me. It's not how other men gawk at me like I'm an object. You're observing me, thinking about me. It's not so much about you but about wanting to react appropriately—for me. At least, that's my take. And I understand the impulse to scrutinize. I make observations for a living. If recording them helps you, why should you stop?"

That boyish smile returned. "The intriguing thing is, when I'm with you, I don't reference the notes or worry about modulating my behavior. Often, I don't worry about anything." He frowned. "No, strike that. *Often* isn't the correct word. I do worry. I worry you're not taking adequate precautions with your health and safety. These reflections make up twenty-five percent of my thoughts when it comes to you."

"What are the other seventy-five percent of your thoughts?" she asked, blown away by this man's careful attention.

He tapped his fingertips on his thigh. "A solid forty percent is spent thinking about your magnificent ass, ten percent on the symmetry of your face, and the remaining twenty-five is spent on how I can't wait to see what you'll do next. I'm on the edge of my proverbial seat, preparing to respond to what you'll say. I'm not sure if it'll make me outraged, enamored, or so goddamned turned on I can't think straight. You captivate me, Bloom. You're an entirely new universe."

Wowza!

His fraction-revelation-universe comment left her slack-jawed. "So, forty percent, my ass, ten, my face, twenty-five percent is spent on concern for my well-being, and twenty-five for everything else."

"Yes, the Isabelle Universe is a solid twenty-five," he answered, straight-faced.

No one had ever rattled off something so wild and so utterly touching.

"I'm confused," she continued. "Why do you believe that you're not capable of reciprocating romantic love? What would you call inhabiting an Isabelle Universe?"

"Simply a reaction. A set of behaviors triggered by your presence. As I've said before, I'm unable to produce the corresponding behaviors required by a long-term partner. This being the case, I've dedicated my life to the town. As the oldest Starrycard, I must ensure its longevity. The autism diagnosis solidifies my decision."

She shook her head. "No."

"What do you disagree with?"

She huffed. "Jesus, plenty! How do you know you can't reciprocate? Have you surveyed your past partners?" she pressed, shifting into scientist mode.

"There haven't been any past long-term partners. I've never maintained contact with anyone I've slept with."

"Except for me."

His expression softened. "Except for you."

"So, you have no data. Nobody's told you that your skills in this area were lacking."

"As I said, I believe the nature of my condition supports my conclusion, but I see your point."

"Did the psychologist tell you couldn't reciprocate?"

"No, but she did suggest improving my communication skills."

"That could be true of anyone. And again, you have no data."

He paused and nodded to himself. "My decision would be bolstered with data."

"Precision is important. You need more information," she pressed.

What was she doing? She was the last person who should dabble in love, yet her heart couldn't give up this opportunity.

"How would you suggest obtaining data?"

"Our situation seems ideal, given we've entered an agreement to maintain a sexual relationship."

"We could amend our no-falling-in-love arrangement to allow for interactions that could foster those feelings—to amass information utilizing a fake love scenario," he replied.

She should stop him. Press her hand to his lips and shut him up.

"A fake love amendment to allow a fake love scenario?" she repeated, not freaking stopping. "Would you be open to changing the agreement? Is that a possibility?" she pressed.

"As your attorney, I'd be remiss if I didn't disclose that renegotiation is possible with nearly every contract. And, of course, loopholes can often be exploited."

This was reckless, but the thought of this man showering her with more attention, more observations, and more of everything that made her body tremble with delight was too enticing to turn down.

"What kind of loopholes exist in a no-falling-in-love agreement?" she pressed.

He pursed his lips, then smirked. "There's the . . . *Cordis* Contingency."

What was he playing at?

"You're talking to an environmental scientist. I'm fluent in Latin. *Cordis* means heart."

"Correct. The clause pertains to matters of the heart. It's an obscure *falsus* legal term." There was that grin—that sexy twist to his lips. And his mountain man scruff only added to his allure.

"*Falsus* is Latin for fake. You made up a fake-love legal term to pretend to love me?"

"You like it when I use legalese creatively."

Her stupid heart skipped a beat. "I do."

"We're not even sure I'm able to love. However, agreeing to fake it via the Cordis Contingency loophole means if we do fall in love, it's not breaking the agreement."

"You're getting too *lawyer-y.*"

"That's not a word."

"Explain it to me like I'm McKenzie."

"Because it's fake love," he supplied.

She watched him closely. "Bullshit love?"

"Yes, not a word I use with my niece. But, yes, I could bullshit love you, and you could report if my behavior elicited the feeling of being loved unless that arrangement would cause you pain."

She mimicked him and kept her expression neutral. "I'm open to it. I'm the one who suggested the need for data. Neither of us is seeking love in the traditional sense, but we could attempt to fall into bullshit love. I'm here for a fixed period of time. I can share my conclusions with you at the end."

"What if we find I'm able to make you feel loved?"

Did she already feel loved?

Her heart knew the answer, but she couldn't tell him—for some nagging reason, she held back.

"It's a data point. You decide how to interpret it."

Did she believe that?

He nodded. "And when it's over, it's over. You'll leave Starrycard Creek," he said, his voice gruff as he borrowed her words from the first night they met.

"Why would I stay?" she asked and held her breath, waiting, but . . . for what? For him? For herself?

His lips parted, then closed, like he couldn't formulate a response.

It didn't matter. They were doing this.

"It's done. I agree to the amended terms." *Reckless, reckless,*

reckless—so reckless. She had feelings for this man. She might even be in love with him. But he'd decided to dedicate his life to this town, and she'd pledged her life to protecting the environment. That was that. There wasn't a reason for her to stay. And he didn't voice one, either.

"Bloom?"

"Yes?"

He cupped her face in his hand and brushed his thumb across her bottom lip. "I'm going to bullshit-love the hell out of you."

Despite not understanding what was happening in her head and her heart, she couldn't help but beam at the guy. "Are you?"

"We'll have mountains of data. Heaps and heaps of precise data."

"Now that gets me hot."

He looked between her dimples, that Starrycard sly smirk on his lips. "And I'd like to begin now."

Well, hello! She was not expecting that.

"Nobody could call you a procrastinator."

He shifted his gaze to her eyes, penetrating her every defense. "Your lips reminded me of another bullshit term."

A thrilling pulse of energy made her tremble. She knew what was coming. "And what term is that?"

"Kissability." He leaned in and caressed her cheek. "The term is bullshit, but it doesn't negate the fact that your highly kissable lips are suitable for, or conducive to, consensual kissing. And I really want to kiss you," he added, then shifted his gaze upward and frowned. "But . . ."

But?

"What's stopping you?" she whispered against his lips, his scruff tickling her chin. She was so damned ready to forget her worries, quiet the voices in her head, and lose herself in this man.

"The butterflies."

She cocked her head to the side. "The butterflies don't want you to kiss me?"

He pulled back and tipped up her chin. "They're behaving oddly. Do you know what they're doing?"

In all the bullshit love . . . *bullshit*, she'd forgotten why they were there. She observed the swarm. They glided across the purple sky, their starry-like, silver markings dotting the air as the last rays of sunlight melted into the horizon and the full moon took center stage.

It was happening.

A warmth spread through her, tinged with the sadness of saying goodbye. "What you're observing is the starwings' celestial farewell dance. The looping behavior serves to gather them and point them in the right direction," she explained as the multitude of winged creatures moved in a lazy, hypnotic loop.

"They're leaving Starrycard Creek?" Kieran asked, gaze trained toward the heavens.

"Yes, they've decided it's time to move on. Time to go." She recalled the rich cadence of Nana Joan's voice. *Say goodbye, Isabelle. When you wake up, they'll be gone.* "It's why we had to come tonight. I had a hunch since the weather conditions were optimal for a departure."

He flicked his attention toward the ground. "Why aren't the ones near us joining them?"

She eyed the eleven insects, sipping nectar, oblivious to their brothers' and sisters' behavior. She knew the answer. "We're the problem."

"But we're not disturbing them."

"Our scent is distracting them. Scientists have hypothesized this, but there's no conclusive evidence—until now. It appears they're hypersensitive to our pheromones." She glanced around the crater and zeroed in on the hot spring. "Take off your clothes," she said, removing her boots and socks.

"I'm on board with getting naked. But why now?"

She peeled off the rest of her clothing, secured them in her pack, then gestured toward the hot spring. "We have to get into the water. If we stay here, they won't join the swarm." She turned, presented her ass to him, and smacked it. "Come on, Birthday Card, tap into that forty percent and get moving."

She headed for the hot spring, taking a detour to steer clear of the nectaring butterflies clustered on a tuft of wild blueberries nearby. The earthy aroma and alluring mist called to her as she approached the spring and stepped into the watery expanse. The balmy heat seeped into her pores, draining away the pain she'd carried year after year. The wet rock beneath her bare feet served as a spiritual connection to the mountain. She sensed the soul of this place, the heart, the layers of stone that witnessed millions upon billions of years of change, life, and death. Wading further into the waters, she twisted her hair into a bun, listening to the rustle of fabric and the buzz of a zipper as Kieran undressed. She continued, and her muscles relaxed. Wrapped in the hot spring's wet embrace, she closed her eyes. Her chaotic mind calmed, and her body became one with nature.

The water hit past her shoulders when a gentle ripple signaled Kieran's arrival. He stood behind her and drew a line from her earlobe down her neck to her shoulder blade with his fingertips.

"You followed me," she said, smiling, but she didn't turn to face him.

He wrapped his arm around her waist as he'd done when he came up behind her in the gift shop. "How could I not? I'll always be right behind you."

She turned and wrapped her arms around his neck. "The ass?"

The man beamed. "The woman. I'm in the Isabelle Universe."

Sweet Jesus. This bullshit love business had cracked him open. His stoic demeanor and measured control disintegrated as he gazed at her for well over seven seconds.

He shivered. "All right, come on, *little* bloom, let's go deeper."

"*Little?*" she protested. "I'm five seven."

"And I'm six five, and the waters barely pass my waist. The temperature is dropping. I'll freeze my ass off if we stay here. Hold on," he said, gripping the globes of her ass.

She gasped as he whisked her into his embrace and carried her in his strong arms. Wrapping her legs around his abdomen, she took in the scenery as they waded into the depths of the hot spring. The stillness of the night surrounded them, broken only by the trickles of water emptying off the rocks into the basin. Stars twinkled in the clear darkness in the moon's silvery glow. She sighed and inhaled the scent of minerals mingling with the star-blooms and wild blueberries. And the butterflies. A spectacular air show fluttered above them in an enchanting, otherworldly scene.

What a night to be fake loved.

"They're remarkable. The looping. The jagged precision. Have you ever seen this before?" Kieran asked, his whispered words piercing the stretch of silence.

"Only once, when I was a girl, but I wasn't this close, and there weren't this many."

"And it's so quiet," he said, keeping his voice at a whisper.

He wasn't wrong. It was a stunningly large swarm. It was so massive that it was hard to tell the real stars from the patterns on the butterflies' symmetrical wings. "It's meant to be quiet," she explained. "Quiet but momentous. Butterflies aren't noisy like buzzing bees and chirping cicadas. Humans can't hear their sounds, and their wings aren't designed to make noise. Starwings are unique. Their wings are thinner than most butterflies, allowing them to be stealthy as they migrate beneath the cover of night."

Kieran leaned back and wet his head in the heated waters. "How long will they maintain this circling behavior?"

She sighed. "Not long. There's not much data on it, but researchers suggest it could be anywhere from twenty minutes to an hour. They don't want to waste too much energy. They'll need their strength for the journey. But they must make sure they're headed in the right direction. Otherwise, they'll lose their way."

He tightened his embrace. "And they'll stay together?"

She met Kieran's gaze. "They'll depend on each other."

"They're never alone," he pressed.

She smoothed his wet curls. "They wouldn't make it alone."

He held her close and traced little circles on her skin with his thumb. "I want to continue observing them, but I'm finding it difficult."

"Why?"

"Because I only want to observe you. Even in the moonlight— no, especially in the moonlight—your symmetry calls to me. I can't get your face out of my head."

"Then keep looking at me. The butterflies won't mind," she whispered.

The way he watched her eased her soul. He observed her like a work of art.

He saw her.

His torso tensed. His hard muscles, taut and tight, pressed against her breasts and stomach. "But that's not all I want to do."

"Tell me what you want. There's no wrong answer. You can say anything. Let the bullshit love flow."

He pressed his fingertips into her supple ass, leaned in, and hummed a beastly, possessive purr of a sound. "I want to kiss you, Isabelle. I want to kiss you like the sun kisses the peak of Starrycard Mountain at dawn. I want to touch you like the creek caresses each stone, every boulder, and each root of the willow and aspen trees that grow near the rushing waters. I want to make love to you. I want to thrust my cock inside you and know that when you're in my arms, you're mine. *All mine.* I want to leave you so spent the only word you can utter is my name. My name on your perfect lips. Is that explicit enough?"

Holy hell!

"Oh yeah, that works. But it's a tall order, Birthday Card. Do you think you can manage that?"

He pressed his lips to the shell of her ear. "We both know I can."

Damn. A little self-assuredness in the sex department never hurt.

She rocked against him, his cock growing rock-hard between her thighs. "You better get started."

He balanced her body in one hand and slipped the other into her hair, holding her head in place, not allowing her to pull back, pull away, or lessen the intensity of their connection. The fierceness of his desire brought tears to her eyes. They trailed down her cheeks, becoming one with the crystal waters. He kissed her like a drowning man drawing oxygen from her breath. And she wanted him to take it—take everything. Because, while he professed to inhabit the Isabelle Universe, she'd crossed space and time and entered the Kieran Dimension. A place where only this man existed. She reached between them and gripped his hard length. In the steamy, mineral-infused waters, she worked him, stroking him, reveling in his massive cock.

"Bloom, that feels so good," he bit out against her lips.

Bloom.

That nickname would be her downfall—or possibly her redemption?

She didn't have time to mull over the notion.

He teased her entrance with his hand that cupped her ass. She writhed against him and arched her back. "Yes, keep touching me," she rasped on a tight exhale. Edging upward, she rubbed her most sensitive spot against his thick shaft. The gentle ripple of water and their audible breaths created a sultry, sexual soundscape.

"I've never done it in water," she confessed between kisses, her arousal building.

He stilled and studied her. Even in the misty moonlight, it was evident he wasn't judging her, wasn't laughing at her inexperience. He stroked her cheek. "Neither have I."

"Really?"

"I've been with seventeen women in fifteen years. Never in a body of water."

"Do you want to know my number?"

He shook his head. "Fuck no. I shouldn't have shared that data point with you regarding my number. I'm sorry. But none of them matter to me."

"I want to tell you my number. It's two."

"Me and Regis?"

She nodded. Her bottom lip trembled. Kieran leaned in and kissed it—a whisper of a kiss as gentle as a butterfly wing's caress.

"I doubt Regis fed you cake while *mucho-fucking* you into oblivion and supplying you with eight orgasms in one night."

She chuckled. "He did not. Before you, my best sex was with a vibrator that, last I saw, was stuck in a pile of alpaca poop on a Peruvian mountaintop."

He watched her for a beat, a smile cutting through his sexy scruff. "Excellent."

"Not weird?"

"What's weird about me being the best sex of your life?"

"Are you getting cocky, Birthday Card Boyfriend?" she teased.

"You bet that perfect ass of yours I am." He kissed her again, his lips deliciously wet with the earthy spring water. "We'll go slowly," he whispered, his words floating in the mist. "Just remember this. Lock it in your brain. I trust you, Isabelle. I trust you with my home. I trust you with my family. I don't want to hurt you. I never want to hurt you. Every cell in my body wants to protect you. I've wanted this from the moment I saw you in that gift shop."

Her heart could explode at any minute. She'd never felt so cherished, so loved.

The midnight-blue water kissed the top of his shoulders. Droplets trailed down his neck. His dark hair, wet and tousled, glistened, catching the moonlight. His scruff softened the sharp cut of his jawline. And damn, he was beautiful. He'd taken her to the center of the crater lake. They were in deep—far too deep if she were alone. But she wasn't on her own. This man, who spoke with a robotic cadence and drove her mad with his sexy flicker of a grin and dry, cunning remarks, could do whatever he wanted with her. He could exert total control. He had the upper hand when it came to strength and power. Physically, he was a beast. But she'd never felt safer than when she was in his arms. If she were braver or more confident of who the hell she was or what the hell she wanted, she'd tell him this—tell him she absorbed his affection like the starbloom, basking in the moon's silver glow.

She threaded her fingers into the hair at the nape of his neck. "You can't hurt data points. You can't damage loopholes," she said instead, shying away from what her heart wanted her to say.

He studied her. His brow furrowed as if he wanted to call actual bullshit but didn't know how.

She peered at the sky, awash in a swirl of butterflies, the creatures' winking wings glinting like twinkling stars. She returned her attention to Kieran. "Kiss me. Make love to me beneath the butterflies."

His hesitation gave way to desire. He captured her mouth, channeling whatever had left him conflicted into the kiss. The mineral-infused waters mixed with their connection and drowned out her fears. With the butterflies above them and the warm water's embrace, it was as if their bodies agreed to let go of what held them back.

He kept her close, rocking her in a steady rhythmic motion, allowing his cock to rub against her tight bundle of nerves. The warmth of the water and the smooth cadence of his strokes had her teetering on the edge. She moaned, anchoring herself to him, permitting each decadent pass of his hard length to take her higher.

He squeezed her ass and increased the tempo. "Give in to the pleasure, Bloom. Take it. You're right there. Don't hold back. I love watching you come."

Her eyes fluttered open, and she found him drinking her in. The ferocity of his expression and the depth of his desire was her undoing. She parted her lips, gasping and whimpering as sweet release tore through her body. She focused on his face and joined the butterflies, soaring and swooping through a crush of endorphins flooding her system. "Kieran," she whispered. It was all she could say. The one word she could manage.

"I could make you come all day. I need to feel you," he rasped, his resolve shattering. He lifted her, slipped his hard length between her thighs, and worked his massive cock into her slowly. His body trembled. His strong muscles flexed, pressing into her softness.

Driven by desire, she kissed him on his lips, his scruffy cheeks, his chin, his eyes. Everywhere, desperate to maintain each point of contact. He filled her to the hilt and rolled his hips. Moving with marked precision. He concentrated on her face, and she locked on to his gaze, observing him as he studied her. The intimacy of unabashedly watching him had her on the cusp of losing control again. And he knew it. He shifted his hand and pressed his thumb to her most sensitive spot, working her in steady circles.

"So. Fucking. Perfect," he bit out between thrusts as a wolfish grin graced his lips.

The rhythm of their bodies enveloped her. His focus left her spellbound, hovering between relishing the anticipation of her release and yearning for the blast of oblivion.

"Go, take it. I'll be right behind you," he said against her lips.

"You promise?" she asked, a raw vulnerability infused into her words.

He kissed her. "Always."

And again, she was swept away into a swirling abyss, flooded by ripples of pleasure. Locked onto the man providing her mind-altering orgasms, she remained mesmerized by Kieran's laser focus as he let go, spilling into her, pumping and thrusting, their bodies grinding in the heated pool. That moment could have lasted ten seconds or ten thousand years. Their connection propelled her into a serene, secret sanctuary where time and regret didn't exist. But as quickly as she arrived, the facade faded. She blinked as she returned to her body. Resting her chin on his shoulder, she inhaled the fragrant blend of flowers, sex, and desire.

Kieran shifted his hold on her. He glanced up, then checked his watch. "Twenty-nine minutes."

She pulled back. "What's twenty-nine minutes?"

"It's nine thirteen p.m. It's taken twenty-nine minutes from when the butterflies started looping until now."

She peered up at the sky as the swarm migrated from the crater. "I can't believe I didn't think to record that. Thank you."

He stroked her cheek. "You appreciate precise information. I simply noted it. It's nothing."

A blend of gratitude and awe swelled in her chest. Moved by his forthright, unassuming kindness, she couldn't hold back the tears building. They trailed down her cheeks.

Concern creased his brow. "Did I say something that upset you?"

"No, but I must correct you. Tracking the butterflies for me is *not* nothing." She held his face in her hands. "It's kind of everything," she added, her voice cracking.

"Does it make you feel loved?"

"It does." She exhaled a slow breath. She had to take the leap. "Is there a loophole that would allow bullshit love to become the real thing?"

The boyish trace of a smile spread across his face. "One of my grandmother's assumptions could answer that for us."

"And what assumption is that?" she asked, another tear trailing down her cheek.

He kissed the salty drop. "When it comes to us, Bloom, I'm starting to believe that anything is possible."

CHAPTER

Eighteen

KIERAN

KIERAN INHALED A TIGHT BREATH. Red-hot desire coursed through his veins as he pistoned his hips and stared at Isabelle's reflection in the bathroom mirror. He pressed his hand against the wall and met the ice-blue gaze that melted his composure. He thrust, moving like a machine as the slap of skin meeting skin peppered the air. Dialing up the intensity, he worked her most sensitive place, reveling in her sweet, wet heat. She tightened around him, arching her back like a cat and taking every inch. A ripple of desire tore through him. Making love to this woman got better with each kiss, each touch, each brush of her skin against his.

He clenched his abdominal muscles, barely able to maintain control. He observed Isabelle. She was close to the edge, teetering on the precipice of release. And it was a damned good thing. He could barely hold back. He focused on her breath, her parted lips, her sexy moans, and her face. *God help him!* That face. Over the last eleven days since they'd found the summit crater, he'd fallen asleep gazing at her and woke to her in his arms. It was like Christmas each day. But now they weren't hidden away at his bungalow or Fiona's cabin. And they didn't have much time. He'd taken a risk bringing her here but couldn't help himself. He had to have her. He drank her in. "Christ, your face is symmetrical even when I fuck you," he growled against the shell of her ear.

She bit her lip, unable to respond. And holy hell, there was nothing better than rendering this symmetrical goddess speechless with his hands and cock.

Isabelle braced herself, gripping the sides of the sink. Her chest heaved, and her dimples winked—the tell, the sign. She writhed against him. Her body tensed. "Kieran," she moaned on a breathy exhale.

"So damned sexy. So beautiful," he bit out. With a primal victory pumping through him, he followed her over the edge, spilling into her and letting go. He soared. He came alive. He didn't think or analyze. He let his body guide him. In this place, with Isabelle, he was a new man. Faking it had become freedom.

She leaned into him and kept her eyes closed. He relaxed and embraced the stillness, coming down from a euphoric high. His pulse evened out as he tightened his hold on her hip, letting her know that he still had her. He wouldn't let her fall. He'd be there, right behind her.

She sighed. "This was not what I expected when you said you had something to show me in the shop. But, oh my God, Birthday Card, you make a tour of Starrycard Creek Paper Company's bathroom a banger of an event."

"It is the Fourth of July—a *banger* of a holiday," he countered.

She chuckled, then hummed a satisfied purr. "It appears I got an early glimpse of fireworks."

He watched her in the mirror. "We aim to please in Starrycard Creek, Colorado."

"You succeeded. You can put that out in the family newsletter. I can picture the headline. *Another Sexual Triumph for Starrycard Creek's Eldest Son*," she announced, giggling.

He took in her sated smile. "Or Isabelle A. Adaire Orgasm Number Thirty-one, A Banging Success."

She tapped the tip of his nose. "You're keeping track of my orgasms? I'm impressed."

He kissed her temple, gently pulling out. "Precision matters."

"Indeed, it does," she replied, then pursed her lips. "And speaking of precision and the importance of keeping track." She'd switched from symmetrical sex goddess to all-business environmentalist mode. An ability he admired and one they shared.

"Yes?" he said, tidying himself and attending to his boxer briefs and pants.

"I need to track down the couple who owns the deli. What's their last name?"

"Brimble."

"Yes, the Brimbles," she replied, smoothing her skirt before carefully removing her paper ring. She handed it to him to hold as she washed her hands.

He eyed the worn item. It wouldn't last much longer. Luckily, he had options.

Isabelle plucked a paper towel from the dispenser and dried her hands. "Ring, please." He slipped it onto her finger. She smiled, admiring his handiwork. "When I presented at the library yesterday, I could tell the Brimbles weren't quite sold on our plan."

He'd noticed their conduct as well. They'd stuck to the back of the room and didn't make eye contact. The behavior could be fear —fear and concern about the future. He'd gleaned this information early on as an attorney. "They'll come around. They've been hit harder than most. The cash award could help them, but we'll make them see that it would only provide a brief respite. Our plan offers life-long growth."

She nodded, employing her mulling-it-over expression as she tapped her fingertips to his chest—another of her thinking habits. "I want to invite them up to Fiona's cabin for a private tour of the crater or a little one-on-one time at the deli if they can't get away for a couple of hours. I know they're busy with this being the town's high season. Don't let me forget."

"It's the least I can do as your counsel on retainer."

She smiled up at him with that dimpled, only-for-him grin. "I'd like to kiss you," she said, resting her hands on his chest. "Or would you like a little more time surveying the expanse of my *mini craters*?"

He raised an eyebrow. "Is that what you're calling your dimples?"

She offered a playful shrug. "Why not? They are a form of a depression."

He cupped her cheek and brushed his thumb over her left dimple. "Were you formed from a volcanic event?"

Her ice-blue eyes sparkled. "It's certainly a possibility. You've seen me when I'm craving sweets. I'm awfully fiery."

"Yes, you are. Fire and ice." He focused on her lips. "And if you're still offering, I'm ready for that kiss."

She pressed onto her tiptoes, wrapped her arms around his neck, and sighed as her lips met his.

And damn, that particular Isabelle sound might be his favorite. As much as he enjoyed making love to her, quietly sharing a kiss fed his soul in a way he'd never expected. Seeking solitude in nature was once the way he recharged. But not anymore. Time with Isabelle accomplished a similar outcome.

He held her close, losing himself to her warmth and jasmine-vanilla scent, then pulled back and wrapped her in his embrace, her head against his chest. Utilizing this move in a prone position was how she'd fallen asleep each night. He'd never thought much of the minutes before he succumbed to sleep. Now, they encapsulated wonder, joy, and keen observation. He'd wait for her to take two slow, steady breaths, then with a whisper of a sigh, her body would relax—and so would he. Completely and utterly at ease, he'd drift off right behind her.

"I like the sound of your heartbeat. It's reassuring and steady," she said, patting his chest.

He rested his chin on the crown of her head and peered at

their reflection in the mirror. Gratitude built inside him like Starrycard Creek swelling after a summer storm.

"I like the sound of us," he replied, watching her, recharging, drawing energy from her presence.

The past eleven days had been one hell of a whirlwind, and he needed this quiet moment with Isabelle like he required oxygen to breathe. They'd divided their time between the mountain and the valley. They worked from sunup to sundown—and well into the night. Isabelle collected data, surveyed the land the charter had opened, and documented the crater while he concentrated on the legal issues and updated the development plan with the engineers. He'd wanted to keep the summit crater a secret, but Isabelle had disagreed and pressed to give guided tours to Starrycard Creek's residents.

It appeared to be the right call.

No longer dubbed Starrycard Creek's *bringer of doom*, she'd won over many townspeople with her knowledge of the land and love of nature. But she didn't stop there. She'd asked him to set up meetings with the merchants and townspeople. Together, they'd held butterfly education events at the rec center and the library. They attended the seniors' breakfast hour at Goldie's restaurant to chat one-on-one with the town's longest-living residents. They stopped by Starrycard Creek Elementary to do a presentation with Hailey's summer enrichment students to engage with the younger generation. They went from business to business and house to house, sharing information and pitching a plan—their plan—that would allow for economic growth and protect the butterflies.

His grandfather had called Isabelle a force of nature after he'd listened to her speak at the seniors' breakfast.

The man was right.

Kieran sharpened his gaze, drinking in every detail of Isabelle's reflection—the same view he'd had the first time he saw her. Her golden hair. Her narrow shoulder blades. The curve of her ass beneath a skirt. She was a fierce force of nature—a force he wanted to keep close and to remain his.

His.

It was possible. With Isabelle, anything seemed possible.

She sighed, another sexy purr of a sound.

"You know what it does to me when you do that," he said, twisting a lock of her hair.

She looked up at him. "Something that has to do with *mucho-fucking*?"

He gripped her hips, then lifted her, resting her ass on the edge of the sink. "Everything that has to do with *mucho-fucking* and *mucho-kissing* and *mucho-touching*." He leaned in, so damned ready to kiss her into oblivion, when a door slammed.

"Kieran? Izzy? Are you guys in here?"

Isabelle gasped. "It's Hailey," she whispered, wide-eyed. "She can't find us like this, Birthday Card. She knows about our night at The Pike, but I told her we were keeping it professional while I'm the land steward. She'll know I lied if she finds us hiding in a tiny bathroom."

He nodded. Her assessment was correct.

Finn and Hailey had returned last week in time for his soon-to-be sister-in-law to teach the summer elementary enrichment session. And in time for McKenzie to share the brain-banging comments and accompanying video with them. And while he and Isabelle didn't want to lie, they needed to prioritize the appearance of an all-work relationship—even with those closest to them.

At least, that was the plan for now.

He eyed the paper ring on her left hand and kept his expression neutral.

"What should we do?" she whispered.

"We'll wait until she leaves and exit quietly through the back."

"Are you here? The kids are asking for you, Izzy," Hailey called. "Twenty kiddos are champing at the bit to finish their butterfly wings with the butterfly lady."

That's what the kids called her. He grinned, picturing her surrounded by the butterflies.

"This is a no-smiling zone. We're mucho fucked!" Isabelle

whisper-shouted, then pointed at the tiny rectangular window near the ceiling, barely the size of a bread box. "Do you think I could fit through it?"

"The last thing we need is you getting stuck in a window. That would only draw more attention and signal we'd engaged in untoward behavior in the bathroom."

"*Untoward?* You're talking like we're in a nineteenth-century Regency romance."

She'd become anxious. He needed to respond in a way that would help her relax.

"Do you feel the urge to curtsy, or does that require the presence of an alpaca?" He kept his expression neutral—the way she liked it when he dropped a salty line.

Her eyes glinted with mischief.

Mission accomplished.

She edged off the counter, extended her arms, bowed her head, and lowered into a deep, ballerina-esque curtsy.

This woman.

He observed her movement, and then it hit. "That's it. That's the answer."

"I was being silly, Birthday Card. I don't think we can curtsy our way out of here. Tossing me out the window would be less conspicuous."

"No, when you completed the curtsy, you pointed to the answer."

She scanned the bathroom. "I did?"

He eyed the tap, then *tapped* the tip of her nose—a gesture she employed when she'd wanted to make a point. Now, it was his turn to copy the playful action. "I'll handle it. I'm about to bullshit our way out of this bathroom without Hailey catching on to your thirty-first orgasm. And a quick note."

Isabelle threw a nervous glance toward the door. "It better be fast, Birthday Card. I hear footsteps."

"While you were talking about the butterflies with the knitting club earlier today, I won a round of the Fourth of July Cake Walk."

"You won a cake? In a game reserved for children?" she asked, the twinkle returning to her gaze.

"Yes. A lemon blueberry cake is waiting for us on the winner's table. This evening, I plan on integrating cake consumption with orgasm number thirty-two and thirty-three."

She drew her fingertips down his jawline. "When you talk like that, you make me want to unzip your pants, drop to my knees, and—"

"Isabelle Ashbourne-Adaire, where are you?" Hailey called.

Isabelle inhaled a tight breath.

He searched her expression. "What is it? We knew she was coming."

Isabelle grimaced. "Hailey's in teacher mode. She used the full-name treatment. She's not leaving."

"Kier? Where are you guys? We saw you two enter but not exit," Finn called.

"Hailey's not alone," Izzy said and chewed her lip. "Your brother is with them. We're screwed. They'll figure out what we're doing. Are you sure you've got a plan?"

He tipped up her chin and kissed the corner of her mouth. "I'm the motherfucking town manager. I always have a plan. *Watch and learn.*" With his shoulders back and riding his watch-and-learn high, he swung open the bathroom door, channeling McKenzie when she projected confidence before recording a tumbling maneuver.

"Holy shit!" Finn belted, jumping out of the way.

Hailey gasped. Her auburn ponytail swished as she collided with Finn.

For a beat, no one said a word. The couples stared at each other until Finn's lips twisted into a shit-eating grin.

Kieran steadied himself. *Best to move on and stick to the plan.* He cleared his throat and turned to Isabelle. "Sometimes, the hot water knob sticks, Ms. Adaire. I'm glad I could assist you in your hand-washing endeavor."

Isabelle stared at him for well over seven seconds. *What was she doing?* "Yes," she stammered as if her brain needed to reboot. "I had to . . . pee, and then wash my hands, as one does in a bathroom."

Hailey glanced past them into the snug restroom. "You pee with the seat up now, Iz? Bold move," she chimed and shared a look with Finn.

Not a good sign. When people shared a look, it often meant they were confirming a hunch—especially Starrycards and, in Hailey's case, an almost-Starrycard.

How would Isabelle respond? He had a *hunch.*

"Yep, seat-up peeing is my thing now, Hails. I like to live on the wild side," the sharp-witted land steward replied coolly and lifted her chin with that air of defiance that got his pulse pumping.

Bravo for owning it, Bloom.

"We need to go," Hailey said, gesturing toward the exit. "The kids are waiting for you in the town square. They want to finish their butterfly wings before the fireworks start."

"Right, right. I've had so much going on that I'd forgotten we were supposed to work on them during the celebration." She moved past him. He hooked his little finger with hers—a barely there touch meant only for them. She looked over her shoulder. "Thanks again for the assistance, Town Manager. You're coming, aren't you?"

"I'll always be right behind you." He glanced at Finn. "Pardon, I mean, my brother and I will be right behind you and Hailey."

"We'll see you guys out there," Hailey said, hooking her arm with Isabelle's, propelling his bloom forward, and breaking the hidden pinky-finger hold.

He listened to their footsteps disappear as the women left through the back exit near the creek.

Finn crossed his arms and resurrected his self-assured grin. "I fixed the faucet before Hailey and I went on vacation."

Kieran switched off the restroom light. "Did you?"

"Yes, but I'll take a look at it in the morning. Maybe something is sticking. It was a good thing you were here to help Izzy," his brother added in a tone that signaled he was calling bullshit.

No need to worry. This was Finn's way.

"I agree," Kieran replied, voice neutral as the men walked through the paper company's cavernous back room toward the exit. It was best to ignore his brother's verbal insinuation. Finn— and the rest of his family, for that matter—surely suspected he and Isabelle were more than colleagues. Now, however, wasn't the time to confirm their suspicions.

Finn opened the back door, letting in a rush of fresh air and the creek's babbling song. "Izzy's great, Kier," his brother said, employing their mother's kill-them-with-kindness conduct.

"She's a gifted environmental scientist."

Finn watched him. "Hailey loves having her here, but we've barely seen you guys since we returned."

Oh, Finnegan. Now, the man was poking around for information, like Goldie, spinning a web.

Luckily, he was ready to deflect. He'd counter Finn's statements with irrefutable facts. "You and your fiancée have been home for six days. And from the moment you returned to town, Hailey's been busy with her summer enrichment class, and you've got your hands full at the paper shop. Under those circumstances, it's not odd that we haven't seen much of each other."

"True," Finn conceded as the men strolled down the path toward the square as music and children's laughter carried on the breeze.

"Also, Isabelle and I have been busy with the land charter development plan," he added, dropping another irrefutable fact.

Finn chuckled—a devious little sound. "I bet you've been busy, Kier."

"We're working, Finnegan. We're committed to our positions and professions," he replied, implementing the stern edge he'd utilized when he was twelve and tasked with watching his siblings.

Finn raised his hands defensively. "I get it. And I'll be the first to admit nobody works harder than you—and Izzy, apparently. Hailey says she's always been a workaholic. But you two are together twenty-four seven. I know a little bit about spending all your time with a Starrycard Creek newcomer. I'm engaged to my former roommate. And Izzy seems to like that paper ring you made for her."

Kieran slipped his hand inside his pocket and smiled. "I see what you're doing, little brother. But a paper ring isn't an engagement ring."

"It's still a ring made from Starrycard Creek paper," Finn countered, shit-eating grin in place.

"Again, I can assure you that Isabelle and I maintain a professional working relationship." That wasn't a lie. They also had a hot-as-hell sexual relationship that had him sneaking her into his family's paper company to engage in carnal activities, but he'd leave out that part.

"I'm just saying," Finn replied, "there's something to the whole 'love is in the cards in Starrycard Creek.' Look at me and Hailey." His brother's cocky expression gave way to a wide grin—a grin like when he was a boy, and he'd figured out how something went together.

Kieran patted his younger brother's shoulder, employing a bonding movement. "And I'm delighted for you, Finnegan. Hailey is a wonderful person."

"You and Izzy seemed to have clicked," Finn added as they rounded the bend, and the town square came into view.

"She's . . ." He trailed off. Isabelle was his universe, but he couldn't say that. "She's a skilled environmental scientist."

Again, not a lie.

Isabelle went above and beyond what the charter required.

He could feel Finn's eyes on him, but he ignored his brother's attention and took in the scene. Downtown Starrycard Creek was teeming with tourists and residents. Along the creek trail, barefoot children and their parents dipped their toes into the crystal waters while, at the wishing wall, a young couple shared a silent moment, tucking their dreams into a vacant crack. Their small slips of paper joined the rocky bouquet of hope and wishes wedged within the old stone wall. Along Main Street, flags fluttered in a mosaic of red, white, and blue as the aroma of hot dogs, hamburgers, cotton candy, and fresh-cut pie filled the air. He gazed at the sky. The light wouldn't last much longer. The sun hung low above Starrycard Mountain. Elongated shadows crept over the ground, and a brisk chill wove through the summer air. He checked his watch. Darkness would fall in a little less than an hour, and fireworks would illuminate the starry sky.

He exhaled. Contented breath. Damn, he hadn't felt this connected to the pulse of his hometown in years.

He scanned the square and zeroed in on his favorite Starrycard Creek newcomer. Isabelle stood a few feet from a trio of tables in the far corner space with two dozen children around her. They listened as she spoke. It didn't matter that he couldn't hear her over the music and the buzz of conversation. He'd observed her tell the story of the looping starwing butterflies twenty-two times over the last eleven days. She raised her arms and waved them in a slow, graceful arc. The children joined her, some circling her, acting out the insects' celestial dance. Soon, every child orbited Isabelle. She laughed and completed a few loops with her pint-sized companions before leading them to the painting table to finish their paper wings project. She stilled. *Could she feel him watching her?* Slowly, she turned her head, peered across the square, and caught his eye. Her expression softened, her cheeks growing pink as she smiled the dimpled smile only for him. *This is where she belonged.* And now he was the one who couldn't avert his gaze after seven seconds.

"Say cheese, Uncle Kier!"

He nearly jumped out of his skin at his niece's boisterous greeting. He turned to find Christian with McKenzie on his shoulders. The kid had Goldie's cell phone in her hand. Had she superglued it in place? He waved to the child and noticed his grandfather ambling alongside them.

"You've gotta say it," McKenzie chided.

Kieran shared a look with Finn.

"Kenz is more like Liza every day," Finnegan said under his breath, a sly grin in place.

"Then we know it's best to do as she asks," he answered, then joined his brother in calling out *cheese.*

McKenzie snapped a photo, then turned the camera toward the crowd and recorded the festivities.

"Kenz, you shouldn't take videos of people without their knowledge," Finn said, eyeing the cell phone.

"I'm not doing anything bad, Uncle Finn. I'm recording the food trucks and tables with sweets so I can remember what I want to eat, and I'm recording the yellow birds in that tree over there and a turtle by the creek, but I don't want to eat them."

This kid.

"Actually, Finn, she can take as many recordings as she likes. We're in public," Kieran countered. "In the state of Colorado, there are no stringent limitations. It's also one-party consent for audio recordings, but you can't use it for commercial purposes."

"I'm not making a commercial. I'm making bird videos. I made one by the creek. I'll show it to you after I finish my butterfly wings. Where's the painting station?"

"At the tables across the square," Finn answered.

"Do you see them, Kenz? Izzy is with Hailey," Kieran added, pointing toward the women and children.

"Hold me up higher, Uncle Chris," McKenzie chimed.

Christian hoisted the girl off his shoulders. He held her above his head, then inhaled a tight breath and flinched.

Christian's shoulder was still giving him trouble, and he was trying to hide it.

"I got her, Chris," Kieran said, gripping his niece's hips and taking over uncle duty.

McKenzie giggled as he lifted her a few inches higher. "Do you see them?"

"I do. I know which direction to go. Put me down, Uncle Kier, so I can migrate like a starwing butterfly."

He set the child on the ground. "Have a safe migration."

McKenzie peered up at him. "I won't lose my way, and it's not *Hailey*. When she's teaching kids, she's Miss Higgins, right, Uncle Finn?"

"It'll be Higgins-Starrycard in December. But yeah, you're right, Kenz. It's Miss Higgins, but I don't think she'd mind if you called her Aunt Hailey. It is the Fourth of July—an official holiday."

McKenzie tapped the cell phone to her chin. "I'll call her Almost-Aunt Hailey today."

Finn tugged on the tail of the girl's braid. "That works. You better get migrating."

"Bye, Great-Grandpa Rex. Bye, Uncle Chris. I'll take a painting video next," McKenzie called, then zigzagged through the crowd toward the cluster of children.

"You guys set a date for the wedding?" Christian asked, turning to Finn.

"I talked up how magical Christmas is in Starrycard Creek, and we decided it would be the perfect time to get married. Plus, Caroline said she'd be back for the holidays, and it's your off-season, Chris. I can't imagine a better time to make Hailey my wife. This place sure knows how to do the holidays," Finn finished, gesturing to the Fourth of July splendor.

"I couldn't agree more. Have you told your grandmother?" Rex asked.

"Not yet. We haven't officially announced a date. But we plan on telling everyone soon," Finn replied as his cell pinged. He pulled it from his pocket and chuckled.

Kieran glanced at the screen. "Why would Hailey send you an axe emoji?"

Finn's grin widened. "She needs my help. I volunteered to be on kid clean-up duty at the paint station. I better head over."

"Me too," Christian said. "I told Liza and Jack I'd watch Kenz so they could help out with the cake table."

"How's the shoulder, Chris?" Kieran asked.

His baseball-star brother mustered a smile that didn't reach his eyes. "Couldn't be better."

Kieran nodded to the man, but before Chris could leave, Rex waved him in.

"Hey, Slugger, you can leave what's in your back pocket with your old grandpa."

"Go easy, Grandpa Rex," Christian replied, handing over a slim flask. "That's Delilah's special blend."

"Will do, kiddo," the man replied, unscrewed the top and took a swig.

Kieran sniffed the air and eyed his grandfather. "Are you drinking Stumble Juice?"

"Christian had some going at the ranch. Seems he's been dabbling in the recipe since you and Izzy *stumbled* upon the crater."

That was nearly two weeks ago.

"Chris has been up at his ranch? How long has he been in town?" Kieran pressed.

The old man took another sip. "Not sure. He's been coming and going a lot more than usual, though. He got his private heli- copter pilot license this past year, and the owner of the Rattlers has been allowing him to use the team's helicopter."

"But it's baseball season. He's never in Starrycard Creek this time of year—even if he can fly down in half an hour."

"Maybe he needs a little bit of home. Take a swig, Kier. We'll worry about what's going on with Chris another day."

Kieran sniffed the bottle, winced, then swallowed the burning liquid. "No wonder they called it Stumble Juice. This'll have you on your ass after a few sips. Those prohibition days must have been something around here."

"This town has quite a history," his grandfather said. His expression softened—or it was the alcohol kicking in.

Kieran eyed the painting area. "It's a special place."

"It's great to see it like this, isn't it? Humming with activity. Alive with joy. The beauty of the creek and mountain," the man gushed.

"It is, Grandpa."

"I can only imagine what our Starrycard ancestors would think if they could see us today," Rex continued, then chuckled.

"What is it?"

"Let's be honest. Delilah would have probably been too drunk to voice her opinion, but I'm sure her spirit is pleased knowing Isabelle found the buried crate that led you to the summit crater."

"Why do you think she hid that journal?"

"I've thought about that. The only conclusion I can come up with is that she wasn't ready to share the data or reveal the crater."

"Perhaps. Still, it's quite a find," Kieran replied.

"I'd say the same thing about our temporary land steward. She's *quite a find*. So sad what happened to Joanie and Jimmy, and her parents, too," Rex murmured and took another pull off the flask.

Joanie and Jimmy?

Kieran eyed the man. "Grandpa," he began, prepared to press for information when movement flickered in his peripheral vision. He concentrated on a group of tourists and glimpsed the side of a woman before she disappeared into the crowd. *What the hell?* He scanned the area.

"Did you see someone you know, Kier?"

"I thought so, but I must have been mistaken," he replied as ice crackled in his veins.

"Kieran, there you are," came a man's voice.

He looked in the other direction as Nelson, Amina, and their two young boys walked toward them.

"It's nice to see you," Kieran said, greeting his friends and shaking off the foreboding feeling. "Grandpa, may I introduce—"

"Introductions aren't needed," Rex said, waving him off. "I

remember your friends from your law school graduation. Nelson and Amina Abadi, correct?"

"Yes. That's quite a memory, Mr. Starrycard," Nelson replied.

"It's just Rex. And who do we have here?" his grandfather asked, looking between the two boys.

"I'm Jamil, and this is Malik," the older boy answered through a gap-toothed grin. He pulled a baseball card from his pocket. "Is that Christian Starrycard over there?"

"Our boys are big Rocky Mountain City Rattler fans," Nelson explained.

Rex nodded. "It is Christian Starrycard. He's my grandson, and I'm sure he'd be happy to sign your card. He's helping the kids make butterfly wings. You should join them."

"Can we, Mom? Can we, Dad? Can we make wings, too?" the boys crooned.

"If it's not too much trouble," Amina replied.

"None at all," Rex assured her. "I'll walk them over and give you three a chance to catch up," he finished, taking each boy by the hand.

"Abadi!" a man called from a stand selling hot dogs.

"I'll be right back. That's dinner," Nelson said and jogged toward the vendor.

Amina gestured to Rex and her boys. "He's a natural grandpa."

Kieran watched the man introduce the Abadi brothers to Christian. "He had six of us to practice on."

"I can tell," she replied. "And you know what they say about practiced behaviors."

"I feel as if I might understand that sentiment more now than when we last spoke," he confided.

Amina raised an eyebrow. "I see. Have you started working with someone?"

"Yes, and I believe I'm in love with her."

The words just flew out of his mouth.

Amina's jaw dropped.

Should he not have mentioned it?

"Did I say something upsetting? I believe my candor is due to our professional relationship. I hadn't meant to speak those words. I'm a bit out of my depth."

"No, you didn't upset me," Amina replied, reverting to her clinical demeanor. "But you caught me off guard. I meant, are you working with a therapist to build on your communication skills?"

"No, I'm not seeing a therapist. I'm working with the woman who's handing your son a paintbrush," he answered, gesturing across the square to the tables.

Amina peered through the crowd. "The blond woman?"

"Yes."

"And you believe you love her?"

He gazed at Isabelle. "I think I could love her. I might be what she needs."

Amina nodded. "Does she feel the same way?"

"I think so."

"You don't know?" the psychologist pressed.

He maintained a neutral front, but Christ, his heart was about to explode. "We share common interests and enjoy being together."

Could he have read the situation wrong? He was so sure that their bullshit love had the potential to be real love. Had his autism caused him to gloss over important details?

"Communication is extremely important," Amina said gently. "Checking in with your partner and confirming you're on the same page is a good way to do this. These discussions strengthen a relationship—especially new relationships. Is this woman someone you've known for a while?"

"No, we met roughly five minutes after you and Nelson left The Pike. Also, nobody knows we're in a relationship. We're hiding it."

"What?" Amina exclaimed, her jaw nearly hitting the floor.

He'd never seen her like this. "I seem to have shocked you."

"I admit that I am surprised. Minutes before meeting her,

you'd told me you were sure of your decision to remain a bachelor."

"And then I met her. And—"

"Don't these look amazing?" Nelson remarked, cutting short the impromptu therapy session. He glanced at his wife. "Everything okay, Mina?"

"Yes," she said, losing the wide-eyed look.

Nelson chuckled. "I rarely see my wife flabbergasted. You must have dropped a doozy on her. What were you talking about?"

Jamil zipped toward them. "Can we eat the hot dogs at the butterfly painting station?"

Amina took the tray of hot dogs from her husband. "Sounds like a plan. Tell your brother I'll be right over with the food." She met her husband's gaze. "Why don't you two take a minute to say hello. Once the boys are with us, it's much harder to chat."

"Ain't that the truth," Nelson replied, swiping his hot dog from the tray.

"It's good to see you, Kieran. I hope we get to talk again soon. The door's always open," Amina said, then followed her son across the square.

"Everything all right?" Nelson asked, then took a bite of his hot dog.

Was everything all right? Kieran slipped his hand in his pocket. He thought he had everything figured out. Could he be wrong? "I'm fine. How do you like Starrycard Creek?" he asked, putting the conversation with Amina out of his head.

Nelson inhaled and exhaled. "We're loving the mountain air! We got in last night and already want to book another trip here next year. How's the land steward situation? Last we spoke, you were pretty salty about it."

Kieran shifted his stance. "It's going well. She's the butterfly lady. The woman with blond hair next to Malik."

Nelson took a bite and nodded. "It looks like she's really fitting in."

"We have a positive working relationship."

"I told you it could be a good thing, buddy."

"You were correct," Kieran replied, keeping Isabelle in the corner of his eye. She was laughing at something Christian had said. His family had grown fond of her. More evidence she fit in here. He couldn't have gotten that wrong.

"And the land charter?" Nelson continued. "Will you be breaking ground soon?"

"That's a trickier situation."

"How so?" the man asked, finishing his hot dog.

"Another developer is vying to build on the land. There are two development plans."

"And the town votes on the one they want?"

"Correct."

"Be careful and do your homework. There are some unscrupulous builders out there. My firm is representing the Redstone Ridge community in Wyoming. They're seeking damages after they were given the bait and switch. They partnered with a developer to expand their winter sports complex. Instead, the company stripped the land's resources, then disappeared. The problem is, the town agreed to it. The contract is comprehensive, almost predatory."

Kieran knew this scenario all too well. "We fear our situation may be similar."

"Tread carefully, man. My firm is in contact with the FBI, the Environmental Protection Agency, the Federal Trade Commission, and the Securities and Exchange Commission. This developer owns a tangled web of companies. He's on their radar, but nobody's got enough evidence to charge him."

"I also have a client who was the victim of an unscrupulous builder. I'm reviewing the contract."

Could Nelson's client be one of Greenstone's victims?

"Does it have an NDA? These guys seem to love slapping those on unsuspecting clients," Nelson continued.

"It does," Kieran answered, noting the similarity.

Nelson sighed. "It gets sticky with those. We're looking for a Hail Mary. Honestly, we need rock-solid evidence of gross negligence. I've cautioned my clients to prepare for the worst."

"I'm in a similar situation with my client," Kieran answered, keeping Isabelle in his peripheral vision.

"Dad, Mr. Starrycard, they sent me over to get you," Malik called, charging through the crowd and taking his father's hand.

Kieran followed a step behind the father and son. Again, he caught a glimpse of a woman in the crowd and the foreboding feeling returned. He tugged at his collar. A cold sweat broke out on his skin. And it had gotten loud—so fucking loud. Snippets of disjointed comments had him clenching his jaw.

"What do you think, Uncle Kier?" McKenzie asked, coming to his side.

He focused on the child, trying to ignore the grating sensations.

She flitted around him, wearing a pair of paper wings. "Do you like them?"

He manufactured a grin, but he couldn't shake the prickle of irritation. "You could migrate with the starwing butterflies," he said, trying to place the woman.

"I painted the wings like the one in my drawing," she said, pulling her picture from her pocket.

"You did," he replied, admiring the picture as the prickling amplified, and he recalled the moment Isabelle entered the hearing. She'd knelt to retrieve the drawing and returned it to his niece. He'd nearly fallen over from shock when she'd burst into the room. His pulse slowed. *Focus on Isabelle. Forget about the mystery woman.*

"Hey, do you have a second?" Isabelle asked, coming to his side.

She was the answer to his prayers.

"I do. For you, I always do."

She glanced at McKenzie and plastered a grin on her lips. But this wasn't a contented expression. This smile had a tightness to it.

Something had happened.

"Let's take a picture first," McKenzie said, holding Goldie's phone for a selfie.

He and Isabelle leaned forward to get in the shot. He studied her face on the screen. The set of her jaw told him she was worried.

"Just one picture, Kenz. I need to speak with Isabelle about a work issue."

"Okay, Uncle Kier," the child replied and snapped the photo.

"McKenzie," Isabelle said, fake smile in place, "can you tell Hailey I need to talk to your uncle for a second?"

"Sure thing, butterfly lady," his niece replied, then skipped to the painting table.

"Is there a problem with the project?" he pressed. He surveyed the tables. The kids appeared joyful and at ease.

"No, the children are great," she said, walking toward the center of the square.

He followed.

She stopped near a cotton candy vendor and gestured toward a group of adults. "Something is going on with the Brimbles and several of the shopkeepers. Do you know who they're talking to? It's some woman with a bunch of papers. They look like zoning and building plans. And I might be wrong, but I feel like I've seen her before."

Kieran zeroed in on the woman—a brunette.

The brunette.

The foreboding chill morphed into an ice storm. Instantly, he recalled Regis's cat-who-ate-the-canary demeanor the day the dirtbag developer sauntered into the hearing room and threw a wrench into the town's plans. Now he understood why the man had a slimy smirk fixed to his lips that day. He had information— compromising information.

"Do you recognize that woman, Kieran?" Isabelle pressed.

Oh, yes, he did. And Christ, he was a fool, and the town was fucked. *Mucho fucked.*

CHAPTER

Nineteen

IZZY

IZZY TAPPED KIERAN'S ARM. *What was going on with the man? He looked like he'd seen a ghost.* "Hey, Birthday Card? Did you hear me? Do you know what the brunette woman is doing here?"

The brunette must have sensed the attention. The woman looked up from her papers and . . . winked.

What the hell?

"Kieran, did you see that? She winked at us. I need you to talk to me. I'm getting a bad feeling about her." She stared at him as that telltale muscle on his jaw twitched.

"I'm sure he heard you, Iz. And I'm damned sure he recognizes the woman, don't you, Mr. Starrycard?"

Izzy's stomach dropped. She'd know that slippery, smarmy voice anywhere. "Regis?" she exclaimed. "What are you doing here?" Wearing boots—the same boots that had never touched a trail—and high-end outdoor clothing, her asshole ex smirked as he held a billowy pink cotton candy wand. The conman developer plucked a strip of sugary fluff from the candy cloud and popped it into his mouth. She glanced at Kieran. The man had turned to stone, his expression unreadable.

"Why don't you tell Izzy who the pretty brunette is, Mr. Starrycard," Regis crooned, chomping on the treat like a horse tucking into a bag of oats.

"Do you know her, Kieran?" she asked, searching his face.

"She's the woman from the bar at The Pike," he said robotically.

Izzy narrowed her gaze. Yes, that was her—the woman Kieran had been eyeing.

"Great memory. I hope you don't mind that we didn't introduce ourselves that night at the hotel. Then again, we knew who you were, but you certainly didn't know us . . . yet," Regis said, eyes glinting with greed.

What the hell did that mean?

Izzy rubbed the back of her neck as the world went topsyturvy. "You were at The Pike? You and that woman know each other?"

"Yes, we were, and yes, we know each other quite well," Regis replied, his slimy smirk still in place.

She wanted to press for details, but her mouth went dry, and her pulse spiked—her body preparing for the worst.

"It was such an opportunity to observe you, Mr. Starrycard," Regis mused and popped another bite of cotton candy into his mouth. "We didn't expect to see you at The Pike. Of course, when we caught a glimpse of you, we knew exactly who you were. We'd researched Starrycard Creek and all the Starrycards. You people certainly stand out in a crowd. It seemed you were on the hunt that night. I can't blame you for ogling Jennifer. My *fiancée* is a beautiful woman."

"She's your fiancée?" Izzy stammered, then looked to Kieran for something, anything, but the man simply glared at Regis. Still, she knew better. A storm brewed beneath the surface of her birthday card boyfriend's eerily serene demeanor.

Regis plucked a tuft of cotton candy from the puffy, pink cloud. "We thought we'd have some fun with you, Kieran. You made it even easier when you started playing peek-a-boo with my girl."

Izzy bit the inside of her cheek, needing the pain to keep her from passing out. *What had Regis seen? How much did he know?*

"And then, to my surprise," Regis continued, zeroing in on her, "little Izzy Adaire showed up. Quite a twist of fate. And it got better. A buddy of mine in the State's Environmental Division tipped me off that Isabelle A. Adaire had been made Starrycard Creek's temporary land steward. I got the text while Mr. Stone-faced here was defending little Izzy Adaire's honor and threatening to break some poor drunk's wrists."

"Stop calling me that," she bit out, hating the shake—the weakness—in her voice.

"But my, my, my," Regis crooned, turning his attention to Kieran, "I had no idea I'd get to observe the two of you *together*. It was riveting to watch you romp around like a pair of carefree teenagers in love." He dropped his half-eaten cotton candy on the ground and pulled his phone from his pocket.

"You're littering," she bit out as she plucked the sticky treat from the ground and tossed it into a trash bin.

"Who the fuck cares, Iz? This place will be mine soon enough." He scrolled through a few shots on his phone. "Ah, here we go. You're an attorney, Mr. Starrycard. Let's call these exhibits A, B, and C. And let me tell you, there's nothing like videos."

Oh God!

The first video showed them in the gift shop. Kieran's arm was around her waist as he berated the drunk.

"Quite a temper, Mr. Starrycard. And next," Regis noted with the mock sincerity of a game show host.

"That's us at the cake tasting," Isabelle stammered, her voice barely a whisper as the grainy video showed his hand beneath her skirt.

"The crazy thing is, Jennifer and I were supposed to be there. It was a sold-out event. You must have taken our spot."

A knot twisted in her belly at the thought of these two following them, recording them.

Regis glanced from side to side. "And this one is not for the kiddies to see. And granted, it's not easy to make out your faces, but I'd be willing to bet Ashbourne Development that's the two of you getting down and dirty against the window."

Isabelle gasped. "Is there no low you'll sink to? You can't do this. You can't record us."

Regis chuckled an evil, maniacal bark of laughter. "Tell her, Mr. Small-Town Attorney."

The muscle on Kieran's jaw twitched. "In the state of Colorado, he can."

"In the hotel room?" she whispered as she blinked back tears.

"We were near the window. They were on the hotel grounds, not trespassing, as they were guests," he answered, his voice void of emotion.

Regis pocketed his phone. "Gotta love the lawyers. I'm always amazed people don't close the curtains in hotel rooms. But you guys were something. What a show!"

"What the hell are you doing here, Greenstone? The hearing isn't for another week," Kieran growled.

"I told you I wanted to return with my fiancée. She's interested in geology. Her family owns a lucrative copper mining business."

"Copper?" Isabelle repeated, her voice shaking. Dammit, she couldn't help it.

Regis's slippery smile widened. "Looks like Little Miss Butterfly put it together. Jennifer and I know about the treks to the crater and tours with the temporary land steward. Residents posted their pictures online. God bless the internet. Jen noticed the malachite. It looks like boring fucking rocks to me, but she saw dollar signs. That's how I knew she was the one."

"What did you put together? What are the green streaks?" Kieran asked.

Izzy swallowed past the lump in her throat. "This land is rich in malachite—a copper carbonite. It's the green veins in the rock. It's all over the summit crater and the mountain. It often indicates the presence of copper ore. They want to mine Starrycard Mountain and strip its resources."

"Strip its resources?" Kieran repeated, wide-eyed.

Speechless, she held his gaze and nodded.

"Sorry to break up your staring game, but I have a feeling you guys will want to hear this. Jennifer's doing a little meet and greet with a few of your merchants since we're here for the festivities. And Iz, you'll want to keep that pretty little mouth shut, or I'll slap you with another lawsuit." Regis walked to the group and wrapped his arm around Jennifer's shoulders. "Did you tell them about the increased incentive, Jen?"

Izzy edged toward the group with Kieran by her side. Each step felt like her legs were turning into lead pillars.

"We'd like to offer twenty thousand dollars to our partners," Jennifer quipped, her voice saccharine sweet.

The shop owners clapped as hopeful grins graced their lips.

"He's a monster," Izzy whispered, twisting the paper ring on her finger as if she were trying to draw strength from the worn fibers.

Regis feigned concern and gazed at his fiancée. "Did you mention the delicate matter to our new friends?"

They must have rehearsed this bit. Izzy scanned the merchants. The shop owners were eating up Regis and Jennifer's act—not suspecting a thing. Prey blindly entering the lion's den.

"I wanted you to break the news, sweetheart," Jennifer answered, batting her eyelashes.

"What news? I hope it's nothing upsetting," Mrs. Brimble asked, her hand pressed to her heart.

"I hate to have to share this, ma'am, but it is upsetting. Still, I can't keep it from you. You deserve to know," Regis replied, fake sincerity etched onto his perfectly tanned face.

"What is it, Mr. Greenstone?" a shop owner pressed.

"There are grave concerns about your land steward and town manager."

Izzy gasped as Regis pointed to them.

"Izzy and Kieran?" Mrs. Brimble remarked with a creased brow.

"It appears they're engaged in a torrid affair—an affair that could cloud their judgment regarding the development of Starrycard Creek," Regis continued, pseudo-sincerity drenching his words.

"What is this? What's going on?" a frowning Maeve Starrycard demanded, joining the group with Hank, Goldie, and Rex. "I'm the mayor. If business is being discussed, it's my job to be a part of the talks."

"This is chat among new friends," Regis answered casually. "I'm introducing them to my fiancée."

"This gal, Jennifer, is with Mr. Greenstone," Debbie Brimble explained. "Instead of ten thousand dollars, they want to give the small business owners twenty thousand dollars to partner with them. And Mr. Greenstone says Kieran and Isabelle are involved with each other and that they might not want to help the town."

"It's inappropriate to make accusations of that nature, especially in this setting. This isn't a public meeting. And you've known Kieran his whole life, Debbie. He's dedicated to Starrycard Creek," Maeve replied, standing her ground.

"No reason to get upset, Madam Mayor," Regis cooed. "As I said before, it's simply a discussion between friends."

"You're not our friend. You're a developer vying to build in Starrycard Creek," Goldie countered.

"Can't we be both, ma'am?" Jennifer replied with a honeyed smirk.

"What about the butterflies? Will you protect them, Mr. Greenstone?" one of the merchants asked.

Izzy braced herself.

Had Regis done his homework since he was last here?

She held her breath as Regis's grin widened. A chill spider-crawled down her spine.

He knew the truth.

"An interesting question. We couldn't find an official sighting report," Regis answered.

"But Kieran and Izzy saw the starwing butterflies in the summit crater," Hank fired back.

"Do they have any evidence? Photographs? *Videos*?" Regis pressed, triumph glittering in his beady gray eyes.

Izzy stepped forward, finding her voice. "We were there. We saw scores of starwings. We witnessed a phenomenon very few people experience."

"And I drew this picture of the starwing butterfly I saw near the waterfall," McKenzie chimed as she held up her drawing. "I showed it to Izzy the day she got here."

Regis gifted McKenzie with a syrupy smile.

He'd figured it out.

"Is that your sighting, Iz? A child's drawing?"

"Isabelle?" Maeve said softly. "There was a reported sighting, wasn't there?"

Izzy parted her lips, but she couldn't utter a word because that's what failure sounded like. That's what losing everything sounded like. Empty, soul-sucking stillness. The sound after she'd had to explain to the Ashbourne employees that she'd sold the company—that she was the reason they'd lost their jobs. She could picture the agony on Pamela's daughter's face.

Starrycard Creek would be no different. Its demise would be her fault. Again, her terrible judgment would bring harm to innocent people. And the Starrycards would never trust her—not after she obliterated their home and their legacy.

"Isabelle and I observed the butterflies, but we don't have any evidence," Kieran supplied robotically. He met her gaze. "It's the truth."

"But . . ." she sputtered.

"So," Regis mused, tapping his chin theatrically, "these good people are supposed to trust you. Maybe you and Isabelle don't want to develop the land. Maybe you've created a story to get what you want." Regis turned to the group. "I did a little digging on the land steward's previous consulting projects, and she's famous for standing in the way of communities' economic progress. Perhaps she and Kieran aren't concerned about the hardworking men and women whose last name *isn't* Starrycard."

"That is a lie," Maeve countered. "Every Starrycard, from William on down, cares deeply for every resident, every business, and every person who honors us with their presence. And I can tell you, my son and our land steward want what's best for this town."

"My fiancé is simply stating facts and raising plausible questions," Jennifer purred.

"Kieran," Mrs. Brimble pressed. "Are you and Isabelle having an affair?"

"That's not our business, Debbie," Maeve chided.

"But Isabelle could be clouding Kieran's judgment," Mrs. Brimble continued. "Doesn't that concern you, Maeve? Isabelle called us—the residents of Starrycard Creek—people who wanted profit over protecting the environment. I thought she'd had a change of heart and was open to building on the mountain, but now, I'm not so sure. And these people, the Ashbourne Development people, want to give us twenty thousand dollars to partner with them to make . . ." She trailed off. "What did you say, dear?" she asked, looking to Jennifer.

"To make Starrycard Creek fulfill its *true potential*," the smirking brunette supplied.

"How dare you insinuate that my family doesn't have the best intentions for our town," Maeve began as the roar of overlapping voices pierced the air.

Chaos took hold of the group. The Starrycards tried to reassure merchants as Jennifer played the innocent, shoving a wedge between the townspeople and the founding family.

Izzy took a few steps back, struggling to breathe.

"Bloom, do you need to sit?" Kieran asked, lowering his voice.

But she couldn't sit. She couldn't collapse. She had to fight—but how?

Regis sauntered away from the verbal sparring sessions and headed toward her. He glanced at the commotion. "This is your fault, Iz. It makes it even more fun to know that I get to put you in your place again. Isabelle Ashbourne-Adaire, the little butterfly princess, the hope for her family's lofty environmental dreams . . . *fails again*. It's too bad my grandpa isn't around. He would have been so proud of me."

"Your grandpa?" she echoed. *What the hell was he talking about?*

"He was an attorney. Years ago, an environmental know-it-all who he was supposed to assist in selling Wilcox Construction ruined his practice after it got out that he'd bad-mouthed her as a client. The Arizona State Board censured him."

"Your grandfather was my nana's attorney?" Izzy said, disbelief coating the words.

His gray gaze hardened. "I told you my family was from Arizona the night we met."

"But he did bad-mouth her," she countered. "He didn't represent her honestly. My nana and grandfather were right to call him out."

Regis scoffed. "You environmental types and your talk of *honesty* and *integrity*. Money and power make the world go round. My grandfather's the one who taught me to play dirty to get what I want. The first time I fucked you over was fun, Iz, but watching you squirm for a second time is the cherry on top of the sundae— or, in your case, a starwing butterfly perched on a starbloom."

"You're doing this to me because you want revenge on my family?" she whispered, her world crumbling.

"You bet your ass it's because of who you are. Jen and I weren't sure we wanted to bother with Starrycard Creek. It's small potatoes for us. But getting to take you down again was too sweet an opportunity to let slip away."

"You're despicable."

He flashed a smug, smarmy grin. "It's just business, baby."

That line. That treacherous, sleazy line.

Regis leaned in and lowered his voice. "Or should I substitute *poor little orphan Izzy* for *baby*? Or what about the sad girl with nobody—no mommy, no daddy, no rich tree-hugging grandparents?" He gasped. "I've got another one! The once-upon-a-time green-build heiress. It appears all of the above apply."

"That's enough," Kieran snarled, fire blazed in his eyes as the beast of a man took a step toward Regis.

"Look, the brick wall speaks," her ex remarked with a condescending huff.

"I warned you regarding your conduct toward Isabelle during your last visit, Mr. Greenstone," Kieran said, his voice eerily calm. "You will never speak to her again. Never. You're not even going to look at her. Don't even fucking think about her. In fact," he continued, then gently guided her a step away. "I'm going to make sure you can't talk for a good, long while."

"And how will you do that?" Regis shot back and glanced past Kieran's shoulder.

Kieran narrowed his gaze. "In the most direct and efficient way possible."

Izzy looked between the men. Kieran curled his hand into a fist as Jennifer pointed her phone in their direction.

Izzy gasped. "Kieran, no, don't. It's what he wants."

But it was too late. The hulk of a man clocked Regis in the jaw. The pop pierced the air as drops of blood dotted the darkened sidewalk.

"Damn, you're strong. Did you get that, Jen?" Regis eked out, cupping his jaw.

"You bet I did, babe," she answered and waved her cell.

Izzy locked onto Kieran's gaze as the melee of raised voices quieted and whispers carried in the mountain breeze.

"Kieran punched Mr. Greenstone. Can you believe it? So unlike him. Could it be Izzy's influence?"

"Why did you hit that man, Uncle Kier?"

McKenzie.

Izzy wanted to crumble, to cry, to hug her knees to her chest and disappear from the world. His niece witnessed her uncle strike a man—all because of her.

She sipped sharp, audible breaths and surveyed the scene. The sun had set, and twinkling lights illuminated the square. If her world wasn't falling apart, she might have noted how much this place felt like home, how the beauty of the town nestled in the valley called to her. Instead, it had become the location of her worst nightmare. Hailey, Finn, and Christian had joined the group. Cast in the hazy glow, they stood wide-eyed alongside Goldie, Rex, Hank, and Maeve. She scanned the rest of the square. Everyone stood stock-still and stared at her and Kieran as Jennifer fawned over Regis and his bloody lip.

Izzy reached for her locket.

"It's gone, Bloom. Remember, you lost your locket," Kieran whispered.

"I forgot." She peered at the shopkeepers and drank in their horrified expressions. She'd made progress with them this week. She'd been so close to winning them over. She blinked, and her vision grew blurry. She turned to the Starrycards. "I'm sorry. I'm . . ." She had no words. All she could do was run.

Weaving through the holiday crowd, she made her way to the trail by the creek and sprinted past the people, tucking their hopes into the stone wishing wall. Meanwhile, her future in Starrycard Creek with Kieran faded, slipping away, lost like her locket, and her dream of finding a place she could call home.

"Isabelle, Isabelle!" Kieran's voice rose above the pound of their footsteps and the creek's watery song.

His voice was her undoing. The dam of tears broke as she kicked up her pace. How could she look at him? The downfall of Starrycard Creek would be her fault. She felt for the paper ring and gasped. "Where is it?" she exclaimed, skidding to a halt as she scanned the darkened ground.

"It fell off. I've got it," Kieran answered. "Please, don't run away."

Gasping for breath, she held his gaze.

"You know I'll catch you," he said softly.

She wiped away her tears. "What do you want, Kieran?"

"I want to show you what I've got in my pocket."

She strained to see what he had in his hand, then gasped. "Is that a ring?"

He turned his hand so she could get a better look. "No, it's the Peruvian coin you gave me to retain my services. It got me thinking about—"

She cut him off with her laughter—a bitter, scathing sound. "Why would I think it was a ring? Why would I think you—or anyone with a brain—would want to marry me?"

"I can protect you if you're my wife, but that's not the reason I . . . *Dammit!*" he hissed. "This isn't how I wanted to broach the subject. I'd been given some advice about communication and thought . . ." He grimaced like he couldn't access his vocabulary. She'd never heard him so tongue-tied, never seen him so scattered. This is what trusting her did to him.

He held her face in his hands. "We can figure this out. We don't have to be alone. We found each other."

Did he not understand his town was screwed thanks to her?

She pulled away, hating to break the connection while knowing it would be the last time she'd touch him. She harnessed the little strength she had left. "Your town is in real trouble, Kieran. And you and I know I'm the reason it's in danger. You heard it yourself. Regis wants to hurt me. If I go, he might get bored and move on. If I disappear, you'll have a fighting chance to be free of him."

"I don't want you to go. I want you to stay with me. I . . ." He grimaced. "I'm good at bullshit-loving you."

"Then we're lucky—at least on that front," she rasped on the cusp of tears again.

He searched her face. "What is that supposed to mean?"

"We're lucky you only *bullshit-love* me. It'll be easier for you to forget me. It's like we agreed. When it's over, it's over. And there is no doubt that, after tonight, it must be over. It doesn't matter that I . . ."

"Tell me."

"That I'm in love with you," she confessed. What did it matter if she said it? She ran her hands down her face. "Look at that. I broke our verbal contract. No falling in love, and of course, with my superb contract track record, I messed this one up, too. Then again, with our fake-love *Cordis-falsus* loophole, my feelings are just a data point. Congratulations, Birthday Card, you've succeeded. Too bad your data comes from an orphaned, broken, untrustworthy source."

The sky erupted with the crackling *pop, pop, pop* of fireworks, scattering white sparkles above them. She gazed at the display, tears trailing down her cheeks. This is not how she'd pictured her first Fourth of July in Starrycard Creek. She'd envisioned sneaking off with her birthday card boyfriend, nuzzling into his embrace, and dreaming of what could be as sparkling light illuminated his beautiful face.

Stupid girl. Stupid dreams. Jesus, what would her family think of her?

"Isabelle, I don't want it to be over," he whispered. His monotone words were infused with such pain that it took everything she had not to wrap her arms around him and never let go.

She stepped back—putting more space between them. "I'm mucho fucked, Mr. Birthday Card Boyfriend. I'm damaged. An orphan. A walking catastrophe. And it's better for everyone, especially for you and your family, if you forget you ever met me."

"I can fix this, Isabelle."

"No, you can't fix it. Only I can do that." She recalled Elder Pachamama's words. *The lone bearer of burdens shall find their own demise.* Oh, dear wool witch, Isabelle A. Adaire had found her demise. Izzy raked her hands through her hair.

"How do you know I can't fix it? What data tells you that?" Kieran pressed, taking the lawyerly step of using her words against her.

Luckily, she had an answer.

"The data is me. I'm the corrupt data point. Corrupt and . . . untrustworthy. Regis wasn't wrong. I lied about the butterflies. I used McKenzie's picture as evidence. A child's drawing! I'm the one who can't be trusted. I'm the one who ruins everything I touch."

He searched her face. "There's so much I want to say but can't. The words are locked in my head. I . . ."

"It's better that way. You won't say anything you'll regret. I've already said too much."

"I don't regret how I feel about you—how I feel about us."

She wiped the river of tears from her cheeks. "You will. You'll wish you never trusted me. You'll hate yourself for it. You'll hate me. And I'll deserve it. That's why I must do what I should have done the second I realized you were the town manager."

"There's got to be another way," he said, his words flat as if he could read her mind. He could anticipate her thoughts. He'd observed her like he loved everything about her, like he enjoyed cataloging her smiles, her sighs, and the tiny behaviors only he'd notice with his perceptive gaze.

She exhaled a shaky breath, her heart breaking as she brushed her thumb across the naked skin of her ring finger. "I have to leave Starrycard Creek and never come back."

CHAPTER
Twenty
KIERAN

"UNCLE KIER?"

"Yes, Kenz?" he replied. And Christ, it took nearly all his energy to respond with an ounce of enthusiasm. He was a husk of a man. An empty shell.

"It smells weird down here," the child noted.

Kieran nudged a clump of earth with the tip of his hiking boot. "It's a root cellar. It smells like dirt and—"

"Great-Grandpa Rex after Uncle Chris gives him a little silver water bottle of Stumble Juice," the child supplied.

"They used to keep canned food and alcohol here, but that was long ago." He studied the darkened space. "Do you want to head over to the summit crater?"

"No, I like it here." McKenzie removed the lid from the once-hidden crate as dim threads of light seeping in from cracks at the top of the cellar's rock walls lit the silver spots on McKenzie's butterfly wings. The kid had been in butterfly mode since Eliza arrived at his bungalow—unannounced—and dropped off McKenzie, citing the urgent need for a babysitter. Minutes after her mother's departure, his niece begged him to take her to Fiona's cabin.

Had he wanted to go?

Hell no.

But he couldn't say no to the kid. So here they were, smack-dab at the place where Isabelle's face materialized in his mind with every inhale of the jasmine-vanilla air. A face he may never see again because he'd locked up—because his autistic brain had held him hostage and kept him from convincing Isabelle that he loved her and that she should stay. Then again, maybe it was just proof he was incapable of being what she needed.

McKenzie shined the cell's flashlight into the empty cavity. "Is this where you found the journal with the butterfly stuff?"

"It is." He peered into the empty hole. Never had he imagined that he could relate so profoundly to a vacant crate.

Christ, he missed Isabelle.

He slipped his hand into his pocket and brushed his finger-tips against his notebook. It now contained two items. The ripped remains of her paper ring and the pressed flower—the starbloom.

Bloom.

The hollow space in his chest doubled in size. He removed his hand and then checked the time. Seven forty-four p.m.

McKenzie flicked her cell's beam of light his way. "You keep looking at your watch, Uncle Kier."

"Do I?"

"Yeah. You punched that guy, and then Izzy ran away. And now you look at your watch a lot. You looked at it seven times when we were at your house, four times in the car, six times when we were hiking to Fiona's cabin, and five times since we got to the root cellar. What are you doing? Did Izzy text you? Did she tell you she's gonna come back? Is that why you keep looking? I know you're sad she's gone."

"Isabelle had other matters to attend to—out of town," he stammered, unable to come up with anything better.

He checked his watch again. Seven forty-five p.m. He'd been fixated on time, obsessively noting it and calculating how long he'd been without her.

"Now it's six times you checked at Fiona's cabin," the child reported.

He clasped his hands behind his back. "You're observant."

"I'm like you. We're good at noticing stuff."

Hopefully, that's all she had in common with him.

He nodded, unable to smile or frown. His insides churned. His demeanor diminished, growing more vacant, more muted, and more robotic by the second.

Isabelle had been gone for forty-six hours and thirty-one minutes. It was 9:14 p.m. when he'd watched her disappear beneath a cascade of fireworks.

She'd called herself untrustworthy, and he'd left her claim unchallenged.

She'd told him she loved him—*loved him*—and he'd let her go.

Actually, that wasn't an accurate description.

To ensure her safety, he'd followed her down the trail and over the bridge until she'd made it to his bungalow. Not that Star-rycard Creek was a crime haven—far from it. But, like he needed to check the time, he couldn't let her out of his sight. He'd followed her. And she'd let him—or tolerated him. She hadn't acknowledged his presence as he walked thirty feet behind her. Perhaps the firework's booms and crackles had drowned out his steps. Or maybe she hadn't had the energy to tell him to piss off. She could have been in her head—lost in a deluge of tormenting thoughts. More than once, she'd stopped, pausing to breathe, her shoulders rising and falling as she'd steadied herself. Her soft sobs pricked the air between the shower of light from above. Each heartbreaking sniffle and gasp hit like a punch to the gut. Yet he'd remained silent.

He'd watched as she entered his bungalow. He could have gone inside and observed as she packed. He could have used that time to plead with her to stay. But he couldn't order his thoughts, couldn't understand how he'd gone from wanting to marry her to wondering if he'd ever see her again. The sensory tsunami had hit and rendered him useless. It's what he'd always feared. He'd confirmed his inability to respond to the romantic social situation. He was autistic, and that meant he had to live a certain way—a predictable way, a solitary way. He'd proved this with his behavior toward Regis and failure to convince Isabelle to stay.

But she occupied space in his head and his heart like he'd never experienced.

He'd thought that was enough—thought bullshit-loving her would have been enough. Still, despite her admission of love, he couldn't be what she needed. At the moment when he should have opened his heart, he froze. He couldn't do more than stand there as her rental car disappeared down the darkened street.

He'd spent the last couple of days poring over the sales contract for Ashbourne Development. He should have been looking for a way to save his town. He would have loved to have shared what she'd told him about Regis but couldn't. It was privileged information, only to be discussed with her council. So, he'd focused on the contract. She'd left it on the table. A part of him hoped she'd come back for it. Maybe she didn't even realize she'd forgotten it. Not that he'd made much progress. He hadn't identified a loophole. The damned thing was ironclad.

He stared into the inky darkness as he listened to McKenzie murmur to herself as she explored the cellar. He closed his eyes and pictured Isabelle's face, recalling the night they ran from the crazy cake concierge and ended up in the butterfly pavilion at The Pike.

The Pike.

That's where she'd gone. She'd texted Hailey yesterday, and Finn had texted him. He must have gotten in his car over a dozen times since he'd learned of her whereabouts. But he never made it out of his garage. What would he say to her? What could he do? He had no plan to get her back, no idea how to fix what was wrong with him, and no strategy to stop Regis Greenstone. He was stuck, so damned mired in this melancholy muck of a mindset.

Tap, tap, tap.

He opened his eyes and observed McKenzie's darkened form as she tossed pebbles into the empty crate. "Put the lid back on, Kenz. We've been down here long enough. I should get you home."

"Not yet, Uncle Kier. It's seven fifty-one," McKenzie replied, staring at her cell's display.

"Yes, it's getting close to sunset."

"We can't go yet."

"Why not?"

"I . . ." she replied, stretching the syllable, "want to take a video of the empty crate."

"Why would you want a video of an empty crate?"

"Because I have videos of everything."

"I'm sure you do," he mumbled.

"Kieran? McKenzie?" Eliza called.

"We're down in the root cellar, Mom," McKenzie hollered back —not at all surprised by her mother's arrival.

What did this kid have up her sleeve?

"What's your mom doing here?"

His niece skipped around the room, her light bobbing with each movement. "She brought the cake, and everybody else should have hidden the treasures around the cabin and hot spring."

He balked. "Cake and treasures?"

"Yeah," she balked right back. "Cake like . . . the *cake* you left on the cake table during the Fourth of July celebration, and treasures for you to find like you hide for me when we go hiking. You said I could decide how to celebrate your birthday. We didn't get to have the muffin party in Grandma Maeve's office, so I was talking to Goldie, and we came up with an idea to surprise you with your cake."

Goldie. Of course, she was in on this.

McKenzie closed the crate and headed up the stone steps. "Remember your cake, Uncle Kier? It's lemon blueberry. Your favorite! We brought it home and put it in the freezer so it would keep."

How was he supposed to hold it together with a giant lemon blueberry cake in front of him?

"What treasures am I supposed to find, Kenz?" he asked, needing something else to go on.

"Five Starrycard Creek paper envelopes filled with love."

"Love?" he repeated.

"You'll see," McKenzie cooed, sprinting up the last few steps. She stood at the top and waved. "Hi, everybody! Uncle Kieran's coming. Are we ready?"

Was he ready? Oh, hell no.

He shook his head and trudged up the steps. He reached the top and eyed his niece. The child looked over her shoulder at him, grinning like it was her birthday. The kid put effort into this birthday surprise—endearing, effusive, Starrycard effort, and he couldn't be cross with her for that. He forced a smile, then relaxed his features when she skipped out of view. He gazed at the sky. Bands of orange and deep red stretched as far as the eye could see. Soon, the fiery canvas would fade into purples and pinks before the stars twinkled in a sea of darkness as the rhythmic rush of water from the falls mingled with the birds' evening chorus of calls. He'd been here thousands of times and knew this place like the back of his hand, but his most recent memories of his time here bubbled to the surface. A handful of days ago, he'd taken in nature's sensory symphony with Isabelle in his arms. Her breath warm against his lips as they made love on the blue faded quilt spread near the edge of the hot spring among their favorite flowers.

"Isabelle," he whispered. Christ, he loved her name, the pleasing syllables. The rolling intonation. Probably his damned brain, latching on to a peculiarity normal people would ignore.

"Hello, big brother," Eliza called, snapping him back to reality. His sister held a cake box in her hands. She watched him for a beat, then admired the sky. "Sunsets on Starrycard Mountain never disappoint, do they?"

He pushed aside thoughts of Isabelle—at least, he tried. "They do not." He joined his sister and tapped the box. "Now isn't the time for a party, Liza."

She looked at him like he'd sprouted antlers. "We're Starrycards. There's always time for a party. And, in news that will shock no one, Grandpa Rex brought moonshine. Chris left it before he went on the road with the Rattlers. You should have a swig or ten."

"That stuff should be illegal."

"That stuff *is* illegal. Just go with it, Kier," she teased. She was trying to lighten his mood. While her expression was breezy, he could see concern welling in her gaze.

He raked his hands through his tangle of hair. "What exactly is going on? What's this envelope treasure hunt?"

"Your surprise."

"Kenz shared that much, but you know what's on the line. I should get back to town. I should talk to the merchants. I haven't spoken to them since—"

"Since you clocked that developer," she supplied.

"Yes."

"Do you want to talk about it?"

"No."

"I'm sure you had a reason to do it."

He glanced away. "I lost my composure." It wasn't a lie, but he couldn't disclose the truth.

"Hailey told us that Regis and Izzy dated, and he hurt her badly," Eliza said, lowering her voice.

He met his sister's gaze. "Isabelle shared that information with me as well."

"Hailey didn't have many details. Izzy told her she couldn't discuss it. It's tied into her family's business."

"That's also true. The breakup was unique due to the sale of her family's company."

"So, you know? I didn't think Izzy could say much."

He slipped his hand in his pocket and felt the Peruvian coin. He'd kept it with him night and day since she'd left. "Isabelle hired me."

"As her lawyer?"

"Yes, to review the sales contract."

"And?"

He stared at his hiking boots. "And nothing."

"Regis Greenstone is bad news," Eliza said with a huff. "I should have known from the second he started talking about doling out signing bonuses that he was nothing but a snake oil salesman."

Every muscle in Kieran's body tightened. The sound of the con artist's name triggered lighting-hot anger to flood his system, but he fought to maintain a neutral demeanor. "I can't comment on Regis Greenstone's business practices, only on what he's presented to the town."

"You left him with a fat lip, Kier. I'll infer your opinion from that action. Does that sound legal enough?"

"It's an accurate inference."

"How do we beat him? How do we convince the town to turn down a plan offering residents and businesses major cash incentives?" she asked, searching his expression.

"I don't know yet. That's why I should get back. The hearing is in five days."

"I get it, and starting tomorrow, I'll help with whatever you need. But there will be hell to pay if you cut out of your birthday party early. Indulge your niece. She worked awfully hard."

"And Goldie, too? I hear she was in on it."

Eliza's lips curled into a sly grin. "And Mom and me. Even Caroline helped from Bali or Bangladesh—wherever she is now. You know Starrycard women. We've always got a plan—especially for our Starrycard bachelors." Eliza leaned in. "And, between you and me, out of all McKenzie's idiot uncles, you might be her favorite idiot."

He chuckled—the first time in days. "Idiot uncles?"

"Well, Finn might not be a complete idiot. He got his act together when he figured out what mattered and asked Hailey to marry him, but the rest of you need a little Starrycard Creek magic to get where you're supposed to be."

"And where do you think I'm supposed to be?"

She smiled up at him—a smile she had since she was a girl. An expression that brimmed with adoration. "A place where you're happy. A place where you're with the one you love. The one meant for you."

"Ah, the Starrycard Creek folklore talk," he mumbled, not prepared to wade into that clusterfuck of a topic.

"You deserve it, Kier. You do so much for everyone," she replied, her expression softening.

"Is that what this is? A birthday push toward a perceived state of happiness?"

"It's a party, asshole," she shot back, losing the adoring glow and drawing on her piss-and-vinegar persona. "Now, check in with your niece. She's over by Delilah's herb garden. She'll tell you what to do."

His sister was one of a kind.

"What will you do?" he pressed.

She adjusted her grip on the box. "I'm going to set this big-ass cake on the table, sit with the adults, drink Christian's batch of Delilah's gazillion-proof hooch, and wait for you to find your treasures. Does that work for you?"

"Yes, but could I take a moment to prepare myself? I only need a minute."

"With Kenz, that's about all you've got," Eliza replied and headed toward the front of the cabin.

Making the most of his sixty seconds, he trailed behind his sister. He rolled his head from side to side, working out the kinks and surveying the scene. While he'd been in the root cellar with McKenzie, his family had arrived. They'd carried the old table and chairs outside and added a linen tablecloth and candles. His parents and grandparents chatted at the table while McKenzie fluttered in her paper wings among the starblooms at the edge of the hot spring. Hailey and Finn were making trips back and forth from the cabin, setting out glasses, plates, and cloth napkins as Owen and Jack poured what had to be Christian's concoction into a pitcher of lemonade.

"We're here to have a party for my old-man uncle Kier. He is thirty-three," McKenzie called, waving to him as she zigzagged toward the table.

His family cheered effusively, clapping and clinking glasses.

"Here's your map. I made it myself," McKenzie continued, pulling the item from her pocket. "There are five envelopes. I marked them with numbers. It's treasure hunt time. Ready, set, go!"

Kieran studied the map and set off. It wouldn't take him long to procure the envelopes, but he made sure to attend carefully to his niece's rendering. He moved slowly, like a conscientious treasure hunter for McKenzie's benefit. "Number one," he called, interjecting excitement into his tone as he plucked the first envelope from behind a barrel.

Predictably, the Starrycards clapped and cheered.

This pattern of behavior continued as he found the remaining envelopes. "Should I open them?" he asked after the last round of applause petered out.

"Bring them to the table, Uncle Kier," McKenzie called, fluttering around him as she led him to the group.

In the time it took for him to collect his treasures, dusk had fallen. The candles on the table flickered in the breeze as wisps of sunlight hovered on the horizon.

He assessed the envelopes. They weren't heavy, per se. They were filled with paper, but not sheets. He rubbed his thumb across one of the envelopes and noted ridges. There were scraps inside.

"Go ahead, open the first one," McKenzie instructed, coming to his side as he took a seat.

He complied, and as he'd guessed, the envelope did contain

slips of paper—Starrycard Creek paper, similar to the slips used for the wishing wall.

"Each piece is made with starbloom petals because those are your favorite. They just made a whole bunch of starbloom paper, right, Grandpa Hank?"

His father nodded. "It's not July in Starrycard Creek without the paper celebrating our town's favorite flower."

Starblooms.

Kieran fought to maintain a neutral demeanor. From the landscape to the paper, Isabelle was everywhere. Following McKenzie's directions, he pulled a slip from the envelope.

"Now read it. Who's it from?" she asked, flitting around the table.

He eyed the slip and noted the handwriting. "Kieran, you introduced me to my love of art and painting the summer you let me borrow your portable easel. Thank you for seeing what I couldn't. Your brother, Owen." Kieran set the scrap of paper on the table and searched the faces of his family. "What are these?"

McKenzie stopped her flitting and pegged him with her gaze. "They're love, Uncle Kier. People wrote about how you showed you cared about them. That's what love is, right, Goldie?"

"Correct, little star," his grandmother answered, pulling her shawl around her shoulders as the breeze picked up.

Owen leaned forward, his elbows resting on the table. "It was a big deal when you brought me here and taught me the basics of painting. I didn't want to go. I was a moody twelve-year-old and one hell of a pain in the ass."

Kieran shrugged. "I noticed you drawing and made a connection to the arts. I simply acted on your behavioral cues. It was nothing."

Owen chuckled. "It wasn't *nothing* to me."

Kieran froze. Isabelle had said the same words when she'd spoken of his kindness.

The woman was everywhere.

"Pick some more," McKenzie instructed.

Grateful for the distraction, he pulled a few slips from the envelope and skimmed the messages, but he didn't read them aloud. He needed to collect the information and process it.

Kier, thank you for helping me figure out who I was supposed to be.

-Finn

Kieran, I'll never forget our walk down Main Street and the kind words you shared.

-Hailey

He looked between Finn and Hailey. "I have your slips here. Again, I merely presented you with my observations regarding your relationship. It was clear you cared for each other."

"Your observations helped us understand what mattered most," Finn replied, taking Hailey's hand.

"I see," Kieran replied, choosing another slip.

You carried my ass all over Starrycard Mountain for an entire summer. I know I pounded my fists on your back and called you Mr. Poopy Head, but I liked being able to keep up with the big kids. You made sure I was always included.

-Caroline

"Jesus, that kid," he muttered, his gaze growing glassy.

"That has to be Caroline's, right?" Eliza remarked.

"Yes, it is."

"I transcribed it for her."

Kieran's throat thickened. He couldn't speak. Instead, he tidied the stack of slips.

One, two, three . . .

He counted the seconds. If he went past seven, his silence would seem odd.

Four, five, six . . .

But he couldn't utter a word. Between his confusion over Isabelle and the kindness of his family, again, like the night Isabelle left, he was stuck. The words were frozen, trapped by a rush of emotion.

"McKenzie and I took a basket of paper scraps all over town," Goldie explained, filling the stretch of silence, her voice rhythmic and soothing. "We visited the library and talked to residents, telling them about our project, a birthday gift project where people could write a note to share how you touched their lives. Some signed them. Some didn't. Nobody refused to participate. Everyone had a story or recalled an event when you touched their lives."

"Uncle Owen had to bring us more paper," McKenzie added.

Kieran nodded, his gaze trained on the neat stack.

"Lots of *good vibrations*, son," his father remarked, garnering a well-earned groan from Eliza, Finn, and Owen for the hip-hop reference. But Kieran didn't join in. That was his father's gift. The gift of lightening the mood and taking the spotlight off someone when they needed time to collect themselves.

"Did anyone mention the Fourth of July?" he asked, finding his voice.

"People want to know if you and Izzy are okay. We've told them there's more to the story, and we're gathering information. They know you, Kieran. They know you care about Starrycard Creek, but they're confused and scared," his mother shared.

They weren't the only ones.

"Hey," McKenzie chimed, pointing toward the far end of the hot spring. "I think I saw a butterfly over there. Do you mind if I fly away from your party and check if it's a starwing?" She hopped from foot to foot as if she'd burst if she couldn't confirm her hunch.

"Go ahead," he replied, straightening his niece's lopsided wings. "But it's probably not a starwing. The starwings migrated through here thirteen days ago."

"Okay," his niece called over her shoulder, zigzagging past boulders and tufts of wild blueberries.

"I'll keep an eye on her," Owen said, rising from his seat to follow the paper-winged child.

Kieran eyed the envelopes. "Would you mind if I opened the rest in private? The gift is touching yet overwhelming."

His mother patted his hand. "Not at all, sweetheart."

"It's a reminder that you have family and friends who are always behind you," Goldie added.

"We're stronger together," Rex said.

"Stronger together," Kieran murmured. That's how Isabelle had described the starwing butterflies.

"Hey," McKenzie called. She'd barely been gone for a minute. The child waved her arms as she ran toward the table. "She came back. She's here."

Everyone rose to their feet.

"Who's here, little star?" Eliza pressed.

"Is it Isabelle?" Kieran got out, his pulse skyrocketing as he peered at the trail leading to the cabin.

Was she here? Had she come back to him?

CHAPTER

Twenty-One

KIERAN

KIERAN SQUINTED, searching the path for Isabelle.

McKenzie removed a folded piece of paper from her pocket. "No, not Izzy. This lady—a girl starwing. Or it could be her sister or cousin. The butterfly over by the far end of the hot spring looks like the one I drew. See." She held up the drawing.

Owen jogged up behind the kid. "McKenzie's right. There's more than one, and they're starwings. More are on the way. They came in over the ridge. They're gathering at the large grove of starblooms near the western edge of the hot spring.

"We need to record this," Goldie said. "This is evidence. The town needs to know."

"Got it!" McKenzie called, whipping out the old cell.

"They're here a second time? Is that typical behavior?" Eliza asked him, taking out her phone.

He drank in the spectacle as the swarm descended on the hot spring. "Isabelle wondered the same thing after sifting through Delilah's data. She proposed they may have adapted to migrate in large waves. There's little information on them because they're elusive and difficult to track. It appears she was correct."

"Come on," McKenzie called. "But we can't get too close. That's what Izzy said when she came to summer enrichment."

"We should spread out and try to get a count," he said, focusing on what he thought Isabelle would do. "We don't get Wi-Fi up here, but we need to take as many videos and photos as possible. When Isabelle and I observed them at the summit crater, we couldn't do that. Let's spread out, but like Kenz says, don't get too close. They're sensitive to our presence."

"They're congregating near one of Delilah's favorite spots," Rex said. "Later in life, my grandmother would sit there on a little wooden stool my grandfather made for her." Rex pointed to a group of boulders a few feet away. "That's it."

Kieran recognized the stool as one of the old items he'd largely overlooked. "It's usually kept in the shed," he noted. "We used to carry it around as kids. And get splinters every time." *Splinters.* "I didn't know it was Delilah's."

"She liked to be close to flowers, down by the earth, which was harder as she got older. And the splinters were because Nathan Starrycard was a papermaker and a lousy carpenter," Rex added with a chuckle.

"I put it by the rocks when we came up to see the summit crater," McKenzie said, then ran toward the boulders and retrieved it.

"I wonder if she liked that spot because of the butterflies. I wonder if it called to her," his grandfather mused.

"Called to her?" Kieran pressed as McKenzie set the stool beside him.

"Your great-grandmother Delilah was highly attuned to the land. She knew things, felt things, heard nature whisper in the wind." The old man shook his head, taking in the butterflies. "I'll be damned. They're back. They're really back. Delilah would have loved to see this."

Kieran stilled and listened. He was connected to this place, too. And there was something about that spot. "I'll head to Delilah's spot and get as close as I can without disturbing the butterflies."

"I'll come with you, Uncle Kier, and we can bring the stool.

"I'll carry it," he said, carefully taking it from the child.

"We'll be careful and respectful of the butterflies. It's very special that they visit us, isn't it?" she said softly as they set off.

"It is."

"The butterflies must trust us," she whispered, taking his free hand.

"I think you're right, Kenz."

The child sighed. "I wish Izzy was here. She'd like to see them. She really loves butterflies."

He gave her hand a gentle squeeze. "That's my wish, too."

She looked up at him. "Your birthday wish?"

Birthday wishes.

He recalled his words to Isabelle as he watched her sleep.

If birthday wishes came true, I'd wish for you.

He observed the butterflies. "Yes, that's my birthday wish."

"You know what Goldie would say," the child continued.

He chuckled. "It can only be yours if it's meant for you."

Was Isabelle meant for him? How would he know?

"What's that on the ground? It's shiny," his niece said, releasing his hand and pulling him from his thoughts as they approached the area Rex had identified as Delilah's spot.

He squinted, peering through the starblooms' ethereal, bioluminescent glow. The petals had begun to open in preparation for the moon. Starwing butterflies flitted from flower to flower. "It's just the butterflies, Kenz. The silver spots can catch the light and glint. They're nectaring now. Eating a big dinner. After visiting the flowers and the blueberries, they'll drink from the hot spring and get the minerals from the water."

"No, there's something on the ground and a little scrap of paper," she said, pointing to the location.

She was right. He set the stool on the ground. Crouching, he picked up the ragged remnant and recognized the midnight-blue painted wing. He turned it over and scanned the words written on the back.

Happy birthday to our butterfly girl.

"Is that a little bit of Starrycard Creek paper, Uncle Kier?"

"It is."

"You could use it to make your birthday wish."

"I could."

"And look! That shiny thing glinted again," McKenzie whispered, recording the ground near the cluster of starblooms with Goldie's old cell.

He saw it now. The object gleamed in the day's final rays of purple light. He reached between the stems, his fingertips trailing across the earth. He stilled when cool metal replaced the scratch of bits of rock and dirt. "The locket," he whispered.

McKenzie scooted the stool closer and sat. "Is that Izzy's? The one she lost?"

Kieran held the necklace and dusted bits of mud from the chain. *Was he seeing things?* Carefully, he opened it and was greeted by her parents and grandparents. "But I looked here. I had to have checked here. I didn't see it," he murmured.

McKenzie recorded as he cradled the piece of jewelry in his palm. She leaned over, zooming in. "Maybe the butterflies wanted to be the ones to show it to you. And Starrycard Card Creek paper is magic. Goldie always says anything is possible with it, right, Uncle Kier? Maybe it was magic and butterflies that helped us find it."

He'd never believed that the paper made from the waters of Starrycard Creek held mystical qualities until now. "That's right, Kenz. Anything is possible."

"I'll tell everybody," McKenzie said, flitting off.

He stared at the bit of gold. "Bloom," he whispered.

"McKenzie tells us you found some paper and Izzy's locket," Goldie said, hurrying over with Rex beside her.

"Yes. It was here."

"In Delilah's spot?" Rex pressed, sharing a look with his wife.

"Isabelle must have wandered here before I found her."

"May I see the locket?" Goldie asked.

"It contains pictures of her parents and grandparents."

Goldie gazed at the images.

"And the paper?" Rex pressed.

"It's a piece of a birthday card her family gave her. The rest probably blew into the hot spring and disintegrated."

"I recognize the painted image. I believe I know the artist," Goldie said, raising an eyebrow.

"I believe you do." His grandfather gazed at Goldie. "You never cease to amaze me. You're a little bit witch, aren't you?"

"You know I am."

Kieran looked between his grandparents. "Am I missing something?" he asked as McKenzie barreled toward him.

She knocked over the stool. "Oops."

Kieran bent to put it upright and stilled when he read a word carved into the back of the seat. "Bloom."

"It's what my grandfather sometimes called Delilah," Rex explained.

Jesus.

"Uncle Kier, can you fix my phone? It says it's out of memory, and I want to keep taking butterfly videos before it gets dark."

Thrown off by the Bloom reference and unable to decipher the exchange between his grandparents, he extended his palm toward his niece as if he were in a dream world. "Yeah, I can help you. You have to delete a few videos to make space."

She handed him the phone. "Delete the boring ones from the Fourth of July. I was trying to take a video of those yellow birds tweeting and singing in the trees, but this lady and man were talking all loud and braggy and messing up my recording."

Loud and braggy? That description snapped him out of his state of confusion.

He opened the video gallery. "What lady and man?"

"The one you punched and the brown-haired lady with the papers."

"What?" Goldie exclaimed.

Kieran scrolled until Regis Greenstone and his fiancée appeared on the screen. The pair sat on a bench beneath a tree.

"What's going on?" Maeve asked as his family hurried toward them.

"Kenz accidentally took a video of Regis Greenstone and his fiancée." He held the phone for everyone to see.

"Let's see it," Rex remarked.

Kieran hit play.

Regis donned a slippery smirk. "Just follow my lead, babe. We'll do what we did in Redstone Ridge, Wyoming."

"Bring in the mining equipment on covered trucks. Put up fences. Lie about needing to excavate to build?" Jennifer supplied.

"That's right. I know who to pay off to get that approved. Then we say we've stumbled upon the copper and tell these small-town mountain morons this will only make the town richer. We'll say we're digging the foundations for the new hotel and ski facilities, which we sure as hell aren't going to build, and mine every bit of copper we can get our hands on. We'll get more bang for our buck if we strip Starrycard Mountain to the bone."

"You are so clever, babe," Jennifer cooed.

"It's foolproof," Regis boasted. "They'll never know what hit them. Texas, Utah, Wyoming, Colorado—it doesn't matter where we go, the courts are too slow to help them. By the time anybody figures out what we're doing, we'll have scrapped the company, and our money will be piling up in our overseas accounts."

The video ended, and no one said a word.

"Nobody's mad I recorded this?" his niece asked, breaking the stretch of silence.

"No, Kenz, you're the opposite of in trouble. You've saved the town," Eliza replied, wide-eyed.

McKenzie beamed. "Did you hear that, butterflies? I saved the town with a phone," she announced, setting off like the winged creatures, joyfully flitting and fluttering.

"Sweet Christ, this guy sounds like a comic book supervillain," Owen remarked when McKenzie was out of earshot.

"This is it. This is the evidence we need," Maeve said, embracing Hank as his family clapped and whooped.

Kieran stared at the screen. "He mentioned Redstone Ridge."

"Yes, I heard him say it. Do you know it?" Rex pressed.

"My friend Nelson is representing them in a lawsuit."

"You'll have to share this with him."

"And we have to tell Izzy. She has to know about this," Hailey gushed. "This will vindicate her. The courts awarded Regis everything she had when he sued her for breaking her NDA."

Finn nodded. "This Regis clown is toast. And it doesn't matter that these yahoos didn't know they were being recorded, right Kier?" his brother continued. "You mentioned this is legal in Colorado. These two are sitting on a park bench in public."

"That's correct. This is admissible evidence."

"I can call an emergency town hall meeting," his mother said, pacing excitedly. "We can share this with the town council. Everyone needs to see this video. Everyone needs to know the truth."

The truth.

Kieran surveyed the video, the locket, the remnant of Isabelle's birthday card, then fixed his gaze on the stool with *Bloom* carved into the old wood. The universe couldn't be clearer. Everyone did need to know the truth—and that included the truth about him. He needed to share it to make peace—no, to embrace—who he was. "I need to share something. Two items, to be exact."

"What is it, dear?" Maeve pressed as the celebration died down with his statement.

He surveyed the group. "It's the truth about me. I have autism. I recently had some testing done to obtain the diagnosis. I thought this condition would justify living a solitary life, a life dedicated to the town. And then, minutes after learning I was on the spectrum, I saw Isabelle, and . . ."

"Your world shifted off its axis," Goldie supplied.

"Yes. Despite telling you that Isabelle and I maintained a professional relationship, I have a feeling you know that I . . ." He paused. *Tell the truth.* "I love her," he said, speaking the words as a lightness came over him. "I love Isabelle, but I made a mistake. I didn't trust in my feelings when she told me she loved me after the incident with Regis Greenstone on the fourth."

"The day she left," Hailey said softly.

"I believed that my autism kept me from loving her. I thought I could only pretend to be the man Isabelle deserved—that giving into my true nature wouldn't be enough for her. I was wrong. I understand love. I'm surrounded by love—by people who love me and people I love. I feared my condition held me back from being a loving partner. But tonight revealed a truth to me. I don't have to do it alone. And she doesn't want me to be alone. She loves me. I need to believe and trust in her love. I also need to figure out how to express my sentiments."

"It's my understanding a gifted psychologist is in town vacationing with her family. Perhaps she'll spare an hour for you."

"I know she would," Kieran answered. He scanned his family —the people who were always behind him. "You're loud and outrageous, and I wouldn't have you any other way. I love you all."

"We're always with you, Uncle Kier," McKenzie said, wrapping her little arms around his waist.

He peered at the piece of Starrycard Creek paper—the paper that had linked his spirit with Isabelle's. "I believe in the magic of Starrycard Creek."

Goldie adjusted her shawl and wiped a tear from her cheek. "Believing in each other is the magic, little star."

"I believe in Isabelle. She doesn't know that I love her—that it's real. She believes she's not trustworthy. She thinks I'm better off without her. But we're going to change that," he said as a plan came together. "I can't do it alone. I have a strategy, but it requires a Starrycard trait I lack." He bit back a grin. "Effusiveness."

"Oh, kid," Rex said with a wry grin, "we've got effusiveness in spades."

"That's what I'm counting on," Kieran replied, excitement

building. "With your help, we'll prove to Isabelle that I love her—that she's meant to be a Starrycard and that her place is here in Starrycard Creek. I want to make this woman my wife and accomplish this task in a way that'll leave no doubt about my feelings."

"Our feelings," his mother added. "We want this for you—and Izzy."

His father wrapped his arm around his mother's shoulder. "Whatever you need. You know we're in."

He glanced at Goldie's cell phone, taking in Regis's smarmy smirk. "This is a two-prong plan," he began, switching to what Isabelle would call watch-and-learn mode. "In addition to the romantic element, we'll also take down an unscrupulous developer, leave him unable to hurt another business or community, and save Starrycard Creek from ruin."

"A little payback. Now you're talking, big brother," Eliza said, rubbing her hands together like an evil genius.

"However, while we hold most of the cards, there's one part of this plan we can't control," he added.

"Isabelle," Hailey supplied.

"Correct," Kieran agreed. "For this to work, Isabelle must return on the day of the hearing—on her birthday."

"She's at The Pike. She told me she'd be there for the next two weeks. I could visit her. I think she'd talk to me," Hailey offered.

Finn nodded. "It's a solid idea."

"It's your best chance," Eliza agreed.

"Let Goldie and I tag along to The Pike," Rex said with a curious edge to his tone.

"Yes, we'll accompany you to Rocky Mountain City," Goldie added. "It's time Isabelle knew everything. And telling her at The Pike is the place to do it."

"What else is there for her to know?" Kieran pressed.

"For starters, why she ended up as Starrycard Creek's land steward," his grandfather supplied.

Kieran stepped back, perplexed. "And why is that?"

Goldie flashed that coy Starrycard smirk and exchanged a glance with Rex. "It's because of us."

"I don't understand."

"Isabelle is here because her family is a part of our love story," Rex replied, taking Goldie's hand.

Goldie's eyes twinkled. "A story that started on a mountaintop in Peru."

CHAPTER

Twenty~Two

IZZY

IZZY peered at the screen of her laptop and typed the email's subject line.

Isabelle A. Adaire's official resignation from Earthwise.

She stilled and stared at the keyboard, then slid her gaze to her left hand. She couldn't help it. She thought she understood loss and believed there wasn't a piece of her heart left to break. She was wrong. She stroked the skin the paper ring had covered as the emptiness threatened to swallow her whole.

She'd brought her laptop to the botanic gardens and found a shady spot close to the butterfly pavilion near the reflecting pool. She sat at a table amidst the foliage. The July sun cast a serene glow. Its rays highlighted the vibrant colors as a gentle breeze tickled the leaves of drooping willow trees. She inhaled the perfumed air. She'd been holed up in her hotel room since she'd arrived at The Pike late on the Fourth of July. Over the last week, she'd fallen back on the one thing she had. Work. She'd meticulously reviewed each report she'd completed over the last four years, correcting her past errors. Naturally, not every mistake could be amended. The harm she'd inflicted on Ashbourne Building and Development, and soon to Starrycard Creek, was irreversible. She'd submitted the Starrycard Creek evaluation to the State earlier in the day. With no physical proof of the starwings return, she'd deemed construction was permissible, though contingent upon following environmental protocols. There was no sense in fighting it, and it was the truth. She could only pray the town wouldn't choose Regis's plan.

Back to the emails. She had two to send.

She clicked over to her notes screen and skimmed the text she'd written earlier.

Dear Pamela, I can no longer fulfill my role with Earthwise Consulting. I submit my resignation. Effective immediately.

Short, sweet, and to the point.

Copy. Paste. Send.

"Happy birthday, Izzy. What a way to celebrate," she murmured, but she wasn't done. She had one last email to send to the mayor of Starrycard Creek.

Dear Madame Mayor,

I can no longer fulfill my role as the temporary land steward. I submit my resignation. Effective immediately.

Why reinvent the wheel?

She hovered the arrow over the send icon and tapped it. "Goodbye," she whispered, her gaze growing glassy.

"Excuse me, ma'am . . . miss?"

Izzy gasped. She closed her laptop and looked up to find a man staring down at her. He looked around her age, maybe a few years younger.

The guy glanced around nervously, adjusted his glasses, then ran his hand through his hair. "Hi . . ." he stammered. "I see you're working, but I was hoping you could . . . you see, this is my girlfriend's favorite place. She loves the botanic gardens at The Pike, and I wanted to get a room, but we're still in college, and money is tight. I also spent a bunch on . . . um . . ."

Izzy studied the odd man. "Do you need help?"

"Yeah, actually, I do."

"Make way! *Vit! Vit!*" came a snippy voice with a French accent. "*Careful, François, maneuver around the cracks in the path. The* cakes must remain perfect and intact. Jacques, protect the lemon blue-berry cake from direct sun."

All hail the snooty *monsieur* cake patrol.

The pastry tyrant tittered around the line of men and women pushing carts transporting the decadent desserts. Izzy turned away from the path, allowing her hair to shield her face. She sure as hell didn't need a run-in with the hotel's high-strung cake cop again.

Once the cake brigade drew closer to the reflecting pool, she returned her attention to her tongue-tied companion. "You seem rather scattered. Do you need me to call someone for you? Maybe this girlfriend of yours?"

Wide-eyed, he waved her off. "No, no! Not my girlfriend. That's why I'm here."

This guy wasn't making a lick of sense.

"What do you need from me?" she asked, about ten seconds away from telling him to buzz off.

"Sorry, I'm a little flustered. Actually, a lot flustered. This is a special day." He extended his hand. "I should introduce myself. I'm Jimmy. Jimmy Bloom."

Jimmy Bloom.

She shook his hand. The names—her grandfather's nickname and Bloom—catching her off guard. "Nice to meet you, Jimmy. I'm Izzy."

Jimmy pulled a compact velvet-covered box from his pocket. "I'm proposing to my girlfriend. That spot by the water, close to where they're setting up those cakes, is where my girlfriend and I met for our first date." He removed his cell from his back pocket. "I was wondering if you could record the proposal on my phone?"

She glanced at her watch. "I'm supposed to be meeting a friend soon."

"This won't take long. At least, I hope it's quick, and she says yes right away," the man gushed, adjusting his glasses.

How could she say no? This guy was a mess and could use some help.

"Yes, I'd be happy to record your proposal."

Relief flooded the man's expression. "Thank you so much." He glanced over his shoulder as a woman in a purple dress with her dark hair pulled into a high ponytail strolled toward the spot Jimmy had pointed out. "That's her. I told her to meet me at our special place. That's my Joanie."

Joanie.

Izzy rose to her feet. *Had she heard him correctly?* "You're Jimmy, and the woman you love is Joanie?"

"Yeah, and hopefully, we'll be Jimmy and Joanie Bloom one day," he replied, his grin widening as he handed her his phone.

"You don't want to keep Joanie waiting," she said, her throat thickening with emotion. "I'll record from behind that hedge."

Jimmy eyed the box before slipping it into his pocket. "Here goes everything."

She patted the guy on his shoulder. "I have a good feeling about you two."

"Thanks, Izzy," he replied, then headed toward the young woman in purple.

Izzy loaded her laptop and cell into her backpack, then got into position as Jimmy waved to the young woman. Joanie ran toward him, wrapped her arms around his neck, and the couple embraced. Izzy couldn't help but smile—her first in days. They made a sweet couple. She reached for her locket, forgetting she'd lost it. Dropping her hand to her side, she gazed at the blue sky. "Is this your doing, Nana and Poppa? Nana, you'd get sentimental if you met a Jimmy and Joanie. I know it. And Poppa, you'd probably rattle off the probability of another Joan and James finding each other. And then you'd look at Nana and tell her that no matter how many Joans were out there, your Joanie was one of a kind." Izzy shook her head. "Focus," she whispered, concentrating on Jimmy Bloom's phone. She tapped record as he took Joanie's hand and led her to their spot near the edge of the reflecting pool. Izzy observed the screen, making sure the image stayed focused and centered. Jimmy dropped to one knee and produced the ring box. Joanie pressed her hand to her chest and nodded, tears streaming down her cheeks as she presented her left hand. Jimmy slipped the ring on her finger, rose to his feet, and kissed his fiancée. And nature celebrated with them. The sun shimmered on the reflecting pool. The couple looked like something out of a movie, surrounded by a living tapestry of vibrant greens, pinks, reds, violets, and fiery oranges. Izzy blinked back tears.

Jimmy pulled back, breaking the kiss. He turned away from his fiancée. "Izzy, she said yes!" he exclaimed, donning an endearing, lovestruck grin.

She stopped recording, gathered herself, and joined the couple. "Congratulations on your engagement," she said, handing Jimmy his phone.

Joanie gazed at her left hand. "I've never been so happy in my whole life."

"What are your plans? You should celebrate," Izzy said, catching Captain No Cake setting out a roped barrier to keep people from entering the cake tasting.

Jimmy's cheeks grew pink. "Between paying for school, rent, and everything else, we don't have much left."

"Let's walk by the cakes, Jimmy. They're so beautiful, and we can smell the sugary deliciousness," Joanie gushed.

Jimmy wrapped his arm around his fiancée. "Joanie is a cake fanatic."

Izzy knew something about that. She glanced at the display as determination flooded her system. There had to be a reason the universe put Jimmy Bloom and Joanie in her path and threw in fifteen cakes within fifteen feet of them.

"You won't be admiring the cakes. You guys deserve to eat cake. All the cake. I've been here before. I know what they're doing. They're setting up for a cake tasting. It's my treat. Meeting you and being a part of your special moment lifted my spirits. It's the least I can do to say thank you."

"That's so kind of you," Joanie exclaimed. "What a day, Jimmy!"

Izzy zeroed in on the Frenchman dressed in black. He stood with his clipboard, checking in couples as they passed into the roped-off area. Trepidation panged in her chest. Things didn't go so well the last time they'd met. Still, he'd probably forgotten about the cake shenanigans. And it was just cake—delicious cake that she and her birthday card boyfriend never paid for. *Oops!* It was a slight error. A misunderstanding. Izzy chewed her lip. If the guy gave her grief, she'd tell him to charge four tickets to her room to pay for Joan and Jim and the night she and her birthday card boyfriend bullshitted their way into the event. The cake cop would certainly let bygones be bygones, right? She'd use the *you-catch-more-flies-with-honey-than-vinegar* approach. Now, should a woman of limited means who just quit her job and will probably never work in the environmental sciences field be spending her last dollars on cake-tasting tickets? She took in the newly engaged couple, mooning over each other. Yeah, this was the right call. It's exactly what her family would want her to do.

Commence Operation Cake for Joanie and Jimmy

She concentrated on the cake cop. "Hello," she said brightly, walking up to the Frenchman with the newly engaged couple trailing behind. "You might remember me from a few weeks ago. I wanted to purchase tickets so my new friends Jimmy and Joanie could attend the cake tasting. Jimmy proposed a few minutes ago. They're officially engaged."

The Frenchman narrowed his gaze and pursed his lips.

So much for letting cake bygones be cake bygones. He remembered her—and not fondly.

"You are a cake thief," he sneered.

He wasn't wrong.

She widened her grin. "I'd like to make amends. I'm happy to pay for this lovely couple and the . . . to-go cake option my companion and I opted for a few weeks ago." *How could he say no?*

"There is no *to-go* cake option. Only cake kidnapping," he snapped, then really snapped, right in her face.

Big mistake, Frenchie.

"You can't kidnap cake," she fired back, losing the grin.

"It's okay, Izzy," Joanie said softly. "We're fine. We'll admire the cakes from here. They're so pretty."

Izzy shook her head. "You're getting cake. You're going to be Jimmy and Joanie Bloom. There's no way the universe would put you *and cake* in my path and not expect me to fight for it."

Jimmy cocked his head to the side and shared a look with Joanie. "I'm not sure what that means. Is there someone I could call for *you?*"

"There's nobody to call, and I'll show you what I mean when I say you're getting cake." Izzy turned to the French dessert despot. "My friends will join this tasting. And they will eat all the *motherfucking* cake."

The Frenchman gasped, then held out his clipboard—that stupid clipboard. "There is no Jimmy and Joanie Bloom on the list."

Izzy leaned in and held the fondant fucker's gaze. "Then write their names on the motherfucking list."

"No! You are a cake crook. I will do no such thing for you or Jimmy and Joanie Bloom. Any friends of yours are most likely cake crooks, too."

Frenchie had gone too far.

"Cake crook?" she seethed, nose to nose with Captain No Cake. "You'll meet my right hook if you don't let Jimmy and Joanie eat the motherfucking cake."

Was this bonkers?

Oh yes. Complete Bonkersville. But she would not back down.

The faint patter of footsteps drew near, then stopped.

"You and your motherfucking cake," came the most robotically sexy voice on the planet.

CHAPTER
Twenty~Three
IZZY

IZZY'S HEART SKIPPED A BEAT. She turned on her heel. And damn, it was him, Mr. Birthday Card Boyfriend. Despite knowing she was no good for this man or his town, she couldn't stop from pulling a Joanie. She leaped into his arms. "What are you doing here, Kieran?"

He embraced her and pressed a kiss to her temple. "It appears I'm intervening in another cake crisis to keep you from ending up in the back of a squad car."

"Hello, Izzy, it's lovely to see you."

Izzy recognized that voice, too. "You're here with your grandmother?"

"Yes."

"And his grandfather. Hello, Izzy, dear," Rex supplied.

Izzy slowly released her hold on the elder Starrycards' grandson. "Hi," she said meekly.

What was happening here?

Izzy glanced past Rex and Goldie. "Where's Hailey? Is she okay? She was supposed to meet me here."

"Hailey's fine. She had to attend to her summer enrichment students. Perhaps we should attend to the matter at hand," Kieran said, sage-green eyes sparkling.

"And that matter is?" she asked. She couldn't think straight with this gorgeous beast of a man grinning down at her like she made up his entire universe.

"Your eminent arrest. What's happening with the cake cretin? Or is this your normal reaction to cake tastings?"

She'd nearly forgotten about the cake tasting and her new friends.

She gestured to the wide-eyed, newly engaged couple. "This is Jimmy Bloom and his fiancée, Joanie."

"Jimmy and Joanie?" Goldie repeated.

"Bloom," Kieran added, his lips curling at the corners as if he knew something she didn't.

Izzy nodded, watching him closely. "They got engaged minutes ago."

"Izzy recorded it for us," Jimmy replied, looking less like a deer caught in headlights.

"Joanie and Jimmy deserve to celebrate. I want them to celebrate. They should enjoy every minute of their love story and get to eat all the motherfucking cake while they do it," she said, her voice shaking.

"My goodness, Izzy is so much like her, isn't she?" Rex murmured to Goldie.

"Very much," the woman replied softly.

"Isabelle," Kieran said and drew his knuckles down her jawline. "I agree with you. The newly engaged couple can be added to the list under the name *Bloom* and should be granted access to the tasting immediately," he said, eyeing the Frenchman. He then gestured to the iced delicacy adorned with blueberries and lemons. He turned to Goldie. "I believe this is your area of expertise."

"It is today," Goldie answered with a twinkle in her eyes. "I assume you're in charge here," the woman said, flicking her long silver hair over her shoulder as she zeroed in on the *cakemonger*.

"*Oui*, madame, I am the maître d'hôtel."

"Excellent. Then I'm sure you insist on the finest ingredients for your cakes."

Frenchie's eyes nearly popped out of their sockets. "But of course! The finest in the state. We pride ourselves on supporting local growers."

Goldie folded her arms. "I see you've got a lemon blueberry cake."

"A very popular cake, *madame*."

"I'm sure you use wild mountain blueberries," Goldie continued, weaving her a web.

Monsieur Cake Controller lifted his chin. "They are a Colorado seasonal delicacy."

"What if I told you I could get The Pike blackballed from purchasing Colorado wild mountain blueberries?"

Frenchie's eyeballs hung by a thread. "I would say you are out of your mind."

"You would be wrong. Over fifty years ago, I brought the special strain of mountain blueberries back to this state. I'm the reason your motherfucking lemon blueberry cake is a showstopper. I know every blueberry grower in Colorado. One word from me, and you're done."

"Is there a blueberry mafia I didn't know about?" she whispered to Kieran.

"Anything is possible," he whispered back.

Good God! This man.

Frenchie tapped his clipboard, snapping her back to the dire cake situation. The man cringed as if his mouth had been stuffed with the lemons adorning the cake. "My mistake. I see Bloom, party of two, right here." He handed Joanie and Jimmy a square of Starrycard Creek paper printed with a number.

"Crisis averted," Goldie crooned with a clap.

These people were something else.

"Thanks again, Izzy," Jimmy said earnestly.

"We'll never forget you," Joanie added.

Izzy patted the woman's back. "I'll never forget you."

"Shall we," Kieran said, gesturing for them to leave. A good call. The less time she spent near the French cake commander, the better.

The foursome strolled past the reflecting pool.

"Is that true, Goldie?" Izzy pressed. "Are you in touch with the Colorado mountain blueberry growers?"

"I believe my grandmother exercised factual flexibility," Kieran replied.

"Sometimes you have to take a gamble and stretch the facts when you know what you want is what's fair and what's just," Goldie explained. "You're a fighter, Izzy. You understand that. You trust your gut when it comes to doing the right thing in this world. It's who you are. And one must let the badass Earth-loving bitch out every so often—even if she has to exercise factual flexibility."

Izzy chuckled. "I appreciate your help with the cake guy. You've been so good to me. I wish I hadn't harmed your town." *The town!* She stopped dead in her tracks and checked her watch. "What are you doing here? The hearing starts in an hour. How will you make it back in time?"

A ping rang out, and Goldie pulled her phone from her handbag. "Rex and I are in charge of transportation. And this is the message we've been waiting for."

"Message me when you're ready," Kieran told his grandparents.

"Talk soon, Izzy," Rex added as the senior Starrycards headed for the exit.

"Kieran, you have to go, too. You're the town manager. You must defend your plan against Regis. The town votes today." She touched his face and frowned. "You've got a little blue smudge of paint on your cheek."

"I was working on a last-minute project, and I'm not going anywhere without you."

"But—"

"Answer this, Isabelle. Do you love me?"

She drank in his beautiful face and those sage-green eyes. "Yes."

"And I make you feel loved."

"You do."

"When we parted, there was so much I wanted to say that I couldn't express. I'm working with a psychologist to improve my communication skills and learn to trust my heart."

"What does your heart tell you?"

He took her hand. "That I want you in my life, my town, and my bed. I want to fall asleep listening to you breathe and wake up to your symmetrical face. My love for you is boundless. I cherish every fragment of your being—even the weird cake obsession."

She chuckled as her gaze grew glassy.

"The depth of my love and esteem for you, Isabelle, is profound and unequivocal. There is nothing bullshit about the love and admiration I feel for you. It was never bullshit. Never. I met the love of my life on my birthday, like William Starrycard. I fell in love with you with two hours and thirty-eight minutes left on that day, and I don't want to waste another minute without you."

Wow!

She searched his face. "How much therapy have you had? I've only been gone a week."

"One session."

"You got all that out of one therapy session?"

The whisper of a cocky grin graced his lips. "I'm perceptive and a fast learner."

"I'll say." She squeezed his hand. "But, Kieran . . ."

"What? Tell me, Bloom."

She blinked back tears. "I can't be a part of hurting your family and town. I love you and Starrycard Creek too much to cause more damage."

He watched her for a beat, his expression unreadable. "Turn around. I have something for you."

"But the town and the hearing and—"

"Turn around," her beast of a town manager growled.

"Fine." Her words seemed to be falling on deaf ears. She sighed and turned away. He came up behind her, and the warmth of his large frame provided such relief, such peace, that a tear trailed down her cheek. Gently, he gathered her hair and rested it over her shoulder. He draped a cool chain around her neck, the weight of it so familiar it was like coming home. The second the pendant rested against her chest, she turned to face him. "You found it," she whispered, reaching for the locket as fresh tears stained her cheeks.

"Friends led Kenz and me to it," he replied, wiping away her tears.

"Friends?" she repeated.

He removed his cell from his pocket, scrolled to a video, and hit play.

Starwings.

She gasped, unsure if she could believe her eyes. Starwing butterflies filled the screen with the rhythmic rush of the waterfall —the Starrycard Waterfall—and McKenzie's bubbly, vivacious laughter in the background.

She drank in the scene, staring at scores of winged creatures with glittering silver markings on their midnight blue wings. "That's the hot spring outside Fiona's cabin. When did you take this?"

"Five days ago."

"They do come in waves."

"It's like you hypothesized. They move in large swarms because. . ." He tipped up her chin. "They're stronger together like us, Isabelle."

She stepped away from him, guilt edging out her joy. "But I make Starrycard Creek weaker. I'm the reason Regis wants to destroy your town."

"Generations of starwing butterflies endured adversity and predators. Their struggles made them stronger. It taught them how to survive. Would you agree with that assessment?"

"Kieran . . ." she said on a tight exhale, shaking her head.

"As a scientist, would you agree with that data?" he pressed, not letting up.

She looked him square in the eyes. "Yes, and while I'm thrilled the butterflies have returned and my assertion is correct, I know how Regis operates. Even with this evidence, he'll vow to follow every protocol to protect the creatures. He'll wax poetic, then break the promises and leave it to the court system to untangle—a process that takes years. A process that most people and towns cannot afford. You know this."

His phone pinged. His expression gave nothing away as he checked the screen, glanced at the sky, and then pocketed his cell. "Do you trust me, Isabelle?"

Was there no getting through to him?

She sighed, unable to lie. "I do trust you."

"And I trust you. I trust your gut, and I trust your heart, and I trust your feelings for me and for Starrycard Creek. And I need you to trust me now and accompany me to the roof."

"The roof?" she exclaimed. *What was he playing at?*

He took her hand and led her inside the hotel.

"Your grandparents picked up the package, Mr. Starrycard," a hotel employee said, coming from behind the concierge desk. "The other items are en route as we speak. This way," he continued, using a keycard to unlock a door leading to a narrow service hallway. "I'll accompany you to the special access elevator."

"Thank you," Kieran said smoothly as they followed the man down the corridor.

The situation was growing more peculiar by the second.

"What packages? What's en route?" she asked, entering the elevator.

Kieran pressed the button labeled with an *R*. "Something for later."

Okay, he was playing coy.

"And what are we doing on the roof?"

"Bypassing traffic," he replied as a low, steady thrum cut through the air, growing louder by the second.

She cocked her head to the side, focusing on the sound. "Is that a helicopter?"

"It is."

"And it's for us?"

"Correct."

The doors opened, and the beat of the chopper's blades was near deafening.

"You want me to ride in a helicopter with you?"

He smiled a boyish grin. "Pretend you're running from a herd of angry alpacas."

This man.

"Kieran Starrycard, I demand to know what we're doing."

"This is what happens when I ask my effusive family for assistance."

He led her out of the elevator toward a staircase with a door at the top that presumably opened to the roof's helipad.

He opened the heavy metal door, and a gust of dry air flooded the snug space.

Isabelle shielded her eyes and peered at the aircraft covered in khaki snake scales and *Rocky Mountain City Rattlers* painted in bold green letters. She squinted and studied the pilot. "Why is Christian at the controls?"

"So he can transport us to Starrycard Creek."

"He flies helicopters and is a major league baseball player?"

"It's his off-season hobby. He's got his private license, and the Rattlers were kind enough to lend us their chopper. My grandparents are already inside. They're waiting to speak to you."

"To me? About what?"

"Your mother's birth announcement, among other topics."

What the WHAT?

"My mother's birth announcement?" she hollered above the roar of the aircraft.

But there was no time to talk. He whisked her out of the doorway and onto the rooftop before she could utter another syllable. He opened the helicopter's door. "You're in the back with my grandparents. I'll be up with Chris," he called over the roar of the blades.

She complied as if she were in a dream, settling into a seat across from Rex and Goldie as Kieran shut the door. The air stilled, and the well-insulated luxury cabin muffled the pound of the rotor blades.

Izzy rested her pack on the seat beside her, then folded her hands on the table, separating her from Kieran's grandparents. Dazed, she glanced around the space.

"I bet you have some questions, dear. Have a muffin," Goldie said, reaching for a plastic tub. The woman set the baked goods on the table.

"Or would a swig of this be better?" Rex asked, holding up a flask.

She eyed the container. "What is it?"

"Stumble Juice."

Why not hit the hooch?

She shrugged and fixed her gaze on the flask. When in Rome, right—or, in her case, in a luxury helicopter, piloted by the baseball player brother of the man she loved, headed to a town where her presence was sure to trigger its complete collapse. Who could blame her if she went full-on Delilah at this point? "I'll go with the liver-busting option B," she replied, accepting the alcohol. She took a sip and grimaced. She coughed and returned the flask to Rex. "That stuff is no joke." Once the fire in her mouth and throat receded, she looked from Goldie to Rex. "You knew my grandparents, didn't you?"

"We did," Goldie answered.

"They never mentioned you to me, or if they did, perhaps I was too young and forgot. Why didn't you say something?"

"Like so many stories that have a connection to Starrycard Creek, this story, the story that connects our families, begins with

Starrycard Creek paper," Rex said as Goldie held out a worn envelope with a faded *Correo Aéreo* stamp.

Correo Aéreo. Spanish for Air Mail.

But that wasn't the only significant marking on the envelope. She read the sender's name on the return address, and her breath caught in her throat.

J. Wilcox
Universidad Nacional Mayor de San Marcos
Peru

"Your grandmother sent me that letter," Rex said, reclining into his seat and taking Goldie's hand.

Izzy studied the item. "It's dated from the sixties. And it's before my nana met my grandfather."

"It's from when she was in college and studied abroad for a semester. Your grandmother and I were from different universities in the states that partnered with Universidad Nacional Mayor de San Marcos. This program allowed students to travel around South America. We were roommates. We became fast friends. Joan borrowed the paper and an envelope from me. Actually, she took it without me knowing. You see, before I left for South America, my family spent the summer in Starrycard Creek. My father was here for work. I tagged along and met a dashing young papermaker." She smiled at Rex.

"A papermaker who didn't want the girl of his dreams to leave and maybe never return," Rex offered. "I was young and fearful she'd meet someone else while she was away. She accused me of not trusting her. And she was right. I said things I'd regretted and regretted not saying what I should have said. I was a frightened fool. I thought I'd lost her forever."

"We broke up," Goldie continued. "I left for South America with Starrycard Creek stationary in my backpack. The day I arrived in Peru, I met your grandmother. My God, Joanie and I were two peas in a pod. Wild, opinionated, and passionate about the environment. It took less than five minutes for me to fall in love with her personality."

"She was magnetic," Izzy agreed, grateful that when she reached for her locket, it was there, solid and reassuring.

"I'd told her about how I'd fallen in love with a papermaker from Starrycard Creek, Colorado, and how it had ended badly. A few weeks of me going on about Rex Starrycard and, you know your grandmother, she had to act," Goldie added with a wistful grin.

"And that's how we get to the letter," Rex said, eyeing the envelope in her hand. "Go on, take a look."

Izzy's hands trembled as she removed the letter from the envelope. She skimmed the text. Her grandmother introduced herself. She'd written the schedule of where they'd be and the dates they'd be there and said she was writing as Marion's friend.

"Marion?"

"I was Marion Gold until this man spent a summer calling me Goldie. It stuck."

Isabelle nodded, then chuckled as she read the last line.

If you've got half a brain, Rex Starrycard, you'll get your ass on a plane so you can tell my friend in person that you trust her and believe in her and your love.

"The half-a-brain part?" Rex asked.

"Yes," Izzy said, touching the worn sheet reverently.

"I took Joan's advice and ended up riding in a cart pulled by a pair of donkeys to a mountaintop village called Encanto de las Alturas."

"Encanto de las Alturas. I know it," Izzy whispered.

Rex and Goldie shared a knowing glance.

"I couldn't believe it when Rex showed up," Goldie continued, a youthfulness taking over her features. "He slept in the barn next to an alpaca pen."

"My back could take the hard ground when I was in my twenties," Rex teased. "Please don't go running off to South America now."

Goldie chuckled. "After making Rex sweat it out for a couple of days, we talked, and the next day, I married Rex Starrycard in that village, with the elder officiating. It was quite a time."

Izzy observed as the couple gazed at each other, lost in the beauty of sweet memories.

Goldie sighed. "It breaks my heart to say that we lost touch with Joan. It was the sixties, unlike today, where everyone has email and social media accounts. But we never forgot her. Five or six years after our semester in Peru, I was happily married and living in Starrycard Creek when we received a request to have birth announcements printed for *Danielle Ashbourne*, the daughter of Joan Wilcox Ashbourne and James Ashbourne."

"My mom," Izzy said, emotion coating her words.

"We were beyond delighted when we got the order and couldn't wait to catch up with Joanie," Rex shared.

"We delivered the announcements in person and spent a few days with your grandparents and baby Danielle," Goldie said, picking up the story. "But life got busy, like it does." She paused as if to steady herself. "Decades passed. You'll see. One day, you're barely twenty-five, building a town and a business with the one you love, and the next minute, you've got grandchildren and a great-grandchild. One morning, Rex and I were reading the paper and came across news of a plane in the northwestern part of the state. There were no survivors, and a list of the deceased included Joan Wilcox Ashbourne, James Ashbourne, Danielle Ashbourne Adaire, and Logan Adaire. We read that you, Isabelle A. Adaire, age twenty-one, weren't on the plane, leaving you as the only surviving family member. We were heart-broken for you. We sent flowers and a note to the funeral home."

Izzy blinked away tears. "I didn't pay much attention to any of that. I apologize if—"

"No, dear, we didn't expect you to respond," Goldie interjected, reaching across the table to take her hand. "But we did keep tabs on you, the best we could, courtesy of the internet and some help from the universe. I subscribe to Rocky Mountain College's alumni magazine and noticed your name printed on the graduates page when you graduated with your master's degree a few years ago. That was the last we'd heard of you until quite recently."

"When the charter opened up Starrycard Mountain for development, and we learned that the State would appoint a land steward," Rex said, pressing on, "I called a friend who'd been involved in Colorado's environmental policy. He shared the consulting firm the State contracted with, and there you were, Izzy, listed as an environmental expert. Unknown to my grandson, I asked my friend to request you for the project, and then Goldie did what she does best."

Izzy eyed the woman. "And what's that?"

"I wrote a wish on Starrycard Creek paper and had McKenzie slip it into the wishing wall."

"What was your wish?"

"It was a birthday wish for Kieran. I wished that his world would get rocked off its axis by love. And it did, by you. My grandson loves you, Izzy. And you've reminded him of something he'd forgotten."

"What's that?"

"Life is meant to be lived. Life can't be all work and no play. Life is wonder and curiosity. Life is believing in love. It was a magical twist of fate that you and Hailey were friends, supplying more proof."

"Proof of what?" Izzy pressed, searching the woman's expression.

Goldie squeezed her hand. "That Starrycard Creek is your home, Isabelle. This is what Joanie and Jimmy would want for you. You're meant for Kieran, and he's meant for you."

"Because God knows nobody else will take him," Rex muttered, but the tears in the old man's eyes gave away his true feelings.

Izzy wiped away happy tears. "I'll take him. I love your grandson. He's very much like—"

"Jimmy," Goldie supplied. "We know, sweetheart. We were quite fond of your grandfather."

She nodded, holding her locket, feeling her family's love as if they were with her. Still, she couldn't ignore what was facing the Starrycards. "But what'll we do about the town and Regis?"

"Haven't you figured it out, dear?" Goldie asked with that sly Starrycard smirk. "Anything is possible—especially in Starrycard Creek. And with a diligent town manager and a perceptive land steward, we're unstoppable."

"And don't forget," Rex added. "Love always wins in Starrycard Creek. Regis Greenstone wants to hurt you and this town. His motivation is greed, which doesn't stand a chance against love."

"So, Kieran has a plan?" she asked.

"He always has a plan, and he let us help with this one to give it a little Starrycard flair," Goldie replied with a wave of her hand.

"Should I be nervous?" she asked, trying to read the couple.

"No, we've got you," Rex answered with a wink.

"Grandpa, Goldie, Izzy," Christian said, his voice flooding the cabin. "We're on our final approach and will be landing shortly. Make sure you're buckled up."

Izzy looked over her shoulder and peered into the cockpit as Kieran looked back at her. "I love you," she mouthed.

"I know, Bloom. We confirmed that piece of data."

My God! This man.

"All right, here we go," Christian said, cutting short her exchange with Kieran.

She buckled her seat belt. Kieran had a plan, but she couldn't ignore the knot in her belly. She peered out the window as they passed Starrycard Mountain and descended into the valley. It only took a few minutes before Town Hall came into view. Christian landed in the park adjacent to the building. Kieran exited the cockpit, opened the main cabin door, and helped his grandparents out.

"Isabelle," he called, offering her his hand.

She grabbed her pack and let him help her out. They hurried toward the building as Christian maneuvered the aircraft off the ground and into the air, heading northwest back to Rocky Mountain City.

She shielded her eyes, watching the chopper depart. "Christian can't stay?"

"He's got a game."

She peered at Kieran. "And what's our game plan?"

His expression darkened. "You'll have to see Regis at the hearing."

"I figured as much. I'm ready to face him. Your grandparents reminded me of something."

"And what's that?"

"I'm a fighter like my nana. I can face him. I'm not alone now, but . . ." She touched her locket. "I've never been alone. They've always been with me."

He touched her locket. "And now you're with me, and I'm going to love and protect you like your family would want. We're a united front. Stronger together."

This man had no idea what his words did to her.

"And rest assured," he continued. "I've arranged transportation out of town for Regis and Jennifer. Our time with them will be brief but eventful."

"Why would you arrange their transportation?" she asked.

"It's in the interest of the public good." He took her hand as they headed to Town Hall.

Strange, but okay.

She watched the elder Starrycards. Rex and Goldie seemed to be headed to Town Hall but passed it and continued down Main Street.

"Your grandparents aren't attending the vote?"

"They're picking up a friend who should arrive at any minute. They'll join us shortly. Also, there's another legal issue we should address."

"Okay."

"As your attorney, I'd be remiss if I didn't tell you new evidence has come to light that will change the parameters of the nondisclosure agreement you signed."

"How so?"

"It will . . . annihilate it."

"Is that a legal term?"

"No. But in this case, hell yes." He held the door for her.

"Can you supply me with specifics?"

"I will, in less than five minutes."

"More cloak and dagger talk," she said, entering the vestibule. There wasn't a soul to be seen. They must have been the last to arrive. She stared at the doors to the hearing room. "I know you've got something up your sleeve. But could you give me a hint about what's going to happen in there?"

Her usually stoic birthday card boyfriend appeared on the verge of giddiness. "One hint," he said robotically, reining in his emotion.

"I'm listening."

"Prepare yourself for fireworks."

"FIREWORKS?" Izzy exclaimed. "I don't know what that means."

"You will. And remember," he said, drinking her in, scanning every inch of her face, "I love you, and everything I do is for you."

Cue the belly butterflies.

Sure, she wanted to know what he had planned. But how could she be cross with him?

"I know." She gazed up at him, her heart ready to burst. While some might see a muted demeanor, she saw love, adoration, and trust—trust that he could be himself and she could be herself, and nothing more was needed. Nothing needed to be explained. They just fit—like her nana and poppa.

"And a final item. An observation," he continued.

"An observation as my attorney?"

"No, as your birthday card boyfriend," he countered.

"Ooh! Let's hear it."

He leaned forward and gave her backside a once-over. "Your ass looks amazing in that skirt."

She laughed, loving how his unbridled honesty shined through. "You do have a thing for my ass."

He frowned and tipped up her chin. "But your lips . . ."

She pouted. "What's wrong with my lips?"

"We'll get to them shortly. And don't worry if you see McKenzie recording everything on Goldie's old phone. She earned phone privileges for the next six billion four hundred and twenty-six years."

Izzy laughed again, an easiness returning. "How'd she pull that off?"

"She negotiated the contract with her parents—with my assistance, of course. However, her parents had indulged in Stumble Juice, which helped sway them considerably." The clock in the vestibule chimed. He held out his hand. "Are you ready?"

She stared at his appendage like he'd strapped a stick of dynamite to it. "You want to walk in holding hands?"

"I do."

"You're not worried about what the town thinks?"

"They're on our side."

She tried to read him. "Our side?"

He offered her that barely there grin. "Trust me, Bloom. Anybody who comes for you has to get through me."

She sighed. "When you put it like that, how can I say no."

"You can't," he replied, taking her hand and lacing his fingers with hers.

He opened the door. The old hinges creaked. She tightened her hold on his hand. Every pair of eyes fell on them as they walked down the aisle. Side conversations ceased. Mouths clamped. The entire town seemed to have taken their cue from Kieran's muted playbook. The packed room was as quiet as a tomb.

"Hi, Izzy!" McKenzie called, her phone in one hand, filming as she pierced the bubble of weighty silence. "I drew a map for you to find a special surprise after the hearing," she said, passing a folded sheet of Starrycard Creek paper.

Izzy accepted the item. "Thank you."

She beamed. "I hope you like my video."

"Your video?"

Kieran patted the child's shoulder. "We'll see you in a bit, Kenz. Everything ready on your end?"

"You betcha, Uncle Kier. Operation Effusive Starrycards is underway."

"McKenzie's in on your plan?" Izzy asked as they continued down the aisle.

Kieran lowered his voice as they approached their table at the front of the room. "Everyone's in on the plan, save for one greedy developer, his scheming fiancée, and the most beguilingly symmetrical woman on the planet."

Holy shit! This man had been busy.

"Nice of you to join us," Regis sneered with his arm wrapped around his smirking fiancée.

She glanced past Kieran and took in her ex. Like always, the poser wore high-end outdoor clothing and shiny hiking boots. But his appearance didn't grate on her as it usually did. She could feel it in the air. A reckoning was coming.

"All right, all right," Judge Ironside uttered, smacking his gavel on the table. "All parties are present. Let's proceed. We're here to vote on items regarding the new land opened for development on Starrycard Mountain. The first item is to vote on the expansion plan." The judge looked from table to table. "Both parties agreed to a yea or nay vote. Mr. Greenstone, would you like to address the town?"

"Absolutely, Your Honor," Regis crooned, running his hand through his blond waves, his smile oozing with mock sincerity. He rose from his seat and turned to the packed room. "It's so good to be back. This place feels like home—like you're our extended family. Jennifer and I—"

Creak!

The door to the hearing room opened. A loud, foreboding screech announced the action. Izzy peered over her shoulder as Kieran's friend, Nelson, entered with an older woman by his side. But she wasn't his only companion. A line of men, women, and children followed him. The group stood along the far wall. Izzy squinted, and her pulse kicked up. She recognized a few faces and a couple of families.

"Birthday Card," she whispered.

"Yes?"

"Those are people from the towns Regis duped—people I tried to help before he sued me. What are they doing here?"

"Watching Regis get mucho fucked. And not in the positive, sugar-rush orgasm mucho-fucked sense."

She stared at the man, wide-eyed. "Like mucho fucked courtesy of the criminal justice system sense?"

His sage-green eyes twinkled with mischief. "Bingo."

"My God, you're good."

He tapped the tip of her nose. "You ain't seen nothing yet."

And holy shit! Kieran Starrycard, ushering in her revenge era, might be the sexiest act she'd ever witnessed.

"Mr. Greenstone, is there a problem? I'd like to move this along," Ironside barked.

"P.S.," Kieran whispered, "the judge signed off on what's about to happen."

This was getting better by the second.

"Did you bring snacks to this show?" she teased.

Regis cleared his throat and tugged at his shirt's collar. "Your Honor, I've said what I need to say. I'm ready for that vote. The sooner, the better. And remember, a vote for the Greenstone Plan comes with that lucrative incentive," he added, scanning the back of the room as the color drained from his cheeks. "And Your Honor?"

"Yes, Mr. Greenstone?"

"My fiancée and I have a pressing matter out of state to attend to. We're . . ." He shifted his stance.

Jennifer popped to her feet. "We're volunteering to plant palm trees in Denver." *What an idiot!* She might know copper, but the woman didn't know a damned thing about Colorado's ecology.

Regis had truly found his match.

"We'll do our best to accommodate your *departure*. Now, Mr.

Starrycard," Ironside said, turning to Kieran, "would you like to address the town before the vote?"

"I would. I have a short video I'd like to share," he answered smoothly as he walked to Regis's table and eyed the man. "While this isn't a courtroom, just for fun, let's call this video Exhibit A."

"A video?" Regis stammered, exchanging a worried glance with Jennifer.

"I'll allow it. Let's play the video," Ironside said, folding his hands on the table.

"Got it," the little old lady who'd walked in with Nelson chimed.

"Who is that?" Izzy asked as the woman set up a portable projection screen.

Kieran returned to her side. "That's Edna, my friend Nelson's mom. She's a whiz with video projection."

"All right," Izzy said, here for the show.

McKenzie ran down the aisle and handed the woman her phone. "Here you go, Edna. Do your thing."

"Are Regis, Jennifer, and me the only people in the room who haven't seen this?" Izzy asked, keeping her voice low.

"Yes. And two-thirds of the individuals will not be amused with the content."

She raised an eyebrow. "And the other third?"

"See for yourself."

Creak!

The doors swung open, and Nico—aka Mr. Tiny Shorts Man—bolted into the room with a to-go food container.

"Isabelle, *bella*, enjoy," the man said, setting the box before her. In the blink of an eye, he sprinted down the aisle and out the door.

"What the hell was that?" she muttered.

"Nico."

"I know it was Nico. What is this?" she asked, gesturing to the box.

"It's your snack."

She opened the lid. "It's a piece of cake and a fork."

A sly grin spread across his lips. "You are still perceptive as ever."

"What's it for, Birthday Card?"

"Some say revenge is a dish best served cold. In your case, I surmised it was best served with a slice of lemon blueberry cake."

She nearly fell out of her chair. "I get revenge cake?"

"You get all the motherfucking revenge cake," he said. And God help her. She loved this man.

"Everybody, look at the screen," McKenzie exclaimed. "And I'm supposed to tell you that in the state of Colorado, the video I took is admissible evidence in a court of law—even though I was trying to do a nature video." She glared at Regis and Jennifer. "And you messed it up with all your bad-guy, supervillain braggy talk."

Izzy peered at her ex and his fiancée. The pair sat stock-still with their jaws on the floor.

"I think I know why McKenzie gets phone privileges for the next billion years," she said.

Kieran rested his hand on her thigh. "Watch and learn, Bloom. And eat your motherfucking cake."

Speechless, she took a bite as the video of Regis and Jennifer played on the screen. And Kieran was right! Watching Regis bloviate and confess to sweeping, persistent, and systematic criminal behavior truly was best paired with cake.

The video ended, and Izzy looked over her shoulder at the men and women from the towns Regis had destroyed. They beamed, sharing fist bumps and high fives. It was everything she'd wanted.

Her heart swelled with joy and gratitude. "How did you find the other victims?"

"Nelson happened to be representing Redstone Ridge. And he brought a few more friends with him."

The door creaked—a sound she was beginning to adore.

A team of men and women in FBI vests barreled down the aisle, their footsteps echoing in the chamber.

"The Feds are involved?" Izzy asked, mid-bite.

"And the Environmental Protection Agency, the Federal Trade Commission, and the Securities and Exchange Commission. They've been watching Regis, but they didn't have concrete evidence. They do now. He'll be going away for a long time," Kieran assured her. He held her gaze. "How's that cake?"

Izzy looked on as Regis turned the color of dirty dishwater. She took a bite, savoring how the wild blueberries and lemon combined perfectly. "It's motherfuckingly delicious."

"Regis Greenstone," a scowling FBI agent barked, "you're under arrest for multiple federal offenses. These charges include defrauding communities, violating numerous environmental laws, embezzling funds from municipal entities, and engaging in extensive money laundering activities. Your actions have crossed state lines, thereby invoking federal jurisdiction and exacerbating the severity of your crimes. We're taking you in."

"What?" Regis stammered.

"Hands behind your back," the agent ordered.

"You said your plan was foolproof. And to think I wore these stupid hiking boots for you," Jennifer whined.

"Iz?" Regis eked out, ignoring his fiancée. "Can't we negotiate a deal?"

She brushed cake crumbs from her hands and stood. Kieran came to her side, and his little finger brushed against her. She lifted her chin, harnessing her strength, her iron will, and the knowledge that she was not alone. No longer the lone bearer of burdens or mired in self-loathing, she stood in solidarity with the man she loved and a town she admired. She stared down Regis. "You are in no position to negotiate. But I do have one piece of advice for you on the eve of your complete and total downfall."

The nervous man swallowed hard. "And what's that?"

She offered him a sugar-sweet smile. "Don't take it personally. It's just business, baby."

Boom!

The families in the back of the room clapped, hooted, and cheered. She pressed her hand to her heart and nodded to them. They'd, no doubt, heard Regis deliver that bullshit line, too. With a satisfying *pop*, the handcuffs clicked, and the FBI agents hauled Regis out of the courtroom, with Jennifer trailing behind the blubbering man.

Judge Ironside banged the gavel, and the cheers faded.

"In light of new evidence," the judge began, "it appears we have one plan to vote on. All in favor of the plan submitted by Mr. Starrycard and Ms. Adaire, say yea."

"YEA!"

"Any nays?"

Izzy scanned the room. Nobody made a peep.

The crusty, old judge smirked. "I didn't think so. The plan passes," he announced to a room filled with clapping and cheering.

Ironside banged his gavel a few times. "Not so fast. There is one last matter in front of me. An issue with the temporary land steward. It's come to my attention that you've resigned, Ms. Adaire. You've left your post as temporary land steward and as a consultant for the State."

Izzy straightened her posture. "Yes, sir. That's true."

"Then you need a job?" the judge replied and cracked a smile. She didn't even know his face could do that.

"Um . . . yes, I need a job."

"I propose we solidify the land steward role as a permanent position, an option authorized by our charter," Maeve called, moving from her seat and into the aisle.

"This is a whole production," she said, holding Kieran's gaze.

"I told you. My family is effusive."

"I second the motion and nominate Isabelle A. Adaire for the position," Eliza added, rising to her feet with McKenzie in her arms. The child held up her phone, recording the proceedings.

"Looks like I won over the opinionated sister," she said to Kieran under her breath.

He gazed at her. "You won over the whole town, Bloom."

"The motion has a second and a candidate. Do you accept, Ms. Adaire?" the judge barked.

Owen passed Kieran a bag. Her birthday card boyfriend removed the item inside and set it on the table. "If you're wondering about the perks, the job comes with a reusable tumbler."

She chuckled and touched his face. "I do appreciate an environmentally friendly tumbler."

"Ms. Adaire, do you accept?" the judge pressed.

She looked from the cup to the town to her birthday card boyfriend. "I do."

That boyish grin graced his lips. "Remember those words."

"Starrycard Creek, Isabelle A. Adaire is voted in as Starrycard Creek's first land steward," Ironside decreed and banged the gavel.

"Go, go, go!" McKenzie called as the room emptied like the place had caught fire.

"It's map time," Kieran said, all cool and collected.

Her head was spinning. "Map?"

"The one McKenzie made for you. We don't have far to go."

Izzy watched as the last of the townspeople exited the room. "How did you get everyone to move so quickly?"

"They were promised dessert."

"Dessert?"

"Yes. Now, where does the map tell you to go?"

She blinked and focused on the sheet of paper. "Looks like the park."

He took her hand. "Don't be distressed if you see giant starwing butterflies."

"Giant starwings?" she repeated as he led her from the room and out of the building.

A pair of children with midnight blue wings adorned with ice-blue starry markings flitted around them, creating a wide loop.

"What is this?" she asked, heading toward the park as more children dressed as starwings joined the dance, fluttering, laughing, and looping.

"An event for the butterfly lady, choreographed by my niece and your best friend."

They passed a smattering of aspens, and a grassy area came into view. Dozens of children giggled, flapped, and flitted, looping around the open space.

Hailey waved to her.

Izzy blinked away tears, so touched by the gesture.

Kieran led her into the center of the activity as the children circled around them, recreating the starwings' celestial dance. He removed a card from his pocket. "Open it."

She lifted the flap and peered at the painting on the cover of a woman with three butterflies perched on her arms and shoulder. She recognized the strokes and shades of blue. She searched Kieran's face. "You're the artist?"

"Remember those paint smudges on my face?"

"Yes."

"I still paint. I've been sending cards to The Pike anonymously since I was a teenager. The profits are donated to the gardens and the butterfly pavilion. My mom helped me negotiate that contract when I was a boy."

"I think I always knew a piece of you had been with me."

"Read it."

"It better not be instructions on how to ice my elbow."

"It's not."

She opened the card.

Marry me, Bloom. Marry me on your birthday like your grandmother married your grandfather on hers.

She gasped. "You remembered it's my birthday."

"I remember everything," he replied and removed a small box from his pocket.

"What's in there, Birthday Card?"

"Something that will last longer than paper." He opened the lid, revealing two gold bands held in place by a remnant of Starrycard Creek paper.

She recognized the painted wing on the snippet. "Is that from my lost birthday card?" she asked, removing the fragment from the gold rings.

"It is. McKenzie and I found it next to your locket. The butterflies led us to it—to you."

"And it's why I am here, Isabelle A. Adaire," came a woman's raspy voice in broken English.

Izzy blinked as a tiny old woman draped in a brightly colored poncho entered the ring. "Elder Pachamama?" she exclaimed, then busted out a curtsy. "Oh my God, what's wrong with me?" she muttered.

Kieran chuckled.

Dammit! No more curtsying.

The old woman bit back a grin. "I am proud of you, Isabelle A. Adaire. You listen to me and take my boom-boom advice. And you send new report. You transformed like butterfly. No more anger. You are the person you're meant to be, strong and fair like your grandmother, my old friend, Joanie Wilcox."

"You knew my grandmother?"

"I did. She and Marion lived with my family when they visited Encanto de las Alturas many years ago. You have your grandmother's eyes."

"Elder Pachamama's grandmother married my grandparents. Goldie invited her here to officiate our wedding," Kieran explained.

She pegged him with her gaze. "Inviting the elder all the way from Peru to officiate is a bold move, Birthday Card. You were pretty sure you'd get the girl, huh?"

"I'm sure of us. The moment I saw that perfect ass of yours, I knew I'd follow it to the ends of the Earth."

"So, my ass is what got us here?"

"Eighty percent ass. Twenty percent magic. You're the wish I've held in my heart—a wish I was too scared to believe in until I met you. You once asked me if I had a favorite thing. I do, and it's you. You've been my favorite since a swish of blond hair and one hell of a perfect ass stole my heart."

"Do you know how romantic that sounds?" she asked, holding the gaze of a man who'd do anything for her.

That sly Starrycard grin curved the corners of his mouth. "It's a statement of fact, not meant to be romantic or otherwise."

She cocked her head to the side.

"Fine, it was meant to be romantic," he conceded. "Now, what do you say, Bloom? Do you want to marry me? However, as your attorney, I should caution you. With this marriage comes family, friends, and nights spent beneath the stars. With this marriage comes me, my notebook, my kisses, my heart, and . . ."

"And?" she repeated.

"Cake," he supplied in his sexy robot voice. "We've got a shit ton of lemon blueberry cake from The Pike about to be delivered."

This man.

She pushed up onto her tiptoes and wrapped her arms around his neck. "There's only one way to answer."

"And what's that?" he whispered, his breath warm against her lips.

"Yes, to all of it—to the kisses, the laughter, the love, and the life with you in my new home. And most importantly. . ."

"Yes?" he purred with a sly Starrycard grin on his lips that hinted at his ability to read her mind.

She drank in the man of her dreams. "Bring on the motherfucking cake."

Epilogue: One month later

KIERAN

"DO YOU WANT IT, *BLOOM*?" he asked, watching Isabelle in all her naked, writhing glory.

She pressed her hands to his chest, rising and falling as she rode his cock. "You know I want it," she said through breathy exhales.

"Bad enough to beg for it?" he growled, on the edge of losing control.

Mischief sparked in her ice-blue eyes. She rolled her hips, taking him deeper.

Holy Christ! There was his answer.

He held a blueberry coated in maple syrup to her lips. She opened her fuckingly perfect mouth, and he stroked the deep indigo berry across her bottom lip before slipping it inside. She hummed that sexy, satisfied little sound that drove him wild.

Now this was how a man enjoyed TBD fucking with a side of syrup-soaked blueberry pancakes.

"I need to taste you." He flipped her onto her back, thrust his hips, and entered her as he sealed his mouth to hers. Their bodies pressed together. Her locket and another bit of metal pressed to his chest.

A key.

Specifically, a key to Fiona's cabin. She wore it on her chain. Of course, she had a key. She was a Starrycard now.

His bloom was his *motherfucking wife.*

Thanks to Elder Pachamama, with assistance from Judge Ironside, who'd expedited obtaining a marriage license, he'd married the woman of his dreams surrounded by the town and children dressed as starwing butterflies.

And they'd eaten cake.

All the motherfucking lemon blueberry *wedding* cake had arrived like clockwork.

He'd never stopped touching Isabelle. He held her hand or had his arm around her waist. Locals brought instruments, and he'd danced with his wife beneath the stars.

They'd spent their wedding night up at Fiona's cabin. It was a strategic choice on his part. The butterflies were still there. As if they were waiting for Isabelle, the starwings had remained. To see his wife with the butterflies again fed his soul. And it was a damned good thing they'd made it to the cabin when they did. Shortly after they'd arrived, the butterflies gifted them with a celestial departure dance. He'd sat on Delilah's stool and held his wife in his arms as the winged creatures bid them a looping goodbye.

His wife.

God help him. He'd never tire of contemplating the word. The simplicity of it. The elegance of the single syllable. The unassuming permanence. And that permanence had him thinking about his legacy. He wanted it all with her. Kids. Memories. A life dedicated to the land he loved with the woman who made him the man he was meant to be. He was the first-born son, and his picture would adorn the family tree with Isabelle by his side. They'd join his ancestors as a team.

And speaking of acting as a team . . .

The man who'd thought he didn't want a wife now shared an office with his life partner.

The town manager and the land steward.

Mr. and Mrs. Starrycard.

Well, Mrs. Isabelle A.A. Starrycard. She kept the *A*s to honor her family.

And how was it spending twenty-four-seven with his wife?

Fucking fantastic. And while there had been quite a bit of actual fucking, the town manager and the land steward had also been busy at work solidifying the future of the town.

And what about Mr. Shiny Boots, Regis Greenstone?

His future looked about as bright as the inside of Delilah's secret crate in the old root cellar. The charges against him were piling up. Isabelle had connected with the communities and businesses impacted by the man's misdeeds and gross negligence. With the assistance of Nelson and his firm, they were well on their way to draining Regis's offshore accounts to help those impacted by his treachery.

But Isabelle didn't stop there.

Ashbourne Building and Development had reverted ownership to her. As soon as this information came to light, he and Isabelle immediately contacted Pamela's daughter, who agreed to return and run the business. Isabelle had also offered jobs to the employees Regis had fired. The company was now owned and operated by the employees. They'd even given Isabelle a spot on their board, which turned out to be quite helpful. Starrycard Creek needed a builder and a developer. Isabelle had wiped away tears of joy when they signed the contract with Ashbourne to develop and build on Starrycard Mountain.

He may have mimicked the *Mimosa pudica* and shed one or two tears as well.

Hey, don't judge! He was a man in therapy, learning to communicate and reciprocate.

And now he needed to communicate that he required his wife to come hard on his cock.

"More," Isabelle pleaded.

He increased his pace. "Like this?" he asked, communicating

like a therapy pro. A bead of sweat dripped from his chest. It landed between her breasts.

"Yes, and pancakes," she answered. "Another bite."

They could screw and eat pancakes at the same time, right? Hell, they saved a mountain. They preserved a butterfly migration corridor. They took down an unscrupulous developer. Last week, he'd slipped his hand beneath her skirt and worked her most sensitive place while Nico presented to the town council. Now, that's multitasking.

He glanced at the tray on the bedside table and tore off a piece of the pancake. "You get one bite, and then . . ."

"Yes?" she whispered and dug her nails into his back.

"I'll make you see stars."

"I agree to those terms."

Music to his ears.

She ate the bite and sucked his fingers. Sticky eroticism took over. He threaded his fingers with hers and pumped his hips. The bed squeaked. The frame banged against the wall. Hello, TBD Bang-fest! Sweet Jesus, he became a beast in bed with her. Their bodies writhed. He kissed her deeply, tasting the syrup and berries while inhaling her jasmine-vanilla scent.

"Kieran, oh my God, Birthday Card," she moaned.

She was right there.

He dialed up the intensity. Something bumped his forearm and clattered onto the ground. *Fuck it!* He didn't care if the roof was caving in. Come hell or high water, he was taking his wife over the edge.

He kissed her earlobe. "Take it, Bloom. It's all for you. I'll be right behind you."

She tensed. Carnal victory flooded his system as she whimpered, riding the ripples of pleasure.

"Husband," she purred, and damn, he liked that word almost as much as he loved *wife*.

She owned him, heart and soul. With the headboard slamming against the wall, he barreled into his release. Now, he was the one seeing stars—stars and Isabelle's face. Her dimples. Her lips. Her symmetrical image was etched into his mind.

She hummed and twisted the ring on his finger. "Birthday Card?"

"Yes?" he answered, catching his breath.

"We have a pancake issue."

He glanced at his arm dotted with a few sticky berries and the syrupy mess on the floor. "I can make more. Also, we're adding blueberry pancake sex to the rotation."

Her dimples winked as she grinned up at him. "Rotation?"

"Yes, that was the fifty-second orgasm I've given you. Consistency is important. But so is spontaneity. A rotation helps me balance the two. It's another strategy I learned in therapy."

She tapped the tip of his nose. "God bless, therapy."

"I'm glad you approve because I plan on giving the woman I love her fifty-third orgasm," he said, plucking a berry from his arm and slipping it into her mouth.

"And where is this orgasm in the rotation?"

"You'll sit on my face."

"A man with a plan. But we should check the time."

"Why? Today is TBD screwing day."

Isabelle chewed her lip. "Oops."

"Oops?"

"I invited your family over to watch Christian's game."

"The game isn't until two."

"I think it might be close to—"

Bang, bang, bang!

"Are you guys in there?" McKenzie called from outside the bedroom door. "Are you guys fixing something in there? I hear banging. This one time, I knocked on Uncle Finn and Almost-Aunt Hailey's front door, and it was really banging. We knocked on your front door, but nobody answered, so I just came in."

"Looks like it's two," Isabelle said and patted his cheek.

"And it's not just McKenzie," Eliza called. "Everybody's here, waiting on you two to finish—"

"Banging!" McKenzie supplied. "They're making something, Mom."

"Oh, they're making something," his sister replied.

God help him!

"Give us a minute, Liza."

"Is that all you need?" the cheeky woman shot back.

"Eliza, we'll be out shortly," he called as Isabelle pressed her lips into a line, trying to hold back laughter. "I'm balls deep inside you with my family on the other side of that door. Is this amusing, wife?"

She picked a berry from his arm and popped it into his mouth. "Yes."

"You're lucky that Dr. Abadi and I also recently spoke about being flexible in any situation."

"I think you're reacting with exceptional flexibility."

"If I had my choice, I'd be testing your flexibility with you on your back and your legs spread wide." He drank her in, mapping every inch of her face. "Luckily, I have a lifetime with you. You, Mrs. Starrycard, are mine."

———

"Let's hear it for the newlyweds. They made it to their own living room," Finn called, eliciting claps and cheers from his effusive family.

The television was on, and the brood had gathered in the living room.

"We'll get the drinks started," Isabelle said and tapped him on the forearm.

They entered the kitchen, and he grabbed the lemonade from the fridge as she took care of the glasses.

"What's Goldie doing? Everyone else is watching the game. What's she writing?" Isabelle asked as she opened the tin of blueberries and craned her neck to look into the living room.

He spotted his grandmother and filled the glasses. "It's what she always does before Chris's games. She pens a note on a piece of Starrycard Creek paper."

"What does she write?"

"I don't know."

"Really?"

He shrugged. "Yes, she won't tell anyone."

"Uncle Christian's up at bat!" McKenzie called, hopping from lap to lap.

Isabelle grabbed a tray. "Have you talked to Christian lately?"

"No," he answered, adding blueberries to the glasses. He'd texted his younger brother three times in the last week and hadn't heard back. He'd chalked it up to Chris being on the road with his team, but it was unlike him to go radio silent.

The crack of Christian's bat meeting the ball pierced the air.

"Why isn't Uncle Chris running?" McKenzie said as the room went silent.

What the hell was going on?

"Is Uncle Chris okay?"

Nobody answered.

Kieran shared a look with Isabelle. Dread washed over him.

It had to be Christian's shoulder.

He hurried into the living room and caught a shot of Christian collapsing to his knees. The man dropped his bat and clutched his shoulder before the game cut to a commercial.

Everyone started talking—speculating. Everyone except for Goldie. She sat silently at the kitchen table.

He went to his grandmother. "You had a feeling, didn't you?"

"I did." Goldie eyed the folded piece of Starrycard Creek paper pressed to her palm. "And your brother's going to need this now more than ever."

Goldie's Muffin Recipe

LET'S MAKE SOME MOTHERF*CKING LEMON BLUEBERRY MUFFINS

I've got a treat for you! You can get Goldie's Muffin Recipe and make your very own motherf*cking muffins. You can even print it off and tuck it away with your recipes.

Books by Krista Sandor

The Starrycard Creek Bachelors Series

A small town rom-com series set in the mountains

Book One: The Business Card Boyfriend

Book Two: The Birthday Card Boyfriend

Book Three: The Baseball Card Boyfriend

The Nanny Love Match Series

A nanny/boss romantic comedy series

Book One: The Nanny and the Nerd

Book Two: The Nanny and the Hothead

Book Three: The Nanny and the Beefcake

Book Four: The Nanny and the Heartthrob

Love Match Legacy Books

Nanny Love Match Series Spin-off Books

Mistletoe Love Match

The Sebastian Guarantee

The Oscar Escape

The Bergen Brothers Series

A steamy billionaire brothers romantic comedy series

Book One: Man Fast

Book Two: Man Feast

Book Three: Man Find

Bergen Brothers: The Complete Series+Bonus Short Story

The Farm to Mabel Duet

Sign up for Krista's newsletter to get all the up-to-date Krista Sandor romance news!

Learn more at www.KristaSandor.com

Acknowledgments

A few years back, while my husband and eldest son were away, I seized the opportunity for a mini getaway with my youngest son to Salida, Colorado. Immersed in the charm of local shops, vibrant outdoor activities, delectable cuisine, and breathtaking scenery, we had an unforgettable time. This enchanting town sparked the concept for the fictional Starrycard Creek, Colorado. I extend my heartfelt gratitude to the wonderful people of Salida for inspiring us and making our journey so memorable.

Indeed, sharing this story has been a collaborative journey, and I owe immense gratitude to many. Carrie, Marla, and Tera, my indispensable editing trio, have been pivotal. Najla Qamber's creative genius gave life to the cover, beautifully complementing Wander Aguiar's photography. The enthusiastic support from countless readers, bloggers, and booktokers has been invaluable in spreading the word. It's clear—it takes a village, and I'm profoundly thankful for mine.

About Krista Sandor

If there's one thing Krista Sandor knows for sure, it's that romance saved her. After she was diagnosed with Multiple Sclerosis in 2015, her world turned upside down. During those difficult first days, her dear friend sent her a romance novel. That kind gesture provided the escape she needed and ignited her love of the genre. Inspired by strong heroines and happily ever afters, Krista decided to write her own romance series. Today, she's living life to the fullest. When she's not writing, you can find her running 5Ks with her husband or chasing after their growing boys in Denver, Colorado.

Never miss a release, contest, or author event! Visit www.KristaSandor.com to sign up for her romance newsletter.

Printed in Great Britain
by Amazon

61435148R00231